BLACK BEAUTY'S FAMILY

BLACK BEAUTY'S FAMILY

Josephine, Diana and
Christine Pullein-Thompson

CHANCELLOR
PRESS

Black Beauty's Clan (containing BLACK
EBONY, BLACK PRINCESS and BLACK
VELVET) was first published in Great Britain in
1975 by Hodder and Stoughton Ltd.

Black Beauty's Family (containing
NIGHTSHADE, BLACK ROMANY and
BLOSSOM) was first published in Great Britain
in 1978 by Hodder and Stoughton Ltd.

This one-volume edition first published in Great
Britain in 1986 by
Chancellor Press
59 Grosvenor Street
London W1.

Printed in Czechoslovakia.
50624

CONTENTS

Book One

BLACK BEAUTY'S CLAN

FOREWORD

BY BLACK ABBOT

Black Beauty's great-great-great-great nephew

Because of the world-wide interest shown in the auto-biography of my kinsman, Black Beauty, I have now taken the liberty of gathering together the life stories written by three other members of my extraordinarily talented family.

These three mildewed manuscripts were found in a loft, in a saddle room medicine cupboard and beneath a pile of rubbish in a deserted loosebox, and, except for the occasional indecipherable word, have been published exactly as they were written.

I feel sure that readers will enjoy Ebony's tale of the 1880's and 90's, his life among the pit ponies, his rather raffish episode as a theatrical horse, Black Princess's story which includes her adventures in the Great War of 1914–18 and Black Velvet's account of the difficult years of the 1930's and the early days of showjumping.

I have also compiled a simple family tree to help those who wish to know the exact relationship each story-teller bears to our famous kinsmen.

BLACK EBONY

✳

by Josephine Pullein-Thompson

CONTENTS

BLACK BEAUTY'S CLAN

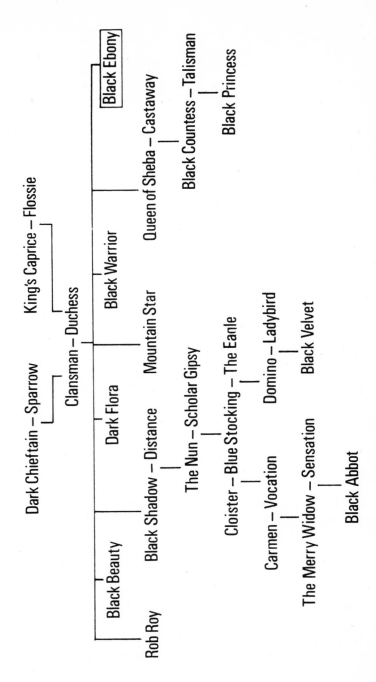

CHAPTER ONE

My foalhood

I did not enjoy being Black Beauty's youngest brother. Our mother, Duchess, had grown very old by the time I arrived; she was rather lame, a little blind and preferred to think about the past rather than the present or the future. Because Rob Roy her eldest foal had died young in a hunting accident, most of her thoughts had centred on her second foal, Black Beauty, and though there had been four fillies and an unsatisfactory colt in between us, it was Black Beauty who was held up as an example of all goodness and elegance and correct behaviour throughout my foalhood. When she talked to the other mares about him he sounded more like a saint than a horse and whenever I misbehaved I was told that Black Beauty would never have *thought* of doing such a thing. I grew to dislike my famous brother very much and I early decided that since I had no hope of rivalling him in goodness I would be as bad as possible and perhaps collect some fame for that.

Farmer Grey's big field was a perfect place to rear foals. There were trees for shade, a large shed in which to shelter from flies or bad weather, a brook for drinking water and a pond for paddling and from which a naughty foal could drive the ducks in wing-flapping hysteria.

I had been named Ebony. The story went that soon after my birth old Farmer Grey and old Daniel, the head horseman on the farm, and Ned his son had been looking me over and they had said, 'Not a white hair on him, he's as black as ebony!' and the name had stuck. My mother always seemed rather disappointed by my lack of white markings. 'Your brother had a very pretty star,' she would say, 'and one neat little white sock.' I never needed to ask which brother, Rob Roy and Black Warrior were rarely mentioned.

There were three middle-aged mares, all old friends of my

mother's, turned out with us and I was supposed to play with their foals but they were all younger than I was and less adventurous and I hankered after the company of the yearling cart colts who lived in the adjoining field. I would watch them at their exciting games and hold cheeky conversations with them over the hedge. My mother was always calling me away, 'They are not our class, dear,' she would say. 'You must remember that you are well-bred and high born, your grandfather won the cup at Newmarket two years running.' I didn't care about being high born, I wanted to play rough games, and when I grew older and stronger I found a low place in the hedge and I would jump over and spend a happy hour racing and chasing, biting, rearing and kicking with the much larger but slower and less nimble cart colts, while my mother and her friends stood in a row watching over the hedge and neighing anxiously for me to come back.

My mother was very shocked by this behaviour, but when Farmer Grey learned what I was up to he only laughed and told her, 'You've got a proper little monkey this time, old Pet.' And he always gave me pieces of bread and told me that I would make a fine hunter one day and that Sir Clarence was already inquiring about Duchess's new foal.

My mother disapproved of hunting. She didn't explain to me that it was because Rob Roy had broken a leg and had to be shot, she just grumbled about foolish men who broke their necks and ruined good horses all for the sake of chasing one little fox or hare, so I'm afraid I paid no attention to her but went off to boast to my cart horse friends that I was soon to be a hunter and must practise galloping and leaping.

I never saw hounds until one day in early spring when I was nearly two years old. In the distance we heard this stirring, musical sound. My mother listened and declared it to be the horn and then, as it came nearer and nearer, all the horses became very excited and stood with their heads high and ears pricked or galloped round their fields. Suddenly hounds came in view: thirty or forty of them black, brown and white, all giving tongue and behind them came the huntsman blowing his horn and behind him a great many people in scarlet or black coats mounted on fine looking horses.

In a flash I was in with the cart colts, in another flash I was over their hedge and following hounds, so excited by their deep cry and the wild thud of galloping hoofs that I scarcely knew what I was doing. Behind I heard the hedge break and crush beneath the feet of the cart colts as they followed me over.

Some of the riders shouted and cracked whips at us but the pace was too hot and the horses too eager for anyone to stop and drive us back to our field. So we galloped on with them trying to take the fences as they did.

I managed quite well for a time. Watching for a horse ahead to blunder, I would follow taking advantage of a smashed top rail or a battered hedge, but then a hedge with a terrible, dark ditch on the take-off side barred my way. My courage failed me and I refused and in doing so turned across the path of another horse. There was a furious shout from the rider and the stinging cut of a whip across my quarters. I wheeled away and then stopped at a safe distance to watch the huge and beautiful horses striding up full of confidence, and skimming over with the greatest of ease. One day, I told myself, I would leap like that.

The cart colts caught up with me and we milled about confused and all dripping with sweat. The tail end of the field was passing us now and a stout cob whinnied to us. We followed his fat round quarters and docked tail to the corner of the field where he bucked over a small stile.

I raced ahead of the cart colts and flew over after him, there was a crack and the sound of splintering wood as the others followed me. The cob's rider was the same square shape as his horse and he wore a rusty black coat and not a smart scarlet one, but he certainly knew the countryside and cutting across two ploughed fields and through a small wood, he brought us up with hounds again. The pace was still fast and I was getting breathlesss and tired. My unshod feet were sore and the heavy, clinging plough had slowed me to a weary canter.

The stout cob was fitter and had the staying power of an adult horse, sadly I watched his quarters grow smaller and smaller. The last stragglers, hounds and horsemen passed me, then the cart colts appeared. 'Let's go 'ome, Eb,' they said. 'Do you know the way?' I didn't, but obviously we couldn't jump back over those fences in cold blood, so we looked for open gates and gaps in hedges and presently, just as the sun was going down, we came to a green lane. We wandered along, stopping to sample the patches of spring grass which had come through in the sheltered corners, for we were now very hungry. Then the lane widened and we saw a group of living carriages or painted wooden houses on wheels. There were two small fires burning and a number of horses and ponies tethered nearby.

We stopped and snorted, but one of the ponies whinnied to us so we went on. Suddenly the shapes of men and boys sprang up silently all round us. I turned in my tracks and tried to flee, but there were gipsies behind us too. One man leaped at me and grabbed my forelock and my ear. Terrified I reared trying to shake him off, but he swung with me, all his weight on my ear and forelock. He hurt me very much and I hated the smell of him and the dark, swarthy face and the rings which dangled from his ears. One hand slid down my nose and he gripped my nostrils with a cruel force.

I plunged and reared violently, I struck out with my forelegs and, still not dislodging him, I reared, higher and higher. He still clung to me and maddened by pain and terror I reared higher still. For a moment I was vertical, then I lost my balance and toppled backwards landing with such force that for a moment I lay stunned.

Then I realised that I was free. There was no hand gripping my ear, no evil smelling fingers in my nostrils, I scrambled up and neighed to the cart colts as I charged the arm-waving, stick-brandishing men who tried to stop me. One stepped right into my path, but I was now so frantic with fear and so determined not to be captured that I would not swerve. My

chest knocked him to the ground and I did my best not to
tread on him as he sprawled beneath my feet.

I neighed to the colts again as I galloped up the lane, not
daring to look behind me. The lane led to a small road and
there on a green, surrounded by cottages grazed one of my
friends. I stopped beside him. We looked back and neighed,
then we listened. There was an answering neigh and presently
a lone figure with a wide, white blaize came galloping through
the dusk to join us. 'They've got Punch,' he said, 'they've put
ropes on him, he can't get away.'

Later we had stopped to graze when we heard the steady

clip-clop of a shod horse approaching at the walk and the sound of cart wheels and an old cob came along. The reins were loose on his back and a snoring noise came from the bottom of the cart. 'Drunk again,' he said crossly. 'It's the same every market day. You young fellows lost?'

We fell in beside him and told him our story as we walked along.

'Better come to our place,' he said, 'you'll be safe there and I expect someone will come looking for you by and by.'

So we followed him along the road and up the lane to his farm. We heard the farmer reproached by his son as he was pulled from the cart and supported indoors, we heard the old cob praised as he was unharnessed, watered and fed. We drank at the water trough and then hung about sheepishly waiting for attention and presently the yard gate was shut and we were thrown a couple of armfuls of hay.

We spent a miserable day or two in that farm-yard wondering whether we would ever see our own farm and our lovely fields again and then at last Farmer Grey came with Dick and Ned in the gig and they led us home.

My mother and all the other horses were delighted to have us back safe and sound, but poor Punch never returned.

CHAPTER TWO

My apprenticeship

This episode with the gipsies, followed by the operation which many colts undergo to turn them into geldings, combined to make me far less trusting. For a few months I was very nervous of all strange men, then the memories faded a little but I was never again the same reckless youngster; I knew that cruelty and danger existed.

I would still jump out of my field especially in the spring when the smell of fresh green grass tempted me from the other side of the hedge, but I never wandered far. I still longed to be a hunter, but I had decided to wait until I was old enough to carry a human guide.

The summer I was three years old Farmer Grey sent me to live in the field by the railway line, as he did all his young horses, for this cured any nervousness of trains and enabled them to trot in and out of railway stations all their lives without the least fear.

Then, at four years old, I was broken in. I was very glad to have work to do for I was heartily bored with my uneventful life and longed to be out in the world. I enjoyed learning to go round in a circle on the lunge rein and to walk, trot and canter on command. I didn't object to the saddle but I found the feel of the girth very constricting at first, especially when it was pulled tight, and I made ferocious faces whenever this was done. I hated the bridle straps pressing close round my ears and I did not care overmuch for the feeling of a bit in my mouth.

However, old Daniel and Ned were so kind and patient with me and they praised and petted me so much that I put up with all these discomforts and gradually they became part of the day's routine and eventually I ceased to notice them. Ned was a good rider, very quiet and calm and I felt quite pleased to carry him. At first his extra weight made all my movements awkward and difficult, but, as I grew stronger, I learned to carry his weight as well as my own and regained the feeling of balance and power that I had always had when free.

The next hurdle was being shod and this I found very hard to bear. Standing in the forge, endlessly picking up my feet. The smoke and smells, the clank of iron, the hiss of water; the strange feeling of having my feet hammered as the nails were driven in combined to make me very fidgety. I was not a very patient horse and if Ned hadn't been there to comfort me I don't think I could have stood it. Afterwards my feet felt very heavy and cumbersome and made a deafening clip clop on the road, but I became used to it all in time.

The weeks that followed were very happy ones for Ned began to take me out for rides. Sometimes we took messages; to the Mill, to other farmers, to the saddler and harness maker and sometimes we just went where we would. I enjoyed trotting through the woods, talking to the charcoal burner and the woodmen watching the teams of huge horses pull the timber wagons laden with great trees. I enjoyed galloping over commons and fields, climbing to the tops of hills so that we could look over and see what lay on the other side.

Everyone seemed to know Ned and we often stopped to chat to the postman on his pony, the carrier with his horse. In the early mornings we would meet all the donkey carts from the small farms on the hills taking the churns of milk to the station and in the evenings we would meet the horses coming home from their work in the fields, their drills and harrows and ploughs left behind, the ploughman would sit sideways on one horse and lead the other.

I had begun to regard myself as an educated horse ready for the world but I soon found that Farmer Grey thought otherwise and, later on that summer, I was broken to harness. I hated being driven. All those straps; blinkers spoiling my view of the countryside and then, when you had gone through the whole fidgety process of putting the harness on, all you could do was to trot tamely along a road drawing a tiresome trap. You couldn't gallop over fields or wind your way through leafy woods, it was just trotting forever on the hard roads. I kicked at cruppers, I refused to push my head into collars when they were held out to me or to back into the shafts. I sulked and stumbled and went with my ears back whenever I was driven.

Ned laughed at me, but he sympathised and presently he gave up the harness work and started to teach me to jump, or leap as it was often called, and this was much more to my taste. We began over a log and a bundle or two of faggots in the paddock, then we tried hurdles and an old gate. Ned would lean back as we landed but he always let the reins slip through his hands a little so that he never caught my mouth and soon I grew to enjoy jumping with him on my back even more than I did when alone.

One autumn morning Farmer Grey came to watch.

'Better take him round the farm and put him over a ditch or two.' he told Ned, 'then we'll let him see hounds.'

Ned and I spent some very pleasant days riding round the farm and jumping whatever took our fancy. We began over the small ditches and the low hedges and rails and, as our confidence in each other grew, we jumped higher and higher. Ned had a lot of sense and he would never let me go on until I was tired and began to make mistakes, so, except for the time I refused the brook and tipped him into it and the time I jumped too big and too boldly over a drop and pecked, we had no mishaps or accidents.

At last the day of my first hunt came. We were fed very early and as we ate Blackbird warned me that it would only be cub hunting because the true foxhunting season does not begin until November the first. But I still set off full of high hopes and Ned, who was looking very spruce in a brown coat and breeches and black boots, gaiters and bowler, seemed cheerful too. The meet was at a remote crossroads deep in the water meadows and I who was obstinately expecting scarlet coats and magnificent horses was bitterly disappointed for only the hunt servants were properly dressed, and even their coats were old and faded, everyone else wore 'ratcatcher', dull browns and greys.

There were a lot of young horses out, many of them much less worldly than I. They stood with bulging eyes snorting at hounds and when we moved off they proceeded crabwise, with wild clatterings of freshly shod hoofs.

Most of the riders looked like farmers, but there were a good many grooms and nagsmen out on young horses, a fair number of children, especially boys, a sprinkling of ladies and gentlemen and two or three soldiers.

'Going to draw the osiers, I shouldn't wonder,' said the old grey horse I fell in beside as we clattered down the road. The horsemen spread out and surrounded the marshy osier bed as hounds were put in and I, who had imagined an immediate chase and seen myself leaping hedge and ditch and gate, grew more and more disappointed as time passed and nothing happened. Ned and the rider of the old grey were discussing the corn harvest and banging the crooks of their hunting whips against their saddles. They gave cries of encouragement to the young hounds when they came out of the osiers and stood looking about them aimlessly or sat down for a good scratch.

At last the old hounds picked up a scent and the deep sound

of their voices echoed up and down the osier bed, but there was still no action; Ned walked me round for a little and the old grey horse told me that cub hunting was usually like this for its whole purpose was to teach young hounds to hunt, and to stir up the fox cubs so that they would leave the family home.

Presently the sun became hot and the old horse slept, until a fox cub peeped out of the undergrowth and there was at burst of crop-banging and shouts of 'Tally-ho bike!' But still no action.

Later we rode on to a small wood, hounds were put in and we went through the whole procedure again, even to the old grey horse falling asleep. Then Ned said that he had work to do and we must go home.

As I ate my second breakfast I grumbled to Blackbird about the unexciting nature of my hunt.

'You don't realise how lucky you are to be taken out quietly like that,' he told me. 'I've known young horses ruined by hard riding. Taken on a fast hunt, galloped nearly to death, broken winded and lame before they'd reached their full strength. And I've known others so over-excited by their first hunt that they could never be calm again, but were always lathered with sweat, sidling, jogging, fighting with their riders from the moment they saw hounds till the time they got home.'

In the afternoon when Ned was grooming me Farmer Grey came into the stable. 'Sir Clarence's man has just been round,' he said. 'They saw Ebony out this morning and were very much struck with him. Sir Clarence is coming over himself in a day or two to try him.'

Ned took the news coldly. 'They'll hunt him to death before he's five.'

'I reminded Sir Clarence that the horse was only five next time and he said that he intended to keep him for his own second horse this season and he would take care not to overdo him.'

'So long as he don't let that dolt Roger ride him,' said Ned.

'I think he's intended for the young ladies,' answered

Farmer Grey. 'He'll make a beautiful horse for a lady in a year or two.'

'Miss Fanny's all right, the other two aren't up to much,' complained Ned.

'Sounds as though you'll soon be off,' said Blackbird when we were alone together again.

Sir Clarence came to try me. Having only had Ned on my back before, I hardly knew how to behave with an unfamiliar rider but Sir Clarence gave much the same signals; he was slower and stiffer than Ned, but equally quiet and patient and I could tell he was a rider to respect. He tried me out thoroughly at the walk, trot and canter, then we had a gallop right round a stubble field and then he put me over several fences. Ned took me when he dismounted.

'He's still a little green,' said Sir Clarence patting me, 'but my word he can gallop and he's got a powerful leap.'

'Yes, jumps like a stag,' agreed Farmer Grey proudly. 'Now come along to the house, Sir Clarence, and try a glass of Mrs Grey's sloe gin.'

'I'm going to miss you Eb,' said Ned sadly. I nibbled his coat lapel trying to explain that I was going to miss him too. Slowly we walked back to the stable.

Next day I was clipped. Farmer Grey told Ned that Sir Clarence had asked for it to be done, because he felt it was too much to ask of a young horse that he should be clipped by complete strangers. And as I felt those tickling clippers creeping over my body I felt sure that I would have kicked any stranger who treated me so. But since it was Ned I accepted it all as a necessary evil and only showed him with a lifted hoof or a ferocious face when the blades grew too warm or began to pull. Then we would stop and give poor red-faced Dick, who was turning the handle of the machine, a rest while Ned oiled the blades.

'If you ask me it's downright unnatural,' Dick complained. 'They wouldn't have coats if they didn't need them, so why take it off?'

'The speed they go hunting is unnatural too,' Ned told him. 'My Father has told me that fifty years ago when they

26

first bred the fast hounds we have today, many good horses foundered and died. Many of the gentlemen would boast about how many horses had died under them and a lot of it was due to the thick coats. But people didn't take to clipping for a goodish while because they thought it made the horses die young and some said it made them blind. Of course we know now that none of that's true.'

CHAPTER THREE

My life at Earleigh Court

Sir Clarence's establishment, Earleigh Court, was very much larger and more handsome than the farm. The stables were entered through an archway with a clock tower above and a clock that chimed every hour. The yard was gravelled with a plot of grass in the centre and the gravel was always kept raked perfectly smooth and without a wisp of hay or straw in sight. The stables, the carriage houses and the harness rooms stood all round the yard and above them were lofts where the hay and straw was kept and rooms for the young grooms; the older, married grooms and the coachman all had cottages nearby.

My stable was a very large loose box, well bedded down with the best wheat straw. One side of it was taken up with an iron manger and hayrack, there were green tiles above the manger and the hayrack was a low one so that I could eat in comfort. The walls and door were of brown varnished wood with iron railings above so that I could see out on three sides but I couldn't put my head out or bite the horse next door.

When I had been rugged up in very smart rugs and Ned had left me I took a sip of water, snatched a mouthful of hay and roamed restlessly round my box. Then, missing Ned and Blackbird, I gave a loud neigh. A very wellbred chestnut head looked at me through the iron bars, 'Kindly moderate your neighs,' it said, 'that noise is deafening. My name is Estella, by Starlight; I imagine you've come to take the place of Patience, she went lame.'

I explained who I was and said that I understood that I was to be Sir Clarence's second horse as it would be my first season's hunting. She told me that four horses, Merlin, Bayard, Sultan and Nimrod were out hunting, but that two should be back at any moment and then she returned to her hayrack.

At three o'clock Merlin, an enormous grey of almost seventeen hands was led into the box on the other side of me and Bayard, a sixteen-two bay was taken into the box beyond Estella. Rugs were flung on and they were offered buckets of warm gruel.

'These are the first horses,' Estella explained to me. 'Sir Clarence and Mr Roger have changed to fresh horses and gone on hunting while Pat and Bert brought the tired ones home.'

'They weren't as fresh as usual,' said Merlin. 'All the second horsemen lost us, they didn't come until very late and they'd covered a mile or two by the look of them.'

'Nothing to what we'd covered,' groaned Bayard when he'd sucked down a mouthful or two of gruel. There was a very fast thing in the morning. We found and he made a straight line for the hills. They killed in a quarry and Mr Roger was very peeved because he wasn't up, but it was his own fault he was coffee-housing – chattering to his friends – when they found and got a bad start, then he expected me to catch the leaders and I just couldn't do it. Then we found again at Fitton Oaks and this one ran towards the river, field after field of water-logged plough and do you think Mr Roger can tell ridge from furrow, not him! No headlands for him either. Straight through the deepest going and no thought of a breather before he rams you at some great bull-finch. I was nearly down several times; he just doesn't give you a chance.'

'Poor old Bayard,' said Estella sympathetically. 'Now Sir Clarence is always so thoughtful. He picks a wide, water-filled furrow whenever he can. He knows that if a furrow holds water it must have a hard bottom and so will be much less tiring for a horse than deep, muddy going.'

'I wish he'd knock some sense into that son of his,' grumbled Bayard. 'I'm quite pumped out. Too tired to eat a thing and so hot, it's stifling under these rugs.'

Bert and Pat came back then having changed into their stable clothes and began to groom the tired and dirty hunters hissing through their teeth as they worked.

'Bayard's broken out,' Pat called, 'What's Merlin like?'

'Dry as a bone,' answered Bert, knocking his curry comb out on the floor.

Presently Pat fetched Mr Johnson the stud groom to have a look at poor Bayard and they stood discussing his exhausted and feverish state and the cold sweat he'd broken out into. Then Mr Johnson went off to get what he called a 'pick me up'.

'Beer, I expect,' said Estella.

The activity in the stable suddenly increased. Lanterns appeared everywhere and as well as the returned hunters being groomed, rugged up and bandaged, Estella and I were being attended to. A small stable boy came into my box with a skip and pitch fork and soon straightened and tidied my straw. My water was changed, my hayrack replenished. Then there were hoofs in the yard, 'Sultan and Nimrod,' said Estella neighing a welcome. I heard Sir Clarence's voice and then a louder less pleasing voice ordering the dog cart to be brought round in an hour to take him to the station.

Sir Clarence came into the stable and looked at Bayard and Merlin and then at me. He was very dirty too, all his fine clothes covered in mud. He had Bert and Mr Johnson with him when he came into my box and Bert had my headcollar on and my rugs off in a flash.

'Not at all a bad-looking animal,' said Mr Johnson as they stood considering me, 'in time he should make up into something very nice indeed. Pity he isn't a hand taller.'

Sir Clarence laughed, 'Never mind he'll make a perfect hunter for Miss Fanny and I think he'll just about carry me; I don't ride as hard as I used to – growing old. The lad at the farm made quite a good job of clipping him.'

'Yes, except for the whiskers, I do hate to see a lot of untidy whiskers on a well-turned out horse,' said Mr Johnson and when Sir Clarence had gone he produced a pair of scissors from his pocket and gently clipped all mine away.

It wasn't until we were fed and settled for the night and the grooms took their lanterns and went away that I began to regret my loss, I'd never realised how useful whiskers are. It was difficult to find my way around a strange stable in the dark, for they feel out the bucket and hayrack for you and save you from banging your nose.

Estella and I talked again when we'd finished our feeds. Bayard still felt done up and was lying down, Merlin was munching hay too busily for conversation and I think she was pleased to have someone to instruct in the way of life at Earleigh Court.

She told me that Mr Johnson was an excellent stud groom and really knew his job, that Pat who did her, Bayard and Jupiter, was very good and careful and took a great pride in her appearance, but that Bert who would be doing me as well as Merlin and Nimrod, was careless and rough. Mr Johnson had to be after him all the time and he'd given her a girth gall once by carelessly pinching her skin when he saddled her. As for rollers he always pulled them up far too tight. Poor Patience had often stood in discomfort all night long because when he rugged her up he'd pulled the roller too tight to permit her to lie down.

'Blow yourself out,' she advised. 'Whenever he does up the roller take a deep breath and hold it, then, when you let the breath go, you'll find the roller comfortably loose, it's the only way.'

'He's not so bad,' Merlin told me slowly and calmly. Estella's so thin-skinned and sensitive and she's always had an easy life. I had a really bad groom once, he didn't clean the water bucket for months and he left a dead mouse in my manger for a week and never bothered to investigate why I wasn't eating up; just went on tipping more feeds on top of it.'

I soon settled down in my new home though I missed Ned and Blackbird, and most of all, my rides with Ned.

Our stables were kept extremely clean and tidy for, as well as being thoroughly mucked out every morning, small stable boys ran in and out with skips all day long. We were groomed and groomed, and the food was excellent.

We were exercised in a body under Mr Johnson's watchful eye, each groom riding one horse and leading another and this crocodile of horses would trot solemnly round the roads and lanes nearly always taking the same route. At a certain spot those horse's that were already fit and working quite hard would return home and I who was considered unfit, a carriage horse who had developed a sore shoulder and so had to be ridden rather than driven, and the two luckless horses that were to carry Miss Grace and Miss Griselda later in the day and so must be thoroughly tired out, went on for another three or four miles.

I enjoyed the companionship of this crowd of horses and the noise of so many hoofs was inspiring, but taking the same way time after time was very monotonous and there seemed to be no chance of a canter or gallop, though we passed many an inviting stretch of turf.

Then Mr Johnson began to ride me when he escorted the young ladies for their almost daily ride, but this too was frustrating. Miss Grace was nervous. She was the youngest of the three sisters and had pale fair hair and eye lashes and weak-looking pale blue eyes. Miss Griselda, the middle one, was a lump with no aptitude for riding. This was not her fault, but her boundless self-confidence and her habit of grumbling at her horse and blaming him for her own short-comings, irritated us all. Miss Fanny was slim and long-legged and high-spirited and always demanding a gallop or a jump, so she would be skimming over sheep hurdles on Estella, Miss Griselda would make a half-hearted attempt to follow and then belabour poor Bayard for refusing while Miss Grace sobbing with terror would plead pitifully with Mr Johnson not to make her canter. I did my best to behave. I stayed close beside Juno so that Mr Johnson could grab Miss Grace's reins whenever it was needful, I opened and shut gates neatly, but I did find it hard to remain at a sedate walk while Estella galloped and jumped, and even the smallest prance of protest brought a wail of fear from Miss Grace and an angry rebuke from Mr Johnson.

At last I was considered fit to hunt and this did enliven my life. Sir Clarence wasn't bold enough for my taste, but I supposed that he was getting on in years and no longer fell lightly and that this cramped his style.

Merlin and Bayard never tired of telling me that I was a hot-head and needed a steady rider. 'Left to your own devices you would have broken your neck a hundred times over,' they told me. And, hacking home after a particularly fast run, Bayard began to lecture me again. 'You're so wild, Ebony. You *never* look before you leap, I know you are only a four-year-old, but we value Sir Clarence and we don't want a good master killed because a youngster can't resist showing off.'

'I once saw a horse land on a harrow, a spiked harrow,' said Estella. 'Farmers just leave these dangerous things lying under hedges, they never think that we may land among the chains and spikes, falling or damaging our legs and feet for life.'

'I was reared in Ireland,' Bayard told us, 'and there you find every sort of rubbish in the hedges and ditches and often a fine fat pig asleep on the landing side of a bank! But there the riders are pretty circumspect, they jump more in the old fashioned way, the way they rode before the Leicestershire style and the flying leap, and the horses hold themselves ready to make a sudden extra effort should they see something waiting to trap them. You wouldn't do there, Ebony.'

However, despite the fears of my stable companions, I finished the season without mishap. Looking back, I can see that this was chiefly due to Sir Clarence's restraining hand, but I was too young and cocksure to believe it at the time.

Hunting ended on April the first and they immediately began to rough us off. During the next month our oats, exercise and rugs were gradually reduced and then some of the horses had their shoes off and some were re-shod with grass tips. Then on May the first the hunters were led away in a long string to the fields where they were to spend their holidays. As I watched Merlin and Bayard and Estella deserting me I neighed loudly and indignantly and dashed myself against the walls and bars of my stable in an attempt to follow.

Juno, the little cob, was hastily moved into Estella's box to keep me company. 'No you can't have a holiday, Ebony,' said the small stable boy who brought her. 'You've only just started work and Sir Clarence says you have a lot to learn before you are fit to carry Miss Fanny.'

The yard was much quieter now that hunting was over, though of course there were carriage horses in the stable opposite, but two pairs of them had gone to London with the family so most of the activity we saw was the spring cleaning and painting of the stables.

I enjoyed Juno's company. I had grown fond of Estella, but she thought too much about herself to be a really interesting companion, she was always wanting her mane admired, or bemoaning some near invisible swelling in her fetlock or complaining of the dull shade her chestnut coat became when she was clipped. Juno was hogged and docked so she was very glad that she was not to be turned out for the summer and left to the mercy of the flies, who tormented her terribly. She had changed hands several times in her life and so had many interesting stories to tell about her other places, but she was such a steady, useful animal that she was always in demand to take messages here, there and everywhere and then I was left on my own.

However I had acquired another friend. A small black cat had jumped down into my loose box one day and spent hours attentively watching a mousehole under my manger. He didn't catch the mouse, but he told me his name was Sambo. He liked my stable and I liked the way he purred and rubbed himself against my face as he marched up and down the edge of my hayrack and manger so we quickly became fast friends and whenever he felt like a nap or a chat he would come to see me.

Mr Johnson rode me almost every day. He would take me in the park and make me practise circling and stopping and starting and cantering with each leg leading in turn. Then he took to riding me in a side-saddle, which felt very strange at first and not nearly so comfortable as having one of the rider's legs on each side to keep you balanced and give signals. I soon learned that a tap with the whip gave the signal on the legless side, but I could not understand why I must now always canter with the off fore leading and straight from the walk without any trotting in between. Juno explained it to me. She said that it was very jolting for the lady if a horse cantered with the near fore, as that was the side she was sitting on, and trotting fast was very jolting too, so ladies' horses were taught to canter straight from the walk and were generally much more carefully trained than gentlemen's horses.

By the time that the family came back from London, Mr Johnson was able to tell Sir Clarence that I was now a suitable mount for Miss Fanny.

There followed a very happy time. Miss Fanny rode me almost every day and seemed delighted with me. Her sisters had given up until a more satisfactory mount could be found for Miss Griselda and, as it was not considered correct or safe for a young lady to ride alone, Mr Johnson or another of the older grooms, riding one of the carriage horses, always accompanied us. Mr Johnson was much more adventurous when not weighed down by the responsibility of timid riders or a long string of valuable hunters and we were allowed long, fast gallops and quite a few jumps. Miss Fanny and I were always on the look out for suitable hedges and brooks, we found stiles and timber and once a five barred gate though Mr Johnson disapproved of this.

For me it was as though I had Ned again. We would see a tempting stretch of turf or a conveniently placed fence at the same moment and know each other's mind. When ridden by Sir Clarence or Mr Johnson I was a horse taking orders, but Miss Fanny and I were partners, sharing the same excitements, planning, sometimes even plotting together.

Though I missed the freedom of the fields these rides, the freshly cut bundle of grass that was brought me daily and the company of my cat kept me contented. Sambo and I often played together and it was considered one of the sights of the stable to see the whole of his tail disappear into my mouth while he purred happily, Miss Grace, being of nervous disposition always screamed. I would push him about with my nose making ferocious faces and he, pretending to be equally angry, would slap my face with his paws, always keeping his claws carefully sheathed. He often slept on my back, comfortable and warm on my summer rug, and then I had to move with great caution to avoid throwing him off.

CHAPTER FOUR

A good horse ruined

The summer passed, the other hunters were brought up from grass, fat, sleepy and rather dull. Grooming, exercising and ever-increasing oat rations began again, but this year I was the fittest horse in the stable. Estella was back in the next box, rather jealous that I had become such a favourite with Miss Fanny and already bemoaning the fact that her beautiful golden coat would soon be shaved away by the clipping machine.

That season I became an experienced hunter. I carried Sir Clarence for several weeks, generally as his first horse, and then he decided that I was behaving in a manner so much more temperate that Miss Fanny would be safe with me.

We were both delighted. She was so light and easy to carry and with the two of us watching to see which way hounds broke we rarely got a bad start. This, with our fondness for jumping, meant that we were always well up and we soon made a name for ourselves. There was the famous occasion of the five mile point from Crowley's Gorse to Austin's Mill spinney when only the huntsman, one very hard-riding squire and Miss Fanny were up and everyone else, including Sir Clarence, had been stopped by the swollen state of the Beverley brook.

Sir Clarence was rather proud of his daughter's riding, but Mr Roger seemed to be jealous and was always making unkind remarks, saying that it was unfeminine to ride hard, that she would never get a husband, that any lady who rode too well became laughing stock in the men's clubs.

Happiness, though pleasant to experience, is dull to read about. I could tell of endless hunts, of hundreds of fences jumped without mishap, of a few falls, of spring and autumn rides of summer holidays fetlock deep in grass, of getting fit and of being roughed off. Enough to say that the seasons passed. That I filled out and became rather more handsome and a great deal more sensible. That Miss Fanny grew up and became beautiful. That Sambo also grew larger and more magnificent and we were such fast friends that sometimes the lads would move me to another loose box just to tease him and then listen laughing to Sam's loud miaows and my answering whinneys until we found each other again.

There were some less happy events. Bayard became touched in the wind and was sold for light work, Estella's elegant legs began to give trouble so it was decided that she should stop work and have a foal and she disappeared to the farm. Bert left to work on the railway and Ben who had been one of the little stable boys was promoted to his place.

Ben's story was a sad one. He had no parents and no relations that he'd ever heard of and was found, ragged and barefoot, living on rubbish from a market and sleeping in a ruined building with a gang of homeless boys, all huddled together for warmth, by the famous Dr Barnardo who started so many homes for starving boys and girls. Sir Clarence, who was a great supporter of this work, hearing that there was a boy who wished to work with horses had found him a family on the estate and taken him on as stable boy. It had turned out a great success for Ben loved horses and we loved him. And, though he never grew very tall, through having been so starved in childhood, he had a nice, kind, freckled face and was always lively and good-humoured.

So four years passed and it seemed to me that Earleigh Court was the world, and happiness the natural state of things. The first blow fell suddenly; we heard that Lady Hilton was ill and must spend the winter in a warmer climate and that Miss Fanny would go with her.

Miss Fanny came to tell me about it herself. She cried a little as she told me how much she was going to miss our hunting, 'But it's only for a few months, Ebony,' she promised me, 'I shall be back in the spring.'

There was a subdued feeling in the stables all the next week and no hunting. But, once Lady Hilton and Miss Fanny had left with Sir Clarence, who was going to settle them in and then return, Mr Roger appeared and began to lord it over everyone. He had grown into a stout young man of twenty-four with a loud, fruity voice and a pompous and sometimes overbearing manner. He was disliked by both grooms and horses so I was not at all pleased at hearing him order me for the meet next day. 'Ebony and Sultan,' he said, 'and I shall ride Ebony first. Send a lad on with them and I'll take the dog cart.'

'Now Sir, you know that Ebony isn't really up to your weight,' said Mr Johnson respectfully. 'Sir Clarence was always careful not to give him a hard day when he rode him; it would break Miss Fanny's heart if any harm came to that horse.'

'If you think he's going to spend the whole winter eating his head off in idleness you're very much mistaken,' Mr Roger spoke rudely, 'He must take his turn with the rest and, since Miss Fanny is abroad, her feelings are neither here nor there.'

'Very well, sir,' said Mr Johnson coldly.

So next day Ben rode Sultan and led me over to Catterick Park. We went slowly but arrived early and stood in the drive outside the large plain house watching the other arrivals. The hunters were mostly ridden up by grooms, the gentlemen came on their covert hacks or in their dog carts. Country house parties came in carriages or wagonettes and the ladies who had come to watch drove up in elegant phaetons and carriages of every description.

It was a lawn meet, which meant that there was a party indoors and menservants came round with drinks and sandwiches for those outside. Ben had a glass of ale and seemed pleased with it. At last Mr Roger raced up in our dog cart, he threw the reins to the groom sitting behind him and strode into the house.

'Oh dear, why doesn't he allow more time?' gasped poor Shamrock who was dripping with sweat. 'We waited at the front door for twenty minutes getting thoroughly chilled and then we came here at such a pace, uphill and downhill, I haven't drawn breath all the way.'

Presently the riders began to come out of the house and the grooms pulled off rugs and tightened girths. Everyone was mounting but there was no sign of Mr Roger, I fidgeted impatiently. At last he came, his face was redder than ever, 'Cherry brandy,' said Sultan sniffing.

Hounds were moving off. I sidled and pranced in an agony of impatience for I could see that we were going to be left behind. Mr Roger swore at me and then at Ben who was trying to hold me still. Even when he was up he was fiddling with his whip and gloves. I snatched at the reins and when he jerked my mouth in retaliation I gave a small protesting rear. At last he let me go and I hurried forward making my way through the press of horses to what I thought of as my right-ful place, the front.

We caught up at covertside and I watched, trembling with excitement, as hounds waded through the undergrowth, their sterns lashing as they found faint traces of fox. At any moment their deep cry would resound through the wood, the huntsman would blow his horn and we would be off across country taking hedge and fence and ditch as they came. Miss Fanny had always understood my excitement and given me a pat or a calming word or walked me up and down a little. But Mr Roger had found a crony; he was sitting side-ways on my saddle smoking a cigar and they were talking in loud voices about a dance they'd been to and discussing the merits of the various young ladies in a very disrespectful way.

I began to fidget and twirl about, forcing Roger to sit properly, for all the knowledgeable riders were slipping away. The Vicar came past on his stout white cob. 'Your sister's horse doesn't approve of your coffee housing, Roger,' he laughed, 'you'd better get moving.'

'He's had far too much of his own way,' said Roger jerking my mouth and kicking me with his spurs. I had stood all I was going to so I gave a plunge and a buck and shot off up the track. We were just in time. Hounds had found and were pouring out on the far side of the covert. The huntsman blew the 'goneaway' as he galloped on with the main body of the pack, the whippers-in were cheering on the tail hounds.

'Hold hard! Hold hard! Give them a chance,' shouted the master, as with one hand held up, he tried to control the eager riders. We horses were wild with excitement, the clamour of hound and horn had gone to our heads. The riders crammed down their hats and shortened their reins and then we were off, across a great grass field with a tall, dark bullfinch ahead. I leapt clearing the solid part of the hedge brushing through the straggling branches above, Mr Roger protected his face with his arm, there was a yawning ditch, I stretched out to clear it and landed in the next field. Hounds were bearing left-handed, I went after them.

I could give you a fence by fence account of that hunt, but I know from my own experience at Earleigh Court, where tired hunters *would* describe in detail every leap they had taken during the day's sport, how very dull such accounts can be. But it was a long and fast run and Roger's weight and riding were a great hindrance to me. He seemed to think that great activity from him was needed at every fence and he would spur away at all the wrong moments. He held me on a tight rein when we went downhill, he sat on the back of the saddle belabouring me with his stout hunting crop when we went uphill. He liked to be masterful but he did none of the things a good master should: picking the good going, steering his horse away from rabbit warrens, choosing the easiest line of country as his horse tires, slowing him for a breather.

We seemed to gallop for miles without a check. I was labouring, rolling in my stride, my breath was coming in gasps. There were very few horses left with us, but I was determined to keep with hounds. I was giving all I had, but those spurs were still prodding my sides, that crop still drumming on my ribs. There was a stile in a hairy hedge. I gathered all my remaining strength for it was uphill and both take-off and landing looked slippery. Instead of keeping me together and sitting very still Roger lurched in the saddle, brandished his whip, spurred me violently and shouted 'Hup'. I suppose he thought he was encouraging an unwilling horse to jump, but he disorganised everything. I slipped as I took off, landed awkwardly and felt a sharp pain shoot up my off

fore leg, but I recovered my balance and galloped on struggling up the hill.

Mercifully hounds had stopped. They were milling round several holes beneath the windswept trees of a sandy knoll.

'Gone to ground, dammit,' grumbled Roger, as the huntsman blew the call. Other horses came struggling up the hill to join us. Their riders jumped off, turned their heads to the reviving wind and loosened their girths. Roger sat slumped on my back, a terrible dead weight. Sandwich cases, and flasks appeared.

As I cooled off I noticed the bitter chill of the wind and I was glad when the huntsman called hounds together and we set off downhill. There was no sign of the second horsemen. Several gentlemen said that their animals had had enough and they would go home, the rest of us jogged wearily to the next draw. I felt very tired and my off fore was still giving me twinges of sharp pain, so I felt no disappointment when we drew the covert blank. We hacked on to a larger covert and still the second horses had not come up.

This time we found and we were soon galloping across

open country, but I felt none of my usual fire, I was jumping carefully saving my off fore. Roger didn't notice that anything was wrong and I feel sure that I was only saved from breaking down completely by a check, and the arrival of the second horses. It was a great relief to have Ben's light weight on my back and to set off for home.

For the first time in my life I failed to eat up and Ben and Mr Johnson fussed over me offering gruels and mashes. Next morning they found that my foreleg had heat and swelling and I had to stand with water from the hose pipe trickling down it for an hour and then have liniment rubbed in three times a day. It soon felt better, but for two days I was only led out for walking exercise up and down the drive. Then, on the third day I heard an angry voice outside my box, 'Well, is the wretched animal lame or isn't he?' demanded Mr Roger. 'I've told you, Johnson, I'm not standing for mollycoddling that horse, he's got to take his turn with the rest. I need six horses tomorrow, for my two friends and myself. If we have Pegasus, Merlin and Jupiter for first horses that leaves Ebony, Sultan and Nimrod for the second string.'

'But you know Sir Clarence's views on hunting a horse two days a week, sir. He never permits it except in very exceptional circumstances,' objected Johnson. 'And two days with heat in a leg is asking for trouble; a strain can so easily become a sprain and then . . .'

'These *are* exceptional circumstances,' interrupted Mr Roger. 'And I think it's a very poor business that with an establishment of this size I can't ask a couple of friends down without all this trouble over mounting them. In my opinion a stud groom doesn't know his job if he can't turn out six sound horses for a bye day.'

'Very well, sir,' said Mr Johnson controlling his anger, 'but I wish it to be clearly understood that you have gone against my advice and that if anything happens to Ebony I am not responsible.'

'Of course you're not responsible. In my father's absence I am master here and I'll thank you to remember it.'

Ben redoubled his efforts with the linament and I felt quite

43

myself again and almost inclined to agree that Mr Johnson was mollycoddling me. So the six of us set off quite cheerfully for the meet.

We saw our stable companions move off to the first covert and then we joined the rest of the second horses and guided by the master's groom, who had a list of the draws, we hacked quietly in pursuit of the hunt.

We came up with them at about one-thirty and found our friends very much exhausted. Pegasus complained of an overreach, Jupiter of a badly bruised knee, while Merlin, who was getting on in years, just stood with his head drooping.

The three young men still seemed very full of spirits. They mounted us and were off larking over fences before hounds had found a fox. At first we entered into it all enthusiastically. Mr Roger knowing of my ability to leap anything in cold blood, challenge his friends first to a brook and then to some park palings that were quite five feet. They were looking round for something else to jump when the master realised what was going on and called them to order. Then hounds found and we were off, our riders urging us on, putting us recklessly at the highest part of every fence and showing off to each other in a very wild manner.

As we grew tired the fun began to pall, but the young men seemed to have forgotten that we were flesh and blood. The run was a very long one, but if they had saved us at the start I think we would have finished, for we were all very fit. As it was, the larking about and racing had taken it out of us and we dropped farther and farther behind. Then poor Nimrod fell, crashing heavily into a ditch and lay there exhausted. He was pulled out, got back on his feet and remounted. We went on, following the tracks of the vanished field into the gathering dusk. Sultan stumbled twice and all but fell with exhaustion. My foreleg was giving me considerable pain and I was soon so lame that even Mr Roger noticed. He swore and dismounted. 'Here's a fine thing,' he said, 'What a collection of old crocks! I'm going to advise my father to dismiss Johnson, the man's useless; then he can send this lot to the knackers and buy some decent horses.'

The friends had dismounted too. 'There's a small farm down there,' said one of them pointing. 'Shall we make for it?'

'Yes, there's nowhere better in sight. With luck the farmer will have some sort of trap and we can get home in that and leave the brutes here for the men to fetch.'

It was a long painful hobble down to the farm and we were all hitched up in the stable while the young men told the farm lad to look sharp and get the trap ready, for he could see to the horses when they had gone. They drove off laughing and then the lad did his best to make us comfortable.

It was a small, rough farm and there was only one old horse rug which he put on Sultan who was trembling uncontrollably, Nimrod and I had to make do with sacks. He brought us warm water and then oats and hay. The oats were musty but the hay was quite eatable. The worst of it was standing tied in a stall, for my leg was very painful and swelling rapidly, and I did not like to lie down. Then my sacks slipped off and I began to feel very cold, the huge cart horse headcollar was rubbing my nose and my leg grew worse and worse. I was a very sad and miserable horse shivering there in the dark and I don't think my two companions felt much better.

It was about two hours later that we heard the sound of the returning trap and then the voices of Mr Johnson and Ben come to our rescue. We whinnied and they came hurrying in with rugs and lanterns and then they fetched hot water from the farm house and made us gruel.

Mr Johnson was very upset when he saw my leg.

'Well he has done it now. No more hunting for you, Ebony, not this season and maybe never. Just look at that tendon! Oh the wicked waste of it, ruining a fine young horse!'

'Whatever will Miss Fanny say?' asked Ben dismally.

'It doesn't bear thinking about, but what can a servant do in such a family matter? Run and ask the farmer's wife to put the kettle on again; a hot fomentation will help to relieve the pain.'

CHAPTER FIVE

A new home

I stayed at that farm for several weeks. They made two of the stalls into a loose box and Ben came over every day to attend to me while the veterinary surgeon would come and shake his head over me several times a week. When I could walk without too much pain they led me home to Earleigh Court and there Sir Clarence came to see me. He seemed very angry as he stood looking down at my misshapen leg, but all he said was, 'Miss Fanny is heartbroken.' And, 'Well, we'll try a summer at grass and then see if he is fit for light work.'

So I was turned out, not with the other horses for Mr Johnson said I would only be tearing about making myself worse, but with Ambrose the old donkey who pulled the mowing machine that mowed the great lawns around the house. We had a pleasant paddock at the back of the stables and only an iron paling separated it from the drive that led to the church. This meant that we had plenty to see and Sunday was a very sociable day. I enjoyed the bells and the singing and the sight of the people streaming up and down to church in their best clothes; some of them went three times on the same day. Most people walked because of the horses having their Sunday rest, but sometimes a carriage came. Best of all I liked the Sunday school children and I used to wait for them by the fence and most of them would stop for a pat and a talk.

Ambrose wasn't much of a talker, but I grew fond of him and he partly made up for the loss of Sambo. I used to miss him when he put on his boots and went off to mow the lawns.

It was autumn when Miss Fanny came to see me. She looked at my leg sadly and then she told Ben who'd come with her carrying the headcollar and the sieve of oats, that she was to be married and would live abroad for several

46

years and, in the circumstances Sir Clarence had decided that I should be sold to a friend of the family. A gentleman who had had a serious hunting accident and needed a well-mannered hack; a lady's horse, narrow and not too tall to mount, for he was still rather crippled from a badly broken leg.

So I was taken up from grass and given light exercise. Mr Arkwright, my new master lived in the north and was connected with the Sir Richard Arkwright who had invented the mechanical spinning machine, so Johnson told Ben. He was a colliery owner with a great coal mine. 'Not an old family like Sir Clarence's,' Johnson said, 'new rich, but educated and gentlemanlike. He was the owner of a fine stable of hunters before his accident.' They all thought it a good place for me.

Mr Arkwright hadn't the time to come south to see me, so he bought me on Sir Clarence's recommendation and I had to travel north by train. It was terrible, especially the shunting. I could stand the noise and the steam and the whistles, but the shunting backwards and forwards and all those jolts and bangs would have unnerved me completely if they had not sent Ben to keep me company.

It was already dark when we arrived at the end of our train journey and left the station for a gas lit street. Ben explained that we were spending the night in the town and hacking on next day and that as the new Railway hotel had no stabling, being built for those travelling by train, we were booked at the old coaching inn, The Bell, in the High Street.

We were greeted by a very old ostler and led into a great gloomy rabbit warren of a stable. He insisted on helping Ben groom me and I've never heard such hissing. He told Ben that he ought to hiss louder for there was nothing like it to stop the dust from the horse's coat going down into your throat and lungs. There were only half a dozen horses stabled there that night, but he told us that they had room for sixty and that twenty or thirty years ago they would be full up nearly every night. 'Them were the days,' he said, 'you'd hear the horn, and there was the stage coach pulling up outside; out with the fresh team of horses, get to work on the dirty, tired ones. Then there'd be all the private carriages and the post horses and on market days you couldn't move for horses, there'd be traps and gigs left everywhere, blocking the roads and alleys. But it's all gone, the railway killed it all.'

'And what happened to all the folk that worked here?' asked Ben rugging me up.

'Lost their jobs, took to the roads most of them, tramped off to find other work. The booking clerks were all right, the railways took them on, but the coachmen – they never got over it. They'd been someone you see, people were proud to know them, proud to sit up on the box with them. They were famous. So when it all went they had nothing. Took to drink most of them, drank themselves to death.'

I spent a comfortable night, my bed of straw was deep and my nearest companion a peaceful piebald mare called Magpie. Ben had been less well looked after and arrived scratching furiously and complaining that his bed was full of fleas. He turned me out very well, saying that I must make a good impression on my new master, and then we set out cheerfully on the last twelve miles of our journey.

Our road led over the moors, the air was very fresh and clear and hills covered in purple and brown heather stretched round us in all directions. Ben was still whistling away and I was still gazing around me fascinated by this new world when we reached a grey stone village and passing through we came to tall iron gates in a grey stone wall and turned up a drive. We passed the side of a fine stone house and turned into a very pleasant looking stable yard.

We were greeted warmly by the grooms, but Ben and I both had difficulty in understanding their Yorkshire accents. I was taken into a large loosebox and word was sent to Mr Arkwright that I had come. He appeared in a few minutes limping badly and walking with a stick, he was a fairly tall, thin man and you could see that he had been seriously ill, from the pallor and the deep lines of his face.

My rug was whipped off and Ben had my headcollar on and stood me up while Mr Arkwright and his head man discussed me. They seemed very pleased and Mr Arkwright asked how I'd taken to the train and the inn.

'No trouble at all,' answered Ben. 'He's a clever horse, if you use him right and give him time and he understands what you want he'll always do it.'

'Well he's certainly a nice looking animal so if he's steady enough he'll be just the thing,' said Mr Arkwright giving me a pat. 'I can't manage a horse that plays up with this crippled leg.'

'If you get on the right side of Eb he'll do anything for you,' said Ben and his voice choked. 'They say Miss Fanny cried her eyes out at parting with him and I for one shall hate to see the old fellow go.'

Then they all went away and presently a strange lad brought me a feed.

I felt very homesick for Earleigh Court and all my friends there and was quite dejected for a few days. Everyone at The Hall did their best for me and they seemed to have been told about Sambo for they brought me every shape and size and colour of cat. I nuzzled them all politely and got scratched and spat at several times for my pains, but in the end a small tabby did decide to stay in my stable, she was a good mouser, but hadn't much to say for herself; I never had another cat friend like Sambo.

Mr Arkwright insisted on trying me first. Draper the head man begged him not to in case I was not as quiet as I was said to be, or had been upset by my journey. But Mr Arkwright, who seemed quite an obstinate man, said that if he couldn't manage a nine-year-old with perfect manners and suitable for a lady, the sooner he was finished off the better.

I was led to the mounting block and Draper held me tightly, but of course I was used to Miss Fanny mounting from the block and once from a gate when she dropped her whip out hunting, so I sidled up as close as I could and stood like a rock to give Mr Arkwright confidence. When we'd got him up we went for a stroll down the drive and then we tried a trot and Mr Arkwright seemed well pleased.

'He is so narrow that he doesn't cause me the pain that the

cob did,' he told Draper, 'and he moves so well there's no jolting.' He patted my neck. 'If it wasn't for the error of reading too much that is human into the animal mentality I'd say he sympathised with me having been a crock himself.' He dismounted gingerly. 'I'll ride him round about the place for a week and then over to Blackmarsh.'

The Hall had been built in a very beautiful spot with the moors on three sides of it and small farms with hilly green fields, enclosed by stone walls and inhabited by flocks of sheep on the other. With Mr Arkwright riding me daily I soon learned to know the neighbourhood. In two directions the moor seemed to go on, wild and deserted, for ever, and we had many rides over it and round the farms. Then one day we took the third road over the moor. It led us across a very high, bleak stretch and brought us to the head of a valley and a very different scene. Columns of black smoke rose from the tall chimneys and great dark mills of the manufactories. Mr Arkwright, who always talked to me a great deal when we were out together, let me stand and look in amazement from the great factories themselves to the railway sidings and the coal for factory engines, to the rows and rows of little blackened dwellings where the people lived, then he said. 'It's mucky and ugly, Ebony, but the source of the nation's wealth. You don't grow rich and powerful on agricultural products and a beautiful landscape.' Then he turned me suddenly and we cantered away.

By the end of the week everyone in the stable trusted me and there was no doubt that Mr Arkwright's leg, health and whole appearance had greatly improved. It was generally agreed that he was now fit enough to ride to Blackmarsh Colliery, instead of using the carriage or the dog cart as he had since his partial recovery.

We took the same road as for the manufactories, passed the head of their valley and then came down into an equally despoiled area. A land of black pyramids, called slag heaps, of blackened grass and blackened trees and even a stream which ran with blackened water. The sharp arid smell of coal filled my nostrils blotting out all other smells. We went

through the wide gates into the colliery. There was a group of grimy buildings and the pit head, a great wheel supported on heavy beams above the shaft that went down deep into the ground. A tall chimney gave forth smoke, a noisy engine gave forth steam. Stout cobs and heavy horses passed me pulling carts of coals. Great trucks brimming with coals stood on the tramways that led down to a railway siding. Men and boys with black faces hurried about their business and over all hung an atmosphere of gritty dust and the overpowering smell of coal.

A bent old man hobbled out and took my rein. 'It's grand to see you on a horse again, sir,' he said, 'and a fine looking animal too.'

'Yes. His name is Ebony and he answers to it,' said Mr Arkwright climbing carefully down from the saddle. 'Look after him, Matthew, he's worth his weight in gold.' Then he vanished into a building labelled 'office' and I was led into another with 'Pony Sick-Bay' written up over the door. This turned out to be a stable, with a comfortable loose-box already prepared for me, and a row of stalls in which were tied several little ponies.

They were exceptionally sturdy ponies and with their strong necks, broad chests and round quarters, they looked like tiny cart horses. Their manes were hogged, every hair of their tails was clipped off close to the bone and they were all stallions. When Matthew had rugged me up and gone away I looked into the stall next to me. A little old grey nodded sleepily. His legs, thick and filled, were bowed with hard work, his body was covered with old scars and his elbows capped with large unsightly callouses.

'What do you little fellows do?' I asked.

The grey raised his weary head. 'We are pit ponies. We work in the mine pulling the tubs of coal from the coal face, where the men cut it, to the cage which brings it to the surface. It's a hard life,' he sighed and lowered his weary head. The bay in the stall beyond was younger. He told me that his name was Pipkin and that he'd been brought to the surface some weeks before because a runaway coal tub had crashed into him, all but breaking a hind leg.

'They've patched me up,' he said cheerfully. 'I'm almost sound now so I shall be going down soon. I shan't come up again until I'm past work like Tammy, unless I have another accident.'

'You live down there night and day?' I asked.

'Yes, there are stables underground, not as comfortable as this one. There's never enough bedding and, as you can see, we all have capped elbows through lying on the bare floor. Tammy can remember the days when there was always an inch or two of water on the floor, but they've drained that away.'

'And is it quite dark?'

'Not when the men are there, they all carry their special safety lamps. A naked light can cause an explosion because of all the gases that abound in the atmosphere. When I was brought up the light seemed so bright it was almost unbearable, but they put me in the dark little stable next door and let me become accustomed to it gradually.'

'Why don't they bring you up for Sundays and holidays?' I asked.

'Because this is a deep mine and so the temperature down below is always very warm and humid and the ponies brought to the surface frequently lose condition or catch chills. Also some ponies are frightened by the movement of the cage and there are terrible accidents when they break loose in their panic and hurl themselves down the shaft to their death.'

'It's the hardness of the work that does us in,' said a tiny chestnut who was called The Giant. 'I'm only eleven hands but I'm expected to pull great tubs of coal for two shifts a day, five days a week. The men only work one shift and we're only supposed to do ten hours, but the good ponies are often taken out twice, which leaves four hours out of the twenty-four for eating, sleeping and resting. You work till you can scarcely stand, your legs go, your wind breaks, cough, cough, cough, day and night. Tammy has seen ponies die at their work, but nowadays they bring us up before we quite come to that, but I'm finished, I'll never be of any more use.' He sighed and we all stood feeling very sad as he gave his hacking cough. Then Georgie, a little skewbald, spoke up from farther down the stable. 'The food and water is dreadful. I can't touch it. There's coal dust in everything. I became quite ill after only a week or two, that's why I've been brought to the surface.'

'The food is not so bad here,' Pipkin told me. 'The horse-keeper is a good one, he keeps the feed bins tightly closed against the dust and he does his best to keep the water supply pure. I've known ponies come here from pits where the water tubs were so foul they stank and yet the ponies must either drink it or go without, and where, though they worked so hard, their feed was a few oats in chopped straw. Here we are well fed, with almost as many oats as we can eat. Our roads are kept in reasonable repair, so that they don't trap our feet, also the roofs, for if the wooden supports are broken they can catch and drag at our collars giving us terrible sores. There are rules about the heights of roofs and the size of pony that may be used when the seams of coal and, consequently, the tunnels are small, as they are here. I have been along tunnels too low for me, one has to crouch and crawl and it is very hard work to pull a load in that cramped position. That is why the tiny ponies like Giant are overworked, there are so many place where only they may go.'

'Mr Arkwright seems such a kind and humane man,' I said, 'and all the horses at The Hall are so well looked after. I don't understand how he can allow you to be treated in this way.'

'It is all to do with money,' answered Pipkin.

Tammy raised his head. 'When I first went down there were old ponies who remembered the days when little children pulled the tubs. They wore a sort of harness and crawled along the tunnels pulling, just like we do now. There were even smaller children of four and five years, who used to sit in the dark all day opening and shutting the trap doors as the tubs came through. Then a law was passed and no women and no children under ten years were to be allowed to work underground, so the ponies were sent down instead. I suppose the coals must be dragged by someone.'

Mr Arkwright was soon in the habit of riding me over to the colliery on four or five days in the week. I enjoyed the ride even in the wintery weather with frost nails in my shoes or, on several occasions, half a pound of lard in each foot to stop the snow balling, and when I got there I enjoyed the company of the pit ponies. Then one day I arrived to hear anxious neighs and I found that Tammy and The Giant had gone and Pipkin and Georgie had been moved into the stalls nearest my box. They both looked very worried.

'What has happened?' I asked.

'They were taken away in a sort of cart,' said Georgie plunging in his stall. 'If I could break loose I would follow.'

'It was the knacker, I think,' Pipkin told me softly and sadly. 'The head horsekeeper and the vet came round yesterday. They examined Tammy and The Giant very thoroughly and I heard the vet say that their useful lives were over. Oh Ebony, I'm afraid they've gone for dogs' and cats' meat, their skins for leather and their bones for glue.'

I know that it is better for an old horse to be shot or poleaxed rather than left out in a cold field to die slowly of disease, but it seemed so very sad that Tammy and The Giant had had so little pleasure in their lives.

CHAPTER SIX

Trouble at the pit

I had belonged to Mr Arkwright for almost two years and he was growing so much stronger that he was talking of hunting again, but Mrs Arkwright was said to be very much against it and there was a lot of talk in the stable about who would win.

Then we heard that there was unrest among the miners. It seemed that the price of coals had fallen suddenly and the owners were refusing to pay the men a wage that had been promised, so they had come out on strike. Mr Arkwright often rode me over to Blackmarsh but there was no longer a busy, bustling scene. The great wheel was still, the engine silent and the railway trucks empty. The men and boys stood at the street corners without work or pleasure.

Some of the women would run after us as we trotted by calling on Mr Arkwright to save their children from starving.

Some children died, it was said, and Mrs Arkwright took to sending soup over to them in the wagonette. The men grew leaner and leaner and took their skin-and-bone dogs poaching for rabbits and other game in the woods and all the keepers stayed at home, rather than come to blows with starving miners.

It must have been after seven or eight weeks that things came to a head. Early one cold, foggy afternoon a message reached the house that there was trouble at the pit. One of the lads was immediately sent off to Bruddersford with a letter and told not to waste a minute on the way, I was saddled and taken round to the front door. Mrs Arkwright was there begging her husband not to go but he said he must and was quickly in the saddle. 'Now Ebony', he said, 'put your best foot forward. The men are planning to mob the manager's house and break up the pit head equipment and I must see if I can do any good by talking to them.'

I enjoyed the exhilaration of an unexpected gallop over

the moors though I had to keep a sharp watch out for rocks and holes, for Mr Arkwright seemed preoccupied with what lay ahead, rather than our present safety. We reached Black-marsh in about half the usual time and found that the gas lamps had been lit and the pit head, the wheel, the chimney and all the buildings looked blacker than ever in the yellow light. The iron gates had been taken off their hinges and thrown down and there were large groups of men some arguing, some agreeing, everywhere.

Their voices grew angry when they saw Mr Arkwright and they began to crowd us answering his quiet words with shouts, swearing and threatening gestures. I didn't like being in the centre of this sea of surging, angry men, I tried to back away for sticks and clubs were being brandished round my head, but Mr Arkwright rode me forward calling upon them to disperse and go home and not to do anything that they would afterwards regret. It seemed to me that we were losing the battle of words and that at any moment we would be set upon and I would have an eye knocked out by one of the vicious-looking sticks. I carried my head as high as I could and tried not to flinch but I was very frightened of the united anger of the crowd.

Just as I decided that our last moment had come, for one man had grabbed my rein and they were pressed round so close that I could see no way to escape, except by plunging into them and trampling on the fallen bodies, there was a shout and a cheer and then a crash of breaking glass across at the manager's house. The crowd turned and then, as more crashes and more cheers followed, they ran to join this new sport.

A crowd of men and boys were pulling up the railings round the manager's garden.

'Where is the Mayor,' muttered Mr Arkwright, 'what the devil's holding him up?' He took out his watch. Every pane of glass had vanished from the conservatory and the crowd were looking round for new victims. A man appeared suddenly with a flaming torch. 'Burn 'em out,' He shouted. 'Get some straw from the stable. Come on we'll burn the

rats out.' Half the crowd cheered, but the other half shouted
against it. One of the women called 'There's children in
there,' but another shouted, 'they don't care if ours starve.'

A lot of people were calling to the man with the torch to
put it out, but he made a sudden dash towards the front of the
house and at the same moment Mr Arkwright said 'Come on,
Ebony!' and we shot forward too. The crowd had cleared
from the front so we had a clear path and reached the man just
as he was thrusting the firebrand through one of the broken
panes. I stopped right against him and for a moment he and
Mr Arkwright wrestled for the torch, there was a smell of
oil and smoke, sparks landed on me. Then Mr Arkwright had
it. I turned. The crowd was shouting and cheering again and
some of the young men were running up for an attempt to
recapture the torch, everyone was pressing in on the side
where the railings were down. The railings which still stood
were a fair-sized jump, but I didn't mean to be trapped in the
garden. I broke into a canter hoping Mr Arkwright's leg was
up to it; if he fell off . . . He was quick to realise my intention.
He had the flaming torch in one hand but I felt him get the

other hand down and grip my mane, I knew he was doubting his leg too. I took the railings as smoothly as I could, the landing was hard, but we were out on our own.

There was a roar, half annoyance and half admiration, from the crowd and then Mr Arkwright was guiding me. He rode to a stone water trough, that was there for the benefit of the coal cart horses, and plunged the firebrand in; it hissed and died. I was thinking that the coal cart horses were not going to be pleased with the taste of oil, charred wood and cloth when there was a clatter of hoofs and a carriage came rattling through the colliery entrance.

'The Mayor at last,' said Mr Arkwright who was binding a handkerchief round his hand.

The Mayor, who seemed to be a very ordinary man with a gold chain round his neck, climbed up on the box of his carriage and while his coachman held a light and two police-men stood guard below he read out something called the Riot Act. There was a lot about dispersing and departing peaceably to their habitations or to their lawful business and the more peaceful miners came to listen, but the less peaceful ones went on smashing up the manager's summer house and breaking the last of his windows. Then we heard the sound of many hoofs on the road and the special jingle soldiers make because of their swords and spurs. The shouting stopped, the crowd began to melt away. The soldiers stopped a little way down the road and one man fired his carbine into the air, the sharp crack made me start, but then they just walked in quietly and the officer came to talk to Mr Arkwright and the Mayor. The horses were a smart-looking lot, strong but not fast, I decided. Mr Wilson the manager had come out and joined in the conversation, it seemed that no one was hurt though his younger children had been much frightened. He and Mr Arkwright began to make arrangements for the repair of the damage and some of the soldiers went to hoist the great iron gates back on their hinges. The Mayor left and at last Mr Arkwright decided that we could go too.

It was very dark and there was no moon but we set off cheerfully for we knew the road well and the night is never so black when you have been out in it a little. We passed the valley of the manufactories and stopped for a moment to look down at the great cotton mills, every window blazing with gas light, smoke and steam and the red glow of furnaces all rising up from the valley and then being swallowed into the vast darkness of the sky.

As we climbed higher we found fog and the higher we went the thicker it grew, swirling round us, nuzzling us with its wet kiss, blotting out everything. Mr Arkwright dismounted and led me. He was limping and I could see that the hand he'd hurt getting the torch was paining him. We were both cold and tired now that the excitement and terror of the evening had died away.

We plodded on wearily, following the road by the feel of its hard surface beneath our feet and noticing the change directly if we strayed on to the turf or heather at the side. Then we began to go downhill and the fog was thinning a little and suddenly I knew we were on the wrong road. I stopped and lifted my head and sniffed the air. Mr Arkwright swore. 'We must have gone wrong at the cross-roads on the top,' he said. 'I don't see how we did it, except that all senses of direction are suspended in a fog. Come on Ebony, we'll have to back.' We turned and I began to hurry I'd had enough of this outing and wanted my supper and stable. Suddenly Mr Arkwirght slipped and fell. For a moment he rolled and twisted in pain, then he half sat up. 'This really is the last straw!' he said. 'I've done something to that ankle and they'll never find me here though they search all night.' He felt his leg gingerly and then he made an attempt to rise. I positioned myself near him thinking that he might like to pull himself up by the stirrup. He took the hint and got himself up on his good foot then he tried to put the other to the ground, but gasped and staggered and would have fallen had I not been there to lean against.

Carefully he lowered himself to the ground. 'I must stay here until I'm found. Well, the weather's not too bad. Many a man has died up here, lost in the snow, but I shall get away with an uncomfortable night and a chill. If only I was not so damnably cold already.' He looked at me. 'Go on, Ebony, home.' He clapped his hands and clicked his tongue. 'Go on, raise the alarm and, even if you can't tell them where I am, at least you'll be in a warm stable and there won't be two of us down with pneumonia.'

I felt very reluctant to leave him, but I set off, reins and stirrups dangling, at a purposeful walk. I went uphill back into the thickest fog and tried to find the homeward road. I was at the cross-roads and wandering uncertainly when I heard the sound of hoofs and the rattle of a trap. I neighed and hurried forward to meet it. Storm's neigh answered mine. I trotted down the road neighing with joy. It was the dogcart with its lamps lit and voices called, 'Mr Arkwright, sir, are you all right?' Then they saw my empty saddle. 'Oh God, the Master's had another fall.' 'Jump down Harry and see if Ebony's all right,' directed Draper. 'Here take the lamp and look at his knees; has he been down?'

'No, not a scratch on him.'

'Well keep the lamp and walk on. Go carefully we don't want to injure him if he's lying senseless in the road.'

'I had no such fear so I dragged Harry along at a brisk pace trying to show him that I knew what I was doing.

'Watch the sides of the road too,' called Draper. 'He may be lying on the grass and we don't want to miss him.'

We came to the cross roads and this time I was certain of my direction and when Harry tried to continue along the Blackmarsh road I refused to follow.

'Here, where do you think you're going, Ebony? It's this way,' he clicked at me and tried to pull me forward. From behind Draper flicked me with the driving whip, 'Come on,' he said. 'No messing about, we've got to find the Master.'

I pulled hard and dragged Harry down the right road, hampered by the lamp he could only pull me round in a circle, and when he tried to get me going again, I jibbed. Both men shouted at me. I still refused to move. They were getting angry, Harry jerked roughly at my mouth, I reared. Draper gave me a sharp cut with the whip. I reared again, higher. And as I came down, narrowly missing Harry with my hoofs, I twisted and plunged and wrenched the reins from his hands. I had galloped a few strides down the road before I trod on the reins flapping round my feet and jagged my mouth severely. They broke. I trotted a few more yards and then turned to see if Harry was following me. He wasn't, so I neighed. He came on and I waited for him. Then, as he got near, I whirled away, he followed me cursing. I did this several times and then Draper began to call from the cross roads. 'Leave him, Harry, come on back, we've got to find the Master.'

Harry wavered. I neighed loudly and then listened. There came on the foggy air a faint answering shout. Harry heard it too. He waved his lamp aloft and shouted. 'there's someone down here.' I moved on hoping that I was going to find Mr Arkwright. Harry followed ignoring the distant shouts from the cross roads. Suddenly a voice said, Well done, Ebony, whom have you brought?'

'Is that you Mr Arkwright?' asked Harry holding the lamp high, and then, suddenly seeing him. 'Oh thank God. We never thought to find you here. Are you much hurt?'

After that it all went easily. Harry ran back to tell Draper. There was a flask of brandy and a rug in the dog cart so Mr Arkwright was soon feeling better and then they lifted him in. Harry made me reins of a piece of cord and mounted and we set off for home. The dog cart took the shortest way, but Harry and I went round by the doctor's house and asked him to come quickly to The Hall.

They made a great fuss of me in the stable that night. Harry gave everyone a very dramatic account of how I had reared and plunged and led him to the Master. Mrs Draper came with a bowl of apples and carrots and brought all the little Drapers to admire me.

As for Mr Arkwright it seemed that he had dislocated his ankle, but as it had never been quite right since his hunting accident, there was hope, that now it was properly put back by the surgeons, there would be an improvement.

He never tired of telling people that I had saved his life, or very nearly so, *and* the manager's house on the same day.

CHAPTER SEVEN

The explosion

Another year passed. Mr Arkwright did manage a day or two's hunting, but we regarded ourselves as old crocks and came home early. The countryside was so wild that speed and jumping ability were far less necessary than in the south, but the pace was more suitable for a horse of my age.

Then spring came earlier than usual for the north and a long hot summer followed.

It was on a particularly hot and heavy day in August when I was standing in the Blackmarsh stable, I was dozing, undisturbed by the familiar sounds of steam engines, clanking trucks and passing coal carts. Then suddenly there was a strange trembling of the ground beneath our feet, followed by a muffled bang and then a much nearer crash. Then men's voices began to shout and alarm bells sounded.

Thoroughly awake I listened. It was impossible to see what was going on, but it seemed to be to the pit head that everyone was running. Then Matthew came in to saddle me. He seemed very disturbed and kept shouting at the boy to bed down the spare stalls and fill all the pails with clean water and put the medicine chest ready. The boy was crying, 'My Dad's down there, and my two brothers.' 'And so are my sons and grandsons,' answered Matthew. 'Now, where's young Wilson?'

Young Wilson came, he was a youth, dressed for the office, but he soon scrambled up on me.

'Take it steady,' advised Matthew, letting go of my rein. We set off at a brisk trot and took the Bruddersford road as we turned out of the gate. He wasn't much of a rider but he had the sense to give me my head and he could click his tongue and cry 'whoa' so I understood him. We went into the town at a steady trot, there was no grass and the road was too hard for a canter.

63

Our first stop was the hospital, he hitched my reins over the railings and ran in. Then we went to the police station where he told them of the explosion from the steps and then on to the telegraph office where I was hitched to some more railings and waited a very long time with flies buzzing round my head. By the time he came back the news had spread and the whole town seemed to be calling to us. 'How bad is it?' 'How many are missing?' 'Are there many trapped?'

And young Wilson called back that he didn't know, that the cage had been damaged in the explosion and so far no one had been brought up.

All the way back we passed groups of anxious-looking women hurrying towards Blackmarsh to ask for news of their menfolk. Many of them had several small children with them and some carried babies.

Young Wilson didn't leave me at the stable but rode me right up to the pit head. I had never been so close before and when I saw the shaft, black and bottomless beneath the shadow of the great headstocks and wheel, I began to snort nervously and back away. The men gathered round the shaft seemed to be shouting to men down below. Engineers struggled with cables, instructions were called from the engine house, people ran to and fro with messages and orders.

'Right, we're ready to try again,' shouted an authoritative voice. 'Stand back, stand back,' became the general cry, someone told young Wilson to 'take that horse away.' We moved back a little but stayed to watch. There was a good head of steam, the wheel was moving slowly. There was a murmur of relief from the watchers, the cage was coming up.

We waited fearfully to see what would emerge when the gates opened and it was a sad sight. Men staggered out supporting damaged hands and arms or holding bloody cloths to their heads or faces, some were carried out by their fellows others had to be laid on stretchers. Mr Arkwright was there directing the long string of carts and wagons that had been collected to take the injured to hospital, and they were laid gently on the fresh straw and driven slowly away. The news was being passed from mouth to mouth, there were so many injured, so many missing, this man had seen his mates killed, that one had been parted from his in the dark and smoke and panic. A huge rockfall was reported here, a fire there. Mr Arkwright was questioning some of the less seriously injured. Young Wilson managed to catch his attention for a moment and told him that the hospital were sending a doctor and a nurse to deal with the most badly hurt and had prepared all their beds; that the police were on their way and that he had telegraphed as ordered. 'Well done,' said Mr Arkwright absently. 'Well put that horse away, see he has a drink. You'll be needed in the office to help make up lists of the injured.'

A great many injured men were brought up before the first pony found its way into the cage, but presently three very frightened, trembling little animals were led into the stable. One was rather burned and singed, another had a severe cut and the third was unhurt. He said that there had been a great wind and then a terrible bang and flash, the air had rushed past him and there had been a dreadful rumbling and falling of rocks. 'My boy unhitched me from the tub,' he said, 'and we ran together.'

The pony who had taken such a singeing said that he had been near the East Stable, drawing a load of pit props and when the explosion came all the wood and hay in the stable caught fire. 'My boy unhitched me and we got away,' he said, 'but the ponies that were in the stable made a terrible noise, pawing and trampling, neighing and groaning, they couldn't get out.'

The cut pony told me that he had been hurt by a pony that took fright and bolted still harnessed to his tub and that there were many ponies down there too badly hurt to be worth bringing up. They all three stood trembling from their fright and the horrors they had seen and heard and I wondered if men really needed coal badly enough to risk all these lives.

Then more and more frightened and injured ponies began to arrive and the stable was soon packed out. There was a veterinary surgeon as well as several horsekeepers trying to deal with them and the unhurt ones were being bundled out into a nearby field. I was taken out and tied to a ring in a wall, for my stable was needed, so I stood watching the carts and wagons coming up from the town to take the rest of the injured to hospital. There were many women standing in silent misery, waiting for husbands and sons who had not been brought up, and there were many children crying. I watched all the ponies coming by, hoping to see my friend Pipkin, but I never did and I fear he may have died in the East Stable.

The offices seemed to have been given over to the doctor and nurse and those who were too badly injured to stand the jolting of the wagons, and Mr Arkwright and Mr Wilson and all the chief engineers were gathered round a table outside. The table was spread with maps and plans and they seemed to be arguing on a plan of action. In the end they seemed to decide on two plans, for Mr Wilson, some of the engineers and a lot of men and equipment, were loaded on several wagons and drove away, the bystanders told each other that this party were going to try to reopen an old shaft on the far side of the rock fall. Meanwhile the other party, led by Mr Arkwright, had equipped themselves with lamps and tools and were preparing to go down in the cage. They were going to try to bore a hole through the rockfall and reach the entombed men that way.

The wheel turned and the cage disappeared from our view. Everyone waited. The sad and anxious women, there seemed to be hundreds of them, were very quiet and resigned. Some of the children still cried, but only softly. In the stable a badly injured pony groaned. The flies buzzed round my head but the heat of the day had passed. There seemed to be no more to do above ground. I rested each leg in turn as I waited.

A boy brought me a bucket of water and a bundle of hay and some ladies appeared in wagonettes and governess carts and began to dispense food and drink to the waiting people. We ate and drank and went on waiting.

The shadows lengthened, the flies ceased to torment me and then, suddenly, I felt that strange trembling of the ground beneath my feet and again it was followed by a muffled bang, this time I knew what it meant, I did not need the wail that went up from the waiting crowd to tell me that something terrible had happened.

The cage still worked and there were still men prepared to go down to rescue their fellows, they vanished and we waited again, this time my heart was heavy and anxious too. At last the cage rose slowly to the surface, but only the second party of rescuers walked out. The others were laid on stretchers and each still form, covered by a blanket, was carried sadly to the office.

Then Matthew came with my saddle and bridle.

'You must take the bad news to The Hall, Ebony,' he

said. 'It's a sad day's work. Mrs Arkwright's only suffering the same as the other women, but his death will bring changes, changes for all of us.'

The news of the explosion, the many deaths and above all the loss of Mr Arkwright, cast the deepest gloom over The Hall, but the plight of the entombed men and ponies made our own futures seem insignificant. We heard that the rescue attempts were continuing that an airway had been drilled, that tapping noises and faint hymn singing had been heard. And there were endless conversations about fire damp, about gases which exploded on meeting a spark or naked light, and gases which were called 'bad air' and killed as you breathed them in.

After three days the news came that thirty-nine men four ponies and a small dog had been got out alive and the rest of the missing were presumed dead. That was one hundred and seventy men and boys and I never heard how many ponies. Then the funerals took place. I didn't go but some of our carriage horses did, for though a great many black horses were hired for the occasion, with so many dead they could not get enough.

That ended the good days at The Hall. Mrs Arkwright was taken ill and had to go away and Mr Edgar Arkwright, the son who came to see to everything, had no liking for the north and said the whole place must be sold lock, stock and barrel. The grooms and the servants were all given their notice and we horses were sent down to the nearest large horse dealer to be sold.

CHAPTER EIGHT

Clarendon Mews

Mr Edgar Arkwright hadn't bothered to find us good homes, but Draper and Harry who delivered us to the horse dealer's yard did their best for us. They gave us all very good characters and explained the sort of work for which we were each best suited. I was to be sold as a patent safety for a lady and the dealer said he did not think there would be any difficulty for, though I was getting on, I was in perfect condition and he knew my history.

He was right, I was sold on the first day. A very large man called Mr Rawlings came with his dark and rather sullen groom, Hopkins. Mr Rawlings announced in a loud voice that he wanted a reliable hunter for his daughters. Good-looking but not too pricey, while Hopkins peered at my teeth and felt my legs. Then Hopkins rode me, he was slightly better than young Wilson, but not much. Mr Rawlings decided not to try me, for which I was very thankful for he looked quite twenty stone, but they put a side saddle on me and the dealer's little daughter rode me. She was really first rate so we put on quite a display and both enjoyed ourselves; I wished she could be my new owner.

Mr Rawlings lived in a tall, town house fronting a wide, tree-lined street and the stables were in the mews at the back. Two long rows of stables and carriage houses, with grooms' quarters above, faced each other across a narrow cobbled road with an archway at either end and each house in the grand street owned a stable in the mews. Our building had four stalls and space for two vehicles, hay, straw and harness. It was rather cramped and dark and not what I had been used to, but I told myself that if there were other horses and if the young ladies were like Miss Fanny I would be perfectly happy there.

Hopkins had fetched me from the dealer's and the moment

we entered the mews he began to swear at a boy of about twelve, called Percy, who seemed to be his only assistant. It seemed that the carriage horses must be put in at once and as the harness was dirty it must be wiped over when it was on.

''Er Royal 'ighness wants to go shopping. Not a minute's peace in this ruddy place,' Hopkins grumbled, thumping on harness and slapping the poor carriage horses when they protested. 'Here Perce, take this rag and clean the worst off them traces. Oh Gawd! There's mud on the floor of the carriage, get the brush, Perce, or she'll be kicking up'. Percy flew about doing the work, the carriage horses wriggled uncomfortably beneath their dirty harness and Hopkins changed into a brown livery. Then they all left, looking quite smart oh the outside.

Hopkins was right when he said that there was never a moment's peace in Clarendon Mews but it wasn't entirely his employer's fault.

Hopkins hated mucking out and he hated us when we lay down and got dirty. He was always swearing at us or at Percy because we were not ready. We never went anywhere without a last minute panic, some piece of harness of saddlery would be found to be dirty, a rein would be broken, a stirrup leather unstitched. It was the same with our food, the corn was always running out, or the chaff wasn't cut or the hay hadn't been delivered.

All this constant noise and chaos made me nervous and irritable especially as I had so little exercise and spent day after day facing the blank wall of my stall. The young ladies did not come to see their new hunter, much less ride him and Hopkins' idea of exercise was a fifteen minute trot round the back streets with him winking and smiling at all the pretty girls.

To add to my discomfort my coat felt neglected and dirty. Out at grass a horse keeps healthy without grooming, but stabled and wearing a rug he must be groomed thoroughly every day and this just didn't happen.

Mr Rawlings left everything to Hopkins, he never came into the stable the whole time I was there, I suppose he was busy with other things and had no interest in our welfare. Hopkins would go to the house every morning at five minutes to nine to get the orders for the day and if there was a change of plan the kitchen maid would be sent running round to tell us.

At last word came that Miss Helen and Miss Beatrice would be riding on alternate mornings and that Hopkins was to accompany them on one of the carriage horses. He was furious for now he would have two saddles and bridles to clean as well as the harness. He would be out riding in the morning and driving in the afternoon and, with the winter parties beginning, the carriage was often out at night as well. It was a lot for one man, but if he had taught Percy how to do things properly he could have been more use.

Miss Beatrice and Miss Helen were plump girls with round faces, round eyes and round mouths that were always emitting little screams and shrieks, which was very unnerving to the horse that was carrying them. They didn't trouble to learn to ride well and Hopkins was no teacher. They prefered to go round the town bowing and smiling to their friends rather than take the road which led out to the country.

I was filled with trepidation when I heard that Beatrice had decided to hunt me. Hopkins was sitting on a bucket reading the racing page, 'Go on, use some elbow grease,' he instructed Percy without looking up.'"'E's got to look a picture Hopkins", that's what she told me. Silly little madam. She's going man-hunting, not fox-hunting. Their Pa thinks they'll meet a better class of young man in the hunting field, that's what I 'eard 'im tell 'er royal 'ighness, so now Miss Beatrice is going to show off her charms to young Lord Beswick and the Hon Walter Pym.'

'I can't reach his ears, honest I can't', wailed Percy.

'Well stand on the manger then.' I hastily lowered my head.

I felt ashamed of my appearance as Hopkins riding Sinbad led me to the meet. My coat was dirty and dull, my bridle was stiff, the twisted curb chain dug into my chin

71

groove, and the saddle had been made for a much wider horse.

Mr Rawlings had driven his family to the meet with Sailor in a borrowed wagonette and I felt even more ashamed as Miss Beatrice, with many little screams, was pushed up into the saddle. I never knew two girls with less spring and Hopkins used to say that it shortened his life by six months every time he legged them up. Once in the saddle Miss Beatrice paraded up and down bowing at everyone, ogling the younger gentleman and giving little screams of apprehension if any of the other horse swung round or pranced.

At last we moved off. Miss Beatrice seemed inclined to ride near the front which pleased me for I had resolved to give her the hunt of her life and teach her what a pleasure it could be. She had manouevred us up beside the Hon Walter Pym and was giving little squeals of joy whenever he spoke to her. He sounded a very dull young man to me. He made a few remarks about the weather and laughed a very loud 'Ha, Ha!' after each one as though he had said something funny.

Young Lord Beswick seemed to have more sense and he even shushed Miss Beatrice when she gave squeal at covertside and told her that she must keep quiet, for she would distract the hounds or, worse still, head the fox.

Hounds found quickly. Some riders cut through the wood and others took the track round the outside. I followed this party for it is difficult to take ladies safely and quickly through trees, there is too much of them on one side. We galloped across a field, Miss Beatrice was already bumping about and out of breath. There was a small hedge and the Hon Walter Pym called, 'Miss Rawlings, follow me'.

I followed his horse, but it ran out and half a dozen other riders cannoned into it. While they were all cursing each other, I circled and popped over. Miss Beatrice hung on by the reins which hurt my mouth and gave a small scream as her hat came off, but hounds were ahead and there was not time to stop for hats.

I gradually slipped into a really fast gallop, it was wonderful, just what I had been longing for. There was a small post and rails ahead, another hedge then round the headland of a ploughed field through a gate and we came up with hounds; they'd checked, the huntsman was casting them. I slowed up and joined the other horses, I was out of breath, but what could you expect with no exercise. Suddenly I became aware that all was not well with Miss Beatrice, loud sobs were coming from my back and several gentlemen were hurrying to her assistance. 'He bolted with me,' she sobbed, 'I pulled and pulled but he wouldn't stop, Oh, help me down. I won't ride another step.'

'I don't think he really bolted,' said young Lord Beswick helping her down. 'He looks a good sort of old hunter, I'd just sit tight and leave it to him.'

'Miss Rawlings finds that she cannot hold her horse,' he said handing my reins to Hopkins. 'I don't think the animal was to blame, she is not experienced enough for the hunting field,' and mounting thankfully, he galloped away.

We went drearily back to look for Miss Beatrice's hat and then turned for home. I was thoroughly depressed, Miss Beatrice was tearful because her hair had come down and she had mud on her face and Lord Beswick had galloped away and left her. And Hopkins was furious because there were three dirty horses, one set of harness, two saddles and bridles and a borrowed wagonette to be cleaned. He didn't do any of it properly. He left our stables dirty and slung our rugs on over mud and sweat and worst of all my bucket wasn't re-filled when I drank it dry so I spent the whole night longing for a drink of water.

I had another ignominious hunt. Two Saturdays later Miss Helen thought she might succeed where her sister had failed, but she didn't take any sensible steps beforehand. She didn't take me out for rides and get to know me, she didn't practise galloping and jumping, so I can only suppose that Hopkins was right and that it was young gentlemen she was chasing and not foxes.

This time it was a lawn meet so she probably enjoyed showing off her new habit in the house, but she took fright

the moment she was put up on me, 'He's going to bolt, I
know he is,' she cried and became so hysterical that Hopkins
had to ride beside us with a hand on my rein. So there we
were creeping along at the back with the little children on
leading reins and the grooms on young horses. I was disgusted. Hounds found at once and we followed at a cautious
trot. Then, even Hopkins' blood rose a little, and he per-
mitted a sedate canter; gradually it grew a little faster. My
eyes were on hounds, they had swung round in a lefthanded

circle and were now only one field ahead. There was a tiny
hedge, Sailor said that he could manage it so we strode towards it side by side. There was a scream from my back and
then, as I took off, Miss Helen flung herself from the saddle.
The new habit caught on the pommel and there was a
rending noise before she rolled free. I stopped and waited,
wondering if she would remount. But she was screaming
hysterically that I had bolted and suddenly I felt that I could
stand no more. Throwing my responsibilities to the wind, I
set off after the vanishing hunt.

I chose my own line and took the fences as I came to them. I was filled with the familiar feeling of exhilaration and happiness. The country was an easy one, the fences of moderate size, so I felt no need of a rider to partner me.

We had a wonderful run and when I came up, out of breath and steaming with heat, after the kill the riders all laughed at me and someone asked, 'Enjoyed yourself, old chap?'

We had finished in stone wall country, miles from town, and there was trouble about getting me home. In the end a second horseman was found who agreed to go a couple of miles out of his way and drop me at Clarendon Mews.

Hopkins was not pleased to see me back. He hit me a sharp blow on the nose, the moment the other groom was out of sight, and used me very roughly as his wisped the worst of the mud off and rugged me up. There was no mash, but I was feeling defiant and not too tired, so I was able to enjoy my feed and hay.

As soon as Hopkins left us Sailor and Sinbad told me that there had been terrible trouble over the hunt. Miss Helen had cried, Mrs Rawlings had stormed and then cried, Mr Rawlings had been furiously angry and blamed Hopkins, I was to be sold.

CHAPTER NINE

I join a fair

I wasn't the clean and elegant horse when I left Clarendon Mews that I had been on arrival. In fact I was dirty and unfit, with a staring coat and a mane and tail that needed pulling, when Percy put an old rope halter on me and led me to the horse sale. Worst of all for an old horse I had no reputation left and not even a respectable stud groom to vouch for my character.

I was tied to a ring in the wall between a shivering and half-starved pony and a stout carthorse and a round paper with a number on it was stuck to my quarters. I turned as far as my rope would allow me and watched the scene. There was a great many people, mostly farmers and tradesmen, but also some very rough-looking men and boys who swore and spat a good deal.

The noise was very great. The sellers were telling everyone what good animals they were offering. The frightened horses were all whinneying and there was an endless clattering of hoofs and cracking of whips as they were run up to show their paces to likely buyers. There were a few men already drunk, though it was not yet twelve, and they were shouting and singing.

It was very unpleasant having my mouth forced open by complete strangers who wanted to see my teeth. Some of them felt my legs, slapped my flank and pulled out my tail as well, before making a disparaging remark about my age and walking on.

The farmers all thought me too well-bred. 'You got to cosset that sort,' they said, or, 'I 'aven't the time to look after a blood 'orse.' The tradesmen all asked if I was broken to harness and Percy, who didn't know any better, said no, I was a hunter. The occasional person looking for a cheap hunter was always horrified by my age. The cart horse next to me was having a better time. The farmers all said that 'he was a likely sort.' He told me that he'd been working on the canals, towing barges, he enjoyed the life but more and more goods were going by rail instead of by water so he and many more like him, were out of a job. But, he added placidly, that he would be quite happy to work on a farm.

At last two men came who didn't dismiss me as useless. The younger was tall and thin with an eager, handsome face, the other short and fat, wearing rather old fashioned clothes and smoking a cigar. The young one, Felix, stood back studying me carefully and then he said, 'I think we've found him, Alf. He's got presence, look at him, and breeding. Trimmed up a bit, well-groomed, he'd be exactly right; stupendous!'

'Except that he's not a mare,' said Alf. He looked at my teeth, 'Past his second youth. Is he sound? That's the question. And can he jump?'

'Oh yes, he can jump all right,' said Percy coming forward and he told them about my riderless hunt.

Felix laughed a lot. 'There, that clinches it,' he said. 'I knew at once he was the horse for us. Personality, looks quiet, friendly; a great jumper and any amount of character.'

Alf seemed less certain. 'We'll see what he fetches; I'm not paying much for a horse of his age. Here, boy, trot him out and let's see now he moves.'

I liked the look of Felix, I felt that he would be a considerate master and all that talk of jumping was music to my ears, but I hoped that he didn't want to hunt me in a fast country for I knew that I wasn't up to that sort of work any more.

Presently my turn to be sold came. I was walked and then trotted up and down amid a sea of white faces and brandishing whips, while the auctioneer called for bids. There was no great eagerness to buy me. A few of the people who'd looked at me bidded, one sounded like the undertaker, another voice could have belonged to the cats' meat man, the third was obviously a farmer. Then I saw Alf waving his catalogue in a lordly manner. At last the auctioneer's hammer fell and I was led away and tied up. The half starved pony was being sold, I hoped he would go to someone who would give him a square meal, and not for cat's meat. Then Felix came up carrying a saddle and bridle. 'We got you for a song, old horse,' he told me. 'Now, where's that boy? I want to know your name.' Percy seemed pleased that Felix was to have me. He put on the saddle, while Felix adjusted the bridle to fit my head, then he sobbed a tear or two as he stroked my neck, but Felix gave him sixpence and told him I should have a good home.

As Felix mounted and rode out of the sale yard I knew that he was a good rider. He felt confident and easy, he didn't attempt to impose his will on me, but just rode me quietly forward while he learned what I was like. In no time we were partners, it was as though I had Fanny or Ned back again and my heart rose as we left the town.

It was a frosty day but the sun was high and warm and had already thawed most of the bone from the ground. Felix sang as we walked and trotted along and altogether he seemed very pleased and cheerful.

We passed through several villages and then we cantered over a short stretch of moor and came to a long lane, between stone walls, that brought us down to a grey stone farm in the valley.

It was rather a tumble down place and the yard instead of being full of pigs or cattle, had a whole collection of living vans within its walls, like gipsy vans they had little chimneys, two windows and shafts for the horse, but the people who came, to greet us weren't gipsies, though there may have been one or two among them. There were a great many children playing everywhere and a smell of paint and cooking filled the air.

Felix led me into a stable. I saw with pleasure that it was quite a large loosebox and when I looked over the low partition into the next box I found the smallest pony I had ever seen. He was skewbald and much smaller than The Giant. He could not have been more than eight hands. He said at once that his name was Tom Thumb that he was the smallest pony in the world and came from the Shetland Isles. Felix was rubbing me down, someone was spreading my straw, someone else brought a bucket of water and yet another came running with a rug so I was soon very comfortably settled. When the humans had gone away and I had eaten my feed, Tom Thumb asked me what I did. I answered that I was a hunter and he didn't seem to find that at all satisfactory.

'I wonder what you'll do here, then,' he said. 'Oh well I suppose they'll teach you something. I jump through hoops, lie down, take handkerchiefs from my master's pocket, chase a boy round the ring and do numerous other tricks. I'm billed as The Clever Pony as well as The Smallest Horse in the World; people pay good money to watch me.'

I felt rather alarmed at this, but Tom Thumb, who seemed very pleased to have a companion, talked on and on. It seemed that he and his master Andrew had belonged to a circus, but there had been a fire and the equipment had all been lost so now they had joined this fair and soon we would all be travelling round the countryside performing.

I asked if he knew what Felix did and he answered that he was an actor and that sometimes a whole company of them went round with a fair, but he thought that Felix was the only one and he had been talking about an equestrian act. Then I asked about Alf and Tom Thumb said he was the Guv'ner and usually called 'His Nibs.' He settled the quarrels and arranged the fairgrounds and lent everyone money.

Felix seemed a very thoughtful master. The very next morning he spent a long time sawing and hammering at my door and when he had finished it was in two halves and the top one fastened back and enabled me to look out and see all the activities in the farmyard. I can't describe the pleasure that gave me. Being tied up in a stall is all very well for a short time and it's not so bad for a horse that is out all day doing slow work and only in his stall at night. But when a hunter or hack is condemned to spend twenty-two out of twenty-four hours, six or seven days a week, facing the same blank wall, well, it's no wonder that horses are driven to crib biting, windsucking and other nervous disorders.

After the boredom of the mews I was delighted with my

view and made Tom Thumb so jealous with my accounts of all I could see that he began to work on the bolt of the door between our boxes. He got the head up and then slid it back with his teeth and pushing the door open and came in with me. Of course he wasn't tall enough to see over the door and he had to balance with one toe on the cross bar. When Felix found our two heads looking out he laughed and fetched a stout box for Tom Thumb's forefeet.

For a few days Felix just took me for rides in the country side. We jumped some walls and hurdles and a gate and he seemed very pleased with me and always told everyone that I was 'just the thing'.

Then one day he took me into the barn. The floor was scattered with peat and a ring was marked out in the middle, it was rather a small space, but I was well enough balanced to canter round it quite fast, which pleased Felix. We practised entering at a wild gallop and stopping dead in the centre. He was very careful of my mouth and threw his weight back as a signal instead of pulling on the reins and, as soon as I understood what was wanted, I did it all on my own. Then we started work on the whole act. After the gallop in Felix would make a speech all about his wonderful mare Black

Bess and then another man called King would come in on one of the caravan horses and he and Felix, who was Dick Turpin, plotted together.

Then a very old coach came in, drawn by four very hairy horses and it was robbed by Turpin and King, several people fell dead and everyone fired pistols which made us horses jump at first though we soon became used to it. After that the police came and they captured King and he called to Turpin to shoot the men who held him, but Turpin missed and killed King by mistake.

Then a great chase began. I would go round and round the ring at a gallop, rush out and come in again from the other side and the pursuers were doing the same though they never caught up with us. We robbed another coach; it was the same one really, but they put a different name on the doors and dressed the people differently, and there was some more firing of pistols.

The next exciting part was when a toll gate was put up in the ring. As Turpin and I came galloping in the keeper shut it to stop us, but Felix would give a shout and I would soar over. After that I had to show signs of tiring and when I could only proceed at a weary trot with my head low we stopped at an Inn and I was given a drench of brandy or ale or something from a bottle, only the bottle was always empty.

Then we came to the city of York and a large cardboard spire was put up and bells began to ring. I was reduced to a walk and Felix dismounted and led me and then it seemed I was supposed to fall down dead. This wasn't easy to learn. Tom Thumb could do it and I was made to watch him, but I found all his advice very irritating and really got on better when Felix taught me alone.

He would take me to a nice soft spot and strap up one of my forelegs, then he would tap my other knee with a whip until I bent it and kneeled down. The moment I did I was praised and given oats or carrots. Gradually I learned to kneel without the strap and whenever he pointed at my knees. All he had to do then was to turn my head towards him and gently push my shoulder until I gave way and lay down on my side. I wouldn't have done it for Hopkins, but Felix was kind to me and made all my lessons enjoyable, so I decided to oblige.

I soon knew the routine and when we reached York and the bells began to ring, I would watch for the signal. When I had died Felix would make a long speech over my dead body and then the pursuers would come up and there was another fight. The first time this happened I raised my head to see what was going on, but this caused a great outcry from the watching children and Felix came and told me I had to stay dead.

The next problem was carrying me out. A great yard door was brought in and slid under as six strong men lifted me, then about twelve of them carried me out. I always hated this part but Felix would walk by my head and stroke my neck to keep me calm, so I put up with it.

CHAPTER TEN

Life as Black Bess

Though there were stablehands among the fair people Felix looked after me himself and by the start of the season I was a picture. Too round and well-covered to be hunting fit I was just right for a public performance, my coat shone, my mane and tail, neatly trimmed, were beautifully brushed out and this was just as well, for there were some very extravagent tributes to Black Bess's beauty in the verses Felix had to say.

On the day we moved out of our winter quarters all the carts and wagons and vans left very early in the morning. Felix and I started much later for we could take a short cut across country instead of going by the roads.

When we reached the fairground which was just outside a large town, Felix rode me to a tent with a large notice about Tom Thumb the Clever Pony and another saying that Captain Felix Fanshawe, late Royal Hussars, would present the stupendous equestrian drama *Dick Turpin's ride to York* with many spectacular fights and a thrilling performance by his famous horse Black Bess.

Inside was our usual ring and the cardboard Inn and spire and the toll gate and a couple more jumps were all ready at the side. I began to feel nervous but Felix rode me round until I was used to the tent and the lights and then he took me out to see the fairground. There were stalls for Hoop-la and ranges for shooting and coconut shies. There was a huge roundabout with brightly coloured and richly gilded horses and a steam engine to work it. There were many little booths with fortune tellers and fireproof ladies and fat ladies inside. There was Professor Lopescu's Flea Circus from Rumania and a Punch and Judy Show and many slides and swings and entertainments of all sort.

As it grew darker more and more lights came on and the steam engines sent sparks and smoke up into the dark sky.

There was a smell of burning coal and hot engines. Then a great steam organ started up. It was painted in bright colours and gilded like the horses and the noise from it was tremendous, as though a whole brass band was playing close at hand. I stood looking at the scene, turning this way and that to take it all in and Felix sat on my back laughing at my amazement.

When we went to the stable tent that I was to share with Tom he was being got ready for his act. He wore a silver and orange bridle, roller and crupper and from his forelock rose a very handsome orange plume. I wondered if I had to dress up, but no, it was Felix who came disguised. He had a curly moustache, a green coat and cocked hat, a belt full of pistols. Andrew was impossible to recognise with his face covered in white, a huge mouth and a false nose, he was dressed as a clown, and the small fat boy Tom had to chase had been made to look fatter than ever by very tight clothes.

When Tom left for the ring one of the stable hands put the finishing touches to my appearance, then Felix stopped brushing his coat and mounted and we walked over to the ring tent and waited in a dark corner.

Tom was pretending to become angrier and angrier with the fat boy and finally he chased him round the ring and out in a very ferocious manner. His Nibs, wearing black trousers, a scarlet coat and a top hat announced Dick Turpin, and Felix took me well back so that we could get up speed for our entrance.

We whirled in and round and came to a very dashing halt in the centre. Felix took off his hat and bowed low, I stared at the lights and the white faces all round me. Then Felix began the verses on how much he loved his bonny Black Bess. As he came to the last verse:

'*Mark that skin, sleek as velvet and dusky at night,*
With its jet undisfigured by one spot of white;
That throat branched with veins, prompt to charge or caress.
Now, is she not beautiful? Bonny Black Bess!'

King came riding in and they began to plan robberies.

We held up the coach, the horses were all looking a good deal smarter than they had at rehearsal and the guard had a horn to blow. There were the usual shootings and several deaths and then we made off with some bags labelled MONEY. King had taken too many and could not control his horse, which was why the police got him.

When Felix's shot killed him all the audience groaned in horror but they cheered up when we took one of the extra jumps and galloped away. These brush fences were not very big but though I was supposed to leap over perfectly the pursuers, especially the police were meant to run into each other, fall off and generally make a hash of things and this pleased the audience very much.

Then we robbed the second coach and came to the toll gate. It had grown larger at every practise and was now a big jump, about five feet. I took it carefully for the lights were casting strange shadows and made finding the right take off difficult. The people cheered and clapped as I soared over. We stopped at the Inn and Felix had another long verse to say which ended:

'By moonlight, in darkness, by night or by day,
Her headlong career there is nothing can stay.
She cares not for distance, she knows not distress,
Can you show me the courser to match with Black Bess?

Then I began to slow down and hang my head, soon I was only walking and then as the spire was put up and the bells began to ring, Felix led me. Right in the middle of the ring he pointed at my knees and I fell dead. The audience were very upset, I think some of them thought I really had died. Turpin was very upset too:

'Art thou gone, Bess? Gone – gone!' he cried out very dramatically. 'And I have killed the best steed that was ever crossed.

'O'er highway and byeway, in rough or smooth weather,
Some thousands of miles have we journeyed together;
Our couch the same straw, our meals the same mess;
No couple more constant than I and Black Bess.'

They fought the last fight and I managed to lie still and not look though it was very hard. Then the door came and they called for volunteers from the audience to help carry out poor dead Bess and I'm certain a great many people went home wondering whether I was really dead or not.

All the fair people thought the performance a great success and Felix kept patting me and saying 'Old horse, you're a natural, a born actor; stupendous!'

After that he became even more ambitious and besides adding new touches to our present act he was always thinking of other acts we could perform in the future and talking about *The Taylor of Brentford* and *The High-Mettled Racer* or,

86

The Fat Farmer, who wore layers and layers of clothes and undressed as he galloped round the ring.

We seemed to be doing well. We moved from place to place sometimes only staying for one day and night, sometimes for five. By the summer we had reached the west country and I was jumping the toll keeper as he ran to bar the way, as well as the gate, we were practising for the *Taylor of Brentford* which called for a lot of acting on my part as I had to push Felix around and make disagreable faces and pretend to bite him.

In some places our audiences were so large that we had to do Dick Turpin three times over every evening. I did get very bored at having to go through it so often and we had to think of new things to do to keep up our interest, Felix invented that I should raise my head and give my thoughtless master a kiss with my lips before I died; this upset the audiences very much.

In the autumn we came near to London and the idea was that we would work our way north and back to winter quarters, except for those who had special Christmas engagements.

Then one night some men came round to the stable when the performance was over. The stablehand was rubbing me down and Felix was unsticking his moustache. They introduced themselves and asked him out to supper. He seemed very excited and changing quickly he went off with them leaving me to the stablehand.

Next day Felix seemed very thoughtful and he had a long talk with His Nibs. Our show went on as usual but we gave up rehearsing *The Taylor's Ride*. I sensed that something was wrong and I lost some of my enthusiasm. But he didn't say anything until one morning when we had just come to a new town. Then he came rushing into my tent, he was dressed very smartly in his best suit. He put his arms round my neck and said, 'I'm sorry, Ebony, I feel a brute, a complete cad doing this to you. You've been magnificent, you did everything you could to make the show a success, you never let me down once and now I'm walking out on you. But you see, old horse, it's the chance of a lifetime, you *can't* refuse a part like this. You just can't!'

'If I had the ready cash I'd buy you from His Nibs and take you with me, but I haven't and no stable to put you in either. I'm truly sorry old horse.' He gave me a carrot and ran out of my stable. I couldn't believe that our happy times together had ended as suddenly and finally as this. For a day or two I thought he might come back, I would look for him in the mornings and when the time for our performance came, I felt sure that he could come bursting in, sticking on his moustache and telling me some new plan. Sometimes I thought I heard his voice and would whinney excitedly, but he never came.

Then I learned, from the talk of the stablehands, that he had been offered a good part at a big London theatre and might well become rich and famous. For a time I clung to the idea that His Nibs was finding another Dick Turpin to ride me and things would go on much as before, but men appeared who looked at my teeth and felt my legs and had me trotted up so I knew I was to be sold.

'Too old for a hunter,' they all said, and 'who wants a circus horse, he'll be doing tricks in the road.' And they haggled with His Nibs over the price.

At last a man with very fair hair came, he said that he owned a large riding school and livery stable in London and needed a reliable, well-mannered horse for his lady clients and was willing to pay a good price for the right animal. So I changed hands again and now belonged to Mr Chandler.

CHAPTER ELEVEN

A popular horse

I was amazed by London. One of our stablehands took me to an inn called The Three Horseshoes and there I was met by one of Mr Chandler's lads, looking very respectable in proper groom's clothes, and he rode me into London.

The height and variety and extent of the buildings and streets amazed me, but the number of horses did so even more. There were pairs of horses pulling omnibuses packed with people, there were single horses in smart hansom cabs thin broken-down-looking horses pulling the four wheeled growlers, coal carts in their hundreds. Brewery drays drawn by three great Shires or Clydesdales. Railway van horses, Mail van horses, teams of horses pulling enormous loads from the docks.

We passed through a poor area where donkeys abounded, carrying every sort of goods in their little carts. We saw sweep's ponies, baker's ponies and butcher's ponies; horses drawing rubbish carts and water carts for laying the dust in the streets, and enormous vans full of the furniture of people moving house.

As we came deeper into London the carriages became more elegant. We saw beautiful horses, perfectly matched pairs, drawing exquisitely painted and polished carriages, with very smartly turned-out coachmen and grooms, in special liveries, on the box. Workman-like carriages and broughams taking the professional men, the lawyers and fashionable doctors about their business and all mixed up with them and crushed together in the street where the pony and donkey carts, the great drays and vans and the omnibuses.

The noise of wheels and hoofs, the shouts of the drivers the crush and the whole scene bewildered me and I was very pleased when I saw trees, a stretch of water and the green of a great park and then we turned down a quiet street and through a pillared gateway into a yard. The groom dismounted and led me up a ramp, it was a wide affair like a road, with a wall on either side and brought me into a great stable on the first floor of a huge building.

It was very light and airy with a high, partly glass, roof and there seemed to be seventy or eighty stalls; most of them were empty, but headcollars and folded rugs, hayracks and water buckets told me that they were only waiting for their occupant's return. There seemed to be some trouble about finding a place or me but eventually I found myself tied up with an empty stall on one side and a large black horse lying comfortably on a good bed of straw on the other.

'I'm tired out,' he said. 'Four funerals yesterday so they've given me a day off. Why all the people die the same week beats me. They say it's the influenza carrying them off. I wish it would carry them somewhere where they don't need black horses. And it beats me why they put all those cemeteries on the tops of hills. Highgate, Finchley, Norwood, whoever fixed that wasn't thinking of horses, those carriages are blessed heavy to drag uphill.'

When he heard that I was new to London, Cardinal began to give me information. He said there were three hundred thousand horses in London and if you put them in single file they would stretch from St Paul's to John O' Groats at the very end of Scotland, or so he had been told. But he knew for a fact that ten thousand horses worked on the omnibuses because an omnibus horse had told him. Their life was a hard one, he said, for all the starting and stopping was a great strain, and they only lasted for five years. 'But take the tram horse, he's done in after four years, and a doctor's horse only lasts six, all that waiting about in the wet and cold, you see, and night jobs.'

I was beginning to wonder how long I would last when six pairs of beautiful grey horses with white decorations on their bridles were led out.

'They're off to a wedding,' said Cardinal. 'People like greys for weddings and if they can't get them they take chestnuts.'

In the evening the horses who had been hired out for the day began to come back. At first it was a trickle and then a flood and I had never seen men work so hard and fast as those grooms cleaning the London dirt from them.

My companion on the other side was a strong active looking horse. He said he was a Cleveland Bay, but that he hadn't been bred in Yorkshire, and that his name was Trooper. He explained that he was kept in reserve, ready to go at a moment's notice when any horse hired out by Chandler and Barlow fell ill or lame. He explained that some people didn't like to be bothered with choosing horses or with keeping the number that were necessary if they were never to be inconvenienced by colic and lameness and chills, so they just hired what they needed from the jobmaster, and he undertook to provide a substitute at any hour of the night or day.

'Where I went today the lady had her own stables and groom, but a pair of Chandler and Barlow carriage horses. When one horse started ringbone she couldn't get out without her carriage, ladies can't go in hansom cabs alone, you see, so the cob boy took me over. I was the right colour but not showy enough to please, so she'll have another horse tomorrow.' He ate a few mouthfuls of hay and then told me that he was trained as a fire engine horse. Chandler and Barlow provided the horses for three fire engines and they had to keep replacements for them always ready. 'They telephone from the fire station and you have to get round there in a flash,' Trooper explained, 'but I'm not a regular fire horse, they prefer greys. They reckon the street clears quicker for a grey.'

I asked Trooper if it was dangerous pulling a fire engine and whether horses were often burned.

'There are a lot of accidents to horses,' he answered, 'but they happen most frequently on the way to the fire, galloping through all the traffic or slipping on the road. Of course the horses have to be trained to remain steady in the midst of heat and smoke, to stand the sparks raining down on them and not to mind the steam pump's engine for that is almost a terrifying to the green horse as the fire itself.'

The next day, after a good grooming, a very neatly turned-out groom mounted me. Two chestnuts, both wearing side-saddles, were brought out and the reins handed to him. So, with a horse on either side of me, I walked through some quiet streets to a large and elegant house.

Here we were evidently expected for a manservant opened the door and said that the young ladies would be out in a moment. Presently they came, very smart in black habits and curly brimmed bowlers. The groom put them up and then we set off for the park. The young ladies rode side by side chattering to each other and the groom and I followed a respectful pace or two behind. They were experienced riders so no demands were made on us and I was able to look about me.

The main streets were very dirty. I suppose with that great crowd of horses passing so constantly it was impossible to keep them clean, but they smelled like a farmyard and where the people on foot crossed the road to the park, a bent old man in a long ragged coat, constantly swept a way clean for them.

The park was very pleasant. There were huge trees and wide stretches of green, and soft peaty rides had been made for the horses. There were roads too for the magnificent carriages. We saw an open laundau drawn by a pair of high-stepping horses, a park phaeton driven by a lady with a pair of cream ponies and a tiny groom called a tiger sitting on a little seat behind. All the ridden horses were good-looking and well turned-out and the elegantly dressed riders were all bowing and smiling and sometimes stopping to chat with each other. We went all round the park and had a very pleasant canter or two and then took the young ladies home. I enjoyed it all very much.

When we were back in the stable Mr Chandler came over and asked, 'How did the new one, Ebony, go?'

'Very well indeed, sir,' answered my rider. 'A perfect park hack, I'd say.'

'Did he shy at all?'

'Not once. No trouble at all and a beautiful collected canter.'

'Sounds all right,' said Mr Chandler, 'but you'd better take him out once more.'

That afternoon I escorted the three Miss Fostergills, who had brown habits and bowlers, and the next morning I was tried out in the school. It was rather a small school, but my training for Dick Turpin's Ride had made me very well-balanced and Mr Chandler soon saw that I could canter and jump without difficulty.

I gave several lessons that day and became heartily tired of that school.

I soon found that being a perfect park hack and a good school horse were great disadvantages in life. All the young ladies wanted to ride me and a good many, supported by their mammas, insisted on having me. Mr Chandler found it very diffcult to say No, partly because he was afraid of losing good custom and partly because he was a good-natured man, who did not like to disappoint any one. The consequence was that I became hopelessly overworked.

All that winter I would go out on the morning ride, the fashionable mid-morning ride and the afternoon ride and give lessons in the school as well. And if the weather was bad, if one of the thick London fogs came down or the morning was frosty I would just work hour after hour in the school instead.

A covered school with its soft going is certainly very kind to a horse's legs, but the boredom of staying within its walls and seeing nothing of the outside world, is very great. Especially when the work itself is monotonous and the horse is learning nothing new.

The young ladies all demanding their favourite, 'their dear Ebony' didn't realise what they were doing and Mr Chandler didn't seem to notice that I had lost all interest and merely plodded round praying for the lesson to end.

I suppose I would have stood up to the work better if I had been in my prime of life, but I was an old horse and I soon began to feel and look like one. I missed Felix and all the change and excitement of our wandering life and I had no one to be fond of, the grooms and strappers changed constantly and had little interest in us horses. I lost all my old pride and became lifeless and at last one of the mammas noticed it, and asked for her daughter to be mounted on something more lively. 'A horse with a little more spirit'.

Mr Chandler ordered me tonic powders in my food and with less competition to ride me I suppose things would have gradually righted themselves, if it had not been for the hoop.

There was a great fashion that spring for hoops. All the children in the parks and streets trundled them along. The boys had iron hoops and a sort of hook to guide them, the

girls had wooden hoops, which they bowled with short sticks.

We had been for a ride in the park, where all was fresh and green. The chestnut trees were out, every house seemed to have window boxes full of flowers and the sun shone. But I had lost my pleasure in it all and just plodded along carrying one of my endless young ladies; I had long ago given up trying to tell them apart. We were walking home along a quiet street when a hoop suddenly shot between my forelegs. If I'd been strong and alert I am sure I could have avoided it, but stumbling along weak and half asleep, with my head low, I was in no position to take sudden action and as it entangled itself with my legs I slipped and fell.

Luckily I fell on my off side so I did not trap the young lady's legs under me and the groom jumped off and soon freed her from the pummels. I lay for a little feeling very sorry for myself. My forelegs were hurting and I was in no hurry to find out just how injured they were.

But a crowd was collecting. The little girl who had bowled the hoop was sobbing and her governess was scolding and several passers by were advising that the knackers cart or the vet should be sent for, so I struggled up. My near knee was gashed and a trickle of blood ran down my cannon bone, but it was the old injury in my off fore that pained me most.

Mr Chandler was very put out. 'I daresay it wasn't the horse's fault but accidents of any sort give us a bad name. And supposing that cut leaves a scar? No one wants to see a daughter mounted on a horse with weak forelegs; on an animal that's been down.'

By next morning both my legs were so swelled that I could scarcely hobble a step and when Mr Chandler came to see me he brought Mr Barlow.

Mr Chandler patted me but he seemed to be very unhappy about my legs. 'He'll be off work for months and just at the start of the season.'

'He's finished,' said Mr Barlow less kindly. 'Waste of money messing about all summer and then poleaxing him in the autumn when we'd get the same price from the knacker now.'

'A grand old horse,' said Mr Chandler mournfully. I felt so poorly that the thought of the knacker didn't bother me overmuch but my masters continued to argue.

Then Mr Chandler had an idea. 'Let Biggs have him. If the sea water does the trick we'll get a sound horse back in the autumn if it doesn't, well, we don't stand to lose. He wrote yesterday asking if we had another crock for him this summer.'

'This one's a crock all right. I doubt you'll patch him up enough to get him to the sea. And what's more, is he broke to harness? Biggs won't be best pleased to have his bathing machines kicked to pieces.'

CHAPTER TWELVE

A reunion

Mr Chandler had won. After a few days in the stable I was led to the infirmary and there shod with a high-heeled shoe to relieve the pain of my old tendon trouble. I wasn't sound, but I could walk without too much pain and presently Mr Biggs was brought by Mr Chandler to see me. He was quite an old man, shabbily dressed and with a shapeless face, but he had a very pleasant voice and he obviously liked horses.

The first thing they did was to slip off my headstall and hold the collar from a set of harness out to me. I remembered the old days at Farmer Greys' and how I'd hated harness in my fierce determination to be a hunter.

But now it was harness or the knacker's and as the pain in my legs grew less I had begun to find some pleasure in life again, so I obediently thrust my head through the collar. This told them that I had been broken to harness. Mr Chandler was all smiles. 'There, that's all right then. And you won't have any trouble with him; a kind old horse, a perfect gentleman, a general favourite.'

'You think he'll stand the work?' asked Mr Biggs looking at my legs.

'A week of sea water and you won't know him,' answered Mr Chandler confidently.

So Mr Biggs and I set off for the sea. I'd always heard that train fares were expensive and now it seemed that my worth as an old crock was less than the fare, so we walked. It was early summer and the weather was kind to us. Mr Biggs wasn't very talkative, but he was a tranquil and good-humoured companion. When we stopped for water and he gave me my nosebag and settled down to his own bread and cheese, I had the impression that he had done this walk many times before.

We were some distance out of London when we met a

worried looking man with a red flag. ''Ang on to the 'orse for Gawd's sake!' he called, 'There's a motor car a-coming.'

And there it was, moving along in a very eerie way just as if a carriage had set off on its own without horses to pull it. I gave a snort, but, used as I was to trains and the noisy machinery of the colliery, I didn't shy or bolt or fall in the ditch as was expected.

'Nasty things,' said Mr Biggs when it had passed. 'And they've gone on and on till they've got the law changed and they'll be going at fourteen miles an hour instead of four this summer and not even a red flag to warn you. The roads 'll be a death trap to horses.'

We spent the night at a farm and went on again next day. I was already feeling better. The new sights, the fresh country air and a good companion had all combined to raise my spirits and though my special shoe forced me to limp, I carried my head higher.

Towards evening the smell on the breeze changed. It no longer carried the sweetness of grass and trees, but had a sharp salty taste to it. Presently we stopped on a hill top and looked down to a vast expanse of grey blue water.

'Well, there's the sea for you, Ebony,' said Mr Biggs. 'Don't know whether you've met up with it before.'

I followed him down a lane between cottages and we came to a field on a cliff. There was a broken down shed with a good bed of straw for me to sleep in. It wouldn't have done for a clipped horse, but I had grown my summer coat and except that I had been too well groomed and had no grease in my coat to protect me from the rain, I could have been turned straight out.

I liked my field, the grass was good and I enjoyed the freedom of pleasing myself, of going in and out of my shed and across to the water trough after so many years of standing in the stable and waiting for food and water to be brought to me.

There were birds and rabbits about, but I longed for a horse companion. There seemed to be plenty of donkeys nearby and when Mr Biggs heard me answering their morning brays and realised that I was lonely he arranged for one to come and live with me.

Moses was his name. He said that a great crowd of donkeys was being collected to give rides on the beach to the holiday makers. He'd done it before and said it was not much of a job. The big boys tried to make you gallop, the stout trippers screamed and bounced about on your back, which was quite painful when they were so large and heavy. And you were expected to toil for long hours on hot days; he prefered the winter when he worked on a farm.

After I had rested for about two weeks, Mr Biggs came into the field one day with a set of harness. It was old and mended but he'd kept it well oiled and he fitted it on me carefully. We went down to the shore, past the smoky houses and on to the sand, for the tide was out. Mr Biggs who was wearing fisherman's boots, walked me along the edge of the sea and let the small waves lap round my hoofs. Gradually we went in deeper and deeper. I enjoyed splashing about.

Then we walked up the beach to where four little huts on wheels stood under the cliff. They all had shafts and a little platform in front, steps down at the back and a little window on either side. Mr Biggs backed me between the shafts of one and hitched my traces to the hooks. Then he led me forward.

I had forgotten what hard work it is to get a vehicle started; you really have to throw yourself into the collar and pull with all your strength. Once they were moving those bathing machines were not too bad, unless their wheels sank into a soft patch of sand.

When we had got going Mr Biggs climbed up on the platform and drove me in and out of the sea several times. Then he made a great fuss of me and took me back to my field and my leisured life. Another day I was taken to the forge and had a shoe with a less high-heel fitted and after that he would put on my driving bridle with a rope rein and ride me bare-back along the beach and into the sea almost every morning.

The days grew hotter and the season started. Moses left

me to give his donkey rides and I pulled the four bathing
machines along to the main beach, close to the pier and just
below the hotels and the elegant villas where the summer
visitors stayed. Mr Biggs put out a large freshly-painted
notice:

BATHING MACHINES FOR HIRE

Prop. E. BIGGS

The visitors were everywhere. Ladies with parasols, nurses
carrying babies; little boys in sailor suits and little girls in
print dresses and sun bonnets, pulling off their shoes and
stockings and running to paddle in the sea. When the tides
were right we spent a lot of time on that beach. Mr Biggs
wore his panama hat and I had a fringe on my browband to
keep the flies from my eyes and a cotton rug to go over me
when, waiting for customers, I stood dozing, tied to a ring in
the sea wall.

There seemed to be special times for ladies and gentlemen
to bathe and they were not allowed to mix, except for little
boys who might go with either their fathers or their mothers.

When they had hired one of our machines they would
climb in and change into their bathing costumes, meanwhile
Mr Biggs would put me in the shafts.

Then, when they were ready, he would jump on the platform or on my back and we would take the machine out into
the water and turn it round so that the steps led directly down
into the waves. I soon learned the routine and directly Mr
Biggs shouted 'whoa' I would stand, while he ran round to
make sure that the steps were safe and that a rope or two was
dangling down from the roof into the water, this gave the
bathers something to hold on to and made them feel safe.
Then he would unhitch me and sometimes we had to hurry
for another customer would be waiting to be drawn up or
down.

When we had all our four machines in a neat line along the
water's edge, I would take a rest until they wished to be
brought up but sometimes, if the tide was coming in, we

would have a great rush to get them all up before they began to float.

On wet days I stayed in my shed and on Sundays there was no bathing and everyone went to church instead, so I had a day of rest in my field. Mr Biggs fed me well and did not expect me to live on grass alone and the sea water strengthened my legs as Mr Chandler had said it would. I began to feel younger, to carry my head high and to enjoy all the company. Some of the children would come to see me every day with an apple or lump of sugar and be quite sad when their holidays ended and we could meet no more.

Then, one hot August day when we were very busy, I heard a voice ask politely if there was a machine for hire.

'Certainly M'am. Just one moment and I'll be with you,' answered Mr Biggs and, as we took the machine I was harnessed to into the sea, I thought about that familiar voice.

When we went back for the next machine I took a good look at the lady. Long pretty dress, hat, parasol, she was accompanied by a small boy and girl called Charlie and Katie. They looked just like all the other families on the beach, but each time the lady spoke I became more convinced that it was Miss Fanny. Dear Miss Fanny from my happy hunting days at Earleigh Court.

At first the children were too excited by the prospect of bathing to notice the horse, but afterwards they came round to pat me as Miss Fanny was paying for the hire. She called to them to be careful, for I was a strange horse and did not know them, but I could hear Mr Biggs assuring her that I was very fond of children and perfectly safe.

Presently she came to fetch the children who didn't want to leave me. 'Oh what a dear old horse,' she said as I looked into her face with pricked ears. 'But he looks too well-bred for this sort of work.' Mr Biggs began to explain about my accident and the excellent effect of salt water and I took Miss Fanny's cuff in my teeth and gave it a playful tug. Suddenly she sensed that I knew her. She turned to Mr Biggs and asked in a strange voice if he knew my name or where I had been before the jobmaster.

'Ebony,' he said. 'And he answers to it, so he's had it a fairish time. And Mr Chandler bought him from some sort of circus that had come down from the north.'

'Then it is Ebony, my old Ebony,' she said putting her arms round my neck and bursting into tears. The children and Mr Biggs all looked horrified so she tried to explain.

'I've often told you of Ebony, the beautiful, black hunter I had when I was young, well I'm certain this is *my* Ebony, look, he knows me.'

I wished I could speak and tell her everything but, as I couldn't I put up my face and gave her the kiss I used to give Dick Turpin before I died. That made her cry the more.

'Don't take on so, M'am, you can see he's fit and well and though he has come down in the world you can tell he has been kindly used, for a nicer-natured horse to handle you'd never find.'

Then Miss Fanny dried her eyes, and apologised for her tears. She gave me a loving pat saying that they would come back next day.

And next day she came again and brought her husband, Mr Cavendish. He patted me and asked Mr Biggs if there would be any possibility of buying me when the season was over. Mr Biggs was very helpful. He explained that I belonged to Chandler and Barlow, and that his interest in me was only until the thirtieth of September, but that he was sure that they would accept any reasonable offer. Mr Cavendish wrote down the London address.

So, by the time their holiday came to an end, Mrs Fanny was able to tell me that it was all settled, that I was to be her's from October the first.

Mr Biggs seemed very pleased. 'You've fallen on your feet, Ebony, and no mistake,' he said when they had gone. 'You'll be thoroughly petted and spoiled there; it'll suit you a lot better than riding school work.'

So the summer ended. I was quite sorrowful at parting with Mr Biggs at the railway station, but I was very happy indeed when at the end of the journey I was led out of the train and found all the Cavendishes waiting for me on the station platform. They had brought their young groom, Sidney, and he was to ride me home while they went in the motor car driven by Mr Cavendish.

The Paddocks wasn't a large establishment like Earleigh Court, but it looked a very comfortable sort of house set in its own meadows and orchards. The stables were near the house and very nice, for all the stalls had been made into loose boxes. Mr Cavendish kept a hunter, Starchaser, and there were two ponies, Dandy and Dumpling. I was to carry Mrs Fanny who had not been riding since she had the children. There were no carriage horses, for the motor car, which lived in the coach house, served instead, but there was a governess cart for the ponies.

It is a very happy home, Sidney is a cheerful groom and Mrs Fanny is very pleased with me. She says that we have both grown old and must take things steadily and not as we did in our wild young days, but we have some very interesting times. The children have become fond of me, especially since they learned I can do tricks, though I won't 'die' for them very often as my joints are too stiff to be constantly getting up and lying down.

Charlie, like his father, is very attached to the motor car and he and Katie are always dressing up as motorists in goggles and veils, huge caps and hats and long coats down to their feet, but they have often told me that they love horses best and me best of all the horses in the world.

BLACK PRINCESS

by Diana Pullein-Thompson

CONTENTS

BLACK BEAUTY'S CLAN

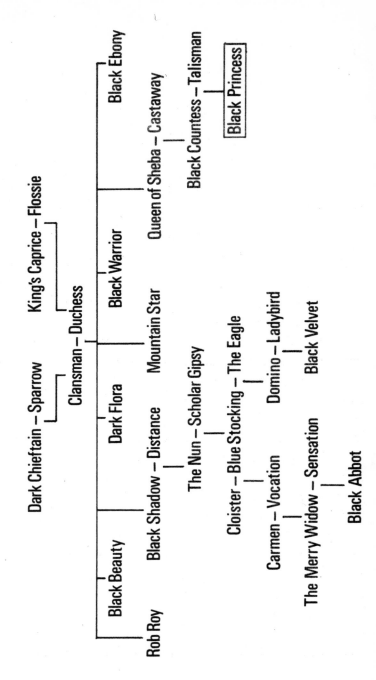

CHAPTER ONE

A quiet beginning

When you are old it is the memories of foalhood which stand out most clearly, shining through time like coach lamps in the half-light, signposts to events in a life whose span is nearly over.

So, looking back now, I see a wide field climbing to meet a line of elms and then the sky, a glorious sea of darkening blue. I smell again the newly mown grass, cowslips, and daisies, the creamy froth of elderberry blossom, the sweetness of the cherry. And I feel on my face the promise of dew and the soft dampness of my native land.

It is my first time out of the hot stable, so deep in golden straw gathered in stooks from the harvest fields. The flies are quiet and still; a few late bees busy themselves in the honeysuckle; a brightly coloured butterfly flashes through the blue light of evening and is gone. It is all new to me as I follow my mother into the meadow which awaits the dusk. My legs are shaky and my eyes very large with wonder at the world. The gate creaks as it opens slowly on its wooden hinges; the grass is springy under my feet after the cobbles of the yard and space stretches before me into eternity. I am afraid. I rush to my mother's side, seeking succour and comfort from the warmth and smell of her glossy black body. She turns and sniffs me, touches me with her lips. And then she is loosed and we are free. Our groom, Will Aken, turns away from us, walks straight-backed, bow-legged to the gate. My mother Black Countess, leads me to the cover of a great oak which overhangs a tall thorn hedge, where I can rest peacefully, for she knows my legs are already tired.

I was my mother's third foal; two colts had been born before me and sold after weaning. They had been, it was said by the grooms, more handsome in foalhood than me, but wilder, and my mother's fine looks and reputation assured that they soon found homes. She had been in her younger days equally good in harness or under the saddle; proud, willing and high spirited, closely related to that famous horse Black Beauty, whose story is still read today.

As a foal I wanted nothing more than to be exactly like my mother, both in character and appearance and I was pleased when Will Aken announced that the Master had decided that I should be called Black Princess.

'You've got a look of breeding in you already,' he said, 'in your head carriage. It marks you out.'

He was leaning over the gate as he spoke, a blade of grass in his mouth, a short, sturdy man with a wide, kind face, smiling and weatherbeaten. Wearing breeches and gaiters, shirt, waistcoat and cap, he smelt of saddle soap, hay and leather, apart from his hair which possessed his own special human tang. His hands were broad and gentle, his voice soft but firm, pleasantly slow in speech. He never hurried and yet he got through more work in a day than two ordinary grooms put together. My mother said we were very fortunate in Will Aken; there were not many of his sort around.

Master was a butcher with several shops scattered on the outskirts of the nearest town. Honest, well-to-do, hardworking and usually modest in speech, he was well-liked by the gentry, their housekeepers and cooks. Horses were his hobby as well as transport for his trade. He kept four for delivering meat to his customers, one for bringing meat from the slaughter house to the shop, and my mother and another mare, Marigold, for breeding. He also possessed a smart hackney, Flyaway, who pulled his gig when he went to market and took many a prize at agricultural shows.

Marigold's foal was born a few days after me; brown at first, he gradually turned a silvery grey with a pinky brown muzzle like the inside of a young mushroom. Marigold, a strawberry van mare, had delivered meat for Master for ten years before becoming permanently lame through a diseased fetlock. Many an owner would have put a bullet through her head once she was no longer able to work but Master, who spent so much time killing cattle, could not bear to destroy a horse. He put her to a local stallion called Seascape and my little silver companion was born eleven months later. Seaspray – for that was the name Master chose – became my greatest friend. We played together imagining every leaf or wisp caught in a gust of wind to be a monster out to kill us. Galloping like wild mustangs, running for our lives. Then, suddenly tired, we stood head to tail like the older horses, keeping each other's eyes clear of flies with our tails, and chewing each other's withers when they grew hot or itchy.

On Saturday evenings the van horses came from the shops and on fine Sundays they were put in the next meadow. And many were the tales they told us, standing under the oaks, resting each of their tired hindlegs in turn.

There was one bay horse I remember especially well. He was what men call a cob, short everywhere with a hogged mane and a docked tail which left him at the mercy of the flies. Although quite heavy in build, Tomtit possessed the quick movements and sprightly manner which had given him his name. Throughout his troubles he had, it seemed, remained cheerful and perky, making the best of many a horrible situation. Broken-in by a drunken master who had been very free with the whip, Tomtit had been sold at three years old to pull a milk float in London. Here, without mane or tail to keep away flies, or forelock to shield his eyes, he found the summer streets a torture. Added to this discomfort was the cruelty of a thoughtless and brutal driver, Bert Brown.

'When he wanted me to go forward, he jerked my mouth, when he wanted me to stop he jerked my mouth and when he wanted me to turn he jerked my mouth. Jerk, jerk, jerk for everything. Can you imagine the pain for a three year old with tender bars?' asked Tomtit. 'Of course in time my bars hardened, but my nerves didn't. The noise and stench of the streets in summer. It was almost unendurable. How I longed for green trees and soft meadows, lush grass and a clear tinkling stream to quench my thirst! Of course there are public troughs in London, but the water grows stale and in summer turns quite yellow, with dead flies and insects floating on the top. It does nothing to comfort a sore mouth.'

'I thank God I have never been sent to London,' said my mother. 'I believe I would lose my senses in such a place. I would rather be dead.'

'There are many fine carriage horses, and until recently many park hacks, but they were, of course, too superior to pay much attention to a poor youngster in a milk float.' replied Tomtit. 'The roads were so hard on our legs. Our fetlocks swelled and we all grew those soft lumps men call windgalls, which made us very ugly. Even at night we could not rest for we were tied too short, which made it impossible for us to lie down.'

'How did you get away?' asked Mother. 'Were you sold?'

'It wasn't as simple as that. This man Bert Brown, used to leave me outside a public house while he met friends for drinks. Often when he came out he was drunk and quarrelsome and then my poor mouth suffered even more than usually. Oh, it was a hard life and pulling Master's cart is paradise in comparison! Well, to cut a long story short, Bert was careless; sometimes when he left me he put on the drag and sometimes he did not. One day when he forgot it, I said to myself: "Why do I wait so patiently outside every customer's house and every tavern or hostelry? Why do I obey this man, who hits me and hurts my mouth? Who dallies drinking and then drives me home too fast, up and down hill, with the whip so painful on my back".'

'But if we do not obey our masters,' put in Mollie a brown mare, 'they shoot us. I have seen it happen.'

'Not always, and Bert was not my master but only my driver,' answered Tomtit stamping in the dust. 'An ignorant man! Well, to carry on with my tale, when the fellow came out of the tavern one day, by jove, I had gone, milk churns, float and all. I would have dearly loved to have seen his countenance at that moment.'

'But where? Go on, don't stop,' I urged, for I greatly valued these stories which told me about the world I was soon to enter.

'Out of town and away. Not too fast or I would have called attention to myself, but at a steady trot. A boy tried to stop me, but a nip on the arm made him drop the reins with a squeal. I kept trotting until I met a tinker's cart and then I fell in behind it, for I could see the horse was a friendly sort, and the man was singing, and I love a good song. The tinker turned off into an alleyway, and then he approached me speaking soft and slow, so that I trusted him and stood quite still. Gently he unharnessed me, and put a rope and canvas halter over my head. Then he painted me with a liquid which turned the hair on my off pastern white so that I now possessed a white sock, a temporary disguise. All this took nearly an hour, but the alleyway was deserted and no one saw us. Directly he had finished this work, the tinker hitched me to the back of his cart and continued his journey.'

'You mean he stole you? He was a thief?' asked my mother. 'I would not serve a thief.'

'He rescued me from a bad home,' said Tomtit stamping again. 'You have always been well treated, working for lords and ladies. You do not know what it is like to be a common cob with no mane or tail and little sympathy. That tinker was a brick with a heart of gold, a poor man earning a few pennies where he could – sharpening knives, soldering pots and pans and so on.'

'A common gipsy,' said Mother severely, 'and a thief to boot.'

'A tinker, I said,' snapped Tomtit. 'A kind, humble man and I am glad he stole me. He never harmed a body except for a rabbit now and then, which he snared for his dinner. He loved the birds and fed them with crumbs, and I've seen him rescue a kitten thrown into a pond with a stone tied round its neck. Now Master here is good to us, but he cares nothing for the bullocks except that they should grow fat to bring him riches. There is often blood on his hands and spattered over his striped apron, and the smell sickens me; it clings even to his hair. My old tinker smelt of trees and earth, of hot metal, wood fires and sweat from honest toil.'

'I can't abide thieves,' said my mother rather irritably swishing her tail. 'I've known many a stable of horses go short of corn, because the grooms have been selling it without their master's knowing. One bad deed leads to another and so on and on.'

'You are preaching like Black Beauty,' said Mollie.

'A great horse,' said my mother. 'Mark you, I never thought to finish my life owned by a butcher.'

'Go on, Tomtit,' urged Seaspray.

'Well the tinker joined a band of gipsies and we all made our way to Kent, where the men, women and children could earn good money picking hops. It was beautiful. The air so clear and fresh and the fields gloriously green, and the trees just beginning to turn. We horses and ponies were not tethered or hobbled any more, but turned out in the farmer's fields.

'For two weeks we rested, and you may well imagine

our pleasure and joy. There was a brook winding between willows, and, although autumn was already in the air, the grass had kept its freshness. It was wonderful to lie down under the open sky again, to see the stars and the moon, a harvest moon large and full and beautiful in the night sky, I would have dearly loved to spend the rest of my days with my tinker friend, for he had a way with horses which brought a calmness to them. He was so near to nature himself, so much part of the earth that it was not possible to be frightened of him. But the farmer had taken a fancy to me. He saw that I was strong, willing and good natured, and persuaded the tinker to sell me to his cousin, a baker in a neighbouring village, so I went on the rounds again, slept in a stall, and pulled a little van. I was still living in the country, and the baker was kind enough, but without the tinker's special understanding. I could not grow to love him, although I liked the smell of yeast which was always about him. You see I was simply a necessity to him, not a character as I had been to the tinker. Do you understand? Do you follow me?'

'Yes,' we chorused.

'Well, presently another baker opened a shop in the village, full of fancy bread and cakes, for this man was half Austrian and knew what the wealthy ladies liked. And in no time my new master, a very plain baker, was pushed out of business. And not understanding horses very well he made no efforts to secure me a good home, but sent me to a sale and that's how I came to be a butcher's horse.'

'I am glad I am too well bred to pull a butcher's cart,' said Flyaway. 'I couldn't stand the smell of blood at all, but Master always looks his best when he takes me out. If you are a show hackney you expect that sort of thing of course.

It's not at all similar to being an ordinary run-of-the-mill working horse.'

We fell silent, Seaspray and I musing on our futures. Then Marigold said, 'Seaspray, do not look so sad, you have thoroughbred blood in your veins. You take after your father and will never have to toil as I have done. Your path will be eased. No windgalls shall spoil your beautiful fetlocks nor spavins your hocks. You will be worth a deal of money, and human beings value money above all else, so they will take care of you. Your father is famous.'

'And Princess?' asked the little grey.

'My daughter has breeding, too,' answered my mother gravely. 'But that is not a complete guarantee against cruelty and ill use. A fall, an accident, a careless groom and, in one week, a horse's outlook and future can be changed through no fault of his own, and once you start moving downwards it is not easy to come up again – you mark my words.'

So the days passed pleasantly marred only occasionally by such seriousness. In the nearby meadows bullocks came and went, and winter arrived with snow and hail, and then Seaspray and I were taken away from our mothers and locked together in a loosebox. How we neighed! And how they neighed back! The yard was full of noise and Flyaway was much irritated by our bellowing, he stamped his feet and kicked his door and snapped at Will Aken's back whenever he passed by. But, after the first terrible night without our mothers we grew calmer, although we missed the sweet warmth of their milk, the comfort of their bodies and the tenderness in their eyes as they watched over us.

When the weather was fair we were put out in the meadow during the day but at night we always came into our fine loosebox which was deep in golden straw. Will soon taught us to be led and handled, and the blacksmith came and filed our hoofs so that they should grow shapely and strong.

When we were three Will Aken put bits into our mouths and left us in the stable to sample them. They were not at all to our liking but presently we started to play with them and make them jingle in our mouths. Then he put sur-cingles over our backs and he fixed reins from the bits to the rings on the surcingles tightening them a little each day until we learned to bow our heads to the pressure from the bits. After a week he took us out across the fields on long reins walking behind us. By now we understood 'Whoa, Steady and Walk!' And, knowing and liking Will, we tried to please him, and so our breaking-in went well.

CHAPTER TWO

A broken gig

I never minded Will Aken on my back, for he was a friend whom I wished to serve. Indeed I loved those early morning rides with the dew still wet and silver on the sleeping fields, and the sky bright with the glow of sunrise; the spiders' cobwebs lying on the hedges like gossamer, and the petals of the wild flowers tightly closed against the last rigours of the night. How I loved then to gallop with the early breeze soft and damp against my face. Sometimes I would buck with sheer joy at my own sense of youth and well being, to be checked sharply by Will.

'None of that! None of that! Mind your manners! Steady there. Now then!'

He knew that my whole future depended upon my good behaviour. And, looking back now, I only wish every youngster could be broken in by so kind and thoughtful a man. For we all must work or die by the gun, and to be soured at the start is a terrible fate for a horse.

But, although I was glad to go out I was also glad to return for I loved the company of my friends. Marigold and my mother now had new foals, long-legged ungainly, handsome youngsters with manes like humans' tooth-brushes and large bright eyes full of mischief and curiosity. We were jealous of these brothers, gaining the succour and warmth from their mothers which would never again be ours.

When I was quiet under the saddle, obedient to leg and rein, I went out with Mollie in the breaking cart. With so steady a friend beside me I felt little fear and quickly learned to obey the stroke of the whip and the command of the voice, although I found the blinkers rather unpleasant until I grew accustomed to them, for no one likes to have their view restricted. After a few weeks Will Aken took me out alone in the gig along the quiet high-banked lanes, rich now with flowers and tall sweet grasses, up hill and down dale, through the thick woodlands out on the plain where the young wheat sprouted green and strong from the dark, rich earth. Occasionally we met young men on bicycles and once three young ladies wearing knickerbockers, with berets with pom-poms on their heads and long scarves wound round their pearly throats. But usually my steel shod hoofs broke the silence of an almost deserted landscape.

One day Master decided to drive me five miles to market, where he hoped to buy a dozen bullocks for fattening.

'She will soon be ready to sell,' he said. 'And you never know we might find a buyer if we show her around a bit.'

The morning was windy, and I hate wind; the trees creaked and shivered like old men, unlatched gates swung to and fro: strange noises seemed to come like whispers of hell from every hedge and ditch. And the road was strange to me. I needed Will or Mollie to calm my nerves and give me confidence, to show me that the road was all right, that no wild cats or dangers lurked in wait for me. Men do not always understand our fears any more than we do ourselves, for they go back to the days when we horses were wild, with speed in flight our only protection. We have no long fangs, no tenacious claws or poisonous bite with which to fight our enemies.

But Master, whose mind was probably on the bullocks

he hoped to buy, seemed unaware of my terror, and merely shouted and whipped me when I hesitated, as though I was being lazy. Presently we overtook a carrier's covered cart pulled by a patient brown mare with a goose rump, then two bread vans pulled by willing but ugly horses and afterwards a wagon pulled by a beautiful Suffolk Punch with a plaited mane and proud carriage. Each time I passed another horse I neighed and the hills caught my neigh and returned it to me, a weak echo of the original, sad as a cry heard through shut doors. Humans, I have noticed, do not like the continuous neighing of lonely or frightened horses and my master was no exception.

'Give over! Enough of that!' he shouted, and sensing his annoyance I felt even more frightened. A lady with a parasol turned my legs weak with fear, a dog scratching and whining like some weird and dangerous animal behind a gate almost stopped me in my tracks. And in front of me, mile on mile, stretched the dusty road, leading me away from my friends and home.

There were two more miles to go. We had just climbed a steep hill, caught a glimpse of the plain below, and were about to round a corner, when I met my first motor car – a carriage, I thought wildly, without a horse, a carriage gone mad running all on its own. In this motor car sat a young lady and gentleman smiling and talking in loud upper-class voices; the gentleman wearing goggles and ear flaps, which made him seem like a giant toad. The lady with a large blue straw hat tied with a white scarf.

Of course I knew about motor cars. Tomtit had seen them both in London and the country. Mollie had met them occasionally on her rounds, and often we had heard them in the distance grinding up the hill, and smelt the vile air which they exuded like poison from their tails. But

when I met this one, face-to-face, I took leave of my
senses; every bit of advice I had received fled with the wind
across the patchwork plain. My heart pounded as though
it would break and the sweat broke out on my flanks.
Indeed I cannot now find words to describe the terror
which gripped me. The gig was forgotten; my master's
shouts were in vain. I stood for a moment stockstill, my
flesh flapping as a fit of trembling overtook me. The
monster was now advancing. It's great brass eyes empty of
colour; a little smoke coming from its front, a rumbling in
its belly. It seemed to be running straight for me; its eyes,
like coach lamps, were on me now; and blind instinct must
have decided my actions for I cannot remember a single
thought crossing my mind, before I had turned on my
hocks, swinging the precious gig over on its side as I
attempted to flee back up the road. The shafts splintered
but the traces held pulling me down into the gritty road,
where the surface grazed my flesh in scores of places.

Master was down there beside me in a moment slashing the traces with his knife. Then he was at my head.

'Hup!' he cried. 'Hup there!'

And then all the drama seemed to end in a trice. With a man at my head I was safe. The monstrous motor was no longer breathing, although its stink still hung in the air. The driver and his lady had dismounted and were standing in the road. And I was shaking from head to foot.

'By jove, I'm sorry! What a devilish thing to happen. I'm afraid my motor frightened him. I thought nags were accustomed to meeting us by now.'

'Are you both unharmed?' asked the lady

'The gig ain't,' said my master, 'and the horse is scratched, and the traces are cut.'

'But no serious damage?' suggested the young gentleman.

'Shaft's broken, that'll cost a mint of money. Most folks in them machines have the good sense to pull into the side of the road when they see a horse coming, and they switch off the engine, that's the civil thing to do. If you'd ever driven a horse yourself you would know better than to keep on coming.'

'Give the poor man something towards the shaft,' said the lady, touching her friend's arm with a gloved hand.

The young gentleman hesitated a moment. His neatly trimmed chestnut moustache twitched twice as though he was a rabbit sniffing the air, then he brought a brown wallet from his pocket.

'Will this help? I'm dashed sorry,' he held out a five pound note.

'Thank you, sir, thank you very much.'

Master was at once all smiles, putting on the expression he wore habitually for his best customers 'Very good of you sir, I'm sure.' He touched his cap, pocketed the note, and pushed the gig to the side of the road. He took off all my harness, except for the bridle, giving me a couple of angry digs in the ribs as he did so, and put it in the cart. Then he jumped on my back, gave me a sharp clap with his hand on the flank, rode me past the stationary motor car, and on to market, where he was greeted with many ribald jokes and remarks.

Returning in the late afternoon, I met two more motors, but the drivers of these stopped and turned off the engines and there were no more mishaps. The gig was brought back later and left at the wheelwright's shop for repair.

Flyaway called me a clumsy fool. My mother said a young horse must learn to control her feelings and fears. 'Otherwise,' she said. 'You will never gain a good position and you could end your life walking in a circle all day cutting chaff.'

Master, who could well have saved himself a broken gig had he been sensible enough to go to my head when I met the motor car, now blamed Will Aken for the accident.

'I've never sold a horse yet which is not tractable and quiet on the roads and I ain't going to have a good reputation dragged in the mire through the fault of a careless horseman.' he shouted. 'It's your good fortune that the young gentleman paid up, Will Aken, or else you would have been going short on your wages till the gig was repaired. Now see to it that this kind of thing does not happen again. I want that mare quiet with motor cars and steam engines. Is that clear?'

Will Aken, who had been gently cleaning my scratches, stood respectfully with bowed head. There were many men out of work and he could not risk losing his job by defending himself. He had of course ridden and driven me on the roads a number of times and it was through no fault of his that we had not chanced to meet a motor car.

Master went on to say the price of horses had dropped. He had hoped to recommend me to a chum at market, but felt he could not when I had just behaved so badly.

'I cannot remember the demand for carriage horses being so low. The gentry are all copying the King and going in for them stinkpots.' he said, 'heaven knows how it will end. But there's no doubt she's a fine looking mare, a pleasure to the eye you might say, and we shall find a place for her in time.'

A month later, when completely quiet in all traffic, I was found a buyer, and sadly left my friends, mother and two brothers.

CHAPTER THREE

A lonely life

My new master was a well-to-do doctor called Miller, portly red-cheeked with a voice which could be soothing and quiet, so long as he was not thwarted when it would rise to a shout which was very unpleasant. A bachelor, he was tended by a valet-butler, a housekeeper and two daily maids. His house was quite new with every comfort an ordinary English gentleman requires, including a bathroom whose overflow pipe came out into the stable yard and was much in use owing to the doctor's liking for very deep baths.

Although quite attached to her master, the housekeeper was heard to say on occasions that he was as selfish as a spoiled child. His weakness was for well bred, charming people; he would bounce their children upon his knees like the most charming uncle in the world, but the grubby village children he would dismiss curtly if they so much as took his hand.

He wanted a smart horse to pull his trap, a horse with naturally high head carriage, now that bearing reins were no longer in fashion, and when he saw me he decided that I would suit his needs, for I had then my mother's air of breeding and my action was straight and lively.

Will Aken rode me the ten miles to my new home, then took a lift in a carrier's cart half-way back and walked the rest, at least that is what he planned to do and I suppose the journey worked out the way he wanted. I was sorry to see him go, for he had been my first and best human friend and, alone in a stall, I felt anxious and bewildered. I neighed and pawed the Staffordshire brick floor until my new groom Alec, a wizened old man, came to calm me.

'Steady my little sweetheart, whoa, my beauty!' his voice was kind, though cracked with age. His hands knotted with disease, soothed me. I could tell by his touch that he loved horses and had spent his life with them. In build and manner he was the exact opposite of the doctor. It would indeed have been hard to find two men less alike.

'I do like a good black,' he had remarked on seeing me the first time 'them's hardy and with spirit.'

Every morning now I took the doctor on his rounds, driven by Alec, who knew how to handle a mettlesome horse. Sometimes if there were many people ill I went out in the afternoons as well. The journeys were pleasant enough, but I disliked waiting while the doctor saw his patients, for I was only five years old with little patience and scant wisdom, and often I allowed old Alec no rest at all. If he stood at my head I would keep pushing him with my muzzle and if he remained in the trap I would not stay still. Sometimes I would neigh for the friends I had left behind in the butcher's fields. But the doctor liked me because I covered the ground at a brisk pace and I was quite happy to trot five miles without a break. We called at many large houses in the district and sometimes the doctor would be asked to stop for lunch. Then I would be un-harnessed and taken to the stables, where the contents of my nose bag would be tipped into a manger. Alec would be asked indoors to eat in the servants' hall or, if the household was modest, in the kitchen.

No one was ever unkind to me. My food was excellent.

My coat shone with health and yet I was unhappy because I lived without one of my kind. Humans do not understand that solitary confinement is torture for many of us. Only these lunch time visits, where often I would be tied close to another horse, saved me from developing a vile and nervous temperament. But however hysterical I felt I was always gentle with Alec, for he was frail, over eighty and also alone. He lived in a little room above my stable next to the loft and he ate in the kitchen with the other servants, and at night I sometimes heard him coughing into the early hours. Although my new master was a medical man he did not seem interested in his groom's cough and frailty.

'Alec's tough as an old boot, live to ninety,' I heard him say on more than one occasion. 'That's what washing under a cold pump at six o'clock every morning does for you!'

But, of course, the doctor would have been horrified had any one seriously suggested that he should follow Alec's way of life for the good of his own health, for he loved his creature comforts, and in winter was always well wrapped with a great muffler wound round his bull neck.

Sometimes the doctor was called out in the middle of the night to attend some very ill person. Once we went ten miles in moonlight to visit a child with pneumonia, who had reached the crisis. I spent three hours in a warm loose box with bars and deep straw which was a pleasant change from a stall. My neighbours were race horses who seemed to speak a language of their own. We came back in the dawn with Master in very good spirits singing in a light baritone voice, because the child had come through the crisis and was sleeping peacefully. Alec, too, had been well cared for by the servants and was reeking of beer, but he was silent as usual.

Another time, a little mite came banging at the doctor's front door around eleven o'clock at night. Ragged and dirty with running eyes and scores round his mouth, he made a pitiful picture. But the doctor, when brought down by Albert, his valet, was not sympathetic.

'What is it this time?' he asked.

'Mamma, Mother, she's all twisted up with the pain. She's crying out, sir, crying out!'

'You should have come earlier. It's a fine time to call a doctor at eleven o'clock at night.'

'We've nowt left,' the little boy said, 'Nowt at all. We can't pay yer.'

'Well, tell her I'll be down presently.'

'I think she's dying, sir, please come quick,' the little mite said.

'I'll be along directly. Now off with you.'

The poor woman only lived half a mile down the road, but the doctor liked to arrive in style, so Albert wakened Alec and I was harnessed and brought with the trap to the front door. The doctor came out twenty minutes later. What he had been doing in the meantime I do not know. I trotted at a good spanking pace but when we reached the cottage the woman was dead and the little boy weeping in the road.

'They always leave it too late,' the doctor complained. 'Yesterday I could have saved her.' But, as his servants said next morning, standing gossiping in the yard, it was hard to ask for help when you had no money to pay for it.

'He should have gone right away,' the housekeeper declared. 'Fancy letting the little mite wait all that time. Now if it had been Lady Louisa at his door that would have been a very different kettle of fish'. Alec said nothing for a while then he cleared his throat. 'There's one rule for gentry and one for the working poor. There always has been and there always will be and them's not going to stir himself for a penniless woman what's had more children than she's any right to.'

'You're getting as hard as the master,' the housekeeper said.

'No, I'm just speaking straight as I know 'tis the truth and it's not only the master who sees it that way.'

'I say it's a wicked shame,' said the housekeeper.

'Things are going to change by and by, you mark my

words,' said the jobbing gardener, leaning on his beesom. 'These trade unions are getting awful strong, and one of these days the gentry are in for a shock.'

'Oh ar! Well, I shall be under the daisies by then I reckons,' said Alec. 'And I'm glad I've lived when I have, 'cos I'm not sure I believe in all these new fangled ways.'

There were many such conversations out in the yard or in the kitchen which opened on it and solitude sharpened my ears so that I could usually hear every word, even when the back door was shut.

CHAPTER FOUR

Illness and pain

I do not think there was any cause for my illness, except perhaps that I was unhappy living alone. It came on quite suddenly as the leaves were falling from the trees and paths of russet and gold led into the murky gloom of the beech-woods. My appetite went, even oats sickened me, but I drank much, for my throat was dry and parched and my tongue thick. My head was like a weight at the end of my neck, so that I could hardly muster the strength to pull the trap along.

Fortunately master was about to take his annual holiday, leaving his patients in the charge of a young doctor who had taken lodgings in a nearby inn.

'And it looks to me as though Princess needs a rest, too, Alec,' he said. 'Either that or she's turned sour or ill on us.'

Soon my eyes were gummed-up with yellow discharge each morning and Alec was tempting me with bran and linseed mashes; his rugged old forehead creased with worry, his knotted hands shaking with an old man's palsy; but I did not mend and two days later Alec consulted his oldest friend, the local farrier, Joshua, who looked me over, peered into my mouth and asked Alec to lead me up the drive and back.

'Them's feverish,' said Alec. 'Them drinks more chilled water than normal.'

Jushua pushed his greasy cap farther back on his head.

'Bleeding,' he said. 'Brings down the fever. It may mean nowt to those with new fangled notions, but I don't know anything better, relieves the pressure on the brain, rests the heart, cools the system. Bleeding and a purge, Alec.' He patted my neck, 'Poor old girl, feel mighty bad, don't you, just want to lie down and die I reckon.' He wiped his hands on his leather apron, which smelt of hoof parings, coal and stockholm tar.

'She will be needing a restorative too,' Alec said. 'Bleeding pulls them down sometimes. I've got a recipe in my cupboard, works like magic. Powdered gentian, Virginian snake root, rust of iron.'

'Yes,' cut in Joshua. 'I know that ball, I've used it myself. It has saffron too, and mithridate, one ounce of sulphurated oil, oil of aniseed, lesser cardamom seeds and a bit of senna, all beaten together with liquorice powder and syrup of roses. My old father used to swear by that recipe, always claimed it saved many a horse's life.'

'Restores the appetite,' said Alec.

'As long as it ain't the strangles, bleeding is the right answer. But it's my belief that the trouble's going to the lungs and there's not a lot of time to lose,' said the farrier. 'I've got Carter's mare waiting to be shod, and then I'll be around.'

They took the blood from a vein in my neck by the light of an hurricane lantern. The prick hurt. I was frightened and wanted to break free, but they had twisted a piece of rope round my upper lip – a twitch they called it – which Alec held in one hand on a stick; any movement on my part caused him to tighten this twitch and then the agony was terrible. I saw the red blood running from a tube into a jar, a quart they took; it was quite dark like blackcurrant juice and the smell terrified me – it seemed

that my life was running out, but I was powerless. Presently they were satisfied. Joshua stitched the puncture they had made and dabbed the place with tar to seal it. Afterwards I felt too weak with pain and fear and loss of blood to move, but not so thirsty.

When the moon rose and all was quiet, a silver light shining through the small paned window at the end of my stall, I lay down in the deep straw, stretching out as much as my rope and ball would allow me. I longed for my first home and all the good friends I had left behind, and, most of all, for my mother with her soft comforting eyes. It was very still; the silence was only broken now and then by the scratching of mice and Alec's snoring in the little room above my stall. He came down once to see me; his face puffy with sleep, his eyes pale as pebbles, a drip at the end of his red-veined nose. He sat with me as I lay, stroking my neck and talking to me in his old, tired voice, pausing every so often to cough.

Looking back now over the years, I see that Alec's life was as hard as a horse's, perhaps it was worse, for he had no one to nurse him through his illnesses, no hand to stroke his neck or calm his fears. Yet like us he was at the beck and call of a master. He had no freedom, little rest and his room in the loft was, I believe, cold and bare of all save a bed, table and chair.

In the morning he pushed a purging ball down my throat. It tasted very strong and seemed to burn my gullet, and later I heard him tell the housekeeper that it was made of Barbadoes aloes, ginger, castile soap, sulphur of antimony, kali and oil of aniseed, all made into a whole with syrup of buckthorn. It had an offensive smell, but I was too weak to resist, and, anyway, I would never fight Alec because I loved him and he was my only friend.

A day after the purging ball my bowels were running, as well as my eyes and nostrils. The pain in my head and chest were like tongs of fire, gripping and easing, gripping and easing; my legs were so weak and swollen that I could barely stand. The days and the night merged. I was hardly aware of light and dark. The two old men looked at me in great misery; there were tears trickling like gentle rain drops down Alec's hollow cheeks and the frowns in Joshua's ancient face were deep and long; his mouth dropped: he scratched his thick grey beard in perplexity. 'More medicine,' he said.

They pushed the restorative ball down my throat and then Alec soaked a blanket in hot water and, after wringing it partly dry, put it over my back so that it hung over my sides under the cover of a waterproof sheet. Every two or three minutes this blanket was replaced by another warmer one, the supply of hot water being constantly replenished by one of the doctor's maids, who brought it across from the house in kettles. After an hour Alec stopped these fomentations and bandaged my legs over the hocks and knees in cotton wool and flannel; then Joshua came and dosed me with Indian Hemp to relieve the pain which was growing in my chest like a furnace gathering strength.

The two men now tried to persuade me to eat, bringing me sweet smelling mashes, scalded carrots and lucerne, but the sight of food sickened me, and the foul taste of aloes still lingered in my throat.

The pain grew worse, until I thought I would die; indeed I wanted to die and have done with a life of such misery and loneliness. Then Alec blistered my chest and forearms with mustard, which he said was a counter irritant to lessen the agony, which was a new and different pain to bear.

The weather changed; the rain beat wildly on my little window and gurgled in the gutters. Outside Alec put a sack over his head to keep his cap dry. Then he fetched the jobbing gardener and begged him to put bars at the end of my stall so that I could be free at last from the rope and ball. The gardener, rolling tobacco in paper, said that I would die.

"E's finished. You can see it in 'is eye. I remember seeing the same look in old Ma Bunbury's donkey the night before it kicked the bucket.'

'Them's a mare,' replied Alec scathingly. 'and the fact that you can't tell a mare from an 'oss proves your ignorance.'

The gardener was annoyed now; he banged furiously

and sang angrily as he worked, caring little for the extra suffering this noise caused me. But when the bars were fixed across I was glad to be able to stretch out my poor burning body in the straw. The housekeeper, a comely woman with dove-grey eyes, stood anxiously looking at me.

'What will master say? It'll be the workhouse for you at last, Alec, if that mare dies, you mark my words.'

Joshua took more blood from me, without a twitch this time, for I was too weak to resist; he stroked my hot head and spoke soothing words into my ear, and I knew then that he was doing every thing he could to save me, and that like Will Aken he cherished horses above all else.

'Not dead yet?' the gardener asked next morning. 'Still hanging on? It's a crying shame that animals should suffer so. Better ask farrier to put her out of her misery.'

'Shut your trap, before I lays into you and knocks your bl . . . block off,' replied Alec, straightening his back and putting up his fists, like some old bantam cock going into battle for the last time.

But I didn't die. All at once the pain lessened; my breath came easier; my aching limbs grew stronger. Night and day separated. There was lightness and there was darkness and a winter sun hanging low in the sky; a skittish breeze sent dry leaves chasing each other down the drive . . . I started to eat with a little pleasure and to listen again for footsteps in the mornings. Old Alec raised his head and began to look people in the face again.

Soon afterwards Master came home, tanned from a holiday abroad, expecting his horse and servant to be ready at once for work. My appearance shocked him and his anger was terrible to see. The sun's gold on his face turned to beetroot red, his small plump hands pounded the air.

His voice was like thunder in the stillness of the yard that soft November day.

'Have you never heard of a veterinary surgeon, you fool?' he bawled. 'This isn't 1850. This is 1911. Bleeding belongs to the last century. Have you never heard that it was bleeding killed poor Prince Albert? They put the leeches on so often they drained away his strength.'

Alec said nothing, but stood, as Will Aken had stood, with hanging head, a wizened figure with bandy legs eyes watery and pale with age. It was hard to believe that the same man had threatened to knock the gardener's head off only a few days ago.

The housekeeper stood in her long grey dress, a shawl about her shoulders, a white frilled apron tied round her waist.

'He did his best, sir, and the mare has lived,' she said. 'He did what he could by his own lights.'

'And damned fine lights they were, too! Soap and aloes, oil of buckthorn, gipsy remedies, witches brews. Good God, we might be in the dark ages! And now how shall I go on my rounds?'

Alec raised his head at last. 'Farrier knows a fine mare at the livery stable, a spirited bay, not young but willing and a treat to watch. Would look grand in your trap by all accounts.'

'I must hire her you mean, while this one rests and renews the blood you have taken? Two horses to keep? It's going to be deuced expensive. I don't know why I keep you on, you old fool.' The Doctor turned on his heel and went back to the house.

The housekeeper put her hand on Alec's arm. 'Come inside and have a nice glass of stout,' she suggested in a voice soft as a southern wind. 'Or a little porter. He'll get over it. Why he looked as though he should lose a little blood himself. I thought he would die of apoplexy. And you up night after night wearing yourself to a shadow! Well that's the gentry for you, no gratitude. But there now, tomorrow he'll be his old self again, as sweet as honey, you mark my words.'

CHAPTER FIVE

Sweetbriar

The bay mare was all that Joshua had promised, beautiful, sweet tempered and willing; her white starred head fine as china; her carriage proud and cheerful, and her manners without fault.

Now for the time being my loneliness was at an end, for in the evenings and early mornings Sweetbriar and I enjoyed many a long talk, our breath rising like steam in the keen November air; the fan tail pigeons, who came in for warmth, padding on our backs, coo-ing gently; the smell of hay sweet in our nostrils.

Like Tomtit, Sweetbriar had lived in London and the impression of that great and squalid city was graven on her heart as indelibly as a brand on a horse's flank. She pitied especially the bus horses.

'The stopping and starting tries their legs to breaking point. No sooner have they thrown themselves into the traces to get the buses running smoothly than it is time to halt to pick up more passengers and they have to go through the whole business again. After six years' of this a horse's legs are finished and his only thank you is a bullet in the head. They start at five years old and are dead at ten, and no one cares! Oh, it makes me so angry that I want to kick every human I see, but I don't my dear, I can't. It isn't in my nature.'

Sweetbriar had been a park hack in London, parading

day after day in Rotten Row, a fine lady riding side saddle on her back. 'Flirting,' Sweetbriar said, 'with all the young dandies. A selfish, beautiful little person, who sold me without a second thought when she married a peer and moved to the country.' Later, pulling a brougham, Sweetbriar had seen much more of London, and on those bright, moonlit November nights she told me about the strange ladies who chained themselves to railings and carried placards asking for votes for women.

'I saw the most singular thing just before I left,' she said. 'A whole procession of ladies led by a beautiful grey horse ridden by a Mrs Drummond, sitting astride the saddle like a man. Londoners call this lady "The General". She commands all those girls who are fighting for votes, whatever those may be. It seems that the men have had votes for years, but do not think the ladies clever enough to have them, too. And the ladies are very angry and will not be denied the right. I wish I was that grey horse, because he looked so beautiful, so loved and admired. I am sure he will be allowed to die of old age as the humans do; he will never finish in a knacker's yard with a bullet in his head, his blood staining the cobble stones. Everybody was talking about Mrs Drummond at the time, the men most cruelly with sarcasm, but many of the ladies and servant girls with much admiration.'

Another time Sweetbriar told me of the destitute in London, under the arches at Charing Cross, covering themselves with newspapers in a vain attempt to protect their thin bodies from the winter's bitter cold. She mentioned children with running eyes and sores around their mouths sleeping on benches; their eyes dark pools in waxen faces pinched with lack of food and care; she spoke of drunk old men, dressed like scarecrows, coughing themselves to death in the street rather than go to the work-houses in which healthy human beings hide away their aged poor.

'Truly they are worse off than us horses, for we are worth something to our masters, and so we must be kept warm and fed and fit. But things are changing. Clarences were everywhere when I left.'

'Clarences?'

'Motor cabs, my dear Princess; they're replacing the growlers. My master at the livery stable bought a beautiful young carriage horse last week – Maharajah, they call him – straight from London. And Maharajah says we are finished in London. Soon men won't need us any more. They've become so fond of motors, don't you see? Why Maharajah says there are only one or two horse buses left in the whole metropolis, and the park hacks are being discarded, my dear, like sacks of grain. The auction rooms are crowded with horses being sold like cattle. Oh, it's good in one way and bad in another. Take St James's, my dear.'

'St James's?'

'A very famous street. I should have thought you would have heard of St James's. Every cab horse dreads St James's for the cobbles are always slippery and more cabs overturn there than anywhere else. There's such a crowd, smart people in a great hurry as smart people usually are, wanting the cabmen to go faster than they should, and all amongst the carriages, the victorias, the clarences and the cabs, are the bicycles. My dear, I can't stand bicycles. They pop up from nowhere and upset one's stride. They are even worse than tricycles because they are less obvious, so narrow; they slip in and out of the horse traffic like little adders, and handicapped as we are with blinkers, we don't see them until they are right under our noses. Oh, I've seen several good horses come down in St James's, and one poor gelding shot where he lay, for it was said his off fore was broken just above the fetlock and he would be of no further use to his master. The poor fellow was floundering and kicking like a bird in a strawberry net, causing such a commotion that quite a crowd collected, but the ladies were escorted away before the farrier put an end to him.'

'What worries me most,' said Sweetbriar after a long silence, 'is not so much men's callousness, as the fact that I've never had a foal. You know, my dear, I would have dearly loved a little fellow gambolling in a field beside me. I dream of it sometimes: a grassy meadow, noble trees, a bubbling stream, high thorn hedges thick with birds' nests and, beside me, a foal tottering on dear spindly legs. I can see it all so clearly, and I feel the fresh spring grass under my hoofs. I smell the flowers as I pull the pasture, my teats heavy. I long to feel the little fellow taking the warm milk from me. It is hard to explain, but sometimes, Princess, the longing is like a pain, but what is the use? I am fourteen and, although I have good blood in my veins, no human would wish to breed from me now. My life is almost over.'

'But you look so young,' I said. 'If you had the chance, you would be a wonderful mother. I have always admired the star on your forehead. It is such a perfect shape. It is like the real stars that shine so bright at night, except for its colour, that is like snow.'

Sweetbriar pulled a mouthful of hay from the rack, chewed a moment then turning her head, said. 'My dear, that is man-made. I was born bay right across my temples.'

'Man-made?'

'You are very innocent. You have not learned much of

human vanity, of dealers' tricks and ladies' fancies. I was bred by a dealer who specialised in park hacks. He knew very well how much store a young lady sets on a white star on a horse's forehead, how she feels such a decoration lends for her romance and beauty to the mount of her dreams. So he learned how to make the stars himself to enhance those youngsters who were born plain. This is how he did it: he cut two holes in my skin two inches apart and then two more at the same distance straight across. He then pushed a skewer into each hole in turn, working it up and down and to and fro until a sort of passage had been made between them under the skin. He pushed two strands of wire along these passages, so that an end stuck out about half an inch long from each hole. These he lapped round with packthread as fast as he could tie it, and finally he covered the whole contraption with pitch to hold it secure.'

'But wasn't it painful?' I asked.

'Oh yes it hurt, but he held a rag against my nostrils which soothed me strangely, then this man put a twitch on, and I dared not move. The aching was worse after-wards. I felt as though hot needles were being pushed under my skin, but after a time this was replaced by numbness.'

'But how long did the wires stay?'

'Only three days, and after they had been removed, he dressed the wound daily with honey of roses and tincture of iodine, pouring some into each hole and rubbing the rest all over the star.'

'It's beautiful now. The hair simply turned white?'

'Yes, I have seen it now and then reflected in shop windows and once in a mirror and it suits me well, and I have almost forgotten the pain, but I have met horses who say it is terrible that we should be so mutilated to suit the vanities of human beings.'

In the New Year Sweetbriar went back to the livery stable.

'I shall miss you,' she said, 'but I am tired of pulling the doctor's trap. There's too much waiting about for a mare of my temperament and your Alec is so old and decrepit. My dear, I prefer a younger, smarter driver with a little dash about him.'

'He cannot help it,' I said.

'No, it's simply his age, but, although I hide my feelings, I do find his cough plays on my nerves most terribly.'

When she had gone, Sweetbriar's influence remained with me, and when spring came her longings became my longings . . . *a little fellow gambolling in the field beside me . . . I can see it all so clearly, and feel the fresh spring grass under my hoofs. I smell the flowers as I pull the pasture, my teats heavy. I long to feel the little fellow taking the warm milk from me.*

The cows were out in the meadows with their calves, the hens pecked in the farmyards with chicks like balls of fluff or peered through the bars of coops with motherly clucks and advice. And I continued trotting down the long, dusty roads pulling my master's trap, blinkered, obedient and sad. I wanted a mate, as every animal wants a mate. I began to sniff the air to catch the scent of a stallion, and the humans seemed unaware of my need, although one day I heard Alec tell the master, after I had shied twice, that mares were sometimes unreliable in the spring.

Then on a fine April day, with the sun playing peep-bo with white scudding clouds, and the breeze stirring the young grass, I thought I had my chance.

Master had been called to visit a young girl of good family with incipient tuberculosis who would not recover in spite of all the love and money lavished on her by doting parents. Master's servants said he liked to call on this particular young lady partly because of her prettiness and charm, and partly because of the grandeur of the place and the glasses of good Spanish sherry he drank with her parents, who were both titled. He was, therefore, in good humour as I trotted the seven miles to the mansion, and bore my rather skittish behaviour without complaint.

After leaving the doctor at the front door old Alec unhitched me and led me away for a drink of chilled water, then tied me clumsily in a stall to wait while the stud groom took him for a glass of porter in the Medicine Room, where the chief grooms usually went for a smoke and chat when they wanted to be rid of the stable boys.

The yard normally a busy place full of comings and goings, hoofbeats, neighs and whinnying, (for the Master here bred thoroughbreds) was now quiet. I pulled at my rope in a sudden mood of impatience, and the knot fell apart, then in a moment I was outside. Nobody was around. Several horses looked over loosebox doors at me, but instinct turned me away from them and within seconds I was trotting along the back drive. It must have been instinct again which guided me in this direction for I cannot remember choosing which way to go. I passed gun dog kennels, a little turreted house and came into a different world of paddocks, white fencing and carefully planted spinnies. And there in a meadow, etched against the April sky, stood a stallion with dark flowing mane and tail and such eyes as come only in dreams, set in a noble countenance. Now I neighed, I flung out my hoofs, carried my head high for, in human words, this was love at first sight.

Seeing me, the stallion came across the field like a deer,

graceful and fleet, but with fine, strong shoulders and high-crested neck; the breath from his wide nostrils making patterns in the air. We touched muzzles. He was barely six for his corner teeth was still short. We ran our muzzles down each other's necks, gave little cries of pleasure and then I let out a little squeal of excitement, which must have been instinct again for it came without any request from me. We moved closer, leaning across the top bar of the fence to sniff each other's forelegs. His lips were very soft, his breath warm and there was a wild look in his eyes. We knew that one of us must jump the fence if we were to come together. I put a foreleg through the lowest bar, then drew it back. The stallion reared, letting out a high shrill neigh which the hills echoed and brought back to us in all its strength. It was a call that lives for ever in the memory, a call of passion belonging to all stallions going back down the centuries and forward into eternity. It was a call of the wild, of instinct and blind nature. But even as the echo thundered across the midday landscape, footsteps crunched on the gravel, human voices spoke my name in the flat, soft tones of country people.

'Whoa, my little Princess, Whoa, steady there!'

And the stallion wheeled in one beautiful pirouette, swift and nubile as a circus horse, and galloped away across the field with his dark mane and tail streaming in the wind. And then I was alone again, standing in my black harness, blinkered and ready for work. I jingled the hard bit in my mouth, shook my head as though to wake myself from a dream, but it had been real, and now I felt as though the very core of my being had travelled across the green pasture with the lovely grey stallion'.

'Poor old girl, wanted a mate, did you?' asked Alec, taking my rein, stroking my neck.

'That's Snow King. She chose well. He's a champion,' said the stud groom. 'His stud fee is a hundred guineas.'

'I reckons every mare should be allowed one foal, the same with every bitch. Well it's nature, ain't it. It's only right,' said Alec, turning my head, starting to lead me back down the gravel driveway. 'Them looked a picture standing there! Come on old lady.'

I never went again to the mansion. Perhaps the fine titled people found a doctor they liked better than my master. Perhaps the girl died. I shall never know the answer. But the stallion is as clear in my mind now as he was then. I see him still etched against the merry April sky his spirit unbroken by man, his eyes full of fire and beauty.

CHAPTER SIX

I lose a friend

Winter came again, and now every morning it took Alec longer to harness me to the trap, for his breathing seemed to grow harsher and more difficult and his hands clumsier. A thin blue film, pale as the plumage on a jay's wing was spreading across his old red-rimmed eyes.

'The cataract,' the servants called it, speaking in whispers so that the old man should not hear their verdict. 'He'll be blind in a year, you mark my words, if he ain't under the daisies, poor soul.'

His large red spotted handkerchief was often dragged from his pocket to wipe his red-veined nose, which dripped pitifully in the sharp frosty air, and he was forever rubbing his hands together in a vain attempt to warm them.

One night Master was called out to visit a farmer's wife, who had collapsed while filling her stone hot water bottle. Roused from his bed in the loft by Albert, Alec crept down the yew ladder to my stable like a phantom, a cough rattling in his throat, his face pale as sand. He struggled to lift the collar over my head, which I lowered at once, then fumbled with the buckles, then could hardly raise the strength to double up my tail and push it through the crupper. While Master started hollering in the yard wanting to know why we were so deuced long in coming.

'The lady will be dead by the time I get there at this rate!'

I backed between the shafts as straight and swiftly as possible. I waited, till Alec was well seated with the reins in his cold clumsy hands, before moving off.

The night was crystal clear, the moon riding like a queen amongst her stars, and everything touched with silver.

My thoughts turned to the grey stallion but I made no attempt to take the road which led to the mansion, for unlike the doctor who refused to see unpleasant facts which might affect his existence, I saw plainly that Alec was very ill. I knew with an animal's instinct that he wanted to creep away in a corner, like a sick dog, and drift into eternal sleep. He could work no more and without work his fate lay within the walls of the hated workhouse.

Master said not a word as we trotted through the moon-lit countryside, although occasionally he cleared his throat with a little cough. Beside the old groom he always looked robust, even portly, with his bright red cheeks, thick jowls and bull neck.

The farm was at the top of a steep hill, looking across a valley, dotted with trees and broken by tall hedgerows, all edged now with silver. In summer it was a pleasant spot, sweet with the scent of thyme and rosemary, but in winter a devilish place, because the east wind caught it, killing all the tenderer plants and shrubs in the little garden, which was normally tended by the farmer's wife.

'Don't unharness the horse. I expect to be out again directly. Wait where you are,' said Master, hardly glancing at Alec as, bag in hand, he strode away to the house.

A dog chained to a kennel started to bark. His coat was matted, his eyes strangely pale in the moonlight. Old Alec put a waterproof sheet over my loins.

'That's better my little sweetheart,' he croaked. He

tried to swing his arms, banging his hands against his sides, to keep warm, but he hadn't the strength, so he took to stamping his feet instead. The moon slipped away behind banks of slate grey clouds and the garden darkened. The east wind whistled down the hill into the valley.

'A warm bran mash when we get home, a warm bran mash,' said Alec.

Half an hour must have passed before the doctor returned.

'Too late! Dammit, they should have called me yesterday. The woman's been in and out of bed for a week,' he climbed angrily into the trap. 'Come on, Alec, what's the matter? Let's get back to our warm beds. Fools, utter fools! Such a nice lady, too!'

But old Alec could not drag himself up into the trap. His watery eyes looked helplessly at the step, and even as he looked the light seemed to be dying in them, sucked from him as dusk sucks away the light of day. He tried; he raised one bandy, gaitered leg, then slipped and fell, and lay still on the frozen, silver earth.

My master, to give him his due, was down in a trice, leaping from the trap like a man half his years. He turned the old groom on his side, loosened his collar, then summoned one of the farmer's sons to help. In a minute or so Alec was borne away into the house, my presence utterly forgotten. The dog barked again straining at his chain; a cow lowed sadly in the frozen meadows, a thin blackbird fell dead from its perch in a young oak tree. Winter was bearing away the weak and old to eternal rest as she had done since time began.

Presently Master came back. 'So you waited, good horse! Well done!' He patted me quite kindly, then he took two swigs from a flask of brandy, climbed into the trap and drove me home at a rousing trot. Albert was wakened to see to my needs.

'So he's finished,' he muttered. 'come on, get over! I never thought to find myself tending a horse.'

There was no bran mash for me that night, just a bucket of water, a handful of plain oats and a nibble of straw.

I never saw Alec again. I heard the housekeeper tell a tradesman that the old groom had died in the night.

'A good way to go! Our Lord was kind to him,' she said. 'But Master should have taken the horse himself, not dragged Alec out in the cold. But there, that's how he is. And, to look on the better side, Alec was past seventy-five and that's a good age for a man to live. Heaven knows, many don't reach fifty!'

I missed the old groom, his coughing in the night, his foot on the ladder, his gentle hands and soft voice. In his place came a red haired youth, an urchin who cared nothing for horses, but needed money for his mother and his fags. 'Fred is just a temporary measure,' the housekeeper said. 'The Master has other plans for the future.'

I felt all at once that I was no longer needed or wanted. I still took the doctor on his rounds but he paid little attention to me, and Fred let my harness grow so stiff through lack of cleaning, that it chafed me. The truth was that my owner had decided to enter the motor age.

'Do my rounds in half the time in a Tourer, might even have time for a rubber of bridge of an afternoon,' he said. 'By jove, it will feel deuced odd to have the afternoon off. I shan't know myself, shall I?'

The motor, a BSA Tourer came just three days later, green shiny, beautiful as the finest carriage with great brass lights, leather seats and a hood that went up and down. The steering wheel was brass too, and there was a horn which made a weird honk when squeezed. The older villagers called this motor car a stinkpot, but the younger ones and Master's servants were as excited as children with a new toy, and many a time the horn was honked when Master was out of earshot. Our jobbing gardener was replaced by a chauffeur-gardener, a smart young man, with a small, well-trimmed moustache and slicked-down dark hair; very slim he was with a cocky air about him and sharp features and eyes bright as beads. The housekeeper said this new chauffeur-gardener was too clever for his own good.

Turned out now in a paddock, my job finished, I felt my solitude even more keenly. Master, it was said, was looking out for a new situation for me. Meanwhile my thoughts turned again to the grey stallion. I tried in vain to force myself to leap the high hedge which parted me from the road, but Will Aken had never taught me to jump and my courage failed me. Every time I heard hoofbeats I was mad with excitement. I neighed and neighed again, galloping up and down as though I had lost my senses, and in the stable I would paw the ground until there was not a stalk of straw left under me. Master grew increasingly irritated by the noise I made, until at last he lost patience with me.

'Take her to next month's horse sale, see to the details, put a good description into the catalogue, Albert,' he said. 'Warranted quiet to ride and drive, and sound in wind limb and eye, you know the form.'

'Yes sir,' said Albert standing in the yard, looking perplexed. 'But who shall lead her over, sir? The new man has no interest in horses, and I know little about them. As likely as not I shall let hold of the rope at the first steam engine we meet.'

'Hire a man from the farm. I leave it to you. But I want that mare away by the end of the week. With that neighing I can hardly think. It's almost worse than having a donkey in the field.'

CHAPTER SEVEN

A move up in the world

I will not dwell on the horse sale. It was like all such events, humiliating for the horses and a sad spectacle of misery and despair. In a great hall showing our paces before a circle of men we were auctioned to the highest bidder. Being one of the fittest there, I went for two hundred guineas. Many broken-down horses changed hands for as little as twenty, and with heavy heads and sad eyes were led away by new masters to end their days dragging carts through the hard streets.

My new owner was a dealer, his yard like every dealer's yard smart on the surface, but dirty and dark if you looked deep into the heart of things. This story will be too sad for you to bear if I relate all the miserable tales I heard and the cruel scenes I witnessed, during my week's stay there. One horse in particular stays in my memory, perhaps because she was grey and I have a weakness for greys; a mare called Moonlight, who was incurably lame in the off-fore and was therefore lamed in the near fore also, that she might not limp. Because she was frightened of motor cars and steam engines, Moonlight refused to leave the yard and much cruelty was employed to make her change her mind; bottles of water were broken over her head when she reared; red hot pokers pushed under her tail. All manner of cutting whips slashed her sides. But these only increased her fear, until her whole body was lathered with sweat, and foam lay about her mouth like milk straight from the cows' udders.

It was Moonlight who was first brought out when my future owner came to the yard, for she was sleek and lovely in appearance with a fine spirited eye and splendid carriage.

And the Lady Angela, come with her brother, Lord Wareing, had said, 'I need a horse, a beautiful horse, something that moves like a dream, a story-book horse...'

'Got a beauty here, see that grey?' said the dealer. 'Lovely little mover, gentle as a lamb. Take first in any show. Here, George, trot her up and down for the lady. Come on, look slippy. Take a side-saddle lovely she does, a grand lady's horse.'

But poor Moonlight having two painful legs, made a bad showing and her stunted gait did not escape Lady Angela's watchful eye.

'The poor creature doesn't step out very freely. What about that black? Can we see her move, please?'

To and fro I went, head and tail up, longing to be away from the dealer's yard.

'She's rather divine, Charles, isn't she,' said Lady Angela.

'Looks a corker to me,' said the young Lord Wareing. 'But I shall see I am not present when you tell Papa you've bought a horse from a dealer's place. Do you want me to try her first?'

'Oh, my dear, certainly not. A saddle on her please.'

'Never tried a side saddle on this horse, milady,' said the dealer. 'Though likely as not she will go well enough, being kind as a kitten.'

'I ride astride,' replied Lady Angela, a trifle haughtily.

And indeed she was wearing breeches and boots partly obscured by her long-waisted riding coat.

'What are you waiting for George? You heard what the lady said. Clap a saddle on the mare,' said the dealer, taking off his cap to scratch his balding head. 'You're the first lady we've had wanting to ride astride, though truth is not many ladies come here any time, I know it's the modern way as you might say.'

'My twin sister could be described as a modern woman,' said Lord Wareing, smiling. 'She's a better rider than I am to be sure and she likes her horse to be a pal.'

While a saddle was put on my back by George, the stable man, I took a long look at the young pair as they stood in the December sunshine, smiling and laughing like those who have never met grief or sorrow, and lovely they were, too; fair-skinned, green eyed, with hair the glorious russet of autumn beech leaves; their voices imperious, a little mocking but full of merriment, as though buying a horse was the biggest joke in the world.

'A great mare this,' continued the dealer, 'only had her a week. Belonged to a doctor who's switched to a motor car. Princess, they call her, Black Princess directly related to the famous Black Beauty. No fault in this mare, no vice, absolutely trustworthy, moves straight as a die.'

Lord Wareing inspected my teeth, ran his hands rather inexpertly down my legs, then asked that I might be galloped so that my wind was well tested. Lady Angela mounted me. Her touch on the reins was light, but her seat in the saddle firm. On the bare field the last of the frost lay like sprinkled silver; the trees in the hedgerow stood still as tired men waiting for a lift in the carrier's cart. I was glad to be out; I pranced and danced and when the time came galloped like a young racehorse.

'She's glorious,' said Lady Angela, back at the gate again. 'She goes like the wind.' She ran her small hands along my neck, patted me. 'How much?'

'Three hundred guineas, worth every penny. You'll never regret it.'

'Too much,' replied Lord Wareing. 'The days are past when a good park hack fetched four hundred guineas, bicycles and motor cars have seen to that.'

My breath rose in the air like clean white smoke. Two pairs of green eyes looked into the dealer's crafty, scarred face. For a moment the world seemed to stand still.

'Worth every penny,' repeated the dealer.

'I am sorry,' said Lord Wareing, turning as if to go, 'but that is more than we are prepared to pay.'

'Not so hasty, not so hasty,' said the dealer, 'I could reduce it a little seeing it would be a good home, as you might say.'

At this, Moonlight, who was tied in the yard gave a snort of derision.

'It all depends by how much. I'm damned sure you didn't pay more than two hundred for this mare, you dealers never go beyond that price as a matter of principle. Come on now, admit it.'

'I'll take two hundred and fifty.'

'Two hundred and twenty,' said Lord Wareing.

'All right, seeing I haven't had the mare long . . .' said the dealer. 'You've a bargain at the price, sir.'

And so I came to be sold into the aristocracy.

CHAPTER EIGHT

The lull before a storm

I now moved to one of England's most gracious houses. Built of mellowed stone it stood on the brow of a hill, looking down into a valley through which a silver river flowed like a satin ribbon. The stable yard behind the house formed a square with a tower and a clock above its arched entrance way.

Lord Wareing's father, the Duke of . . . , still kept a coach and four, with beautiful Yorkshire carriage horses, matching bays, named after stars: Venus, Mercury, Jupiter and Gemini. There was also a phaeton pulled by two grey ponies, Flotsam and Jetsam, and other vehicles too numerous to list. The bustle and busyness of the Duke's well-run stable made the doctor's establishment seem like a grave in comparison. Here the routine was so regular that after only a few days I felt as though I had spent half my life within its walls. And I may as well say now that there is nothing a horse likes more than a good routine, which is very calming for the nerves, just as uncertainty and disorder are very upsetting. At five minutes to six each morning every pony and horse was looking over his loosebox door for the arrival of his groom. Mine was a twenty-five year old called Terence, a fair freckled man very quick and efficient at his work, but not at all affectionate; indeed he rarely patted me or the five other horses in his charge, but along with the other grooms he always appeared as the clock's hands reached the hour of six, often with a joke on his lips.

And how fine it was not to be tied! To be able to look over a loosebox door again to see all the happenings in the yard; the arrivals and departures; the tradesmen coming and leaving the back door; the servants busy about their work. This was a world in itself with its own rules. The stud groom, Jim Watkins, expected to be treated with respect and he gave nothing away. The local tradesmen tipped him well, so that he should bring the Duke's work to them. It was said by the younger grooms that the saddler and farrier each gave him five pounds'a year and the corn merchant ten. In addition he received many a tip from visitors who came to the Hall. He was said to be a religious man who read his Bible each night. His sons were well disciplined and his daughters demure and shy, but he was not liked because he kept all the tips to himself never sharing any of them with the under-grooms.

There were many week-end parties, especially in the shooting season, for the Duke was a fine shot and his coverts full of game. The beaters were out early then, driving the beautiful pheasants up into the sky to meet their death from the gentry's cartridges. We horses hated these times, for the bangs tried our nerves and the killing disgusted us. One of the ponies used to take a cart up into the coverts to bring the dead pheasants home, and a gelding called Nutcracker took the older gentlemen with their guns in a dogcart to a clearing in the woods.

Once King George V came and there was a great fuss all because he was a king. The servants' children put on their Sunday best clothes and some of them were given flags to wave. The grooms worked twice as hard as usually till our coats were like satin and you could see your faces in the coachwork. Yet to me the King looked a very ordinary man, bearded, balding, rather short and stocky with a stomach a little too large to be healthy, not nearly import-ant enough to receive such homage. But he was a crack shot. He used three hammer guns with two men to assist him, one to load and one to cock them, and one day he brought down six hundred birds, rarely missing. Nut-cracker heard the beaters say that there had been a record that day, a total of one thousand, one hundred and two birds. Heather, who pulled the cart was sickened by the rows of corpses, but the people on the estate looked forward to shoots, because they received most of the game; the rest being given to the Duke's friends or stolen by the game-keepers to be sold to publicans and butchers.

Lady Angela and her brother took no part in these shoots, which they called 'ritual and barbaric slaughter'. Their friends were not sportsmen, but would-be authors and artists and their like, handsome young men and pretty girls, sometimes brave and reckless, nearly always indolent and spoiled. Lady Angela took a delight in telling people how she had found me without Jim Watson's help. She called me 'her little adventure' and congratulated herself on her skill and judgement as a horse buyer, not seeing how deeply annoyed the stud-groom was by her behaviour.

She took me out most afternoons sometimes with friends, sometimes alone, but rarely without a good hard gallop. Now and then she would race me against other horses urging me with whip and voice until I thought my wind would break and my heart burst. I wanted to please. Some of her wildness entered into me and I was willing to gallop until I dropped, but although I could beat most of the Duke's hunters on races of a mile or less, I was a loser on a longer course and regularly beaten by a young thoroughbred owned by the Squire's son, a poet studying at Oxford University.

So life galloped by; summer came and went; the great beechwoods were aflame with colour; autumn smells were everywhere: wet leaves, cobwebs on the hedges, Michaelmas daisies, chrysanthemums, roses, bonfires and the dying bracken. Cub hunting started and the grooms came earlier to our stables, but I stayed home because the twins, did not hunt. Murmurings of war were in the air. Germany and the Kaiser were words now commonly used. Long serious conversations took place amongst the servants. What did it all mean? We horses hardly knew. The oldest of the Duke's hunters, a great dun called Napoleon, had known a cavalry horse who had taken part in a war called the Crimean.

'It's a wicked thing, war,' said Napoleon. 'It brings nothing but grief. There's no sense in it, no sense at all. Nothing but muddle and mistakes, cold, hunger and disease. A horse is lost. There's nothing to cling to.'

But war there was, next summer, and many farewells as men on the estate left to join the Colours.

My Lady Angela's friends still came to discuss ways to end the conflict and took us for many a long ride over hill and down dale, through deep woods and open plains, their conversations grave, and sometimes angry. They spoke of Russia and revolutions, a revolt by working people against their masters. They cursed Britain's leaders as fools and talked of uniting the world's artists, authors, musicians and philosophers, who would put an end to the useless slaughter of men to satisfy the needs of the world's rich. I could not understand what all this meant. Strange names spattered their conversation: Rothschild, Litvinov, Lenin and Trotsky, Lloyd George, Haig and Joffre are just a few which lodged in my memory. Yet it seemed surprising to me that Lady Angela should so bitterly dislike the rich when she lived amongst them in a mansion and had never known want in her life.

Winter came; the frost was hoary again on hedges, the fields lay like iron waiting for the blacksmith's furnace to soften it. The sun often lay low in the sky, a great red ball behind the elms, powerless against the bitter cold. More men left. Our routine suffered. The Duke put his phaeton aside and Flotsam and Jetsam were found new homes with local children.

. The remaining servants were often sad. Terence, my groom, was said to have been killed at the Front. Posters started to appear in the village appealing for army volunteers.

Jim Watson started to make nasty remarks about the Duke's children. Why should the young Lord Wareing amuse himself with talk and parties, while others more humble went out to fight for their country in France?

Then suddenly, without warning it seemed, both Lady Angela and her brother left, suffering, people supposed, a sudden change of heart. The servants talked of the young pair driving ambulances in France. And now all at once it was suggested that the Duke was unpatriotic to keep so many horses, for the army had lost many in the first disastrous battles in France and Belgium and needed more to replace them.

A man came in uniform from the army to look round the Duke's stables and Jim Watson, who had never forgiven Lady Angela for buying me without his advice, suggested that I would make a fine charger. 'Plenty of spirit and tough and no use to us here, now that the young mistress is a v.a.d.' he said. Money passed between this brisk broad

shouldered moustached man from the army and Jim
Watson; and overnight I suddenly changed hands. You see
Napoleon was right; there is no security in war. Changes
come suddenly without warning. One day I was a lady's
hack and the next on my way to a Remount Depot, the
property of His Majesty's army. It was very distressing.

The Depot was a huge place with so many stables you
lost count of them. The regular army horses were steady
enough, but the rest of us were uneasy and irritable. On
arrival each one of us was branded with a number on the
hoof. The heavier horses also had their manes hogged, but,
earmarked as an officer's charger, I was spared the clippers.
And I soon found myself with a master, a fair, open faced
young man with the unusual name of Augustine Appleyard,
known by most of his friends as A.A. He was a very fine

young man with a loud infectious laugh, gentle hands and a kind nature, and I liked him from the moment I set eyes on him. He was a friend to me as well as a master, and I trusted him as I had trusted no one since I parted with Will Aken. Not knowing my name, Augustine decided to call me Emily after the brave suffragette, who had died for her cause under the hoofs of a racehorse in the Derby. (Oh how I pity that horse, for not one of us would wish to kill a human being.)

'You have spirit, too, haven't you Emily? You are a good brave mare who will face everything. And we shall have to face death, Emily, you and I together. We may die together, you and I'.

Often I believe, Augustine spoke his thoughts aloud to me, thoughts which he kept secret from all his fellow men. Now as he spoke he pressed his face against my coat; his hair smelt of soap and fresh straw and his skin of a young man much in the fresh air. His kindness and affection made me feel safe.

Life now seemed to pass again at a gallop; days flashed by. Snowdrops pushed through the earth, their little flowers like tiny paper lanterns, forsythia shone like bright stars in cottage gardens.

'It's France for us, Emily. This is it,' said my young master one February morning. 'Tomorrow we go to strike a blow for England!'

Sure enough the very next day it was all change again, and I found myself, trembling and shaking in a railway truck racing across the Kentish fields bound for foreign soil. With me were four stouthearted artillery horses: Pioneer, Floss, Joey and Sampson. It was a long and tedious journey with many halts. But, soon after we smelt the sea, the train drew puffing and spitting to a halt, and we were hurried down the ramp into the soft grey light of an English dusk with the wind blowing from the south west and the waves throwing up gentle foam like the head on a glass of porter.

After a drink of chilled water, we were quickly led down another ramp into the very bowels of a cross-channel steamer. Here we stood tied in the dark with aching legs and dizzy heads listening to the sound of feet on deck, the shouts of men and the strange honking of ships' hooters.

'I trust we won't be here many days,' said Floss, jerking at her rope.

'Sometimes these journeys last for weeks. I've been in the artillery long enough to have heard many a tale, I can tell you,' said Pioneer tossing his handsome liver chestnut head, 'but I'm tough. It's the quality horses like Princess who take the rough life so badly.'

My nerves were already on edge. When at last the ship started to shake and vibrate, I felt my heart pounding with fear, and sweat broke out on my flanks. But it wasn't very long before we were off the steamer and on another train rattling through the flat French countryside. There were many stops and delays; darkness came and went. Through the slats in our truck we saw dawn breaking over red rooftops, tall foreign trees, sleeping shuttered houses. At each stop Augustine and his two gunners came to visit us. At one station he spent a long time arguing with Frenchmen in peaked high-crowned hats.

'Fourrage' and 'Foin' he kept saying. Later on in the war I learned that these words meant fodder and hay, and I knew then that he had been doing his best to find us something to eat. At that station he was unsuccessful, but at the next stop he brought us hay which, foreign though it was, tasted very good to our empty bellies.

After many hours, as the shadows lengthened over the long white roads, we drew into a station crowded with soldiers. Our truck was disconnected from the train and shunted into a siding, and presently we disembarked, led by Augustine and the two gunner privates.

Evening was again in the air, keen now with the promise of frost; the foreign sky blank and white. The men made a shelter for us out of hop poles and sacking, and we learned that we were to join a battery on the following day. Far off we could hear the rumble of guns like distant thunder, while overhead a monoplane buzzed like some lonely hornet lost on the wide horizon.

CHAPTER NINE

All hell let loose

The war was long and terrible. Names of places and battles live like little fires of hell in my memory, and sometimes, when the wind is low, I seem to hear again the songs of the soldiers: *There's A Ship That's Bound for Blighty*, *Tipperary*, and *It's a Long, Long Trail Awinding*, tunes sung occasionally to different words than the composers intended.

My friends, Pioneer, Joey, Floss and Sampson, were all wiped out somewhere on the Somme, pulling a gun through mud deeper than any we had seen in our lives before. I can recall it all now so clearly: the great flash followed by a boom like thunder; the earth caving in, the struggling horses. For me it was the first disaster, a taste of the future. They had been only ten days at the Front. Soon the rest of us retreated, the shells following us, pitting the ground with craters, our ears battered by the noise, our flesh flapping with fear. Farther back were the kite balloons, from which men of the Observer Corps watched the enemy through binoculars. Now and then a mono- or bi-plane buzzed overhead in the grey, French sky. For a horse it was all strange and frightening. It was as though the whole human race had gone mad.

We usually went into action before a battle, moving up the big guns with which to batter the Germans so that the infantry could advance while the enemy was still suffering from our fire. It was Augustine's job to see the guns reached their positions, directed their fire in the right direction and were replaced, if possible, when put out of action. We were normally moved farther back once the bombardment had started. The men covered their ears immediately after firing a shell, but, of course, we could do no more than lay ours back, and sometimes we felt as though they would be blown out by the noise and vibration.

These battles were very frightening, but, worst of all was the steady, unending misery of cold and mud, the lack of proper shelter and shortage of food when things went wrong. Sometimes we stood out night after night in dreadful horse lines, our rugs saturated with sleet and rain, freezing against our backs, our bellies often empty and aching. Most of my friends, the artillery horses, were hardy and tough, former dray horses or vanners, but the better bred horses, the officers' chargers, suffered terribly, for they had spent all their lives cossetted by grooms in warm stables or taking their yearly holidays in summer fields. Many died in the horse lines of pneumonia, for which the army vets had no cure, and, later a terrible horse influenza took its toll. It was a time of great sadness and bewilderment and I think some of us who survived would not have minded dying just to escape from the misery of it all.

Twice I was tied next to captured German horses, stout hearted strong fellows with hoofs like saucers. They were used to pull our guns and worked as well as any British gunners' horses. From them I learned that the Germans thought the human's God was on *their* side, that Sunday after Sunday they held church services kneeling sometimes under bare and angry skies, as the British knelt, to ask the same God for help and succour. It seemed strange that people believing in one God could fight to destroy each other. It was very confusing, for both countries seemed to have many good and noble men. I was told that early in the War that, one Christmas, German and British soldiers had crossed the strip of earth between them, known as No Man's Land, to make friends and drink each other's health, but the generals had put an end to that and had ordered them to continue fighting.

One day, after a lull, my master was one of three men ordered to reconnoitre to see whether several big guns could be moved farther forward to bombard the enemy before an attack.

'Just to have a little look-see,' someone said. 'But keep your eyes skinned for rookies.'

The sky was overcast. The evening air for once empty of the rumble of guns, so that we could hear the birds singing and farther down the valley, the trickle of water. A.A. was silent, too, but I knew by the way he gripped the reins that he was tense. No one quite knew where the enemy was . . . Every so often our riders brought us to a halt so that they could scan the landscape through their binoculars or consult a map or compass.

We came into a wood, not yet flattened by guns, a place of peace with sand-white anemones like little spots of snow against the bright russet of last year's bracken. I stopped for a moment to paw the ground for I longed to lie down and roll, being like many soldiers from the trenches, itchy with lice. But Augustine urged me on.

'Good old Emily,' he whispered. 'What would I do if you weren't with me? What will we all do when this is over, if we come through? Come on, no time to stop.'

He straightened up. At the same moment the fire from a shell flashed across the sky like a white sword of flame.

The boom of the gun followed together with the weird shriek with which we were now familiar. And then suddenly it was as though all hell had been let loose. A pit was in front of our hoofs, trees were falling like matchsticks and, sharper than everything else, was 'a-rat-a-tat-tat'.

'Machine gun post!' shouted Augustine. 'Back, back.' The enemy had moved up into the spot we were to reconnoitre. I saw a steel helmet. Someone was crawling through the woods on hands and knees. Augustine fired his revolver, and the man rolled back, but the 'rat-a-tat-tat' came from behind gorse bushes farther up, and was more than a match for us. Darkness was coming down like a curtain, but too slowly to protect us. 'Rat-a-tat-tat-rat-a-tat-tat'. Now, like grey ghosts, in the half-light more Germans advanced. Augustine swung me round. 'Come on, Emily!' I needed no second bidding, for my own heart was pounding with fear.

We started to gallop back down a narrow path that wound crazily through the trees. Another machine seemed to start up and suddenly Augustine said, 'I'm hit. Go on, Boys, don't wait!'

His hands were limp on the reins. His legs no longer guided me. His body slumped. I should have stopped, but the firing terrified me. There seemed to be bullets everywhere. His voice was very matter of fact, as though he had always expected this moment, had even lived through it in his imagination many times. The other horses, Piper and Blossom, were ahead of me, their hoofs throwing up mud, but I slowed my pace. Augustine's body slid from the saddle and came to rest in fern, tipped with the greenness of spring. His face was the colour of gruel, his khaki uniform already wet with blood.

Piper's rider, a young man from Cornwall, turned back a moment.

'Done for,' he said. 'Poor devil!'

For a moment I was alone standing under a sky rent with the sounds of battle. Then I turned too, and followed the other horses.

I came out of the wood. Below me lay the poor battered valley shrouded in mist; above me the guns rattled. Piper and Blossom had gone. Barkless trees shone through the gathering darkness like white milestones. The firing stopped. I sniffed the air, heavy now with the bitter odour of cordite. A green Very light rose in the sky, pretty as a plaything.

I trotted down a path, saw at last the light of camp fires and came back to the horse lines. My saddle empty.

CHAPTER TEN

A new master

Someone must have blundered, for after Augustine's death things seemed to go from bad to worse.

There was a long and dreadful retreat with the enemy harassing us all the way. Some horses were left behind, their drivers dead. Others were without food.

Desperately hungry, I was ridden for miles by Augustine's friend, another gunner officer, David Bellamy, a nice enough young man but often silent and moody. The days were long and raw, the nights bitterly cold, moonless and dark. The men were dispirited, although at times they joked and occasionally raised a song. We had abandoned many guns, but, after two days, we met new supplies coming up, which included two tractors which were to take the place of horses.

At last there was a halt. We came to new billets. A line of motor ambulances were on their way to pick up the wounded, and the men gave a cheer and wave because two girls were sitting beside the drivers of the first pair.

David Bellamy urged me on. He was cold and tired and wanted a meal, but something made me hesitate. The girl who leaned out to wave back was the Lady Angela, her red hair peeping out from under the nurse's cap.

'Your horse is just like one I had at home. We called her Black Princess.'

David Bellamy stopped, smiled, took off his army cap.

'This one is Emily, until recently Augustine Appleyard's charger.'

'She's the image of my Princess, but thin, poor thing. Here, come on, there's a good girl.'

I turned to nuzzle the Lady Angela.

'Her eyes are different. She's thinner. Princess! Is it you Princess? If only horses could speak.'

'Then their riders would learn a thing or two,' said David with a quick laugh.

But now the ambulance was moving on. 'Goodbye, good luck, Princess Emily!' It was the last I saw of Lady Angela.

We rested in barns until the May sun had dried the mud and flowers bloomed again in cottage gardens, and then we went back to the Front again, where we met a new horror, mustard gas. Now the men often donned gas

masks, which made them look like pigs and frightened the new horses which came over from England from time to time. Those who did not, often lost their power of speech, died or were sent home incurably ill. Sometimes the smell of gas seemed to hang in the air for days on end, making us all feel very depressed.

There were many attacks and counter attacks, crazy attempts to gain a few yards of No Man's Land, a derelict place pitted with shell holes treacherous with mud and eerie with death.

One day the great General Haig visited us on his spirited grey charger, looking very healthy and clean. The soldiers were polite in his presence, but afterward very bitter. They invented coarse rhymes about the General and asked one another what he knew about the realities of war. It was all very well to ride about on a fine charger, but wasn't it time some of the leaders spent a time in the trenches or battled their way across the mud and barbed wire of No Man's Land.

So the war went on and on until we thought it would only end for us in death. Another winter came. Our heels cracked open in the horse lines and a young private lost his footing on the duck boards and drowned in the mud while attempting to feed us.

In early summer we took more guns forward for another bombardment. People began to talk of the 'Big Push'. Monstrous machines, called tanks, ground their way mercilessly across the countryside. Hopes began to rise in the British ranks; the gunners started to sing again as they groomed us and, with fairer weather and southern winds, the mud began to dry again . . . New fresh-faced boys straight from school came to replace the hundreds lost in battle.

Soon we noticed more German prisoners of war coming in, sad, broken men putty-faced and hollow eyed. I learned that, after bombardment, many enemy soldiers had given themselves up and our advancing infantrymen had found trenches deserted.

Soon my brave friends pulled the gun carriages across No Man's Land, dragged them up to the crest of a hill from which our artillery shelled the retreating Germans in the valley.

It was, although we did not know it then, the beginning of the end. The cavalry began to move up at last for action. I caught a glimpse of Symphony, a mare I had known at the Remount Depot, looking blythe, untouched by the deeper horrors of war. They charged in the old fashioned style, while we, the gunners' horses, so much more experienced in the ways of battle, rested our weary legs farther back, while the guns we had moved rumbled and thundered.

Autumn came and peace at last. All France seemed to be loud with the cheers of women, old men and girls. Garlands of flowers were lovingly hung round the necks of smiling British soldiers. We saw for the first time American troops who had come over to help towards the end, Indian troops in white turbans, and blacks from Africa, and the West Indies. We saw dogs and doves, who unknown to us, had carried messages when field telephone lines were cut.

Our side had won the war, but what did this mean to us? We longed for home, for green English meadows, high thorn hedges, the special smell of our native land.

Some officers bought their chargers from the army and took them back to England, but David, who wanted to be a great actor, had no need for a horse, and no special affection for me.

The French people were tired and often hungry. Would they eat us like bullocks? They had, we were told, a fondness for horseflesh. Billeted in warm barns we waited patiently, while men far away decided our fate.

CHAPTER ELEVEN

Exile

Most of the cavalry horses now returned with their regiments, but many of the artillery horses were aged and of little further use to a branch of the army which was being rapidly mechanised.

So on a windy day in March I found myself again at a sale, standing next to a fine gun carriage horse called Big Ben, who had suffered shell shock but was otherwise sound. The French peasants, farmers and cabbies looked at us much as their English counterparts would have done, inspecting our teeth, running their hands down our legs picking up our hoofs, pulling down the lower lids of our eyes and lifting our tails. Most of them seemed to be more interested in the horses that had pulled the guns than in me. The cabbies were gradually changing over to motors. There was not much call for carriage or riding horses in those hard days following the war when many people were struggling for survival. Finally, I was sold for less than Big Ben, in spite of my breeding, to a man who could barely read or write.

Monsieur Bernard Forel was a peasant who had been lucky enough to inherit a few acres of land from an uncle. The smell of garlic, alcohol and sweat seemed always about his spare, stunted frame. There was rarely a smile in his brown, leathery face which was pierced by two eyes, small and sharp as ferrets', and crowned by a balding head

with two sad tufts of grey hair on either side like little
bushes guarding a bare track. He had good reason to be sad
because both his sons had been killed in the war.

Madame Forel was a small, wiry person with a face
smooth and brown as a walking-stick handle which has
seen much use. She always wore black, although sometimes this colour was slightly relieved by an apron of
coarse sacking-like material. Her greying hair was severely
pulled back into a tight bun as though she resented it and
wished it out of the way and forgotten. Her eyes were the
colour and shape of coffee beans and a line of dark hairs

running along her upper lip gave the impression of a moustache, which was confusing in a lady. She smelt pleasanter than her husband, the scent of herbs and fresh dough sweetening the garlic.

I now started a very hard part of my life. Monsieur Bernard Forel ran a small market garden and farm, and every morning but Sunday, I had to take his vegetables and fruit to market, trotting briskly down a long straight road between Lombardy poplars for seven miles to the nearest town. A poor riser in the mornings, he always left a little late so I was forced to hurry most of the way. Now, had my cart been as light as Dr Miller's trap, this would have been no hardship for the mornings were usually fresh, the dew had dampened the dust, and the birds were singing blithely as indeed they had sung throughout the war. But Monsieur Forel's cart, was both heavy and badly sprung, with iron-rimmed wheels and shafts that were too wide and too long for me. The harness, too, had been made for a larger animal and rubbed me in the wrong places so that I was often overtired and sore and wanted nothing more than a good long sleep under a shady tree in deep cool grass.

While my master sold his goods at his stall, I was left standing under a tree in the market place, with a nosebag of chaff, mixed with a little bran and wheat flyers which are the husks which remain when the wheat is ground at the mill. It was dry, tasteless fare on a hot day, but better than nothing.

Other horses stood with me in the Square and some-times Big Ben was amongst them and then we would greet one another with soft neighs, but we were tied so that we could not touch or smell each other. My other companions were French, some bright and cheerful others sad with dull coats, weary eyes, swollen fetlocks and hips standing out like cliffs in their poor thin bodies.

France's victory had left Master poorer in every way than he had been in earlier days and this irony ate into his soul and drove him to find solace in the brandy bottle.

So on the way home he would usually slip into drunken slumber, and I could set my pace to suit my mood. If it was cool I would trot most of the way, but when the sun was fierce and bright I dawdled, even allowing donkeys to overtake me.

My master's farm was divided into narrow strips, each one cultivated as fully as possible all the year round. In the late afternoons I was tethered on the bits and pieces which were left over, along with his two cows. At night I was tied in a smelly stall, alongside his pigs, who were very noisy at times and reminded me of the gas masks. I was always harnessed or tied, never free, which was very irksome.

On Sundays I took the Forels five miles to a grey turreted village on a hill, to see their relations. For these occasions Monsieur Forel would shave the grey stubble from his chin, don a suit and occasionally replace his black beret with a straw hat. Madame Forel would change into a slightly newer black dress which sported a little lace on the cuffs and collar. Sometimes she would take a lace shawl which she would wear over her head on the homeward journey when the sun had gone down and the blue light of evening drowned the landscape.

As the weeks went by, I found this Sunday journey growing harder. The long climb up the curling grey road to the hilltop village seemed to drain me of strength. I found my breath coming quickly in gasps and every so often a harsh cough rose in my throat as the dry food, hard work and dust increasingly affected my wind. My body too was losing its beauty. Untended sores on my withers and back festered, my fetlocks swelled, my proud head carriage disappeared as my step became slow and reluctant. The days ran into one another with little respite. Dawn was no longer a joy but a summons to further toil. In summer the nights were always too short to revive me for my master worked me until the light had gone from the fields, and farrowing sows often kept me from the nocturnal doze so essential to hardworked horses. I grew careless and clumsy, for as time wore on, I did not care whether I lived or died.

One afternoon coming home from market I tripped, falling on my knees and breaking their skin. In England such a fall would have been considered a tragedy, for I was now broken-kneed, a grave condition because it meant that I could never again fetch a high price. But my French master was not at all upset, and I realised then that he intended to work me until I died. Indeed the poor man's despair and apathy, were so deep that he did nothing to tend my wounds. It was Big Ben's master, a splendid young farmer, who defeated the flies that clustered on them, by simply coating my knees and all my sores with stockholm tar.

My owner's despair now entered into me and the cheerful willingness which had survived as part of my nature throughout all the terrors and misery of war disappeared. I became sour towards animals and humans alike. Leaning down one day I bit a little child in a pinafore who came to pat me, as I stood waiting for my nosebag under the lime trees in the Square. I also kicked my owner's dog, a miserable mongrel who spent much of his time barking at the end of a chain.

A bitter winter came. The cold seemed to eat into my poorly covered bones, and my left eye, already irritated by dusty roads, was red and sore. Lice returned to my coat. Monsieur Forel shook powder along my back and mane and rubbed it into the roots of my tail to deal with these, muttering angrily in French. He even took to grooming me a little, perhaps because one or two men at the market had remarked on my poor condition. Indeed some of the horses that stood with me under the trees had improved during the summer and I was now one of the most decrepit looking in the group.

Although at the time I hated my master and blamed the French character for my condition, looking back now I see that there were many Frenchmen who cared for their horses. Indeed Big Ben's owner had two beautiful Percherons of which he was justly proud, and Monsieur Forel's relations often rebuked him for neglecting my welfare and sometimes his nieces brought me sugar and carrots. Just as in England, many men here were kind to their animals, a sizeable number neglected them and a few were deliberately cruel.

CHAPTER TWELVE

The end of the road

There is an old saying that it is always darkest before dawn, perhaps we should never despair, for we cannot know what forces are at work to save us from final disaster or early death. Fate is full of surprises.

I was now without hope, convinced that I would be pulling my ill-fitting cart until I dropped, living forever in a country whose language and customs I did not understand. For the first time in my life I felt no joy at the coming of spring. The fresh green grass, the young leaves and first flowers no longer lightened my spirits. Yet the French countryside, recovering from the ravages of war, was beautiful; the skies each day as clear as crystal the sun at noon a glory of gold and red. And at the time, unknown to me, rescue was almost at hand; a chain of events was leading me nearer home. Letters were being written on my behalf, men harassed in London and chivvied in France. I had become very important to two people on the other side of that grey stretch of water known as the English Channel, and if horses' ears burned as humans are said to do, mine would have been red-hot.

But my first indication of rescue came on one of those sleepy noontides when all the world seems still and the heat lies on hot cobblestones, so that dogs creep into doorways to take their midday naps. I was dreaming, too, my eyes half closed; the scent of wine, garlic, coffee and ripe melons in my nostrils; the drowsy flies busy around my eyes. And the English voice which broke this stillness was at first part of my dreams, and then it was real, and I saw that it belonged to a long-legged English lady who came striding across the square with head high and arms swinging in a way which could never belong to the French. Behind this lady was a tall thin girl in a cotton summer dress and a straw hat like a pudding basin, and behind her the postmaster, a fussy little man with a white moustache, gesticulating helplessly as though he had lost an argument.

'Black,' said the English lady. 'No not cavalry, artillery, no, not a gun carriage horse, an officer's charger. Noir cheval, noir. Oui, Anglais. Ici?'

She stood looking at me, her head on one side, her face oddly familiar.

'I don't know, this doesn't look like an officer's charger. Dear me, she looks more like a poor cab horse. But she's the only black, isn't she, and they said under the lime trees. These are lime trees, aren't they, Rosemary?'

'Oh yes, I'm sure. They're the same as in Granny's London Square,' the girl answered in a voice which reminded me suddenly of Augustine.

'Well, come on, don't be a mutt, pick up her hoof, and see if it's stamped with a number. I wish this little man would go away. What a poor creature she is.

The Postmaster was now joined by Big Ben's master.

'You are in difficulties, Madame, yes? I speak a little English, Yes. Can I help? I try.'

'Oh good, oh, thank you. We are looking for my late son's horse, an artillery officer's charger . . . You understand? You follow me?'

'Yes, Madame. I buy horse from English army. Big

horse. Here. And Monsieur Forel, he buy also, smaller horse, charger, yes? Charger. This one you have . . .'

'At auction?'

'Sorry, I do not understand it is too difficult for me.'

'Never mind,' said the English lady. 'Come on, Rosemary . . .'

'I do it for you, a minute.'

Big Ben's master had my leg up before you could say Jack Robinson and there was a cry of delight from the English girl when she saw the number on my hoof.

'It's Emily. Oh, Emily, we've found you.' She flung her arms round my neck. 'And now we shall keep you for ever, you shall never work again.'

'My son wrote to me just before he was killed, I believe he had a premonition,' went on Augustine's mother for that is who she was, 'saying that he had this wonderful mare, Emily.'

'Emily, Emily, yes I believe the name was in the cata— how do you say it?'

'Catalogue,' said Augustine's mother rather sharply. 'Now let me finish my story. My son wrote to say that if anything happened to him we were to see that Emily came back to England and was cared for in her old age. He said he owed his life to her, and that she had been his dearest companion. I'm afraid I thought at first, what sentiment! I did nothing. The letter lay in my desk, but the words haunted me and, after a year, I wrote to his fellow officer, Bellamy, who told me the mare had been auctioned somewhere in this part of France along with others in the regiment. After that it was a matter of getting round red tape, and then coming over here and talking to the local populace in my appalling French.

'And now Madame you find. It is good,' said Big Ben's

master, who clearly had understood very little of Mrs Appleyard's statement. 'Now I fetch Monsieur Forel, yes? Just a minute, I return.'

Presently he came back with my master whose grasp of matters was somewhat handicapped by the cheap brandy he had been drinking. At last his ferret-like eyes lit up with interest.

'Mon Cheval. Ah so, mon cheval. C'est bon. Combien, Madame?'

'How much you pay?' translated Big Ben's master.

'Ten pounds.'

'Pounds, pounds, C'est impossible. Cette jument est bonne, très bonne, compris, madame?' The old man gazed up at Mrs Appleyard, his face like cracked leather, his eyes small and quick.

'N'est pas vrai,' said Big Ben's master, sharply, pointing to my broken knees, my lean flanks and staring coat. Then he continued in rapid French; the two men moved away and Mrs Appleyard followed them. Before long money was

changing hands, and I knew that I had been sold again, as swiftly and suddenly as the day I left the Duke's Hall. My master was well pleased, although he continued to grumble as though he had lost a good horse too cheaply.

Mrs Appleyard started to make inquiries about transport. Big Ben's master said I could spend the night on his farm and he would find a lad to lead me to the railway station the next day. Quite a crowd had now collected, for the Appleyard's foreignness was like a magnet to the people of this sleepy market town. Another horse was found to take my master's cart home and Monsieur Forel was recommended to buy a mule to replace me, because they are hardier than horses.

I spent an agreeable night in a stall next to Big Ben who was pleasant though a little strange owing to the shell-shock.

A few days later after two wearisome train journeys I was again on a steamboat tossing on the English Channel. I came out of the hold of the ship into the soft watery light of an English sky. There were white cliffs and customs houses, and Englishmen with bright cheeks and soft, slow voices. And I swear the air was different, the meadows greener, the trees more beautiful than anywhere else in the world.

But when ashore, travelling from boat to train and from a village railway station to my new home, I saw that this was not quite the same England as I had left in 1915. The ladies skirts were short now, their legs visible; maid servants no longer curtsied to their betters, black bowlers and homburgs had replaced the top hats and deer stalkers. Only old men still boasted side whiskers, beards were few and I saw several young men with cheeks smooth as pumice stones.

Walking through the English dusk, I passed again a carrier's cart pulled by an old grey mare. I saw two great Shire horses bringing a felled oak from a forest on a long wagon, cars buzzing through the drizzling rain like grounded wasps. And there was electric light in many shops, tremendously bright, much stronger than gas. Here and there we passed petrol pumps and once a great bus, very frightening with lights burning inside its wooden frame.

So at last I came to my new home, a manor house of soft red brick, flanked by beeches, where Augustine Appleyard had grown to manhood.

It was a long wet summer's day, grey as the guns belching fire and death over those sad and broken fields of France, grey as the soldiers' faces after a long battle, grey as Monsieur Forel's despair. And yet through all the greyness I now saw hope, quietness and peace. Such was the tranquillity of the house and its paddocks, the atmosphere created by all the people, the dogs and horses, the hens, yes even the hens, which had known happiness in the shadow of the house and the trees which were so much older than any of us.

A horse knows when he enters a yard whether or not it is a place of happiness or misery; the odours of cruelty and kindness are quite different from one another. So I had entered the dealer's yard with misgivings and the Lady Angela's with a light and easy step, so now, walking under the arch over which the red roses spread with wild abandon, I knew that I had come home, for the buildings seemed to encircle me, to protect me from all horrors of the past and the future, almost to greet me as a friend. Yet there were no horses here now that Augustine was dead.

The paddocks were let to a sturdy farmer, a man with a

broad, jovial face and eyes like violets faded in the sun, a man with thirteen children and a wife with coal-black hair, and dark flashing eyes, and plump arms adorned with bangles that jingled as she moved. This farmer kept two Clydesdales, lovely big bays, called Punch and Judy with beards of dark hair and long whiskers and splashes of white like spilled milk running down their faces. Beside these gentle giants I felt narrow, small and old. My terrible experiences, my life in foreign lands seemed to set me apart from ordinary, English horses. I felt withered by my part in the war, by events too awful to relate to these kind simple creatures, who had never known a cruel word or deed. But the Appleyards bought me a donkey to keep me company while Punch and Judy were at work, a little biscuit-coloured fellow with a black list down his back and the mark of the human Christ's yoke across his shoulders. They called him Daniel. Donkeys are the holy men amongst us horses; around them hangs an aura of quietude that brings peace to the most agitated of us.

So, now that I am at the end of my story, I want you to picture me under the beeches with Daniel, Punch and Judy, a fatter Princess with a coat sleek as a panther's paw, hoofs well trimmed, eyes bright. At the creosoted five-barred gate stand Augustine's parents, his mother with all the elegance of an ageing greyhound, his father of wider, squarer build, a man smelling of tobacco, whisky and tweeds, rather loud-voiced, a trifly lazy I suspect, but kindly. Rosemary, grown gawkier still, with bobbed, fair hair, observant grey eyes and Augustine's wide, frank smile. They are looking not at me, nor the donkey, nor the Clydesdales, but at someone much smaller and newer to the world; a little being lying beside me, a blue roan, who may turn darker or lighter as the weeks pass, a little body which slipped out of me so easily without help then waited for my tongue to break the envelope and set her free. She has, this little foal of mine, great eyes under lashes black as night, a stumpy tail like a scrubbing brush and long legs like stilts. I hope she will be grey like her father, Harvest Moon. Miraculously, unbelieveably my dream has come true. The Long, Long Trail, in the song the soldiers sang, has led me to home and a longing satisfied.

The farmer joins the Appleyards; his wide, country face creased in smiles. It was he who brought Harvest Moon to me, 'She's getting old, but it's worth a try,' he had said. For the farmer only has to see an animal to want it to multiply. His yard is full of puppies, chicks and kittens; his meadows with calves and next year Judy is to have a foal. He is looking forward to his own grandchildren.

'Will she be big enough for me to ride?' asks Rosemary, 'for I mean to learn you know.'

'What the little-un? Don't you worry, she'll make fifteen two. That's a grand foal, that is.'

I turn then to nuzzle my foal, and I hope that there will be no wars for her, no dealers, no purges, bleedings and restoratives, that she will live here for ever in the shadow of the beeches; her life passing gently and kindly, her good nature and looks winning admiration and affection everywhere.

BLACK VELVET

❋

by Christine Pullein-Thompson

CONTENTS

BLACK BEAUTY'S CLAN

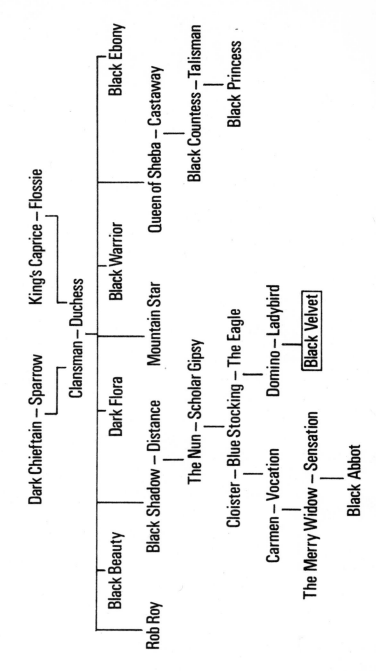

CHAPTER ONE

A fair beginning

I was born on a farm. It lay in a valley with gentle green hills on each side topped by tall trees. The fields were fenced by high hedges so there was always plenty of shelter from driving rain and clumps of trees gave us shade in summer.

My mother was dark brown with a beautiful head and a large, kind eye. Our master called her Ladybird and she was a great favourite with him. He rode her to hounds and about the farm. Sometimes on market days she pulled the high-wheeled trap.

There were five other horses on the farm, Merlin and Mermaid, the Shire horses, which pulled the plough and the wagon at harvest time. They were grey with huge fetlocks, and so large that even my mother, who was sixteen hands high, looked small and slender beside them. There was Rosie, a cheerful chestnut mare who did all the odd jobs, carting mangolds and kale to the cattle in winter, helping out when times were busy by pulling the harrow and the hay rake at harvest time. She was used on market days as well when the cart was needed instead of the trap. She did more work than any of the other horses on the farm, but I never heard her complain. Smallest of us all was Sinbad, the little piebald pony which our master's children rode, and who pulled the governess cart when our mistress went shopping or visiting friends.

We were a happy bunch of horses, well-fed and kindly treated. I was the youngest and came in for a good deal of teasing; but my mother always took my side, and I knew my master was proud of me for I heard him say once, 'You've really produced a good 'un this time Ladybird. He's the best looking colt I've seen for a long time.'

And though my mother told me I was wrong to listen to what was being said, she also told me that my father was one of the best looking horses in England.

'He's a relation of that great horse Black Beauty,' she said, 'and he's as black as you are, but with a star.'

It was a long time before I saw my father, but one day he came to the farm and stayed the night. My mother neighed with joy when she saw him. He was led by a small bandy legged man called 'a stallion walker' who slept near his loosebox. I was very proud when I saw my father. His coat shone like satin and he carried himself like a king. I neighed to him over the field gate, and he threw up his head and arched his beautiful neck and neighed back. That was the only time I ever saw him, for the next day he was led on to another farm which was how he spent his life moving from one farm to another all through the spring and summer.

There were cows on the farm as well as horses and a dairy where often our mistress worked with the three dairy maids. There was always a lot of laughter coming from the dairy and sometimes singing as well. There were two farm men as well as the dairy maids, the older carter Matthew who watched over all us horses though his main duty was to Mermaid and Merlin. A younger man called Mooring who did a lot of the other work like cutting the kale and carting it and feeding the pigs. And a boy called

Bob, who helped where he was needed. I believe he was Matthew's eldest boy. They all lived on the farm and seemed happy enough – at least I never heard them grumble though once we heard Matthew talking about something called, 'the general strike'.

'There's no trains at all,' he said. 'And no letters either I don't know what the world's comin' too. Supposin' we went on strike. Who would feed the animals then?'

'It's all money these days, everyone wants more money. One can't blame them; it's hard enough trying to live on thirty shillings a week, even with a spot of garden,' replied Bill.

'And working all hours as well,' put in Bob.

'But it 'urts everyone in the long run, even the master,' replied Matthew. 'That's the worst of it.'

We were all worried by this conversation. The dairy maids poured away a lot of milk because there were no trains to take it to London. And our master walked about with a worried frown on his face.

My mother said that everything would be all right in the end but we horses sensed that something was wrong. The men had less time for us and there were less oats in our mangers and less singing from the dairy. The general strike ended. No more milk was poured away, but things didn't get any better and after a time one of the dairy maids left.

Our master had little time for us now and one day we heard him saying to Bob, 'It's time you moved on; there's no future in farming any more. No one wants our butter. The world's changing Bob. I can't afford to give you a rise, and I'm sorry for it because you're a good lad I've never had a better. But the way things are going, I don't know how we'll be next year.'

Soon after that Bob left. We missed him, especially Sinbad who had been a great friend of his. Our master took off his coat and helped Matthew and Bill himself, which was something he had never done before. He didn't have time to hunt any more, which saddened my mother, who loved hunting more than anything else.

I was four now and black all over except for a splash of white on my left fetlock. My master called me Blackbird. I was used to having my feet rasped, and quiet to groom and handle. No one had ever spoken in anger to me, so that when my master and mistress came to the field gate, I was the first to greet them.

'It's time you were working,' said my master to me one day stroking my neck. 'When the hay is in, we'll make a start. You should make someone a fine young hunter.' He looked much older and I rubbed my head against his sleeve trying to tell him that I would always do my best.

'Don't do too much George,' pleaded our mistress. slipping her arm through his. 'Let old Matthew break him in. You know Dr Simmonds said that you were to rest.'

'Rest!' cried our master. 'When everything is going to rack and ruin. When the bills pile up on my desk and no one wants our butter because New Zealand's butter's cheaper. No, my dear, I can't rest till things are straight.'

'Straight!' she cried. 'They will never be straight till we sell up and go.'

'And that I will never do,' replied our master quietly. 'I was born here. The soil is like a mother to me. And where would we go?' I have always been a farmer as my father was before me. I know nothing else, so let's talk no more of going.'

They walked away arm in arm, while my mother shook her head sadly.

'There are bad days ahead for all of us,' she said. 'You are young and strong Blackbird. Always do your best whatever happens.'

Two weeks later we heard that our master was dead. Gloom hung over the farm affecting all of us. People think animals don't understand much. But we knew that things were bad. There was no more laughter, everyone looked worried. Matthew feared for his home. His children walked about with their heads down silently weeping. Bill Mooring stopped tending his garden and was late to work in the mornings. A notice was put outside the farm saying, FOR SALE.

The funeral day was saddest of all. Black horses with plumes on their bridles pulled the hearse and my mother was led behind by Matthew, her saddle empty. All the mourners were in black, our mistress with a veil hiding her face, the children weeping bitterly.

We horses watched the cortège over the field gate, as it wound its sad way to the church less than a mile away.

'We won't be wanted any more,' Merlin said, shaking his wise grey head. 'We will all be sold. And who wants a farm horse these days?'

'I worked in a town once,' said Rosie. 'It was a terrible place. Our stables were high up, with gas lighting. I couldn't bear to go back.'

'I shall be all right,' said Sinbad. 'Children always want piebald ponies. I shall be found a kind home. The children will see to it. Why our mistress says I'm better than a nanny.'

Mermaid said nothing. She was the oldest of us all and not worth much any more.

Later my mother came back. We all pleaded for news, but first she washed her mouth out at the trough; then she rolled twice, once for each side of her. After that she shook herself and said, 'This is a bad day for all of us. If a good master comes, we will be all right. If not, we will each go our separate ways and most likely never see each other again.'

'But I don't work on the farm. I am separate. I belong to the mistress and the children,' said Sinbad. 'I won't be sold with the farm. They'll find me a good home somewhere.' And he cantered round the field, while the rest of us put our heads down and grazed, each afraid of what the future might hold for us.

CHAPTER TWO

I start a new life

It was not long before we had a new master. He was a
young man with hard blue eyes and a moustache waxed
at both ends. He had bought the farm cheaply and intended making a profit out of it. He walked round the
farm with Matthew, poking the buildings with a stick,
laughing at the way things had been run in the past.

'That horse plough can go for a start,' he said. 'I'm not
having horses here. The farm is going to be run by
machinery. And the hedges will have to go too,' he
continued. 'They use up valuable space. If we are to beat
the colonies, we can only do it by farming like them.'

Merlin and Mermaid hung their heads in despair. Rosie
said, 'That's that then.'

'A lot of trees will have to go too, and the dairy will
be modernised. There will be no more dairy maids,'
continued our new master.

Matthew touched his cap respectfully. 'And me too sir?
Is my job to be done by machinery?' he asked.

'Yes. We don't need a carter, and you're too old to
learn new ways. I shall need your cottage for a younger
man. I will give you a week to clear out.'

'But where shall I go?' replied poor Matthew. 'No one
is taking on farm hands these days and I'm knocking sixty
sir. I was born in the cottage as my father was before me.'

'That has nothing to do with me,' replied the young

man harshly. 'The cottage is mine now and I can do what I like with it. You can apply to sweep the roads. The council are paying a fair bit these days.'

'But where can I live? And what about my Missus? asked Matthew.

'That's your business. Now show me the horses. What you do with your life is your own affair. I'm here to make money, and make it I will.'

We stood together in a corner of the field. Matthew called us but we didn't go to him as we usually did. Our new master looked us over as though we were bits of machinery. He did not speak to any of us. We knew he was deciding how much he might get for each one of us. My mother looked quite frightened. She had been treated kindly all her life and talked to as a equal by our poor late master. She had expected to live on the farm until her end came.

At last, our new master spoke. 'The young horse might fetch a bit,' he said staring at me. 'But the others aren't worth much. They can go to the sale at Stansbury next week. I shall be ploughing the field; I'm trying the modern way, one crop one year, one the next. That way you get more out of the land.'

'The master would have wanted them to have good homes. He thought the world of them,' said Matthew.

'And that was his undoing,' snapped back the young man. 'There's no place for sentimentality in modern farming.'

'Shall I be taking them then?' asked Matthew. 'I understand them sir. I can put in a good word for them; they'll fetch more that way sir.'

'No. You will be gone by then. I want you out in a week. And I mean a week,' said our new master.

The next day our mistress and the children came to say goodbye. The children cried into Sinbad's mane. Our mistress stroked my mother's nose. 'I'm sorry. He wouldn't have wanted it this way,' she said.

My mother rubbed her nose against her shoulder as she had done to me when I was a foal and needed comforting. The children cried louder than ever. Then they all went away, their arms round each other, and everything was suddenly quiet and I wondered how our field would look with the grass ploughed under and the trees gone.

A few days later a young man, wearing a cap on the back of his head, started moving furniture into Matthew's cottage sighing and grumbling meanwhile.

'Ain't there no water closet,' he asked Matthew. 'And where's the cooking range. How do you manage with the one fireplace?'

'We cooked with a pot hung over it, and reared six children as well,' replied Matthew.

'There's no running water either.'

'There's the well at the bottom of the garden and a good sty for a pig and a couple of old apple trees,' Matthew answered.

When Matthew and his family had gone, we felt as though we had no friend left. No one came to visit us in the evenings to see if we were well. Our water grew low in the trough and we were all bad tempered with worry. Merlin and Mermaid bullied poor Rosie unmercifully and my mother called Sinbad 'an impudent young fool'.

The old farmhouse was empty now and only the young man and a girl milked the cows. Then the day came when we all stood together for the last time under the elm trees. The next morning some rough looking men came, put halters on our heads and led us away from the farm for ever.

It was five miles to Stansbury and we took an hour and a half to reach it. I had never been so far before and I was scared of everything I saw. A man called Jim pulled me along and a man called Fred whipped me from behind while my mother kept whinnying to me in a distracted fashion saying.

'Do your best. Don't be frightened. Follow me.'

But I had never seen a car close up before, nor a bicycle. I could not understand how they moved without legs or heads. People shaking mats out of windows scared me and so did yapping dogs and children playing in the street.

By the time I reached the sale, I was soaked in sweat, with whip marks all over my quarters. There were a great many men shouting, some carrying whips and horses everywhere in all shapes and sizes. There were stalls ladened with fruits, and cars going backwards as well as forwards.

It was too much for me. I stopped and stood trembling

with fear, my legs braced under me. Jim jerked at my rope. Fred whipped me from behind.

My mother called, 'Don't be afraid. They won't hurt you.' But I was in such a state now that nothing seemed to make sense any more.

If someone had spoken to me kindly then I think I might have calmed down, but all I received was blows from behind and jerks from my halter in front and a flood of bad words. So I stood up on my hind legs and then plunged forward in a wild leap scattering the by-standers. Jim held on shouting, 'Fetch a bridle'.

A man seized one ear, another my nose. A bit was forced between my teeth, while more men put a rope round my quarters. Then Fred whipped me again and Jim held on to my head while the bit cut my mouth cruelly. All my friends had gone on by this time. The crowd had cleared a space. I was shaking in every limb. I started to spin round and round fighting against the pain of the bit. I reared again, plunged and then came down in a heap on the cobbles. A man in gaiters leapt on my head. I could feel my heart thumping against my ribs and my breath coming in gasps.

'Hold him there for a bit. Let him calm down,' said someone. The bridle had blinkers on it. My mouth was bleeding.

After a time I was allowed to stand again. I was still trembling and my sweat dripped on to the street. A quiet man came and took the reins from Jim. He patted my neck and spoke kindly. 'You shouldn't whip a young horse like that,' he said. 'All he needs is a little kindness.'

He reminded me of our late master though he was a younger man. He had the same quiet strong way with him. I saw my mother tied to a railing in the centre of the square, and still shaking with fright, I was tied up along-side her.

She looked at me sadly, 'If our master could see you now, his heart would be broken,' she said.

I stood tensely straining against the rope that held me. I shook all over. Men walked up and down looking at us. They forced my mother's mouth open and picked up her hoofs. She was very patient, though I could see how their rough treatment pained her.

No one touched me; one look at my wild eye sent them on to a quieter animal. I think if they had touched my mouth I would have gone mad.

The sale had started now. There was a great deal of noise. A man sat high up holding a hammer while horses were trotted up and down. He shouted all the time and when a horse was sold he banged his hammer on a table. Merlin and Mermaid were separated; their wise heads were furrowed with anxiety. Poor Sinbad stood with his head low, let down by his mistress and the children. Rosie knew about sales; her shoulders were dark with sweat.

Merlin and Mermaid were sold. They neighed pite-ously to each other as they were led away to await their new owners.

My mother said, 'Always do your best my son. Man is cleverer than we are; he will always win.' Her turn was next. She went calmly her head high, her beautiful eyes shining. She trotted steadily over the rough cobbles while the man with the hammer shouted, 'Who wants this twelve year old mare, quiet to ride and with hounds? How much am I bid? Come on ladies and gentlemen. Fifty pounds, who will bid fifty pounds?'

Men pushed forward to feel her legs, to open her

mouth once again with rough fingers. Someone whipped her from behind. She trotted faster over the cobbles, her neck wet with sweat.

I strained against the rope which held me. I neighed 'Don't go. Don't leave me.'

They wrenched her round on the cobbles and I heard her hoofs slipping. A boy hit her with a stick. Someone said, 'Forty.'

'I'm bid forty,' shouted the auctioneer as though it was a victory.

She was sold for forty five guineas and led away. Now it was my turn. A man untied me, jerking at my bridle. I trotted over the cobbles my unshod hoofs making no noise. I couldn't see the crowds on each side because of the blinkers, but when a man touched my quarters I lashed out catching him on the side and I reared when a large fisted farmer touched my mouth.

The auctioneer shouted, 'Who wants this high spirited young horse. Only four, and what a looker. By a great stallion, out of the mare you've just seen. A certain winner in the right hands. Come along ladies and gentlemen, how much am I bid?.'

I stood with my legs braced trembling with fear. In the distance I heard my mother calling to me.

Then a man in breeches and boots said, 'Well I'll risk him. No horse has beaten me yet.' And people laughed and a man said,

'That's right, have a go Sid. You can only break your neck once.' A farmer bid twenty. Sid bid twenty-five. I was dragged across the cobbles again. The farmer bid thirty. Sid bid thirty-five. I heard the hammer fall. I was dragged away and tied up with the other horses which had been sold. Mermaid and Merlin were together again.

I longed for a drink, but though there was a trough in the square no one watered us.

After a time, Rosie was led away by a bent old farmer.

The town square reeked of beer and sweat and horse dung. A small boy led my mother away. He spoke kindly to her, stroking her neck. I never saw her again.

I stood in the square for a long time. Horses were taken away in ones and twos. The sale ended. Evening came and I still stood tied to the railing longing for a drink.

At last my new master came out of a pub yard leading a chestnut cob. He pushed her between the shafts of a cart. He was unsteady on his feet and it took him some time to buckle the harness.

He tied me to the back of the cart while the cob snapped, 'And don't hang back young fellow. I've got enough to do without pulling you home.'

I felt too exhausted and bewildered to fight any more. In the pubs men were singing. Sid whipped up the cob. My head was sore from pulling against the railings. I could not see much because of the blinkers. I just followed the cart. I don't know how far we went but my unshod hoofs were sore and split when at last we turned into a yard and stopped.

A small man came out of a building with a lantern in his hand. 'So you're back Gov.' he said.

'Yes and ready for me dinner,' retorted my new master. 'And I've bought myself a black rogue with the devil in him, for you to pit your wits against Joe. Put him in the end stall and give him nothing but straw to eat and just one bucket of water. We'll have to starve him before we break him.'

There were rows of stalls inside a long stable. The little man led me to one at the end. He spoke kindly to me and fetched me water and filled the hay rack with oat straw. He looked at my hoofs and sighed. He looked at my teeth with gentle hands and sighed. 'And only a four year old too,' he said.

Then he went away carrying his lantern. The straw tasted rough in my sore mouth. I drank the bucketful of water and was still thirsty. I remembered the field where I had grown up. I thought of Matthew turned out of his cottage with nowhere to go, and the world seemed a rough cruel place.

CHAPTER THREE

I'm broken in

My new master was a horse dealer. He had fought in the Great War and had been wounded in the head. Part of his skull had been replaced by a tin plate and he drank to kill the pain from it. Joe had fought in the war too. He had a scar from his right eye to his left ear and three fingers missing on one hand where they had been blown off by a shell.

They were not bad men, but they had suffered. They had watched men stay at home and make money, while they fought in the trenches. Now they had their own code of honesty which included making money out of us horses by fair means or foul.

My education began the day after I arrived at my new home, which was called Little Heath Stables on account of the rough heath at the back.

In the morning I was given only half a bucket of water and straw again in my rack and not much of that either. I had hardly slept all night and felt weak and listless. There were always nearly twenty horses in the yard and only the two men to look after them; so only the ones about to be sold were groomed regularly; the rest of us stood in our stalls for hours at a time bored and ill tempered dreaming of the fields where we had grown up. I stood next to a handsome dark brown gelding called Solomon. He was very well bred and had been a hunter, but had fallen on the road and was now scarred on both knees. Sid was doing what he called, 'doctoring them up' in the hope of making a profit.

My education began with the dumb jockey. It was a strange contraption made of wood and leather straps which Joe strapped on to my back while Sid held my head. Then a bit was forced between my teeth and reins attached from it to the dumb jockey. And so I was left, my head too high for comfort, my nose tucked in towards my chest. I could move little in any direction. I tried pulling, but it hurt my mouth. I tried lowering my head, but that was impossible. In the end I put my hind legs under me to ease the pain and stayed in a sort of sitting position until I could bear it no longer. Next I put my hind legs out behind me and hollowed my loins. Soon my neck muscles suffered from cramp and my hind legs ached unbearably.

I thought, if only we horses could weep like humans,

people might know how we suffer. But hours passed and no one came to relieve my agony. Solomon was taken out for exercise and brought back. He looked at me sadly over the partition of his stall.

'They call it mouthing,' he said. 'I wish someone would mouth them.'

My mouth dripped blood on to my scant bedding. Joe was working overtime preparing a rangy bay for a prospective buyer, so it was Sid who came at last to loosen the reins and let me stretch my aching neck. He took the dumb jockey away and fetched me hay and clean water. The bay horse had been sold for a good price and he was cheerful. He called Joe to me.

'He can have hay from now on, but no oats, and give him a brush over when you have time.'

They were not cruel men. Joe worked harder than any of us. He was in the stable by six in the morning and often still there at nine at night. And our master when he was well, was kind enough in his way, but when his head began to ache, he turned to the bottle.

The dumb jockey was the fashionable way to break in a horse in those days and it suited the dealers well enough because it was quick. It broke our spirits and the quicker this was done, the quicker they could sell us and make a profit.

So the next day the contraption was strapped to my back again and, though I longed to fight, I remembered my mother's words, and stood still until my head was strapped into the desired position again. I can't tell you the agony I suffered that day for my muscles still ached from the day before. I had constant attacks of cramp, my tongue felt swollen in my mouth and my hind legs seemed to have no strength left in them.

For the next three days I wore that dumb jockey for hours every day until gradually the pain became less as I grew accustomed to standing for hours in the unnatural position it demanded.

On the fourth day, Joe attached a long rein to my bridle and led me outside to a small paddock behind the stables. He carried a whip and soon I was trotting round and round him in a circle. It was lovely to smell fresh air again after my dingy stall, but I did wish that I could stretch my neck. However Joe was well pleased. 'He's quick to learn and willing and all the fight's knocked out of him,' he told our master.

Two days later I was shod. Joe talked to me all the time while the shoes were nailed on and the farrier was a quiet, gentle man who took the trouble to make friends with me from the beginning.

After that I was lunged with a saddle on my back and how good it was to be able to stretch my neck. Then my master held my head, while Joe gently slipped on to my back. I was led up and down the paddock and though I felt tense and my joints and muscles still ached from the affect of the dumb jockey, I didn't buck. And so I was broken in. Most of my spirit was gone by this time and my ribs showed through my dirty coat; but there was no fight left in me. I knew now that humans are stronger than us poor horses and however strange their commands we must obey them.

Joe had been a rough rider for the army and he had a firm seat and good hands. He took me for rides when he had time and I soon grew accustomed to the few cars and bicycles which we met, and learned to go how he wished. I looked everywhere for my mother and friends on these rides, but I never saw them. Sometimes I wondered whether they would recognise me if we did meet because I was so much thinner now.

Some weeks later, Sid and Joe started to break me to harness. First of all I pulled a heavy log about the paddock, then I was put in a breaking cart and after that in a carriage with another horse of my own size called, Tom. He was old and bed-tempered and if I went too fast, he bit me, and if I dawdled he would kick. At first I was very frightened of the sound of the wheels running behind me, but after a few weeks I ceased to notice them and Sid seemed well pleased.

'We can call him quiet in harness now, not that there's much call for harness horses these days,' he said. 'But sometimes it just tips the balance. Now all he needs is some jumping lessons, then he'll be ready for sale and worth a good price too, I should say.'

A few days later, Joe started popping me over logs in the nearby woods and my food was increased. A brush fence and gate were put up in the paddock and soon I was jumping these with ease.

I was now four and a half, and sixteen hands high. Joe began to groom me more and I wore a checked rug in the day and a warmer one at night. My time at the dealer's yard was coming to an end as I was now considered a schooled horse. I could walk and trot on either rein with my nose tucked in. I never pulled against the reins because I knew that a dumb jockey would never give, so I was considered to have a 'good mouth!' I would stand quietly to be mounted and while my rider opened a gate. I could jump fences of three foot six from a trot or canter. I went equally well in a double bridle or snaffle. I would go in harness. I was fast, but no one knew how fast, because, since wearing the dumb jockey, I was afraid to extend myself. I tired easily because carrying my head so near my chest was not natural to me, but to most people who wanted a well-schooled horse, I appeared to be one.

'You wouldn't recognise him as the horse we bought at Stansbury sale,' said Sid one evening watching Joe rug me up. 'We'll ask one hundred and fifty guineas for him and if we get it, there's a fiver for you Joe, that's a promise. I'll advertise him this week.'

CHAPTER FOUR

I'm sold again

Two days later an elderly lady came to see Solomon. She had high cheek bones and a voice which expected to be obeyed. She wore breeches with long socks and men's shoes and a khaki shirt. Solomon had been well groomed, his mane was plaited and Joe had covered the scars on his knees with boot polish.

The lady knew how to handle a horse for she went straight to Solomon's head with a lump of sugar in her hand.

'You've known better days I can see,' she said.

She bent down to look at his knees and then looked at Sid and said, 'You may as well take the boot polish off. I'm not a fool'

Joe rubbed the polish off with a cloth while Sid hurried off to fetch a side saddle muttering, 'I can see that Madam.'

'And I don't need that,' she replied when he returned. 'I ride astride, and I'll have a snaffle bridle please.'

She rode Solomon in the paddock at the back of the stables and afterwards he said that she had the best hands he had ever known.

'And now my man, we'll talk about money,' she said dismounting. 'I'm not paying what you ask for a start. He's a horse of quality but his legs are ruined as you no doubt know.' They went away to discuss a price and the next day she brought a man over to ride Solomon to her house. He was a quiet gentle groom, who slipped a snaffle bit into Solomon's mouth with great care and then put a light-weight saddle on to his back as though he was made of china.

'You've fallen into good hands Solomon old fellow,' he said pulling up the girths. 'No one's going to work you to death. The Countess only hacks around the estate and there's the old pony in the orchard for company. 'You'll last another twenty years with us.'

I neighed goodbye and he answered with a quick nod of his head. I had never met a finer horse than Solomon. I knew I would miss him but I hoped that at last he had found the happiness he deserved.

The next day a cream mare was moved into Solomon's stall. She was a vain, proud pony with a long flowing flaxen mane.

'What a nasty stall,' she said looking round with dislike. 'And how it smells! I come from fine stables where I always had my own loosebox. I'm not used to being tied up.'

'You will have to get used to it then,' I replied.

'That I never will. I shall keep turning round until the head stall rubs me raw; and then I shall dig up the floor and kick the grooms,' she replied with a toss of her head.

'There's only Joe. He won't have time to bother with you,' I answered.

'I'm a weaver. I shall weave then.'

'What do you weave?'

'I keep swaying, moving my weight from one hoof to another. It's a dreadful habit,' she said starting to do it. 'In my last home I was never exercised; sometimes I stood in my box for days on end, though my mistress visited me every day and gave me sugar and my mane was groomed until it was like spun silk, and my hoofs oiled till they gleamed like polished tortoiseshell. Oh, my mistress loved me all right. She called me her Fairy Queen, but how bored I was! I thought I would go mad with nothing to do day after day. I dreamed of beautiful stallions, of racing the wind. My sides were soon as fat and round as butter. And when at last I was taken out, I couldn't trot without puffing. But my mistress thought this beautiful too. 'Look how she blows, just like a little train!' she would cry, clapping her plump hands with glee. She didn't mind my weaving either. 'It's like a circus trick,' she said and she would throw her arms round my neck crying, 'Oh Fairy Queen, you are so adorable.'

'She wanted you to be as fat and silly as she was herself,' I said. 'There are many humans like that; we are supposed to resemble them, though we may be quite different. But what about the grooms?' I asked. 'Had they no sense either?'

'They followed their orders, though I heard John, the stud groom, saying once that it was a shame to keep me so, and that I would look well in a phaeton or a circus – a circus I ask you? And then one day my feet started to hurt. They felt as though they were swelling and swelling; only hoofs can't swell, can they? The pain was terrible and there was no way of relieving it. At last I sank down on the straw and lay there groaning. John found me and then what a hubbub there was! The vet was fetched. I was led outside and stood in a pond and fed branmashes. And I was made to walk though my hoofs felt on fire. How painful that was! And look at my hoofs; they are no longer beautiful; they curl up at the end and everyone can tell that I've had laminitus, and no one wants me now; not even my mistress, though it was her fault. Oh the injustice of it! And how often I longed to gallop, to pull a phaeton and show how fast my little hoofs could trot; but no, my mistress wanted me to be as idle as herself. And now I'm a weaver and my hoofs are spoilt, and I've never done anything; never had any fun.'

I didn't know what to say. Fairy Queen started to dig up her bed. She had been given nothing but musty hay in her rack, which she refused to touch. Soon she was standing on bricks. Then Sid came in.

'What a fool you are Queenie,' he said. 'Come outside and get some exercise. We can't have you digging up the stable.' She looked pleased and rubbed her nose on his sleeve, and I thought that although Sid was a rough man, at least he understood us.

The next day I was groomed and plaited early and given an extra ration of oats. 'You behave yourself and you'll find yourself with a good home,' Joe said.

'So you're going,' whispered Fairy Queen from the next stall, 'just when I was beginning to like you. I shall have some cross old horse put next to me for certain. Some crusty old thing which never answers and I shall be more bored than ever.'

'You will be sold soon yourself,' I said. 'You are so pretty, no one will resist you.'

'Not with my weaving and my hoofs. Look at them,' she cried. 'Just look.'

Shortly afterwards Joe came for me. He undid my rope and led me outside to where a young man was waiting, dressed in breeches and boots and a checked jacket with cap to match. He had a small trimmed moustache and carried a cane.

'You'll never find a better horse than this,' said Sid slapping my neck. 'He's not five yet, but he never puts a foot wrong. And as for jumping, well I've never seen one which will beat him.'

The young man was called Richard Bastable. He ran hard, cool hands down my legs. He opened my mouth and checked my age. He stood behind looking at my hocks.

'Trot him up and back. I want to see how he moves,' he said.

Fairy Queen heard my hoofs on the gravel and neighed.

'Yes, he moves well enough,' said Richard Bastable. 'He's for a young lady, so he must have good paces. Now perhaps your man will show me how he jumps.'

Joe threw a saddle on my back; then he put on the twisted snaffle he rode me in normally and mounting, rode me to the paddock. He walked and trotted me to loosen up my muscles; then cantered me in circles while Sid straightened the brush fence and put up the gate. I had stood in the stable for two days with hardly any exercise and was eager to jump; so that when Joe turned me towards the gate, I snatched at the bit and fairly flew.

'What did I say? Jumps like a stag!' exclaimed Sid rubbing his hands together.

'I do a spot of jumping myself,' said Richard Bastable sounding pleased.

I jumped the brush again, then they put the gate up to four feet six and I took it easily while Joe stayed as though glued to my back.

Then Richard Bastable mounted. Every rider has his own particular style, Joe gripped tight with his knees, his hands went with you, but if need be, they were like a vice. Richard Bastable rode with longer stirrups, his

228

weight further back in the saddle, his reins longer. At first I missed Joe's firmer grip. I felt like bucking; instead I shied at a bit of paper and pranced a little.

'He hasn't been out for two days,' called Sid anxiously from the gate.

I was determined to do my best. I cantered on either leg, keeping my nose bent inwards, and jumped the fences easily, without fuss.

'I like him,' said Richard Bastable sliding to the ground. 'I'll pay you what you're asking if he passes the vet.'

'Passes the vet? Of course he will. I'll warrant him sound myself,' exclaimed Sid.

They went inside for a drink, while Joe led me back to my stall. 'I expect you're sold,' said the Fairy Queen.' I hope it's to a nice home, but I shall miss you terribly.'

Her entire bed was now at the back of her stall, and she had rubbed herself raw fighting against the headstall. Joe hit her from behind. 'Get up you fool,' he shouted. 'You'll end up pulling a baker's van. It's work you want and plenty of it.'

He rubbed vaseline into her sores grumbling all the time; then he turned her loose in the paddock. I stood wondering about my new home. I had grown used to Sid's yard. I knew the routine and what Joe wanted. But a loosebox would be nicer than a stall and I dearly wanted to roll again, to lie stretched out in the sun, to sleep under the stars. One way and another I was ready for a move.

CHAPTER FIVE

A new home

Richard Bastable rode me to my new home. It was fifteen miles .by roads and lanes. The countryside was pleasant all the way; once we were clear of the heath there were lush meadows on each side full of cows, and little farmhouses nestling in the valleys.

My new master lived in a pretty white house with a cedar tree on the lawn. He was still an un-married man, but had a housekeeper and Bowles, a cheerful ginger-haired man of around forty who looked after both his motor-car and his horses. There were three of us, myself, a grey hunter, and a brown cob which had pulled my master's dog cart before he had bought a car.

Our stables were modern with four loose boxes which looked towards the house, and when I arrived Richard Bastable took my tack off himself and fetched me hay and water. I was greatly surprised by this having expected a groom to be waiting for me. He then patted my neck for a long time saying, 'May will be here tomorrow and what a surprise you'll be. She's twenty-one tomorrow, quite an age for a young gal and by jove, she's a pretty gal. You'll love her. Everyone does.' Then he went away whistling and the horse in the next box looked over his door and said,

'Who are you? What's your name?'

231

'I don't know. I'm usually known as the black un,' I answered.

'And that's no name at all,' he replied. 'But they'll soon give you one, at least May will. I'm Warrior. You've come to a good place here. You'll have every attention. Mr Bastable does a lot himself, though he's a proper young gentleman and Miss May, she's a sweet young lady.'

'I'll do my best,' I answered.

'And that will be good enough for them,' he said.

The next morning a young lady came into the yard. She wore breeches and boots and a riding jacket. She came straight to my box. 'And who are you?' she asked.

'Your birthday present,' cried Richard Bastable bobbing out from behind a tree and hugging her. 'Later we'll drink your health in champagne, but now I want to see how you like him. He hasn't a name. You must choose one for him. He's only five, but he has a mouth like velvet and he jumps like a stag.'

'I shall call him Black Velvet then,' she replied making friends with me, patting my neck, finding me an apple from under the trees while Warrior leaned jealously over his door blowing through his nose and stamping his hoofs impatiently.

'Can I try him now?' May asked.

'I don't see why not. He's had a good night's rest.'

Bowles was busy with the car, so they tacked me up together, laughing and kissing one another, so that a happier pair it was impossible to imagine.

'I'll come out with you on old Warrior,' said Richard Bastable. 'He's as jealous as a cat.'

May had light hands and a firm seat. 'He's behind the bit,' she said after a time. 'He must have been broken in with a dumb jockey poor darling, and now he's afraid to extend himself at all. But his paces are lovely. I shall re-school him. I shall follow Santini's advice and Caprilli's and of course Paul Rodianko's and in a month you won't recognise him.'

'I'm sure I won't,' laughed Richard. 'But why you want to follow the advice of a bunch of foreigners I can't imagine. But he's yours so do as you like with him.'

Richard Bastable's house was called The Grange. I was happy there. We were well fed and well looked after and best of all whenever the weather was nice we were turned out into one of the paddocks. Miss May's schooling was hard work but pleasant. Slowly she undid all the harm the dumb jockey had done. She made me go forward driving me on with her legs, she taught me to do shoulder in and shoulder out and how to curve my spine. She taught me to rein back and circle with my neck and back flexed; after two weeks she pronounced me ready to jump and what a revelation that was! I wore only the plainest snaffle and, as we jumped, May leaned forward her hands going with me so that I could extend myself freely. I found I could jump far more easily in this way, my movements became smoother and more flowing, and though Richard would never admit it was a better way of jumping, I knew it was.

Winter came and on a lovely frosty afternoon May Chantry and Richard Bastable were married in the grey Saxon church in the village.

We horses were not needed, but we could hear the church bells ringing joyously and everyone seemed happy that day. Bowles whistled and chatted cheerfully to the jobbing gardener who came three days a week. The housekeeper, Mrs Roberts, announced that there wasn't a better matched pair on earth. 'And I shall pray to God every night that they shall be happy,' she said. 'And have sweet children and everything they want.'

After the wedding they left in Richard's yellow car and we three horses had a holiday. We had not been clipped yet so were turned out every fine day in the paddocks and brought in each night. We liked each other; Warrior was patient and Brandy the cob good natured, so that one way and another we got along very well together. Warrior had gone to the Great War as a four year old and was one of the few in his regiment to come back. Brandy had been a farmer's cob. Neither had been ill-used or beaten and because of that they were happy and contented with no vice in them.

We were clipped before our master and mistress returned from their honeymoon and that winter they hunted us regularly, always bringing us home before we were too tired. Bowles would be waiting for us, the electric light shining out from the stables, our loose boxes deeply bedded in deep golden straw. The three of them would settle us for the night together and there were always hot mashes with salt and grated carrot in them. So the winter passed and spring came and I was very fit now and moved easily and well. I had jumped many a five barred gate in the hunting field and my master wanted to ride me in point-to-points, but this my mistress forbade.

'Too many men have been killed racing,' she said. 'And I couldn't bear to lose you Richard, besides two races with you would undo all my schooling. No Richard darling, I intend to show jump him this summer, if you have no objection.'

'None at all, though I don't suppose you'll have much

luck. I've yet to see a lady rider beat the gentlemen,' he replied laughing.

'Then I shall be the first,' she replied.

So Bowles was put to building jumps and, while Warrior and Brandy lounged about the paddocks, my mistress schooled me, always riding me forward in the Italian style. I was very careful.

If I hit anything May would scold me and I would feel ashamed and jump better next time. She never lost her temper and when I jumped well she would dismount at once, reward me with sugar, and that would be the end of the lesson. She taught me slowly, never making the jumps too high or too difficult until I was ready for them. One day Richard was watching and he called out, 'By jove he's doing well. How about the local show next month, there a novice class and not too many entries I believe?'

'How high are the jumps?'

'Not more than three foot six, but they might go higher in a jump off,' replied Richard.

'Well, I've jumped him over five foot in the hunting field and four foot six at home, so that should cause Black Velvet no headaches,' said my mistress patting my neck. 'Let's enter him tonight, and if he jumps well there we can go on to something better before the summer's gone.'

I felt very proud as I returned to my stables. Neither Warrior nor Brandy had ever competed at a show, nor had my mother.

'We must win Black Velvet,' said my mistress taking off my bridle. 'We must show everyone that the forward seat is best. People may laugh at me in the hunting field for the way I sit over fences, but they won't laugh any more if they see us winning prizes. Then they may lean

forward too and stop trying to hold up their poor horses by brute force, and there will be a lot of happier horses around.'

Warrior shook his head. 'They won't take a blind bit

of notice of a lady,' he said to me afterwards. 'Now if it was the master things might be different.'

I knew he was jealous, so I said nothing more about it, but I made up my mind that I would do my best come what may.

CHAPTER SIX

A show

Many of the horses I had met hunting were at the show. The master's bay, called Benjamin, was there and a subscriber's flashy chestnut mare called Wildfire. There was the cob, Moonlight which carried an old lady to hounds, ridden by his groom and a roan pony of fourteen two ridden by a girl. May had plaited my mane. Bowles had groomed me till my coat shone like black ivory.

Of course, I had never been to a show before, so everything was new to me. But May was calm and kind. She talked to me and let me look around, so that when it was my turn to go into the ring I was quite at home.

I shall never forget that first competition. I felt so proud to be carrying my mistress. She was the only lady competing and I was determined to do my best.

The first jump was a brush fence, the second a gate. May allowed me to gallop on. I heard someone say, 'It's a lady, astride too, well I never.'

'And what a pace she's going,' commented someone else.

Then we were turning towards the wall. It was painted red and grey and I snorted a little with surprise.

'Go on, it's all right,' said May. 'You can do it Velvet.'

I could feel the strength and determination in her hands through the reins. I increased my pace and then we were over the wall and cantering on towards the stile. This was a narrow fence and like all the other fences had thin slats of wood along the top, and, if you knocked one of these down, you were given half a fault. But I didn't touch anything. An in-and-out followed the stile and then some rails. Another second and we were racing down the centre to the last and largest jump, the triple. May urged me on and then we were over and the crowd was cheering and someone shouted, 'A clear for Black Velvet ridden by Mrs Bastable herself.'

Richard Bastable met us. 'By jove, that was great,' he cried. 'Well done both of you!'

May slipped to the ground and filled my mouth with sugar.

In the ring the jumps were being put up.

'There's one other clear,' said Richard, 'so you'll have to go round again.'

'The forward seat must win,' said May. 'Leg me up again Richard.'

The jumps were higher, but it didn't matter. I think I could have jumped anything that day. Benjamin went first with the master of our hounds riding him, but he brought the slats down off the wall and refused the gate.

I was prancing to go in. I knew I could do it and I did. I came out to a great roar from the crowd and then May rode me in again to stand first in the ring.

'That was pretty good for a lady, Mrs Bastable,' said the judge lifting his bowler hat.

'That was the forward seat in action Colonel Rivers.' replied May quickly. 'It has nothing to do with being a lady.'

Benjamin snapped at me. 'I can still beat you in the hunting field.'

'We'll see about that next season,' I said arching my neck proudly.

After that we went to several shows and I was always in the first three.

At one a large man on a half-hackney half-thoroughbred offered three hundred pounds for me.

But May only laughed. 'I wouldn't sell him for all the tea in China,' she said.

'I could make him into one of the best jumpers in England,' replied the man. 'So don't forget will you? The name is Chambers.'

'I shall forget just as soon as I can,' replied May.

'Because you jump with the backward seat and I with the forward. If I sold Black Velvet it would be to a rider who practised the forward seat. Good afternoon Mr Chambers.'

A year passed pleasantly, then another and another. They were happy years. We were content, well fed and well ridden. Then a blow fell on us all like a thunderclap out of the sky.

It happened one early morning when May was helping Bowles to groom us. Richard came rushing out of the house with a newspaper in his hand.

He didn't see Bowles but rushed straight to May. 'We are ruined,' he said. 'I've lost everything, I gambled it all and lost!'

'But on what?' she asked only half believing.

'On pepper.'

'On pepper?'

'On shares, on pepper shares!,' he cried. 'Oh what does it matter on what? It's gone. All of it.'

May turned pale. She put my rug straight with trembling hands. 'But there's still *my* money,' she said at last.

'It's gone too. I gambled it too.'

'What, all of it?'

'Yes, every penny. Oh I was mad, I see that now. I thought I was going to make a fortune for both of us. I can't forgive myself.'

May shut my box door. 'Will we have to go, leave, sell up . . .?' she asked, her voice shaking.

'Yes everything . . .'

I could see tears trickling down her face. 'How could you? You fool,' she said quietly. 'How could you let us all down?'

We watched them go into the house together, filled with foreboding.

'We will be sold,' Brandy said. 'I shall pull a hay cutter and you will be worked to death.'

'I shall go to the kennels,' said Warrior. 'I'm good for nothing else.'

The house had been mortgaged. The mortgage couldn't

be paid. May came to the stables and wept. Men appeared with vans and took the furniture away. Bowles stopped coming. The yellow car was driven away by a strange man in a peaked cap.

Then one morning, May came into the stable and stood weeping with her face buried in my name. Richard soon followed. He seemed a changed man.

'I will be master in my own house,' he shouted. 'I tell you Velvet will go to Mr Chambers whatever you say. We can't refuse three hundred guineas.'

'You gave him to me. He was my birthday present,' wept May.

'That was years ago. Things were different then.'

'Yes, they were,' replied May with much misery in her voice.

'Well I've sold him anyway,' replied Richard roughly. 'Mr Chambers is fetching him after lunch and a dealer's coming for the other two. Black Velvet will have a good home. He will become a champion jumper and he loves jumping, and just forget about the forward seat . . . It's not important.'

May fed us the last of the oats. 'I can't bear to see them go,' she said in a broken voice. 'You must load them up, or send them off which ever it is Richard. I can take no more. If only you had given me time, I could have found them all good homes.'

'There is no time,' Richard replied. 'I owe everyone money and they must be paid somehow.'

'But why did you have to gamble. We were so comfortable,' she said. 'Why?'

'I don't know myself. It's like a madness,' he said.

So we all went our different ways. A horse box came for me and Mr Chambers himself led me up the ramp. He was a heavy man with a red face and a loud voice.

'Tell your Missis, he'll be all right with me and that she'll see him jumping at Olympia before I've done with him.' he said.

'I will, I will,' replied Richard Bastable in a distraught voice.

I had never travelled in a horse box before. I found it rough at first, but after a time I learned to keep my balance and travelled comfortably enough.

Mr Chambers kept a farm with six or seven loose boxes for his show jumpers. The boxes were comfortable though the doors were too low for a horse of my size, and if I was scared suddenly I frequently hit my head on the roof. However there was plenty to eat and good company and I thought at first I would be happy. I liked show jumping and, though Mr Chambers was much heavier then my late mistress, I was determined to do my best and win him many prizes.

CHAPTER SEVEN

A beating

Sometimes determination and goodwill are not enough. I wanted to win and I did, to begin with. I could jump round novice classes from a walk. But when the jumps were over four foot I needed to stretch myself, to go on a bit. May had taught me to jump like that and I could jump anything given my head. But my new master had other ideas. He liked his horses to jump with precision. He rode at the fences at a slow collected canter and he never let go.

Even when we were in the air we could still feel his heavy hands on our mouths. Without being snobbish, I must say that his other horses were not as well bred as I am. Most of them had carthorse blood and they could stand heavy hands and pain better than I could.

I fought my master and because I fought him, I couldn't attend to the jumps and knocked them. I grew careless and disheartened, all I wanted was room to extend myself, nothing more. But he wouldn't give in to me. He changed my bit for a stronger one which hurt my mouth. I stuck my head in the air to avoid the pain, so he attached a martingale. I fought against the martingale, so he attached another one. I shook my head, so he changed the bit to a curb.

I went on hitting the jumps so he attached hedgehog skins to them to prick my legs. The pricks from the skins made me more frantic, because I wanted a chance to jump in my own fashion and avoid them; so my forelegs were bandaged with tin tacks in the bandages. Sometimes I thought I would go mad. The other horses were friendly enough. 'Go the way he wants. Stop fighting. Humans are stronger than us. Give in,' they said.

I wished I could. I wished I could jump the fences slowly like they did, but I wasn't built that way.

I couldn't jump out of a slow canter. I had not their short springy action which made it possible. Soon I was dreading shows and even more the endless practising beforehand. Mr Chambers was an obstinate man. He had paid a good price for me and he didn't mean to be done. When the hedgehog skins and tin tacks failed, his groom would rap me as I went over. Bert the groom was not a bad man, he merely did what he was told. He never gave us a kind word nor did he beat us or ill use us in the stable, our boxes were none too clean but they were mucked out once a day and there was no shortage of food or bedding.

I don't think he liked the rapping, I heard him say once, 'It won't do any good with a high spirited horse like Velvet.' But my master didn't listen. He didn't listen to anyone, not to his poor frightened mouse-like wife, the vicar nor anybody else. He was a law unto himself.

So Bert ran with a long stick and as I jumped, he hit my legs trying to make me jump higher.

And soon I was looking at him instead of the jumps so that sometimes I hardly jumped at all.

One day, my master lost his temper completely and beat me viciously. He swore and shouted and said that if I didn't jump he would shoot me, while I stood dripping with sweat and trembling all over, my head strapped down, my bandages full of tin tacks, my legs bleeding.

His wife chose to come across the field then with a mug of tea for him, but he knocked it straight out of her hand.

'Wouldn't a little kindness be better?', she asked in a timid voice. 'A little kindness all round?'

Another day a man was riding past on a splendid thoroughbred and stopped to watch. After I had been thoroughly beaten he called from the gate, 'Can I make a suggestion?'

'I don't want any suggestions, I've been riding since I was four. I don't need help from anyone,' shouted back my master.

'I just want to say that no animal can jump with his head strapped down like that,' shouted the stranger. 'Beating won't help. He can't jump like that, poor devil.'

But my master made no answer, so after a moment the stranger rode on.

At last the show-jumping came to an end and we were clipped for the hunting season. My mane was hogged to save trouble and I was hunted in the same dreadful curb and the two martingales. I did my best, but my master was a heavy man. He leaned back over every jump and thirteen stone on your quarters is no help when you have been hunting all day and there are still high fences to be jumped. No one knew me in this part of the country and I doubt whether they would have recognised me if they had, for my coat was a dull black now which no amount of grooming would alter, my mane was gone, and I did not go well any more, but fought and shook my head unceasingly.

My master was for ever jerking at my mouth and shouting, 'Walk you b . . . horse.' But I could not walk well with my head strapped towards my chest by two martingales.

That winter was the worst I had suffered. I felt years older when spring came with the first shows. Mr Chambers had been certain that 'a spot of hunting' would put me right, but it hadn't. I was more run down and nervous than ever.

The bandages were put on again with the tin tacks; the hedgehog skins were nailed to the poles. Bert and Mrs Chambers held wire above the fences which they raised as I went over to catch my legs and make me jump higher, but still the slats fell.

I went to the shows with the other horses. Last season I had won too much to be classed a novice any more, so the jumps were higher now. I fought more. I refused to go into the horse box without a fight, I refused to enter the collecting ring.

One day I felt a soft hand on my neck and heard a voice say 'Velvet'. I was sweating, waiting to go in, dreading every moment which was to follow.

I turned and saw that it was May. She had changed too, she was thinner, sadder. She stroked my neck and said, 'Do you need two martingales and a curb Mr Chambers? Once he had a mouth like velvet.'

My master looked down at her. 'He's mine now Mrs Bastable,' he said. 'And I will ride him in what I like.' He dug his spurs into my sides and a moment later we were in the ring. I never saw May again.

I cleared five fences but I could not jump the spread fence that followed. It was four feet high and wider than I had ever jumped before. I came into it far too slowly and stopped. You need speed to jump a spread, I tried again while my master spurred me on holding me at the same time with his hands and I knew I couldn't do it. The third time I jumped, but landed in the middle of the poles and

my master fell into them very slowly. The crowd laughed
loudly, while my master stood up his face red with fury
and I stood waiting trembling in every limb.

He remounted and we jumped the last fence and left the
ring. He took me to the box and called Bert.

'Shut up the ramp when he's in. We're going to give
this one a lesson for all time,' he said.

'Do you think it will do any good?' Bert asked leading
me up the ramp.

'Yes, he's still fighting. He's got to be mastered. When
he's mastered, he'll jump.'

Bert said no more. They threw up the ramp and
climbed back into the box and laid into me with
whips. My master calling all the while, 'That will teach
you a lesson you stupid animal. That will teach you to
make me a laughing stock.' I reared up and hit my head.
I ran backwards but I couldn't escape. When they had had
enough they left me still in my tack with my girths still
tight, Bert came back after a while with the other horse
which had come with us. He was a thick-set cob called

Gimlet. 'I told you man is stronger. Why do you go on fighting? You'll always get the worst of it. Just do your best,' he said.

'But I can't', I answered, 'not in a curb with my head strapped in. I wish I could.'

After that dreadful day, things went from bad to worse. I lost my nerve completely. I started to refuse at every show. Bert and my master beat me unmercifully and one day, when I saw my chance, I fought back. I started to kick. I caught Bert on his arm and my master on his back and then suddenly everything was quiet, the shouting stopped, the whips were still. Then I saw that Bert was holding his arm saying, 'It's smashed', in a surprised voice. And that my master was lying in a corner of the box without moving.

A little later some men came and let down the ramp and carried away my master. Still later Bert returned with his arm in a sling, and took off my tack. 'I always knew it would end like this,' he said in a subdued voice. ''Im and his temper, and all that drink as well.'

A strange man drove the box home. Another man came to help Bert with us horses. The next day I learned that I had broken my master's back and that he would never ride again. We were all to be sold at once, I with my reputation in ruins.

CHAPTER EIGHT

I'm sold again

We were sent to a sale. There was much interest in the
other jumpers, but news travelled and no one would look
at me for a jumper.

I felt very dejected though Bert stood up for me as best
he could saying, 'He's not a bad horse. It was the master's
temper which did it. He's not a vicious animal . . .'

Finally a man with a hook nose and blue veins on his
face opened my mouth and said, 'He's quite a young horse
though his legs have been banged about.'

'That's jumping,' replied Bert quickly. 'It isn't work
that's done it. If you want a cheap horse, he won't fetch
much and there's plenty of work still in him.'

The man ran his hands down my legs and looked into
my eyes.

'I don't like blacks myself.' He muttered.

Later he bid for me standing firmly in the crowd with
his legs far apart, one thumb in his waistcoat pocket.
There was only one other bidder and I was sold to Mr
Smith for the small sum of thirty pounds. Soon afterwards he mounted a bicycle from which he led me home.

My new owner lived five miles from a town and ran a
hiring stable.

His stables were dilapidated; built of packing cases and
corrugated iron; they leaned lopsided against a bank.
There were no windows and what air there was came

through the gaps in the walls. There were horses standing in stalls but none of them raised their heads when I entered; they were all too busy picking up wisps of musty hay from the floor.

My stall was at the end. I was offered water from a trough; then tied to a ring in the wall. There was a pile of musty hay in a corner. I was accustomed to wearing a rug; to moving about a loose box, but at least here there were no tin tacks or hedgehog skins. The whole place smelt damp and dirty. I heard my master shut a door and latch it. All was total darkness now.

An ugly horse showing much white in his eye raised his head and sniffed. 'And who are you?' he asked.

'I'm Black Velvet, a show jumper.'

'You won't show jump here,' he answered.

I felt very miserable. I knew I was going down in the world. There was damp sawdust under my feet and the hay was hard and tasted damp.

'You'll catch lice,' said another voice. 'We all have lice.'

'Don't talk, please don't talk. I'm so tired and to-morrow is Saturday,' said a plaintive voice from the other end of the stable.

'And what happens on Saturday?' I asked.

'You'll soon know,' replied the ugly horse next to me. 'Don't talk any more. We must rest.'

I spent a restless night, racked by hunger and thirst. In the morning I could see the other horses better. There were not many of us, and the others looked a motley crowd. Their ribs stood out, their quarters had deep poverty marks; their poor necks were thin and looked as scraggy as a crow's neck. Most of their hoofs needed shoeing; their eyes were dull and listless.

We were all offered stagnant water from the trough;

then more hay was brought and dumped on the floor of our stalls.

The ugly horse next to me said, 'You look fat enough young fellow. But you won't stay that way long.'

A small pony nickered. 'Here come the potato peelings.'

'I'm Major, that's Silver,' said the ugly horse.

The potato peelings were tipped into our mangers, which smelt rancid, our master shouting all the time, 'Get over will you. Stand up, or I'll teach you a lesson.'

He was very rough with me, jerking at my head muttering 'And if you so much as lift a hoof you're for it.'

After that we were brushed with an assortment of worn-out brushes and then a strange collection of saddles were brought in. Most of them needed stuffing. Major had an old piece of blanket put under his and wads of cotton wool stuffed under his girth. He stood resting a foreleg, his old head hanging, deep hollows above his eyes.

Further down a mare called Mouse wore a new saddle which looked as though it had never been cleaned. Her withers were high, her poor back very thin from lack of food. She looked very weak. 'I shan't last much longer. I know I shan't,' she said.

'She used to pull a cab by the seaside,' said Major without raising his head. 'She has been here some time, about five years she thinks. She was here when I came.'

Silver wore a felt saddle. He must have been a pretty pony once, but now his tail was stained yellow, and his eyes had a dull, hopeless look about them.

'What is this place?' I said to Major.

'A hiring stable they call it. People come here from the town to ride us; it's fashionable you see among the town folk. They don't know anything of course; if they did, they wouldn't come would they?

'Yes they would,' replied Silver. 'They wouldn't care. They couldn't ride us if we were well; we would be too lively for them.'

'I will never be lively again,' said Mouse.

'Nor I,' agreed a large grey, white with age. 'I find it hard to trot. I'm always stumbling; one day I shall fall and won't have the strength to get up again.'

'That's old Twilight. He carried a master of hounds when he was young. He's never forgotten it.'

An old hunting saddle was put on my back and then two bits were forced into my mouth, a curb and bridoon. The curb had a port and a curb chain.

'That's it then, Jake', said my new master. 'You just behave yourself and you'll be all right.'

We were all ready now and presently our riders started to arrive. They wore all sorts of clothes. Some carried hunting whips, others sticks cut from hedges, one man came in boots and spurs and a young lady even rode in shorts.

They came in droves, all day long with hardly a break. We always went the same way – up a lane across three fields, through a wood and back down the lane again. Most of the riders knew nothing, though I was given the best. They didn't consider us and we were forced to canter along the rough lane, and often to gallop through the fields however tired and blown we were.

Twilight was given all the heavy riders. They sat far back in the saddle and many couldn't so much as rise, but hung on by the reins. He looked very tired and dejected and stumbled constantly. Mouse was given the ladies to carry; they were lighter, but they sat anyhow and talked and smoked and kicked her incessantly with unsuitable shoes. As the day wore on, her poor neck seemed to grow thinner and several times she stopped to cough.

I felt very dejected. I wanted to do my best, but carrying one heavy handed rider after another took every ounce of pleasure away. As I have said, I was given the best riders, but they rode me hard. By evening the soles of my hoofs were bruised from the stones in the lane and my back ached.

Work ended with darkness. Our master collected his last few miserable shillings and led us to our stalls. Our saddles were removed. Our bridles taken away. We stood patiently waiting without moving; too tired to protest at anything. Twilight lay down. Outside there was a dark sky and a rising moon, inside it was humid with an over-powering smell of horse dung.

After a time we were watered and given hay; then the door was shut and the day was over. Though we were hungry, we ate slowly. A rat ran from manger to manger. Mice squeaked around our hoofs.

Presently Mouse lay down. There was no sound from Twilight's box.

'Sunday is worse than Saturday,' said Major. 'My off fore is very painful tonight.'

'I've lost a shoe,' said Silver.

'If it rains they won't come, no one will come,' said Major.

Twilight was dead in the morning; his poor grey head pathetic on the dirty yellow sawdust. Our master said it was old age which killed him, but we knew differently.

'I shall be the next,' Mouse said. 'I keep coughing. I hope it will be soon.'

They tied ropes round Twilight's thin fetlocks and dragged him away. We were very sad.

'You will carry all the heavyweights now,' Major told me. He knew Twilight wouldn't last much longer.

Sunday was worse than Saturday. People kept asking where the old grey was.

'Died in the night,' our master said. 'It was very sad. He must have had a weak heart.'

'Poor old thing, what a shame,' said our riders. 'We shall miss him. There's nothing like a white horse.'

Mouse looked very dejected. It was a dry warm day with a cloudless blue sky. The wood was full of flies; the ground in the fields was hard and unyielding to our tired legs.

Men rode me in ancient hunting boots, in shiny black shoes, in trousers, in plus fours. 'He's terrific, they said. 'Can I have him next week. He's very fast.'

My mouth was sore now and bleeding at the corners. They gave me lumps of sugar and said that I should be called Highwayman.

They came and went pressing shillings into our master's hand, until at last darkness came like a welcoming blanket to shield us from work.

We lumbered exhausted into our stalls. Twilight's was empty reminding us that our turn might not be long in coming.

'They could ride bicycles. Why must they ride us?' asked Silver.

'It's fun,' replied Major bitterly.

We were given old cabbage leaves mixed with chaff and a handful of oats. Our master was in a hurry because he wanted to spend some of what we had earned at the pub. He didn't wait for us to drink our fill of water. Ten minutes after the last saddle was taken off, the doors were shut.

Major was resting his off fore again. 'It's Monday tomorrow. We'll have more of a rest.'

Mouse was coughing; after a time she lay down. We were all afraid she would die in the night, but in the morning she was still there.

Soon I had lice like the other horses. They sucked my blood and my skin itched and I felt ill tempered. A little powder would have killed them, but our master either didn't know or didn't care.

Day followed day. I grew thinner. My feet had thrush in them. My eyes smarted from a combination of sawdust and ammonia. I began to tire easily. I was popular with the customers and one day one of my regular riders asked to take me hunting.

'Hounds are meeting just over the hill. I'd like to take

my young lady as well. She's never been hunting before,' he said.

I could see our master hesitating. He knew how badly fed we were; no doubt he was wondering whether I could stand up to a day's hunting.

But the young man was persistent. 'My young lady would like Mouse,' he said. 'And we'll pay a pound for each. We won't go fast.'

He took two pound notes from his wallet and held them in one hand.

There was a short silence. 'Make it two pounds ten shillings,' said our master, his eyes shining at the sight of money.

'Fair enough.'

'What time do you want them?'

'The meet is at eleven at The Horse and Groom. So ten o'clock will do. We'll want a drink at the meet,' said the young man lighting a cigarette.

CHAPTER NINE

The hunt

Next day and the day after Mouse and I were fed oats. We were groomed with extra care and on the third day we were fed early and had our tails bandaged and our hoofs oiled.

Then we were led outside to stand in the yard waiting the arrival of our riders. It was a misty morning with dewy cobwebs still festooning the hedgerows. Poor Mouse stood with drooping head and straggling legs. I felt better for the oats. The air felt fresh and I longed for the cry of hounds.

Presently the young man, who was called Dick, and his girl friend Jane arrived. They both wore bowler hats. Jane wore an ordinary tie, checked coat, breeches and wellington boots. Dick wore a white cravat, a black coat with tails, white breeches, black boots with spurs attached. They were soon mounted and riding away laughing and talking together. Mouse had not my long stride and found it difficult to keep up. She coughed twice and kept trying to turn back towards the stables. We met a few cars on the road and a great many bicycles with people on their way to the meet.

Quite soon we saw hounds and a collection of horses outside a pub. Our riders pushed us on. Mouse coughed again, while Jane bumped up and down on her back, sometimes rising sometimes not.

Outside the pub all was merriment. Dick fetched drinks and they sat on our backs laughing, smoking and drinking calling the hounds 'dogs', and everyone in a pink coat a huntsman. People looked at us curiously. Someone said, 'That mealy mare over there looks poor doesn't she, nothing but skin and bone?' But Dick and Jane did not hear, or if they did they pretended otherwise. Presently we moved off, Dick and Jane talking all the while and bouncing up and down on our poor backs like balls on a tennis court.

Hounds drew a copse. Dick lit a cigarette. Mouse hung her head. Soon there was a holla from the far side and I, intoxicated as usual by the sound of the horn and the cry of hounds, forgot poor Mouse and galloped wildly across a field in the wake of fifty horses. But Dick yelled over his shoulder, 'Come on Jane. We're getting left. Use your crop dammit.'

I reached into my bridle, my sore mouth forgotten, my heart thudding against my side, ready to go until I dropped. Dick pulled me up at the top of a hill and waited. Mouse was coughing again. Dick was angry and red faced.

'We are missing everything,' he yelled. 'Make the blasted mare go,' and he thrashed her himself with his own lash and thong.

I could see the hurt in Mouse's eyes as we went on. Her breathing was laboured now. Jane held on to the saddle with both hands. Hounds were checking. Dick stopped me and waited; then we rode on more slowly. 'We've hired a dud. That's obvious,' said Dick angrily. 'She just can't or won't keep up.'

'I have been whipping her,' said Jane. 'When she gets her breath she'll go better.'

Sweat was dripping off Mouse's side, her neck was lathered with it. She looked at me and said nothing. I thought, if we could only speak or weep.

Then hounds found once more and we were off. We checked again in a field with sheep bunched in one corner. Dick lit a cigarette, his hands trembling with rage. Jane was beating Mouse up a hill without mercy. I thought she was going to die; there was agony in her eyes and her nostrils were extended and her breath was coming in sobs. A farmer on a cob was watching. He rode up to Jane yelling, 'Put down that whip. Leave her alone. Do you want a dead horse under you. Get off at once. Loosen the girths.'

Jane dismounted reluctantly. 'I don't know where the girths are,' she said in a plaintive voice.

The farmer dismounted and let the girths out himself. 'You should be ashamed of hunting a horse in that condition,' he said. 'She's nothing but skin and bone and her wind's broken. Now you take her straight home before I have the police or an RSPCA Inspector after you. Where do you come from?'

'Mr Smith's livery stables. We've hired these two horses. We've paid a good price for a day's hunting and that's what we intend to have,' said Dick.

'And that you won't have,' replied the farmer. 'You take your poor animal home this minute or I'll speak to the master myself.'

'We paid the Secretary,' replied Dick. 'And hunt we will.'

'I'm going home,' replied Jane. 'Before Mouse dies. Just look at her Dick and have mercy.'

'And there's a sensible young lady. There's some things beyond and above money; there's some things money won't buy – and one is a clear conscience,' replied the farmer.

And now a lady had joined the farmer. She looked at us with pity. 'Someone should be prosecuted,' she said.

'Don't worry, m'lady,' replied the farmer. 'I shall be seeing Mr Smith tonight. I shall see this never happens again.'

'We had better go,' Dick said. 'Get up on your wretched horse Jane.'

'I would rather walk,' she replied fondling Mouse. 'If only I had known I would never have come. What is a broken wind?'

'It's her lungs. They've been strained,' said the lady.

'Won't she ever get well?'

'No.'

'Poor Mouse.' Jane was crying now. She walked away leading Mouse with Dick reluctantly following. The hunt had vanished, but the farmer and the lady set off in hot pursuit, while Dick jerked me in the mouth and kicked me with his spurs and Jane walked with one arm over Mouse's neck weeping bitterly and muttering over and over again. 'If only I had known.'

We were earlier than expected and Mr Smith was not at home.

Dick knocked on the back door of the house and after a while, Mrs Smith answered. 'Tie them to the wall,' she said. 'They will be all right there.'

'Mouse needs a veterinary surgeon,' called Jane, 'she's ill,'

'He will attend to that. He understands horses. Just leave them. You have paid, haven't you?' she asked.

'Yes, and far too much,' replied Dick angrily turning on his heel.

They tied us to two rings on the stable wall by our reins; my girths were still tight. Mouse looked very tired.

Jane wanted to stay and wait, but Dick insisted that if they were quick they could have a drink before the pubs closed. He swung his car with a handle, grumbling all the time about Mr Smith's dishonesty in sending out two unfit horses.

When they were gone everything was quiet and I could hear Mouse's laboured breathing. She tried to lie down but the reins were tied too tightly to the wall. She coughed and started shivering. A cold wind whipped round the yard and soon I was cold too and very thirsty. Slowly afternoon turned to evening and then at last Mr Smith returned whistling merrily. He was surprised to see us back, but soon had us inside the muggy stable. Mouse lay down at once with a sigh and was not interested in her hay, or the oats he brought later. None of us felt like talking. I think we were all too worried about Mouse.

Then we heard a great commotion outside and the farmer who had sent us home from hunting, rushed into the stable with Mr Smith on his heels.

'This place should be pulled down,' he shouted furiously. 'What are you feeding your animals on? Let me see. Come on, show it to me, or by George I'll have you prosecuted.'

Then he saw Mouse and kneeling down beside her he said, 'And how are you pet?' so gently that he might have been speaking to his own child. He stroked her poor thin neck and put his hand against her labouring sides. She raised her head a little and nuzzled him.

He put his head against her side and listened to her

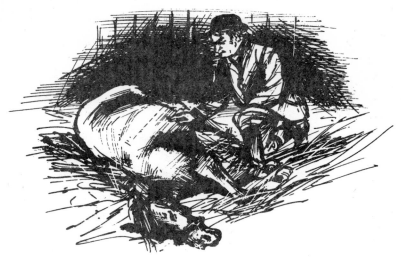

heart. He stood up slowly and stared at Mr Smith muttering, 'Poor little mare.'

'She needs a vet,' he said. 'I'll send mine over at once. I think it's too late, and while I'm away I expect these other horses to be properly fed and watered. Try the mare with a mash, a nice warm bran mash with some treacle in it.'

He looked round the stable in disgust kicking the sawdust with the toe of a hunting boot. He picked up a wisp of hay and smelt it. Then he patted us each in turn muttering 'Poor horses, poor old devils,' and left.

Later a man came in a car. Mr Smith took him straight to Mouse. We had all been well fed by now and the sweat had been brushed from my coat. They were a long time with Mouse. They wanted to take her outside, but she wouldn't move. We heard Mr Smith say, 'She's only twelve,' and the other man replied, 'More's the pity.' And there was a bang which made us all jump in our stalls and Major said quietly, 'She's gone.'

After that, we were given better hay and more of it and

at least one feed of oats and chaff a day. But the work was harder without Twilight and Mouse and I could feel my strength going. My legs had windgalls and were often stiff in the mornings from lying on damp sawdust. Then in March Mr Smith bought a new horse, a big chestnut named Starlight. He was a handsome horse with badly scarred knees. He soon became a great favourite with all the better riders and I found myself carrying most of the beginners. We now had our diet supplemented with cut grass and sometimes a boy would help in the stables at the week-ends. I was so quiet now, that my double bridle was changed for a snaffle which was more comfortable.

The blacksmith painted the inside of my hoofs with some tar which cured my thrush and sometimes on Mondays we were turned out in a small paddock behind the stables. Here we would tell each other our life stories while we stood head to tail swishing at the flies.

CHAPTER TEN

Another war

I won't dwell on the next few years. Gradually life grew
worse again. Another Christmas came and passed. Major's
leg became worse until even our customers complained
that he was lame. So one beautiful day he was taken out
and shot. We all missed him a great deal.

Then Silver was hit by a car and after that shied a good
deal and was considered unsafe. He was sent to a sale and
we never saw him again. Starlight developed ring bone
and complained constantly about the pain in his hoof. A
new horse was bought who reared and broke a young
man's arm. He was sold for dogs' meat I believe. A bay
mare came, a kind hardworking animal who because of
her willingness did a great deal of work. Another year
passed. My eyes were very bad by this time and my coat
had come out in patches.

I stumbled a good deal and sometimes I wished I could
just lie down and die as Twilight had. More children came
to ride us and at least they were light and anxious to
please. A skewbald pony was bought for them and called
Clown. He talked a great deal about things I had never
heard of.

'My last owner was a member of the Pony Club,' he
said. It's a club formed to make people understand us
better, to give us a better life. He would take me to rallies
and gymkhanas.' But after a time Clown's enthusiasm

faded and he became like the rest of us, depressed and dejected. I was known as Old Jake now; I was fifteen years old with a hollow back and deep hollows above my eyes.

I still tried to do my best, but the week-ends seemed to grow harder and our food less plentiful. Our master had aged too. He moved more slowly and his face grew increasingly red. One day his wife was taken away to hospital on a stretcher and after that he was more bad tempered and drank more.

Tractors ploughed the fields now and it was rare to see a horse pulling a plough as Mermaid and Merlin had long ago. I often thought about the past but mostly about May and how happy I had been at The Grange.

Then one day our master came into our stable very drunk singing, *It's a long way to Tipperary*. 'There's going to be a war,' he yelled. 'You'll be all wanted in the army you bunch of old crocks.'

We shrank in our stalls, while he walked up and down singing and shouting alternatively. His breath smelt very bad and several times he nearly fell; then he went out again singing *Pack up your troubles in your old kit bag*. And we could hear him throwing things about in his house.

What is a war?' asked Clown.

'A fight,' I answered wishing that Major was still with us because he had known everything. 'I knew a war horse once,' I continued. 'His name was Warrior. He was the only one to come back out of thousands of horses.'

'I couldn't fight,' replied the bay mare. 'I'm too weak.'

'Where did he come back from?' asked Clown.

'From over the sea, in a ship.'

The next day everyone was talking about a war. Our master felt very ill after so much drink and beat me about the head with a pitch fork. I had a sore on my back from an ill fitting saddle and I felt restless and unhappy.

Three weeks later, the war started and very soon Mr Smith's hay ran out. There was none coming from Australia or Canada any more, and the fields of England had been allowed to go to waste. Soon there were no oats either. The young men and women joined the army, while we horses grew thinner and thinner. Then one day Mr Smith came into the stable very drunk. He hit Clown for not moving over quickly and threw a bucket of water over Starlight who laid his ears back at him. Then he reeled from one side of the stable to the other, talking wildly, with sweat running down his face. Then his breath started to come in gasps and he sat down on a truss of hay his face slowly turning blue. A few more minutes and he was dead.

We all knew death by this time, but for a while none of us spoke, then the bay mare who had been called Mimosa asked,

'Who will feed us now?'

And Clown said, 'And who will water us?'

'No one,' replied Starlight. 'We will die in our stalls.'

And we, who had hated our master, all wished he would come alive again. The day passed. Our mangers were empty; we had eaten the last wisps of foul smelling hay which had lain in crevices around our mangers for many a long day. The mice ran squeaking round our feet searching out the last few precious spilled oats. The rats looked at us in dismay. Day became night. It was a long uncomfortable night.

'We will die,' said Mimosa when daybreak came, wrenching against the rope which held her.

I had been there longer than any of the others and I

felt very weak; I was the thinnest. Clown pulled on his head collar and neighed. 'No one will hear you,' said Starlight.

'On Saturday our riders will come,' replied Clown.

'We'll be dead by Saturday.'

I could feel my tongue swelling in my mouth. My stall was foul with dung. Clown kicked the walls of his partition. Ponies have a stronger constitution than horses: they can live on less. He would not give up, but kept up a continual neighing and kicking. The doors were closed. We could see nothing but each other and our dead master. The rats came back with the dusk. Finding no food the

mice were already leaving. The rats hovered round our legs, waiting for us to grow weaker, waiting to eat our poor starved flesh. Clown killed two daring ones with his neat pale covered hoofs. Another night passed.

The next day we thought we heard voices, but whoever came went away again without opening the stable door. I was too tired to stand up any more. I lay down on the dirty sawdust in my own dung waiting for death.

Clown had stopped kicking and neighing. I could see the rats' sharp eyes, watching, waiting. I remembered my mother. How happy we had been on the farm together.

Hours passed. Then at last we heard voices. They will go away again I thought. We are doomed to die along with our master.

Clown found the strength to neigh. We could hear hands trying to open the stable door and a voice said, 'Go on trying. Mr Smith must be here somewhere.' I didn't move. I was ready to die now. The rats scurried away at the sound of human voices.

Mimosa gave a low whinny deep in her throat. The door opened and two small faces with crash caps on their heads peered in.

'Mr Smith,' one of them called nervously. 'Mr Smith, where are you? It's Sally and Chrissy. We've come for our ride.'

They stepped into the stable timidly like children into an ogre's den, looking round them with frightened eyes. They saw Mr Smith's body and their mouths fell open with surprise.

'Mr Smith, Mr Smith are you awake?' they called before the smaller one screamed. 'He's dead. Can't you see? He's dead'

They ran outside again.

'That's that,' said Mimosa.

'They must tell someone,' replied Clown.

We heard them ride away on their bicycles. They had left the door open and fresh air came in like a gift from heaven. The rats scurried out of the door.

'They will send someone,' said Clown with hope in his voice.

We waited; rain was pattering now on the old tin roof. Then at last there were voices, more and more voices, policemen, a doctor, an ambulance. They took our master away on a stretcher and then they looked at us.

'Crickey,' cried one. 'They are like walking corpses.'
'They are only fit for the knackers,' said another.

They fetched us hay and fresh water from the house, such water as we had not tasted in months.

The house was full of police. An old man came and cleaned our stalls. Someone went away and came back with oats, though oats were supposed to be unobtainable just then. The old man groomed us making a hissing noise, reminding us of our younger days. Next day a man of around forty came in uniform. He looked at us in dismay. He ran his hands through our staring coats, and said, 'They're covered with lice. I'll borrow Dad's bike and go down to the farm and see if they've got something to kill them.'

He had fair hair, a round face with a fresh complexion. It was difficult to believe that he was our late master's son.

Later his wife came with their four children. They took everything out of Mr Smith's house and the wife wept over us.

He only had three days' compassionate leave from the army, but he did his best. He found us food from somewhere and scrubbed out our stalls and bedded them in fresh golden straw. He deloused us and wormed us and paid the old man to go on looking after us. Then he went back to his unit.

The old man said, 'No one will want you. They're shooting horses as it is.' He brought a gas mask every day with him and hung it on a nail.

We grew stronger. We were advertised for sale and people came and looked at us, pulled our mouths open, felt our legs and said, 'They're not even fat enough for meat.'

Then Chrissy and Sally came one day with their

mother. They kept saying, 'Please, please we must have him. Please, please, please.' They threw their arms round Clown's thin neck and begged. 'We can ride to school,' they said. 'We can buy him a cart, please Mummy please.'

Finally their mother gave the old man ten pounds and they led Clown away.

No one wanted Starlight because of his ring bone, but presently a farmer bought Mimosa to pull his hay cutter.

I was better in body but becoming more and more dejected in spirit. 'If no one comes for you tomorrow it's goodbye old fellow,' said the old man. 'That's my orders. I was to wait a week.'

I had been ready to die but now I felt better. I looked out of the stable door which was open all the time now and smelt spring coming, the sap rising in the trees, the grass pushing it's way through the damp earth. I remembered the pleasure of rolling, the taste of dew drenched grass.

I shifted my weight from one leg to another. My strength was coming back.

'A lot more are going to die before this war's finished,' said the old man.

'I've heard people say, "It's always darkest before dawn". And that is how it was with me. The last day came. Starlight and I looked at each other sadly wondering which of us would go first.

Then a lady came riding into the yard on a dun mare. She dismounted and called, 'Hoi. Are you in charge? Have you a horse here called Black Velvet?'

'Not that I know of,' replied the old man. 'Though we have got an old back horse inside.'

'He was once a show jumper,' she said. 'A man called Bert told me he was here.'

'I'll hold your mare while you look,' said the old man.
She had short wavy hair and an upturned nose.

She said, 'Poor old chap, so you were once a show
jumper with a mouth like velvet. What a shame.'

'You are only just in time. I have orders to call the horse
slaughterers after I've had my dinner,' said the old man
through the doorway.

'He's twelve pounds, isn't he. I've brought the money,'
she answered opening her purse.

I wondered why she wanted me as the old man led me
out into the daylight, saying, 'You're in luck after all.'
And I was sorry for Starlight, for I knew now that he had
no future, only the humane killer.

'I'm leading him home,' said my new mistress mounting her mare. 'It's twelve miles. Do you think he will
make it?'

'If you take it slowly he will.'

'I promised an old school friend that I would buy him.

Her name is Bastable. Her husband was killed last week in France.' She said. 'He's going to live in honourable retirement.'

Starlight neighed. I was sorry to leave him to his fate alone; I wished that he could have come with us. If I could have spoken I would have pleaded for him, begged for his life, as it was I neighed a long sad farewell and hoped that his end would be swift and painless.

CHAPTER ELEVEN

My last home

It was a long way. I grew very tired. We stopped to rest me and once I recognised the landscape and saw that we had halted nearby to where I was born. But everything was changed. The old buildings were falling down with neglect; the hedges had been replaced by sagging barbed wire. The trees under which we had stood on hot summer days were gone and, worst of all, the paddock near the house had houses on it. I felt very sad when I saw the change. The fields were being ploughed by two tractors. A different breed of cow was waiting to be milked.

We went on, my new mistress, who was called Jean, whistling as we went, the dun mare saying, 'Can't you walk any faster? I want to get home.'

I wondered whether Starlight had been shot yet. There were pill boxes [machine-gun positions] at the side of the roads, but not many soldiers to be seen. Then we saw a sandbagged post with a large gun pointing towards the sky. Soon afterwards we turned down a lane and came to an old white cottage with roses climbing up its walls.

Two children and a dog came to greet us. The boy was called Paul, the girl Sonia. They both had fair hair like their mother.

'Gosh he looks awful,' Sonia said.

'Do you think he's going to live?'

'Yes, if he has the chance.'

'Mummy, I've milked Tiddlywinks,' said Paul.

'And I've fed Jemina,' said Sonia.

It wasn't a smart place. There were no servants. They did everything themselves. But it was a happy house, perhaps the happiest place I had ever known. Every animal had a name and was loved and looked after. If the chickens were ill they were taken indoors to be warm, if the cat had a bad foot it was tenderly bandaged up. Oats were rationed and I and the dun mare, who was called Amelia, did not qualify for a ration, but there was always plenty of sweet smelling home-made hay. The children rode Amelia and were members of the pony club. They spent hours learning stable management from books. They fussed over our food, as though we were invalids.

On wet days they played a gramophone to us to keep us amused. They fought over who should wind it up and tried to decide which record we preferred. Sometimes they dressed us up in their own clothes. The stable was only an old cow shed, but they had made it into two boxes and they were always bedded down in plenty of straw, so we were always warm and comfortable. Gradually the shine came back to my coat; my sides started to fill out, the poverty marks on my quarters grew less pronounced. Amelia was only six. She had never had a bad home. She was fourteen hands high and full of life. She would never believe my stories.

'Humans are not like that,' she would say. 'Humans are lovely.'

'You wouldn't say that if you had belonged to Mr Smith or Mr Chambers,' I answered.

'Well I haven't and I don't believe they exist,' she would answer with a snort. 'You wait until you see our master, he's lovely too.'

She would spend hours licking the childrens' hands, while I stood aloof, too nervous to approach, afraid of a sudden blow.

The days grew warmer and the sky was full of planes. My new master came home one evening exhausted, his face blackened, his eyes crying out for sleep. He said that things were going very badly and that soon the Germans would be coming and that we must be ready and he gave Jean a gun to use on herself and the children if things got bad. Then he bought a cart and a set of harness and he said that one of us must be put to use to help the war effort. Then his leave was over and he disappeared again and Jean and the children sat and cried, and for the next three nights all we heard was gunfire. It made me feel very nervous but Amelia who had never been ill treated was not afraid. She insisted that it was nothing but thunder, but I knew differently for Warrior had told me about war. After that there was gunfire and bombs and great lights wheeling in the sky night after night and no one slept much. Sonia and Paul would go out early in the morning looking for bits of shrapnel, while Jean waited sad-eyed for the post to come. Everything was in short supply. But Jean never grumbled. She would say, 'We're the lucky ones, because we live in the country and can grow things.'

Then one day we saw planes chasing each other in the sky.

'They are only playing,' said Amelia.

I knew differently of course – I knew that the men inside were trying to kill each other, and I wondered why man is always fighting and killing. Then one of the planes started coming down in a pall of smoke, and Jean and the children came running from the cottage. Soon

we could see men like toys dangling from the sky on parachutes and the children started to shout and wave.

Then Jean said in a strange voice, 'They are Germans. Go for help one of you.'

Amelia was tearing round the field by this time, her tail up over her back, snorting like a mustang. Sonia fetched a head collar.

Jean said, 'It will have to be Black Velvet.' Can you manage him?'

'I'll try,' replied Paul. It was many months since I had been ridden, but I stood as quietly as I could and pushed my nose into the head collar. Paul jumped on my back off a gate.

The Germans were untangling themselves from their parachutes two fields away.

I turned quickly. Paul gripped me tightly with his small bony knees.

'Be careful. Godspeed,' shouted Jean.

We galloped up the lane and turned left, Paul crouching on my withers like a jockey. I wasn't fit, but I galloped as fast as I could along the tarmac road. Outside a cottage, an old lady stood staring over her gate. 'Have they come?' 'Is it the invasion?' she cried.

'No. They've been shot down', yelled Paul. We had reached a police house now. Paul slipped off my back and rapped on the door. A policeman came out carrying his helmet.

'A German plane has been shot down,' shouted Paul. 'Some men have landed by our house.' The policeman ran for his bike.

Paul patted my neck. 'You're lovely,' he said. 'Better than Amelia even.'

He rode me slowly back.

By the time we had reached the house the men were being taken away. One had his face bandaged, another had half an arm missing. They looked fine young men. I felt very sad when I saw them. I could see the charred remains of the plane and Sonia stood waving a bit of wing triumphantly. After that the children and Jean started to ride me quietly and then they put me in the cart and soon I was trotting up and down the empty wartime roads to the shop and back.

I was glad to be of some use. Horses can become bored just like humans and I was tired of my retirement.

CHAPTER TWELVE

Bad news

There followed a long hard winter. It was very cold; sometimes so cold that the children didn't even go to school. We spent the nights in our warm loose boxes, but there was nothing but hay to eat and once, for a few days, only oat straw.

I lost condition again but continued working, pulling the cart, which was more of a farm cart than a carriage. More than once I heard Jean say,

'I don't know what we would do without old Velvet.'

The children drove me to nearby woods and came back with the cart loaded with firewood. It snowed for days on end. The holly trees were bright with berries. But at last spring came.

Jean borrowed a harrow and I harrowed the fields. Summer came and I pulled a hay cutter. One day Jean came outside with a letter in her hand. The children were cutting nettles to make us nettle hay.

Her face looked crumpled and exhausted. She called: 'Come over here please.' She put her arms around them and said, 'This has just come.'

'It is about Daddy isn't it? He's dead,' said Paul. Sonia didn't speak.

'It say's he's missing, believed killed,' replied Jean. 'But only believed. They haven't found him.'

'Found him?' asked Sonia.

'His body,' replied Paul.

They stayed close together without speaking and I was very sorry for them. 'The master's dead,' I told Amelia.

'We don't belong to him, we belong to Jean, she feeds us,' Amelia replied.

'Silly ignorant mare,' I retorted though I am not usually rude. 'He's dead and he was a fine young man and it will affect us all.'

The next day there was much talk of selling the farm and leaving. I knew that if that happened there was no hope for me. I was twenty years old now and very tired. My back was hollow, and old saddle sores had left grey hairs on my back and withers. Lack of oats made me tire easily and, though I did my best, I knew I couldn't work as I had when I was younger.

Jean and the children understood this and let me go at my own pace and, as I always did my best, they never used a whip or stick.

I was worried now. I had been very happy. I had no wish to start again in a new home. Fortunately after much talk, it was decided that Jean and the children should stay where they were to the end of the war.

Jemina died and the children put her body in a black box and put me in the cart and dressed themselves in black. I had to pull her coffin to a small grave by the pond where she was buried. It seemed odd to bury a little duck with such ceremony when so many young men were dying all over the world.

Another winter came. Everyone had become accustomed to our master being dead. Paul tried hard to be the man about the house, chopping the wood and digging the vegetable patch. Sonia rode Amelia most of the time now.

She was too silly to pull the cart so she was kept mostly for pleasure, though sometimes she was ridden into the nearby town to do the shopping.

Jean looked very worn. She was trying to make a living out of the land and soon I was carrying vegetables and fruit into the nearby town on market day. Then two cows were bought and more chickens.

Then one night, Paul came running out to the stable with a torch.

'Wake up Black Velvet, you're needed. Sonia's very ill. And there's no petrol anywhere and the bikes are punctured. You'll have to take her to the doctor in the cart.'

He pushed my head into the collar and threw the rest of the harness over my back. I pushed my head into the bridle. I had been to market once already that day and was tired, but I knew by the urgency in Paul's voice that this was a matter of life or death. He dragged me outside and pushed me between the shafts of the cart. There was a bright moon shining and everything was frozen. Jean came out carrying Sonia wrapped in blankets.

'I'll be all right soon,' said Sonia between chattering teeth. 'If only it didn't hurt. I'm sorry Mummy. I know I'm being a nuisance, but it does hurt.'

'A nuisance? Don't be so silly. You've got an appendicitis and if I hadn't been so busy with the cow calving, and it being market day and everything else, I would have noticed hours ago.'

And with that she put her gently into the cart propped up against the seat with pillows and got up herself, her face very white. Paul jumped in the back.

'Steady. Go gently Black Velvet,' Jean said.

I did my best. The road was covered with ice. How I

stayed on my legs I shall never know. Sonia was moaning all the time and I could hear Paul's voice saying, 'It's going to be all right Mummy.'

'What do you mean – all right? If her appendix bursts the poison will be all over her body; and it will be my fault if she dies, because I didn't know it was so bad when she complained earlier. I shall have killed her Paul,' replied Jean.

I heard Sonia say, very quietly, 'No Mummy,' And Paul said:

'She'll be all right. We are going to get there in time.' But I could hear how worried he was and knew he was only trying to comfort his mother.

'Sometimes I think I have had enough,' she went on. 'If your father was coming home, if the farm paid, if anything went right it would be different.'

'You're tired,' Paul answered. 'Tired to death.'

We had reached the Doctor's house. Paul ran to the door and started beating upon it with his fists. Presently a window was opened and a lady said, 'What is it? The doctor's gone to Pickwicks. There's been an explosion. A bomb I think. There's lots of dead.'

'My daughter has an appendicitis,' shouted Jean. 'It's urgent.'

'There's many dead and injured,' replied the lady shutting the window.

'Let's try another doctor. We can telephone from the kiosk,' Paul said.

He jumped out of the cart and ran up the road, but was soon back saying, 'It doesn't work. The line is dead. We had better drive on to the hospital. We may meet some-one. Come on.'

Jean jerked the reins and I set off as fast as I could on the slippery road. Sonia had stopped moaning. Jean kept saying, 'Faster Black Velvet. Come on. Move on.'

The road was empty. There were houses, but you couldn't see them because their windows were blacked out. We had no lamps at all on the cart. Snow started to fall in small, white flakes.

'I can her something coming,' shouted Paul. He leapt out of the cart and stood waving in the road.

'Are you going into town. We've got a sick person here. She's dying,' he shouted.

The car stopped. A man leaned out. 'Jump inside,' he shouted.

'Go on Mummy,' yelled Paul. 'I'll take Black Velvet back.'

The man helped Jean lift Sonia gently into the car. She couldn't move her legs by this time and she was groaning all the time.

'Right you are,' said the man and the car was gone.

'Home,' said Paul, fighting back tears. 'I'll walk with you Velvet. I'm so cold it may warm me up.'

It was a long cold road home before Paul put me away in the stable. 'I'm sorry there's no mash for you, no oats,' he said giving me a carrot. 'One day this war will be over and we'll give you a great bucketful of oats, but now I must go in, though I would rather stay with you, for the fire is out and the house is freezing.'

Jean came back the next morning on the bus. She had not slept all night. 'She's not out of danger yet,' she said. 'It burst. I just came back to milk the cows.'

'I can manage, but I would like to see her sometime,' said Paul with a break in his voice. 'Is she going to die?'

'They say so. They say there's no hope.'

The next few days were terrible, even Amelia was

affected, because she thought the world of Sonia. We hardly saw Jean, neighbours came and fed us when they could and a strange boy milked the two cows.

Gloom hung over the little farm like a big dark cloud, none of us cared much if we lived or died.

Then one morning Paul came running down to the stable crying 'She's out of danger; she's going to be all right. She's saved Velvet – saved.' And he put his arms round my neck and buried his face in my mane.

Then, after some weeks had passed Sonia came back looking pale and fragile and needing extra food which wasn't there, though there was plenty of milk now because of the cows, and eggs too, and vegetables, so we were luckier than most people.

The roads were crammed with soldiers now in tanks and armoured vehicles; they came down to the farm for water. There were many Americans and Canadians. They said they had come to save us from the Germans.

Then suddenly they were all gone and people seemed a little more cheerful and there was talk of when the war was over. But Jean never talked about it though once I heard her say,

'When peace comes I shan't feel like celebrating, because I shall know then that Alan will never come back.'

Sonia grew stronger. Paul grew taller and we could all see that soon he would be a man. And then suddenly part of the war was over and people lit great bonfires and danced and there was much singing.

Jean stayed inside with the children without saying much, though a few days later she said, 'We will have to sort out our future soon. We can't go on here. It's too isolated for just us three, and what shall I do Paul when you go away? When you are grown up.'

'I'll stay with you Mummy,' Sonia said. 'And there's always the horses.' But Jean was determined to go now. 'You need friends she told the children and you will never make friends here. You'll want to go to dances.'

Then the rest of the war ended and the church bells rang, and all the houses were lit up again, and then the soldiers started to come home.

Everyone was much merrier in the village and there was talk of more food soon.

Jean decided to sell the farm. 'I want to be near to relations,' she said. 'I can't stand the loneliness any more. We can find Amelia a nice home; but Velvet will have to be put down.'

We were all older. Sonia and Paul were fifteen and I was well past twenty. I stood under the trees a lot now remembering the past. I had seen many changes. I had lived through a fearful war. I had seen the emergence of a new style of riding. I had witnessed horses being driven from the farms by tractors and watched them come back in wartime. I was content to go peacefully. I had been very happy on the farm. I was grateful for the years there.

A notice was nailed up at the front of the house saying FOR SALE. The children cried. The cows were sold. Amelia grew anxious now. I wanted to give her good advice but she would not listen.

'You are too old,' she said. 'You don't know anything. Times have changed.'

'But human nature hasn't. There will always be good and bad masters', I said.

'Masters, Mistresses! We call them our owners, now–

adays,' she retorted. 'I shall teach my next one a thing or two, I can tell you.'

People came to look over the house, complaining that there was no telephone and only one bathroom, and no central heating, just as they had complained over Matthew's cottage all those years ago.

Then one day a tall gaunt man in uniform came walking up the path. One of his sleeves was empty and his hair was grey. He looked at the notice before he knocked on the back door. Jean came out her hands dirty from cleaning the grate. 'I see this place is for sale,' he said. 'Oh Jean!'

She stared at him and said 'Alan! It can't be.' But she kept staring at him.

Amelia and I watched without speaking.

'I built a railway. I was in prison a long time. But I'm Alan, all right minus one arm of course,' he said.

'It doesn't matter.'

'How pleased the children will be. They're at school,' gasped Jean.

'Oh Alan I thought I would never see you again.'

'The thought of this place and you, kept me alive. Let's take down the notice, we're not leaving,' he said, stooping to kiss her. She started to cry. 'I'm so happy,' she said.

They fetched a hammer and took down the notice. 'I was going to sell everything. The cows have gone already.' Jean told him.

'Not any more,' said Alan, his one arm round her.

They talked for a long time. He had been sent to Australia because he was like a scarecrow. 'They fattened me up there,' he said. 'You should have had a letter. Something went wrong.'

'It doesn't matter now,' she said. 'I was going to have Black Velvet put down and sell Amelia, but they can stay now can't they? Black Velvet saved Sonia's life you know. No other horse could have stood up on the roads that night. They were covered with ice. I think he knew how ill she was . . . I never stopped hoping you would come back. Not until the war was over. I couldn't celebrate then,' she said.

'We'll have our own celebration this evening,' he promised.

Sonia and Paul came home later and a great bonfire was lit in the paddock. Amelia and I watched as they danced round it singing old war songs. I felt very tired but happy too for I knew now that this was my home for ever. Amelia pranced up and down snorting at the flames, but I wasn't afraid because I knew I would never be hurt again.

Later they said good night to us.

'You really are going to be pensioned off this time,' Sonia told me one arm round my neck. 'You are going to live here to the end of your days and, when your time comes, you will be buried under the apple trees with a gravestone with *Black Velvet* on it, for all to see.'

I remembered how Mouse and Twilight had died, and poor Starlight killed because of ringbone. They had all been quite young. I was old now. Soon I would be ready to go to wherever horses go. Perhaps I would meet my mother there and all the other horses I had known – my own generation. They would be sound and young again and we would talk about the old days, not about owners and the pony club, but about masters and mistresses and carriages and phaetons, about the days when tails were still docked and we pulled the carts and ploughs of England.

Book Two
BLACK BEAUTY'S FAMILY

Foreword

BY POT BLACK

Black Beauty's great-great-great-great-great nephew

The three stories discovered by my late sire, Black Abbot, and published under the title *Black Beauty's Clan* brought a great spate of letters from horses believing themselves related to Black Beauty and a deluge of hoof-written manuscripts.

Checking the authenticity of these relationships and life stories has been a heavy task, but I am now in a position to set a further three bona fide autobiographies, written by members of my extraordinarily talented family, before the public.

Nightshade, a thoroughbred born in the reign of George III, writes of his life as a racehorse, of the robbery and violence of the roads when he found himself carrying a highwayman. He describes the world of factory children and chimney sweeps, which he saw when a manufactory owner's horse and finally the part he played in the Home Defence during the Napoleonic war.

Black Romany's story is set in the 1840s and tells of life in a stately home, a visit from Queen Victoria, a hunt with the Consort, Prince Albert. She goes on to relate her incredible adventures when trekking across England: confrontation with a ghost, near-death by drowning.

Blossom, a great-great niece of Black Beauty, starts a life full of problems caused by the unfortunate marriage of her dam, Black Tulip. Forced into drudgery as a working horse at the end of the nineteenth century, Blossom's story is of a lost foal, of carting coal, working in the fields and then, at last, of unexpected success.

I have appended that portion of our family tree which shows the relationship which our three storytellers bear to Black Beauty.

NIGHTSHADE

✳

by Josephine Pullein-Thompson

CONTENTS

❧Black Beauty's Family❧

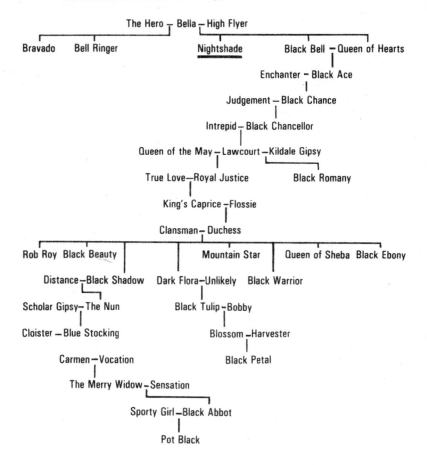

CHAPTER ONE

Thorngate Manor

When I was young I thought myself a very lucky horse. I seemed to have been born into a perfect world. Squire Lovelace, my owner, was a great man in our locality and his estate, Thorngate Manor, was situated deep in the countryside far from any town or city. We, a peaceful party of mares and foals, lived among grassy hills and stately trees in a wonderful state of contentment.

All through my foalhood I was proud and happy. My mother often told me that we were aristocrats among horses for we were descended from two of the great arab stallions that had been brought to England from over the sea. Both my parents were thoroughbreds with pedigrees and their names were in the new Stud Book. My name was to go in the Stud Book too: Nightshade, black colt, by Highflyer out of Bella. All this made me walk proudly and carry my head high and I am afraid that I boasted and bragged of my breeding to the less high-born foals.

My mother, Bella, was still quite young; I was only her third foal. She was bright bay with a broad white blaze on her face and white socks. I thought her very beautiful.

My sire, Highflyer, was a very well known racer and I early showed that I had inherited his exceptional turn of speed. I was overjoyed when I found that I could outpace the other foals with the greatest of ease.

The leader of our group was an old grey mare called Cobweb. She had been the Squire's favourite hunter until lamed in an accident and, though not well-bred or fast, she was very wise and I noticed that my mother always listened to her with great attention.

Cobweb could remember the Squire as a young man when things had been very different. Our park had been the common field where the villagers grazed their cattle and ponies and their pigs, with rings in their noses that they might not root about too much and spoil the turf. The Squire had bought out the commoners' rights, fenced and improved the land and made the long, winding drive, that visitors might have plenty of opportunity to admire the house before they reached it.

We would graze early in the morning and then, as the day grew hot, retire to our shelter of thatch and poles to escape from the flies, which were a great plague to us foals with our soft and tender skins, and to the mares, who, except for my mother, were all cocktails. One day I asked my mother why she alone had such a fine, full tail and she told me that all horses were provided with them by nature, but it was the fashion for all but racers to have short tails, so men cut them off. And, not content with cutting off the hair, they cut through the bone of the tail so it could never grow long again.

'It saves our grooms the trouble of brushing tails and they think it is safer for driving as the reins cannot be caught under a cocktail,' said Rosetta, a brown mare who was chiefly used in the Squire's carriage.

'I have heard that its main purpose is to make our backs grow stronger,' added Cobweb, 'but it is difficult to see why a racer does not need an equally strong back.'

Whatever the reason, I was very glad that being a racer meant I could keep my tail.

Rosetta was a stout, talkative mare with an opinion on everything. My mother said that carriage horses travelled a good deal and saw much of life and Rosetta had stayed at inns as well as private houses and even in London, for several months once, when the Squire had taken a house for the season.

Snap was even more heavily built and drew the coach or chariot with three other chestnuts when she was not in foal. She pointed out to us one day that Mischief, her filly, was a much finer, better bred looking animal than she was. 'Up-breeding is all the rage nowadays,' she told us. 'I heard Squire talking to Buckle a little time ago and he was saying that with more and more turnpike-roads coming into use all the carriage mares must be put to finer-bred stallions, for it was speed, not strength, that would be needed in the future as the better roads encouraged the building of lighter, more elegant carriages.'

'True enough,' agreed Rosetta. 'I well remember the effort it used to be to drag that heavy, old, broad-wheeled carriage. And the roads! We'd be stuck fast half a dozen times between here and town in the rainy season, but now, once you're on the hard surface of the turnpike, the carriage spins along with no effort at all.'

'Yes, it is very well once you are *on* the turnpike,' said Snap, 'but if you take these modern coaches into the more remote areas, along the old fashioned byroads, their wheels sink deep in the mud where the old broad wheels would have gone over the top, and you dare not take to the fields on either side as you used to do when the road became impassable.'

'But all these new hedges and fences prevent that anyway,' Rosetta pointed out. 'They force the road to continue along its usual track even though a drover taking two or three hundred cattle up to the meat market in London has just turned it into a hock-deep quagmire.'

'These new fences are a confounded pest in the hunting field too,' Skylark told us. 'Leaping from morning to night, that's all the young men think of nowadays and the Squire's grown nearly as bad. When I started a couple of stiles and a few ditches would be all you'd meet in a day's sport, but now every other field is fenced. And the speed they go! A hunter has to be almost as fast as a racer these days.' She looked at Ringleader, her foal. 'His sire *was* a racer so he should be fast enough for them.'

The abundant grass enabled our mothers to give us plenty of milk so we foals grew apace and were very strong and forward. In the cool of the evenings and early mornings we would race and wrestle and, as we grew older and dared to venture from our mothers' sides, we would make our way down to the fence that ran close to the drive, and watch the comings and goings.

Elegant carriages and chariots, curricles and chaises would bring the neighbours calling and relations and friends from further afield for longer visits. Our own horses took the Squire's wife and daughters to the town or to repay the calls and visits, in equally elegant vehicles.

The Squire and his sons did most of their travelling on horseback and they would start out across the fields rather than bother with the long, winding drive.

As I have said I was possessed of an exceptional turn of speed and I would frequently challenge the other foals to races and beat them easily. Even Ringleader, whose sire was a racer, could keep nowhere near me. Sometimes I would let them all start and then, coming from behind, I would exert myself to the very top of my speed and flashing by them in turn, be the victor once again.

My mother would not praise me for these efforts, but the other mares looked on and talked admiringly of my spirit and 'bottom'.

'He'll be a celebrated racer and no mistake,' they told my mother.

She would only blow and sniff as she grazed. 'So he ought to be,' she admitted at last, 'since his sire and dam and his grand-sires and grand-dams have all been racers before him, but it's not much of a life.'

'Why not?' I asked. To me racing with the wind in your mane and tail seemed the height of happiness, far better than drawing carriages, dragging carts or even being a hunter.

She stood staring into the distance, a few blades of grass dangling from her lip as she answered me, 'It is wonderful enough when the cheers of the crowd are ringing in your ears and you are in the lead; when you gallop first past the post to the delight of your jockey and master; but it is not always like that.'

'Why not?' I asked disbelievingly as I tried to imagine the sound of a cheering crowd.

'Because you can lose. You can gallop for all you are worth, until your lungs are bursting and your brain is dizzy with the effort, and still the other horse is ahead. The whip cuts your flank as you struggle to catch up, but the cheers are for the other horse and you stand, spent, with heaving sides and watch him led in in triumph.'

'*I* won't ever lose,' I told her. '*I'll* be the fastest horse in the land.'

My mother had sighed. 'You have a great deal to learn, Nightshade,' she said.

The other mares liked my answer, they said I had plenty of 'bottom'.

When I asked my mother what 'bottom' might be, she answered that it was really another name for courage and perseverance. 'It is the spirit and doggedness,' she went on, 'that keeps some horses galloping though they are struggling for breath and scarce able to see; it makes them keep going through a long day's hunting or pull and pull to get their cart out of a slough. That is what men call "bottom" and they are full of admiration for it, in horses and in each other.'

I was very glad when I heard this that I had 'bottom' and I determined to practise having it so that I possessed more and more.

CHAPTER TWO

The Lovelace family

My first summer passed without event. But in the autumn I began to see more of life for Ringleader and I, with our mothers, were taken into the stable each night.

Two stable boys, generally Bob and Dick, would come across the park calling us and shaking a sieve of oats. They would put halters on the two mares and lead them to the stables with Ringleader and I trotting along behind.

We would go through a gate into the back drive, past the midden and the forge, past the barns that held the hay and straw, the granaries and the coachhouse into the stable yard. This was a modern brick–built square with stables below and grooms' quarters in the lofts above. Two turrets faced each other, one holding a dovecote and the other a clock that struck the hours. Above the clock, a gilded weathercock showed where the wind lay.

The stables were thought very fine, fitted up with every modern convenience, my mother said, and Mr Lovelace brought any new acquaintance to see them and to admire every detail.

As the weather grew colder my mother and Skylark would trot across to meet the boys and when winter came on they would find us waiting at the gate whinneying at them to hurry and take us in.

One night instead of sharing a stable with my mother I was put in with Ringleader, just the two of us shut away in a great loose-box. A feed of crushed oats was put in the manger and soft, sweet hay in the low hay rack, but we felt very indignant at this trick and neighed at the tops of our voices, wanting our mothers and our accustomed milk. We heard their voices neighing back from distant stables, but they did not come. At last, worn out by our protests, we ate the food provided and lay down disconsolately together in the thick straw.

From that night our mothers vanished from our lives. We spent a few mournful days together in the loose-box and then Bob and Dick led us out to a little paddock behind the stables. They told us that we were grown horses now and must stop crying after our mothers, for they would be having new foals in the spring and must gather strength for that and not feed great colts like us with their milk.

We saw a good deal of life from our paddock and perhaps this was intended, for a young horse, reared in some very secluded pasture or moor, is likely to be in a continual state of fright when taken into the larger world and will spend much of his time starting and shying. We had something to watch every minute of the day. Besides all the carts and wagons belonging to the estate there would be visitors like the miller, his men and horses white with flour, the coal fetched in carts from a barge on the canal. Wagons from the cities bringing new furniture and carpets and once, when Mr Lovelace's old aunt died, mourning coaches and carriages drawn by black horses with black plumes on their heads; we thought this a very fine sight.

The children's ponies: Squirrel a red chestnut, Fidget a dun, elegant bay Julius, and tiny brown Sparrow, were often turned out in the paddock next to ours. Squirrel and Fidget belonged to the two younger boys, Georgie and

Harry, Julius carried Miss Polly and Sparrow, who was not as tall as Ringleader and me, had taught all the Lovelace children to ride and now belonged to the youngest, Miss Cassy. Mr Tom, the heir, who was almost of age, and Mr William both had several hunters and a road horse apiece. While Miss Lovelace, the eldest daughter, had a very pretty mare called Grace.

When the Christmas holidays came we saw a lot of Georgie and Harry for they liked the company of our stable boys and a great deal of boasting, wrestling and sham fighting would go on in the hay barn beside our paddock. If Mr Buckle caught our boys at it he would soon send them back to work and then, with no playfellows, Harry and Georgie would get their guns and blaze away at everything that moved. No bird was safe from being blown to pieces and they would fire at the stable cats and stray dogs if no other targets offered themselves.

Ringleader and I spent a good deal of time talking to the ponies over the fence for, Sparrow especially, knew a great deal about life and about the Lovelace family.

We learned that there had been eleven children born, but four had died of one thing or another, as was quite common, and Mrs Lovelace was thought lucky to have as many as seven children living and all in good health.

Fidget said that he couldn't answer for Masters Georgie and Harry remaining in good health much longer. He and Squirrel were being rammed at every new fence they met and he thought it likely that both boys would have broken necks before the season was over.

We saw Mrs Lovelace only occasionally. Sparrow said that she kept to the house in bad weather. She looked to us quite an elderly lady, much older than the short, square, red-faced Squire, but Sparrow explained that she was in poor health, mostly due to having borne eleven children.

The whole family gathered at Thorngate Manor for Christmas and Mr Tom came from his University, bringing with him a Bull Terrier and a fighting cock. The dog was renowned for killing rats and we learned that this was a popular sport among university men. They would put a dog in a pit, specially made so the rats could not get away. Then empty in a whole sackful of rats and timed how long he took to kill them, laying wagers on which dog would kill the most in the shortest time.

Mr Tom's dog had become the champion and Sparrow, who went up to the house each day to take Miss Cassy out, reported that the Squire was as proud of Mr Tom for possessing the champion rat-killer as many fathers would have been if he had passed his exams or gained some great honour for learning.

The fighting cock was less fortunate. It seemed he was only a second rate bird and not worthy of the big fights that the Squire attended, but before long Mr Tom managed to arrange a match with an untried cock.

The weather being fine, they made a ring with boxes and trusses of hay between our paddock and the barn and the Lovelace sons, their friends and our stable boys assembled to see the fight. We all leaned over the fence to watch. We saw the cocks, two very fine looking birds, taken out of their baskets and some very long metal spurs attached to their legs. Squirrel and Fidget, who had experience of being spurred at large fences, were very much shocked at the length and sharpness of these weapons and said the birds would tear each other to pieces.

When the cocks were thrown into the ring we could

not see very clearly, for the excited spectators jumping up and down obscured our view. But we saw the cocks leap into the air and meet with savage fury. We heard their flapping wings. as they prepared for fresh attacks. We caught glimpses of them pecking fiercely at each other's heads, we saw the blood on their combs and wattles. We could tell how the battle went by the cheers or silence from our family and our stable boys, who supported Mr Tom's cock to a man.

The great flapping of wings grew weaker as the combat went on, but the excitement of the watchers became more feverish.

At first all seemed to be going the way of Mr Tom's bird and he and Mr Will were betting heavily on their victory, but then there came a change of fortune and the voices on our side began to swear and call on the cock to show some pluck.

Then suddenly there was silence and then, in the midst of the silence, came a triumphant crow and we knew that the fight was over. The winning cock was taken up by his owner and carried away to his basket. Our bird lay on the ground until Master Harry picked him up and asked if he might not be revived with brandy.

'No, dead as a doornail,' said Mr Tom. 'Give him here,

I'd better save the spurs.' And, having unfastened them, he took the poor bird by the legs and flung him up on the dungheap.

'I'll get myself a better one, with more bottom to him,' he told Master Harry and then called to his friends to come up to the house and try the strong beer.

My second summer came. Ringleader and I were yearlings now and growing fast. He was a beautiful gold chestnut, I a sober, shining black with one white sock. We were no longer biddable foals and we would play up Bob and Dick, rearing and bucking, trying to break away from them as they led us in and out of the stable.

The Squire and Mr Buckle had a conference and decided that we had better be made obedient to man's will and accustomed to wearing saddles and bridles before we grew any stronger or more unruly.

After that Stephen, the second man, took us in charge and we were made to go round on the lunge rein, to wear saddles and bridles and taken to the forge to have our feet trimmed. We were also put in separate stables and every day we were tied up and made to submit to a thorough grooming.

I did not care for all this discipline, but most of all I hated the bridle, the feel of straps over my head and a bit in my mouth, was a great source of irritation. And, when we were led out in our bridles, the boys had far greater control over us and we were forced to walk soberly, without horseplay.

Looking back now I see that the Squire was right. If a horse has to submit to the commands of man it is better to teach him to do so early rather than to wait until he is a strong and rebellious horse, accustomed to liberty and with a will of his own.

Mr Tom was the focus of all events that summer, for it was his coming of age. He was not universally popular with Squire Lovelace's people for he showed little consideration to those beneath him. His orders were not given with politeness and they were often followed with, 'and look sharp about it,' which annoyed the older men, while his habit of forcing his attentions on laundry maids and dairy maids caused frequent uproars. But most of all it was his constant need to be best at everything that was disliked. A man had only to say that his horse could trot so many miles an hour for Mr Tom to cry out that he had one to beat that easily and suggest a match. He would bet on how many miles he could run, how many bottles of wine he could drink, before falling in a stupor under the table, and one day, on how many swallows on the wing he would shoot in half an hour. I think his friend, another university man who was staying in the house, felt certain of winning this one for Mr Tom finally agreed to shoot twenty in as many minutes.

But fetching his guns and Mr Will to act as loader, he stationed himself by the barn and shot the poor birds as they flew in to feed their young in the beautiful little nests under the eaves.

The friend lost his money, the birds lost their lives and the fledglings must have starved to death, but Mr Tom went off very pleased with himself at this clever idea.

The coming of age was a great occasion with the quality entertained to an elegant ball in the house one day and the tenants and work people and all the poor from the villages for miles around, invited to a great feast in the park the next. A whole ox was roasted on a huge fire and great quantities of ale were drunk.

We horses heard the proceedings very plainly, but we saw little save the glow in the sky, for we had all been taken out of our stables and put in farm buildings and barns for the night. Our stables were bedded with fresh straw and given over to those who were too drunk to make their way home, of which there were a great number.

Next morning we heard nothing but groans and complaints and the yard was full of people waiting to put their aching heads under the pump. Our stable folk were among the sufferers and it was several days before life returned to normal.

Soon after this our early education was considered complete and Ringleader and I were turned out in a great meadow that took in two sides of a valley as well as a copse. Here we were reunited with the colts we had known as foals and joined a number of hunter geldings turned out to rest.

CHAPTER THREE

A racer's life

The spring that I was two years old I was separated from my friend Ringleader, which was a great blow to me, but it was on Squire Lovelace's orders.

He came round the stable one morning, with Mr Buckle as usual in anxious attendance, and, looking at Ringleader said that he would grow into a valuable hunter by and by and had better be turned away for another year. But that Nightshade, being destined for the race course, had better be sent over to Clinton Lacey to commence his training with Simpson; it having become common practice of late to race two- and three-year-olds.

I could see that Mr Buckle did not like this overmuch, but he did not dare argue with the Squire; he mentioned one or two horses who'd raced very young, but whose successes had been short-lived.

'There may be truth in what you say,' admitted the Squire, 'but it suits my plans to have a good horse on the turf as soon as possible. I need some return on the enormous sums these animals are costing me and I count on Nightshade here to provide it.'

Clinton Lacey was a matter of ten or twelve miles from Thorngate Manor, but the countryside was very different. The village was in a hollow below a high, bare down, growing nothing but the short, sweet grass so beloved of sheep. Their baa, the bark of dogs and the whistles of shepherds were the sounds that filled the air.

The house was a comfortable sort of farm house which

had been given over to Mr Tom as a hunting box. It was considered good enough for him in his bachelor state, but the Squire was said to have great plans for turning it into a gentleman's residence should he decide to marry.

The racers, of whom there were upwards of half a dozen, were kept at some distance from the house in a new-built stable block and I soon found that we were kept very much apart, our large comfortable loose-boxes being entirely cut off from each other, to avoid the spread of coughs and other distempers.

Simpson, the Squire's training groom, was a thin man with a limp, blackened teeth and a crooked nose from being thrown in various accidents. He had a very quick temper, not that he vented it on the horses. It was kept for the poor stable boys and he would lash out at them with a whip for the most minor of faults.

I was given a little lad called Andrew. He was some years older than he looked, being about twelve, he thought. But lack of proper food had made him small and stunted, though with a rather wizened and careworn face. He was fair with blue eyes and, being very timid, lived in mortal terror of Mr Simpson. I was the only horse in Andrew's care, but he was expected to groom me to perfection and his lack of strength and stature made it hard work for him.

I found my new life, shut up in a loose-box on my own, very hard to bear. The four walls quickly became a prison to me and I fretted for my lost freedom and companions. The door of my stable was always kept shut and the window was set too high for me to see out, so there I lived in solitary silence and, after being my own master in the meadows at Thorngate Manor, I found it very terrible.

I made a friend of Andrew and would listen hopefully for his coming as the long hours dragged by. He understood horses and would talk to me as he groomed. 'Mr Simpson's in a rare old mood,' he would tell me or, 'Two of the boys 'ad a turn up and Christopher's nose won't stop bleeding though they've 'ad 'im under the pump these ten minutes.'

After a few days of being driven round on the lunge and led out in a saddle and bridle, Mr Simpson decided that I was ready to be backed and Andrew was legged up into my saddle. He weighed nothing, but it seemed very extraordinary to have him perched up there and I felt I must move with extreme care lest he should come tumbling down. But having seen so much riding and driving going on, I thought it quite the usual thing and was not terrified as wild horses are, so I raised not the slightest objection and very soon the feeling of strangeness passed off.

After that my education went on apace. I was taught to turn and stop and set off again at signals from Andrew's reins and legs and, when I understood them, we went on to trotting. Soon Mr Simpson, who was always there overlooking the proceedings and would shout furiously at Andrew, damning him for this and that if he made the least wrong move, decided that I was ready to go out with the general string of horses.

This made a great improvement in my life for I now had company for some two hours a day. At first I was so excited by the sight of the other horses that I almost tipped Andrew off with my prancing about, but recollected myself just in time. When he was back in the saddle and Mr Simpson had ceased his shouting and swearing, I was allotted fifth place in the string and we set off up a miry lane to the Down. Mr Simpson led the way on an old grey nag, followed by a full grown stallion and two three-year-old colts and behind me came a couple of very pretty fillies and a boy on a pony.

I found carrying Andrew up the long hill to the Down very hard work and I was glad when I reached the soft turf of the training area, that no galloping was required of me. I and the younger of the two fillies were walked about while the other horses galloped and Mr Simpson cursed and roared.

Andrew told me that one of the colts was half brother to me. He was a beautiful bay like our dam and I felt very proud when I saw his fine carriage and his turn of speed.

I settled down to my new life fairly well after this and, after I had been ridden up and down to the Down for a few weeks, Mr Simpson said I had to start my training proper and, to this end, I was physicked. The forcing of a ball of evil-smelling medicine down my throat with a long stick was bad enough, but the next day I developed terrible pains in my stomach. Andrew was sorry for me, but he said that it was for my own good and the physic would drive out all the bad blood and humours from my system. After a day or two's ill health I recovered, but I cannot say, in all honesty, that the medicine did me the smallest good.

Now I began to be fed on a rich diet of rye bread and split beans as well as oats and cut grass and carrots and I joined the older horses in their gallops. I enjoyed carrying Andrew and sharing the feeling of speed. I enjoyed the wind in my mane and the soft turf beneath my hoofs and the feeling of strength and power that grew in me as I became fit.

One day the Squire came to see us gallop. Mr Simpson

paraded us with pride, pointing out our glossy coats and hard muscles, and then we were lined up.

We set off steadily and at first Andrew held me in behind the other horses. My brother, Bravado, was the leader and we thudded across the Down in a close-knit bunch.

There were whitewashed stones to mark the furlongs and, at the third, Andrew began to ride me on. The other horses quickened too and we began to race, all delighting in the feel of speed. Then Andrew urged me on again. I lengthened my stride and suddenly I was amazing myself with the speed at which I could travel; I seemed to be flying. I flew past my stable companions one by one. I galloped neck and neck, stride for stride with my brother. Then, at Andrew's urging, I drew away and suddenly I was alone, out in front; the winner.

We pulled up at the appointed place and turned back. The Squire was full of excitement, his red face glowing with triumph. He dismounted and hurried to slap me on the neck and praise Andrew. Then he began to talk about the horses I might be matched with.

'He'll beat any horse in these parts,' he told Mr Simpson, 'and the best of it is we'll take them by surprise. You must bid the boys keep quiet upon pain of dismissal. I'll plunge heavily and win a fortune on his first appearance. You must put him into full training at once, Simpson. He's too fat; you sweat him well and he'll beat any horse in the kingdom.

'Bella's colt! I knew Highflyer would be right for her. We'll put him in next year's Derby; how should you like that, Simpson? To train a Derby winner, eh?'

'You don't think we should keep him for the Derby, Squire?' asked Mr Simpson. 'A dash race like that is far less strain on a young horse than the old system of heats. It would be a shocking pity to knock him up by asking too much of him.'

'Oh damn you for an old cosset,' said the Squire. 'Look, I'll tell you plain, I can't afford to go on laying out money with no return. With Mr Tom's debts on top of my own, I'm in no position to wait. Nightshade must win me a packet, and quickly.'

From that day I was exercised all wrapped up in horse clothes and a hood. I did not enjoy my sweating sessions overmuch and at first I looked very askance at the exotic food I was being offered. The best oats were dressed with beaten eggs, a dozen at a time, Andrew told me, and ale, and I was given drinks of barley water flavoured with syrup of lemons and syrup of violets. While every day at noon my legs were rubbed with oil.

It seemed that Andrew was not to ride me in my race.

The Squire had decided that he dare not risk his money with a greenhorn in the saddle and had engaged an experienced boy, called Sam Tilney, who had many races to his credit, and he would come and ride me in a trial gallop.

Andrew was very disappointed at this, but when the day for the trial came he was mounted on a pony and came to watch, while I carried Sam. Sam was taller than Andrew, but being dreadfully thin, weighed much the same. He had a dark, gipsy-looking face and no front teeth, which made him talk with a lisp. He was very much a man of the world and was soon setting our boys right about all matters to do with the turf.

It seemed that I was entered for a plate for two- and three-year-olds at Newbury. The prize was only fifty pounds but Mr Lovelace was known to have made several large wagers with other gentlemen, notably the owner of the favourite, a grey called Pegasus.

Sam was a more forceful rider than Andrew. He was always pushing me on or holding me back or thrusting me through a small space between Lady Jane and Bravado and he seemed to be up to all sorts of tricks like making a great noise with his whip to put them off their stride. Not that we needed tricks, for I just galloped away and left them standing.

The Squire and Mr Simpson seemed well-pleased with this trial and it was settled that Andrew should lead me over to Sir Peter Cardew's stable, where I would stay overnight, and then walk me to the course next morning. Andrew was given very strict instructions by the Squire. He was to sleep in my box and let no one come near me lest they tried to ruin my hopes with a nail in the foot or a last minute bucket of water.

'And don't go bragging about his chances,' finished the Squire. 'Keep your mouth shut and if anyone questions you play the clodhopper. If all goes well you shall have a handsome present.'

CHAPTER FOUR

Triumph and disaster

I enjoyed the walk to Knighton Park. We set off early in the morning when all was fresh and dewy and made our way through lanes and byroads with one stretch along a turnpike, for which Andrew had to pay one penny at the tollgate. He said it was for me as pedestrians paid no dues.

At Knighton I was kept very much to myself and being a young, untried horse did not cause much of a stir. Mr Simpson sent my food over in a little cart so that I should have no change of diet. On the morning of the race Andrew gave me toast soaked in wine, which was supposed to give great energy. 'Most boys drink the wine themselves,' he told me, 'but I 'aven't, not one drop.'

It was late in the morning when we set out for the course and when we reached it I was amazed to see all the people and bustle. There were a great many booths and little tents erected everywhere; gipsies told fortunes, strong ale was sold and many other things.

A large number of gentlemen and farmers were there on horseback, careering all over the course, the ladies were mainly seated in carriages that were placed in a row along the rails to give a good view.

Andrew asked for the rubbing house and when we came to it we found Mr Simpson and Sam waiting for us. Then Andrew got to rubbing my legs with oil and Mr Simpson offered me more toast soaked in wine, while Sam took my saddle and went to be weighed in on the scales by the rubbing house.

I looked with interest at all the activity. The great crowd of gentlemen, in their round black hats and frock coats, clustered round the betting post, the quieter ladies with their long dresses billowing out around them and their wide-brimmed hats.

The Squire came to watch me saddled and Sam, very elegantly dressed in a red and white striped silk jacket, breeches, boots and a velvet jockey cap, was legged up. Mr Lovelace's face was a deep red, his talk louder and his oaths more frequent than usual. Though he had told Andrew not to brag of my chances he never ceased from doing so and all his friends were called over to inspect me.

Many of the gentlemen were in an even greater state of drink and excitement and thieves were picking pockets in the most open way, the crowd seeming to view it as the most normal thing and doing nothing to stop it.

Sam cantered me down to the start alongside Pegasus who was still favourite to win. The starter, a portly man in breeches, frock coat and a high-crowned narrow-brimmed hat, came forward carrying a flag. He spoke severely to the jockeys about lining up correctly and not trying to break away before the others.

Ignoring the great crowd of horsemen pressing round us, I watched the flag with Sam and when it fell I leaped forward and there was no need for the sharp jab with the spurs he gave me.

Two miles is a long way and Sam did not want to make the running so he tucked me in behind the favourite and we stayed there easily enough.

At the mile post Pegasus began to quicken and Black Tommy and I quickened with him, but the other two, Merryman and Defiance, had shot their bolts and fell back out of sight.

I stayed with the leaders very easily and when Sam began to make a lot of noise with his whip on his boot, I drew alongside Pegasus, leaving Black Tommy behind. As we came to the carriage stand the two of us raced neck and neck and the roar from the crowd was immense. When Sam urged me on I swept by Pegasus and raced on alone, proud of my easy stride and the speed that put lengths between us.

As Sam pulled me up I felt a hero. Many people cheered as we walked back to the rubbing house, though some were too busy cursing the loss of their money.

I was soon surrounded by my own people who seemed delighted by my success and as Sam went off to be weighed again, Andrew got busy, scraping the sweat from me with his old piece of sword blade and then rubbing me with a cloth.

I was munching wine and toast when the Squire came over, so cock-a-hoop that one would have thought he'd run the race himself. Then the wagering began again and Andrew told me proudly that I was now favourite. After about fifteen minutes I was saddled and I realised that I was expected to go through the whole performance again.

Down to the start we went and though I did not feel quite the same enthusiasm for the race, I did not think that any of the other horses could beat me.

This time I jumped off smartly to avoid a jab from Sam's spurs. Black Tommy took the lead and Pegasus followed right on my heels, which I did not like at all, while Defiance and Merryman pressed close on either side of me and in this way we proceeded steadily for the first mile. Then the other jockeys all seemed intent on putting me off, they all banged their boots and crowded in on me. But Sam held me very steady for another half mile and then he began to ride me. I was still game and responded willingly enough, lengthening my stride, I burst out of the knot of horses and raced away. Not one of them could keep with me. The crowd roared with pleasure and I passed the post two lengths ahead of Defiance, who came second.

The effort had been considerable and my head was not so high, nor my step so proud as I walked back to the rubbing house for the second time. But my people were even more jubilant as all the weighing and scraping and rubbing down was gone through again.

I thought that having won twice should be proof enough of my superiority, but I soon learned that I had to run *yet* again.

'Win once more Nightshade and you'll be the clear leader and won't 'ave to run again a fourth time,' Andrew told me as he walked me up and down to prevent me stiffening after all my exertions. But I didn't feel like running again. Four miles is a long way for a mere two-year-old, which cannot have the stamina of an adult horse, and I felt tired out and saw the possibility of defeat.

Mr Simpson saw it too. I heard him advising the Squire to hedge his bets as he was afraid that I might not pull it off for a third time, but the Squire would have none of it. Purple-faced and reckless, he shook Simpson off angrily, 'The other animals are just as done up. Take a look at Defiance, if I ever saw a horse cooked it is him.'

Wearily I cantered down to the start, without enough energy left to study the condition of my rivals. I resolved to do my best, but if that did not win me the race I was not going to care. I had proved myself the fastest horse and

this running again and again seemed senseless cruelty to
me.

We all started slowly. We galloped, but not near so fast
as previously. The way seemed very long and my breath
grew short before the first mile was done. As we went
into the second mile it seemed to be Sam who was
holding me together. I could feel myself rolling and
lurching, my breath came and went in painful gasps and
the green track ahead seemed to stretch on for ever and
ever. Another panting, grunting horse came alongside
me, and we seemed to be almost leaning on one another
for support as we staggered on and on. Winning or losing
meant nothing to me now; I just kept going. Sam was
sawing on my snaffle, spurring my sides. Then he began
to lash me with the whip, burning, red-hot cuts on my

heaving sides. I made one last effort to escape from the pain. Then it was over. We pulled up.

Head down, panting for breath, I stumbled back to the rubbing house too exhausted to care for cheers. I was still trying to get my breath as Andrew began to scrape and rub.

'You won, you beat the favourite. Well done, Old Nightshade,' he was telling me.

Interested bystanders and sporting men came to inspect me. 'What a turn of speed!' they said. 'What bottom for a youngster!' Only one man looked sadly at my hanging head and mangled sides and spoke angrily against the butchery of heats; wishing that they might be abolished in favour of dash races, for the sake of the horses.

As I recovered from my exhaustion I became more and more conscious of my spurred and lashed sides. I walked back to Knighton in a very dejected state and not at all pleased with my triumph.

Mr Simpson beat up eggs and ale into a drink and poured it down my throat through a cow's horn, Andrew brought me a warm mash and bathed my torn sides, my straw bed was made thicker than ever. But none of this attention could make up for what I had been through and it was several days before I regained my spirits.

Back at Clinton Lacey we fell into the old routine and it was some time before the date of my next race was decided. Andrew told me that Mr Simpson constantly pleaded for its postponement as he felt another severe trial so soon would destroy me, but the Squire, who cared for nothing but the restoration of his fortune, insisted that I ran at Hungerford Races.

328

This time I started favourite, for my fame had spread. But, knowing what lay ahead I husbanded my strength, winning each heat by the narrowest of margins.

The day ended with the Squire triumphant and drunk, his face purple, his wig askew, while I was spent and exhausted and in much pain from Sam's reckless use of spurs and whip.

So my life went on. The Squire, regarding me as invincible, backed me heavily every time I ran and it was soon being said that I had earned him some forty or fifty thousand pounds.

Fortunately Simpson managed to convince him that the modern dash race would preserve my strength longer and Andrew and I walked many miles through the countryside that summer to reach the courses where they were held. Those walks were very pleasant to me for I enjoyed the new surroundings and the escape from my hot, solitary stable.

When winter came I rested quietly, but great events were taking place in the outside world. The French people, who had been in the throes of a revolution for some time, cut off their King's head and declared war on England, but, though it was said that both prices and taxes had risen alarmingly, things seemed to go on much as usual at Clinton Lacey.

In the spring I reached three years of age. Mr Simpson wanted to give me one or two dash races before the Derby, but the Squire, who was running short of money again, had other plans.

It seemed that I had become altogether too well-known and people did not want to match their horses or lay bets against me. There had been talk of a brilliant three-year-old from one of the midland shires and a four-year-old from Oxford, but their owners were not prepared to take the Squire's vast wagers at even weights. They demanded that I should be heavily handicapped and, much against Mr Simpson's advice, the Squire agreed.

I never care to remember that day. My heart sank from the moment I was saddled and Sam legged up, for I felt the weight of the extra lead that I was to carry in my weightcloth. I knew at once that I had been given a very severe penalty and the wet state of the ground made the extra weight even more of a burden.

I won the first heat, but only with great labour. I carried off the second heat too, but only by a nose and I was totally exhausted by this hard fought battle with the Oxford horse – Baytree – who was a year older and carried no dead weight at all.

When the half hour of scraping and rubbing was over, I could scarce drag myself down to the start of the third heat and then, try as I would, and despite all Sam's spurring and lashing, I just could not draw ahead of

Baytree. We battled together the whole way up the course, we fought for every inch and, at the end the weight told and he just managed to get his nose in front.

I had won two heats and been second once, Baytree had won once and been second twice. Gold Dust was out of it, but if Baytree won the final heat and I was second it would be a draw. If he won and I was only third he would win the match.

The Squire came over half drunk and in a very ugly mood. He cursed Mr Simpson for not having me fit and then he turned on Sam and said if he did not win next time he would never employ him again.

'I'll do my utmost, sir, but the weight is telling on the horse,' Sam answered respectfully.

'Damn the weight,' roared the Squire. 'I've wagered a fortune on this race. You get that horse first past the post. I don't care if it kills him, you're to win, boy. D'ye hear me?'

'Yes, sir,' said Sam, 'I'll do my utmost.'

He did. When we came to the last mile I began to fail. I was grunting for breath and rolling in my stride, but I suppose the other two were in much the same state, for they did not pass me, though Baytree seemed constantly alongside.

With five furlongs to go I could no longer see. My breath came in hard, unbearably painful gasps, my legs were scarcely under my control, but the cruel spurs and whip forced me on and on. I think I was slowed to a stumbling trot when I passed the post and when the whip and spurs stopped I staggered and fell.

For a time I hardly knew what went on around me, but gradually the mist over my eyes cleared and I found

Andrew stroking my neck and Mr Simpson calling for wine or ale.

I cared nothing for the crowd pressing round me, all telling each other that I was done for and advising Mr Simpson that it would be a waste of good wine to pour it down my throat. I just lay there in a state of exhaustion, unable to move.

Then I heard the Squire's voice, 'Is he done for, Simpson? Well, small matter, he's more than paid for his keep. If you do get him on his feet, sell him for whatever you can get. I doubt if he'll make a full recovery.'

I could feel Andrew's tears falling on my cheek and as I moved my head a little to escape them he called to Mr Simpson, ''E moved. There's life in 'im yet.'

'Can you lift his head? Some of this might revive him.' I was quite indifferent as to whether I lived or died, but Andrew and some of the bystanders heaved me into a position from which they could raise my head and pour wine down my throat. Then they let me lie again and I could hear talk of sending for the knacker's cart.

But, gradually the wine did revive me. I stirred and found I could raise my head and look about me. And then, after about ten minutes, I felt able to get to my feet.

Andrew, seemingly overjoyed, put on my horse cloth and led me slowly to Knighton.

'What will the Squire do when 'e finds you 'aven't sold Nightshade?' he asked Simpson fearfully as they fed me that evening.

'He won't remember, men don't when they are three-parts drunk as he was. He'll never say a word if the horse recovers. I'll only hear about it if he lingers on an old crock, but he won't remember.'

Andrew nursed me back to health, but there was now

no hope of my running in the Derby and indeed it seemed as though all my old fire and spirit had gone. I would walk up to the Down with the rest of the string, but when they wanted me to gallop with the other horses I became very nervous. Sweat would pour off me as I ran backwards and refused to start. Andrew did his best to calm me, but it was no use; I could no longer bear the thought of running in a race.

'He's turned sour,' said Mr Simpson, 'I knew it would happen. All we can do is take him steady and hope he comes right in the end. I'll talk to the Squire.'

I suppose the Squire thought he knew better, for I found myself in training again and suffered the indignity of being chased by boys with great branches of furze or gorse when I ran backwards and refused to start.

I gave up this fight mainly to oblige Andrew, but though I consented to canter gently with the other horses I had made a firm resolve that I would never try to win a race again.

Mr Simpson could see I had changed, but when the Squire came to watch he said that the fault lay with Andrew, who wasn't man enough to put me straight, but with Sam in the saddle I'd stop all that nonsense and show my old form.

When the day came to set off for the next race meeting both Andrew and I were in very low spirits. We knew what sort of man the Squire was now: he would kill me in order to win, but as his anger at losing would be uncontrollable, the outcome was bound to be unhappy.

When we reached the course, when I saw the booths and tents, the white rails and the people, I began to sweat and shake with anxiety. Andrew tried to calm me with stroking and soothing words, but it was no use. The

333

dreadful memories of my last race kept flooding back and filling me with a terrible agitation.

Mr Simpson took one look at me and went off to tell the Squire that he must hedge his bets before my state was generally noticed.

Sam's face also became glum at the sight of me.

'Try to use him gently,' said Mr Simpson, legging Sam up, but I knew that I was not going to trust myself to him again. I was not going to race and I did not care what they did to me, it could not be any worse than the treatment I had gained by trying to win.

I went down to the start lathered with sweat and in a great state of turmoil. I began to lash out as we lined up, confusing the other horses with my display of anger. The starter shouted at Sam to control me, but I had no intention of being controlled and when the flag fell I was facing in the wrong direction, kicking and plunging as I had never done in my life before. When Sam dug in his spurs and began to lash me with his whip I became almost unrideable. I flung myself backwards like a mad thing, I reared, I plunged, I kicked and bucked. I no longer cared for the safety of my rider and, when he persisted in his attempts to make me join the race, I redoubled my violence until at last I threw him off. Then, still half crazed by painful memories, I fled into the crowd. Eventually I found Andrew and let myself be caught. I was disqualified, disgraced.

The Squire came purple-faced, almost bursting with rage.

'Pole-axe him, knock him on the head,' he roared at Simpson. 'He's cost me thousands, the damned, sour faint-hearted screw. He can have his eyes put out and turn a mill-wheel, that's all he's fit for. Get him out of my sight, he'll not even do for stud now he's disgraced himself.'

Andrew hurried me away and, acting on the assumption that the Squire was three-parts drunk, Mr Simpson didn't have me pole-axed, but told Andrew that he might ride me home.

CHAPTER FIVE

A gentleman of the road

I never knew what took place between the Squire and Mr Simpson. But it soon became plain that my career as a racer was over. The Squire's revenge was limited to having me gelded. I suppose he thought that I had not bottom enough to father future racehorses. Then I was turned out in the familiar valley meadow at Thorngate Manor with a collection of untried colts and lame hunters for companions.

I was more neglected than I had ever been in my life. There was grass in summer, hay in winter. A stream for water, a copse for shelter, but as for oats and beans, eggs and ale, toast soaked in wine, I never saw them. I was unkempt and ungroomed, but wonderfully happy.

As the weeks stretched into months and the months into a year I began to feel that I had been forgotten. But one day as summer ended, when autumn mists hung over the valley and little children came with baskets and pails to pick the mushrooms that had suddenly sprung up everywhere, I saw Dick, quite a man now, coming across the meadow and he was calling my name.

In the stable Mr Buckle sighed over the white hairs that had grown where the spurs wounded my sides and told his boys to get to work on me. In no time I had a short tail, a trimmed mane an almost clean coat and a set of shoes.

Life was different now. After the horrible process of physicking had been gone through I started exercise, walking and trotting round the lanes with a string of hunters. I had become an ordinary horse, living in a stall and treated just like the others. I missed my loose-box at night, for I could no longer lie down and stretch out, but the pleasure of having the other horses all round me made up for this.

I was not looking forward to my career as a hunter for the Squire and Mr Tom were known as hard riders who cared little for their mounts. Only Mr Will, it was said, spared a thought for the horse that carried him. But then something occurred to change my life.

The Squire came home from Scotland in a high good humour having shot more birds than any of the other gentlemen in his party, but this mood vanished when Mr Tom returned from foreign parts and confessed to having run up gaming debts of a considerable sum. The uproar over this had scarcely died away when a young man calling himself James or Jem Lovelace appeared at the house.

There was great excitement in the stable over this visitation for the young man was known to be a bastard son of the Squire's – it was said he had six or seven – who had come to claim relationship and assistance.

He was a pleasant well-dressed young man and his likeness to Mr Will struck Mrs Lovelace and the young ladies so forcibly, that they pleaded for him to be allowed to stay the night at the house and not turned straight out into the storm as the Squire intended. The result was permission to sleep in the stable. He came in with us hunters, his face black as thunder at the reception he had received from the Squire, and, wrapping his cloak around him had flung himself down on a pile of straw in an empty stall.

But when all was quiet and our boys asleep in the loft above, Jem Lovelace rose up and began to prowl about the stable. He obtained a lantern and went from stall to stall closely inspecting us horses.

At length he seemed to decide on me and, to my amazement, I was saddled and bridled and cloths were bound round my feet. Then, with the utmost caution, I was led out and across the yard, the cloths muffling the ring of iron on cobblestones. Outside, by the barn, he mounted and, in the grey cold of first light, we cantered silently and swiftly up the back drive. Behind I heard the voices of my friends calling to me, but I left willingly enough. I felt that any master would be preferable to Squire Lovelace.

At the end of the drive Jem stopped to pull the cloths from my feet and then we rode on, but at a less rapid pace.

Dawn came; a wet, misty morning, and from the light coming behind me I knew that we were heading westward. My new owner seemed very pleased with himself and with me. Several times he patted my neck and then he said, 'Nightshade, by Highflyer out of Bella, quite an aristocrat and a very fine piece of horse flesh, if I may say so. What do *you* think of carrying a by-blow, a Lovelace bastard? Or don't such things concern even aristocratic horses?

'You are my Patrimony, Nightshade,' he went on after a pause. 'My Father flung me a guinea and said I might eat in the servants' hall, so I have stolen the fastest horse in his stable, a good saddle and bridle, a pair of pistols and set myself up in a business more to my taste than the apprenticeship he provided. I am too much of a Lovelace to be content with putting up a draper's shutters and sweeping his shop.

'I don't suppose you've heard of the Foundling Hospital, Nightshade, but that is where I was brought up. Neither parent having the least use for me, my Father paid ten guineas that I might not starve. Ten guineas! How does that compare with what he has spent on the education and pleasures of my proud brother Tom? But never mind that, I begin to feel more equal now that I am mounted on a fine horse. And we must go to work for I have nothing but the Squire's guinea, having spent every penny I possessed on fine clothes to impress my family.'

By noon we'd left our tame and cultivated country with its frequent villages, its rectories, farms, manors and halls and entered a wilder, bleaker county. Windswept hills and downs stretched away on either side of us and the turnpike-road lay ahead. My master rode along singing cheerfully, showing no haste to begin the work he had spoken of, until he caught sight of a tollgate. Then he said, 'We had best save our penny,' and, riding me through a weak half-grown hedge, took to the fields.

Some way on, well out of sight of the pikeman, we regained the turnpike and found ourselves approaching a small market town.

'A two hour bait for you, Shady and a good dinner for me,' said Jem as we clattered into the innyard. He called for the ostler, in a very confident and gentlemanlike way, and stayed to see me watered and fed before vanishing into the inn.

I was glad of the food, but did not get much rest owing to the great noise and constant comings and goings. The clatter of hoofs, the harsh rattle of the iron tyres of the carts on the cobblestones, never stopped for a moment and the voices of men calling for ostlers and ostlers calling for stable boys were near as bad, while the cries of the traders selling their wares in the market place added to the general turmoil.

When I complained of the uproar to a stout chestnut horse in the next stall, he looked at me in surprise, 'O 'tis nothing,' he said. 'You want to come on fair day, then 'tis bursting over and you can't get in nor out of yard for carts.'

Later, when my master called for me, a new saddlebag was strapped to my saddle and when we had made our way down the main street, which was as crowded as any race course, and out into the open country beyond, he began to talk. 'I laid out the rest of my money in town, Shady. I am equipped with powder, ball and the means for casting more. My father's pocket pistols shall earn us a good living.'

I was glad to hear that the pistols were to earn our living and went on happily enough, enjoying the new scenery that constantly unfolded before my eyes and listening to my master's songs, which he sang very cheerfully, considering they were all about being crossed in love or dying young.

We saw few people for this was grazing country and great numbers of workers were not needed, just cowmen and drovers for the cattle. No great armies of people to plough and sow and harvest. The hamlets we passed through were very poor places. One-storied hovels, built of mud and straw, housed the people. The doors stood open to the road, for there were no chimneys to let the smoke out, and the window was frequently covered with paper or rags for want of glass. The difference between these one-roomed cottages and elegant houses like Thorngate Manor struck me very forcibly and I could see that the Squire's horses had been better fed, housed and

clothed than the ragged families who came to their doors
to watch us ride by.

My new master seemed to know where he was going.
Once he asked for directions from an elderly crone
gathering cresses from a stream and once from some
ragged children picking up 'sticks, to whom he threw a
penny. We rode down green lanes and across fields and
then, on the crest of a hill he halted and exclaimed, 'The
Bath road, Nightshade. That is where we commence
our business.'

The road was still some distance away, across a stretch
of grass, and Jem suddenly urged me into a gallop. I was
quite happy to show my paces and I think he was amazed
by my speed and the way we covered the ground. When
we pulled up he patted me delightedly. 'You'll do excel-
lently, Shady,' he said. 'I'd defy anyone to catch me when
riding a horse of your speed. I foresee a very long and
profitable partnership between us. We will both live like
gentlemen for very little toil.'

I was surprised to find Jem a practised horseman and
wondered at the time how a foundling apprenticed to a
draper could have accomplished this, but later I learned
that the draper, being in business in a very big way, had
kept a stable of horses, mainly for deliveries, in which
Jem had started work as a stable boy.

When we reached the Bath road my master became
nervous and uncertain. He said we must find a suitable
spot, but this proved far from easy. One place was too
close to a house, from another he could see a church spire,
a third offered no hiding place. He had almost settled on a
hollow at the foot of a long hill, when he recollected that
most coachmen 'spring' their horses, that is whip them
into a gallop, at the foot of a hill so that the carriage is

taken half way up by the momentum, and this would not suit our purpose. We climbed to the top of the hill and Jem found a spot there that would do.

'Those coming up the hill will be blown and those coming the other way will be going slow and wondering whether to put on the drag,' he said, 'and there is that clump of trees for us to lurk in.'

We went into the trees and there he took out his pocket pistols and inspected them in turn. Then he waited, listening and watching the road with impatience.

We heard a rumbling, the sound of hoofs and bells and soon a covered wagon heavily laden with goods and drawn by six great horses came in sight. Rattling and clanking on its great broad wheels it passed slowly by. Behind it came two farm horses, clopping leisurely. A smocked carter sat sideways on one and there was a smell of new shoes about them. My master fidgeted and sighed. Then, as dusk was thickening, we heard the rattle of light wheels and the spanking trot of well-bred horses. In a moment my master tied a piece of black crepe round his face, his eyes seeing through two slits, drew a pistol and urged me forward into the road.

A handsome carriage drawn by four roan horses was slowing as it came to the downhill; a private carriage with two postilions in blue jackets and jockey caps riding the nearside horses.

'Stand!' shouted my master in a loud and commanding voice and riding into their path, he pointed his pistol at the leading postilion's head. He was a decrepit grey-haired old man and the other just a boy so they offered no resistance and came quickly to a halt. My master rode to the carriage door and pulled it open. The lady and gentleman inside were both middle-aged and agitated.

'Sir, Madam,' said Jem in very polite tones, 'I am sorry to inconvenience you but, being the natural son of a gentleman with no fortune of my own, I must extract contributions from those in happier circumstances. Your money, sir.'

'Money, yes, of course. Let me see . . .' The gentleman searched his pockets and held out a handful of coins. My master took the two golden guineas from among them and said, 'Your purse, if you please,' thrusting his pistol into the carriage to emphasise his words. The lady screamed and the gentleman began to scuffle hurriedly inside his coat and brought forth a small leather bag. Jem looked inside and seemed well satisfied. 'Thank you, sir,' he said. 'May I wish you a pleasant journey.' And, wheeling round, we took to the fields.

Safely away we stopped to count the coins. 'Eleven guineas, Shady! Eleven guineas. That is the beginning of our fortune, though I should have taken their watches too, but clean forgot in the excitement. Still, guineas are a good deal safer. Well, that is our work done for today. We'll go on towards Bath and find an inn.'

We put up at a small inn some distance from the highway. I found myself stalled between a bagman's pony and a doctor's horse that had lost a wheel off his gig and was waiting at the inn while the wheelwright carried out repairs.

The landlord's son, aged about ten years, was our groom. He brought me a large feed and an armful of choice hay, gazing at me all the while with great admiration. I don't think he had ever had a thoroughbred in his care before.

The bagman's pony, a hairy bay with a ewe neck and a hollow back, was a very talkative fellow and when I confessed that I had no notion of what a bagman did for a living, he soon explained. It seemed that many villages were beginning to have a shop for the first time. This saved the poorer sort of people from a long trudge into town every time they ran out of tea or some other grocery they could not produce for themselves. The bagman rode round these village shops taking their orders and collecting the debts on previous deliveries of goods which were sent by wagon or pack pony.

The bagman's pony said that it was a good life except that his master was a terrible rider, 'By my troth 'e'd be off an 'undred times a day if I didn't see after 'e. As for stumbling or starting I just daren't risk the like of it, 'e'd pitch straight over m' 'ead for sure.'

When my companions enquired as to the occupation of my master, I found myself saying that, as I had only been his for one day, I hardly knew as yet, but he seemed a very pleasant young fellow and might have private means.

As I lay down on my thick bed of bracken, I thought that my master's profession was going to involve me in many lies and deceptions and I wished, most heartily, that he had chosen some respectable occupation.

For the next few days we rode about the countryside, dining and sleeping at different inns, while my master seemed very taken up with observing the lie of the land and studying maps.

Then one day he told me that our money was running out and towards evening we set off purposefully and came at length to a highway which he said was the Exeter road.

By reading the milestones, we found a particular spot which was midway between two post houses, the inns where the stage coaches and the post-chaises changed their horses. It was a very lonely place, without a habitation in sight, and there was a thicket close to the road in which we took up our station. There Jem checked his pistols and put on his crepe mask.

We waited. The faint wintery sun sank behind a hill, the evening closed about us cold and damp; my master shivered.

Then we heard hoofs. A great number of hoofs and the rattle of several carriages. I waited ready to swoop out into the road, but the order never came.

'Outriders,' said Jem, as two grooms in green livery on matching chestnuts went by, and he cursed under his breath. Then came a very handsome chariot, also drawn by chestnuts and with postilions in green livery, then more liveried grooms. They were followed by several less outstanding carriages, carrying children and nurses, servants and boxes, while more grooms brought up the rear. We could see that it was a rich family moving from one estate to another or coming home from a visit.

'There were far too many of them for us to take on,' said Jem as the cavalcade passed out of sight.

It was not long before we heard a single set of hoofs coming along at a very brisk pace, as though anxious to reach home before dark.

As we burst out of our hiding place I saw that it was a very stout, hairy-legged grey, ridden by an oldish man, with a lady in a long cloak and a bonnet riding behind him pillion.

'Stand!' called my master. 'Stand, sir, or I fire,' and he waved his pistol aloft in a very threatening manner.

The man reined-in the horse, but the old woman shrieked at him to take no notice, but gallop on and she

was belabouring the horse's rump with the bag she carried.

'Strike the villain with your whip,' she cried. 'Ride him down, he'll not fire.'

But the man, I took him to be her groom, was grey faced with fright and dared not ride on. He shook his head, when Jem demanded money again, 'I've but a few pence,' he said through chattering teeth.

'Madam, your money,' said Jem pointing his pistol at the lady.

'You won't frighten me, that's never loaded,' she answered scornfully.

'If you try my patience much further, Madam, you

shall have proof that it is,' said my master in a cold voice. 'I will begin by putting a ball in your old horse,' and he clapped the muzzle of the pistol to the horse's head, which I felt very unfair. Let the humans rob each other as much as they like, I thought, but they should leave us horses out of their quarrels. So I backed away and resolved to rear up if he fired and make the ball go wide.

However the lady had been convinced by Jem's manner and was fumbling inside her cloak. She brought out a little bag on a string and handed it over with many scoldings and threats that she should see Jem hanged before long.

'Thank you, Madam,' he said bowing. As we galloped off I could hear her berating the poor old groom for his cowardice.

'Six guineas,' said Jem stopping to count them. 'And now I think we will move on, for that ferocious old woman will be back if she can find a few stout lads to help her.'

We rode westward. It was almost dark, but soon we heard a carriage and saw lights approaching. Jem stopped to put on his mask and draw his pistol, then we took up position in the middle of the road.

'Stand!' shouted my master very loud. 'Stand and deliver or I fire.'

The postilion, there was only one for it was but a pair of horses, tried to whip them into a gallop. My master fired a shot over his head and quickly drew his other pistol. The chaise window opened and a deep voice called, 'Pull up, postilion, we want no loss of life.'

'Your money, sirs,' said Jem looking into the carriage.

'I am afraid we have but little on us,' said the deep voice. 'We have met with so many accidents and delays on the road that we are almost penniless.' He rattled a few coins in his hand.

Jem ordered them both out and told them to stand by the carriage lamp. They were well, but soberly, dressed. City men by the look of them for they had white hands and faces and none of the ruddiness of country folk.

They turned out their pockets eagerly, demonstrating their emptiness in the most affable manner. Jem brandished his pistol and ordered them to take off their coats. They stripped off great coats and frock coats and waistcoats, the last most reluctantly for the night air was cold. Still finding no hidden money bags, Jem ordered them to take off their boots.

The sudden fall in their spirits told me that he had hit upon the hiding place, and, as the boots came off, a shower of guineas fell upon the ground.

'Hand them up,' ordered Jem and when he had been given some twenty-five he seemed satisfied and, apologising for the great inconvenience he had given them, we set off westward again.

He kept laughing to himself as we walked slowly along the dark road, hoping for the moon to rise. 'An excellent evening's work, Shady,' he told me. 'I'll never forget their faces when I hit upon the boots.'

CHAPTER SIX

'To be hanged like a dog'

For some weeks we went on in much the same manner. We kept on the move, never robbing two nights in the same spot and changing frequently between the Bath and Exeter roads so that the poor travellers might never know where to expect us.

As winter came on there were fewer travellers. Though the regular coaches, The Salisbury Diligence, The Green Dragon, The Expedition, went up and down our roads with great horn blowing as they went through the villages or approached the post houses, my master did not like to take them on single-handed. He said they all carried an armed guard as well as the coachman so it only wanted one stout-hearted passenger with a pistol for him to be outnumbered. Instead we took to preying on the farmers going home from market and, since they had frequently drunk away some of the proceeds of selling their cattle and corn, they were easy victims.

At the post inns we could sometimes gather information about the travellers staying overnight and several times we rose in the early morning and waylaid our fellow guests a few miles along the road. Again my master was cautious; *one* naval man, newly paid off and travelling home alone, he would attack, but *two*, travelling together, might keep their money.

'I want to live to be an old man, Shady, and to die in my bed,' he told me, 'so discretion shall be the better part.'

As the winter grew increasingly bitter, he decided that

we needed more permanent quarters and we made our way to the Cranborne Chase, a great forest on the borders of Hampshire and Dorset and there we found an isolated farm that took us in.

It seemed that this was a very desperate and lawless neighbourhood, which welcomed such a man as my master. I soon heard tell of the terrible bloody battles that took place when the poachers went after the deer, for Prince and Queenie, the two stout ponies that stood next to me, were used to carry home the carcases when the poachers had made their kills.

They had witnessed many ugly scenes and battles, for the gamekeepers and poachers would kill and maim each other without a thought, and they told me their stories on the long winter nights, when the wind moaned round our stable, the rain pelted down or the snow fell, thick and silent.

We were fairly comfortable inside. My master had procured me a horse cloth. It was a little faded and moth-eaten, but warm enough and as the farm boy slept in the stable with us, he had taken great trouble to stuff all the cracks and crevices with rags and make the place snug.

But outside many people lost their lives, for the cold was intense and we even heard of folk being frozen to death on their way home from market.

I was always happy enough if I had good food and company and there it was strange company. For sometimes at dawn the smugglers' ponies, carrying tea and lace and spirits that had come into the country without paying duty, would arrive and hide away in our stables until darkness enabled them to move on again with their packs and panniers of contraband goods. They had many stories of fights with the Excise men and though the smugglers themselves were often desperate men, the buyers of the contraband were most respectable people and the ponies said they left many a cask and package on squires' and parsons' doorsteps at dead of night.

It seemed that my master was keeping company with a very pretty milkmaid and had decided that during the cold weather one or two robberies a week should be sufficient to keep us. We continued to terrorise the folk going home from market, but as we took a different market each week, no sooner had one set of people decided to arm and organise themselves, than we had gone elsewhere.

At the first sign of spring my master became restless and irritable. As the days grew longer we would ride to Salisbury and watch the cockfighting or bull-baiting. The second was a very cruel sport, I thought, for the poor bull was fastened up by a chain and then the dogs were set upon him. As he could not run, he had to stand and fight and, with the dogs sinking their teeth into him in the most ferocious manner, he would toss or gore them with his horns.

I longed to tell them all to stop, for this was a fight purely got up for the pleasure of men, who watched in a great state of excitement and laid wagers on the result, which was frequently the death and maiming of several dogs as well as the death of the bull. I never saw bear-baiting, though a lot of it went on, but I was told it was much the same and very horrible to watch.

One day my master bought a fine new suit of clothes, which put him in a very good humour. Then he paid the carter to trim my mane and tail and give me a very thorough grooming, and, soon afterwards, we set out on our travels again.

I was sad to part with Prince and Queenie and the pretty milkmaid sobbed most pitifully to see us go.

As we rode through the countryside I was very much shocked to see the state of the animals that had wintered out on the commons belonging to the villages. Many of them were walking bags of bones and had evidently not seen oats or hay all through the bitter weather. Ponies, donkeys, cows and goats, it was pitiful to watch them searching for each new blade of grass as it came through, there being not a scrap left to eat on their bare pastures.

One day, when my master was drinking a mug of ale at the door of an inn, I talked to starved pony that had been put to pull a cart, despite his condition, and looked so feeble that it seemed to be the shafts that held him up. He explained that he belonged to a cottager who had but a very small amount of land on which he grew vegetables for his family, but had no room for hay or oats. His master had grazing rights on the common, but so had all the other village folk, and their great quantity of animals over-grazed it even in the summer, with the result that in a hard winter like the last, many animals died of starvation.

In one village we passed through there seemed to be more organisation and the whole common was given over to geese. A great flock of several hundreds honked and grazed and two or three very little boys and girls were minding them.

Yet another common was newly fenced and my master enquiring about it was told that the villagers had sold their rights to a rich farmer under the enclosure laws. But now, having spent the money, they deeply regretted what they had done for they had nowhere to graze their cows and when they sold them, no milk for their children. Added to this they had lost the right to cut furze for their fires and now many cottages were without fires for days on end and those that had them would be boiling their neighbours' kettles as well as their own.

As spring came on with balmy air and flowers and blossom everywhere, my master talked to me about his plans. He had heard that there was talk of setting up a special patrol to capture him and earn the forty pounds paid to thief takers, so he had decided to leave our old neighbourhood and move across to the Southampton road.

We kept on the move all that summer and robbed a great many travellers. Though I had grown accustomed to sleeping in a different stall every night, I often felt the want of a regular stable and some of the ostlers were careless, some rough in their grooming and others dishonest. If my master did not stay to see me fed, it was quite likely that I would get nothing but hay, my feed of oats being spirited away in a sack to be sold or fed to the ostlers' own goat or poultry.

When winter came we returned to the Cranborne Chase. There I enjoyed the company of Prince and Queenie and the local farmers, coming home from market with their hard-earned guineas, were again at the mercy of my master.

It was sometime during this winter that Jem Lovelace took up with another highwayman called Edmund Evershaw. Evershaw had been robbing coaches on the Norwich road and then moved to Hounslow Heath and now being wanted for the murder of a guard, he had come to lie low in the Chase.

His previous horse having gone lame on the journey, he had turned her loose on a common and stolen a good chestnut hunter, called Harkaway, who was now stabled next to me.

I did not like Evershaw. He had a hard, cruel face, deeply pitted with smallpox, and he cared nothing for Harkaway except as a means of conveyance. I also feared his influence on my master, who was younger and had seen less of the world.

Of course it was understood that with two of them, they could take on greater numbers and more reckless endeavours and Harkaway and I soon began to feel a great dislike for the night's work.

Evershaw had a double barrelled pistol of which he was very proud and he would fire it in the wildest manner. On one occasion the ball went through the window of the carriage, narrowly missing the people inside and causing an elderly lady to faint, and all this after they had pulled up and were handing over their valuables.

Another night we robbed two clerical gentlemen coming up from the cathedral at Exeter and Evershaw swore most horribly at them when they failed to hand over as many guineas as he expected. Having had almost all their clothes off, he seemed inclined to kill them out of spite, when he found that they were speaking the truth and had no more money hidden. If my master had not been there to drag him away, I am convinced there would have been bloodshed.

And once he was very cruel to a lady who could not remove the ring from her finger. He threatened to take the finger too, if she did not hurry up and actually got out his knife.

Then, as summer came on, the rogue somehow heard of a mail coach that would be carrying vast numbers of bill notes from a bank. He knew that there would be a guard travelling with it and perhaps two, both armed, so he persuaded my master that another highwayman should be asked to join them.

When we set out for the scene of the robbery, it was to take place somewhere near Andover, a loutish youth, called Billy Hind, came with us. He was a great bragger and before we had gone many miles we were all heartily tired of hearing how much his pistols had cost him and how fast his lumbering gelding could trot.

After some disagreement, they settled on a suitable spot and my master checked his pistols and put on his mask. Evershaw never wore a mask. I suppose he thought his ill-favoured countenance almost as good a weapon as his pistol.

Poor Harkaway was very nervous and kept sighing and wishing that he could return to his life as a hunter, while Billy boasted in a loud voice how many pints of ale he could drink at a sitting.

We waited and the drizzle which was falling, thickened into rain. The men swore and turned up their coat collars; we horses bowed our heads and tried to put our tails to the wind.

At last we heard the coach, the four horses trotting briskly. It wasn't dark, just wet and dismal, and, as we burst into the road with our masters shouting 'Stand! Stand and deliver!' we could be seen quite plainly.

Evershaw, who always carried at least three loaded pistols, fired off one of them, the ball passing dangerously close to the coachman. The guard fired in return and Billy Hind cried out and dropped his reins. My master closed with the guard, demanding his blunderbuss and making him and the coachman get down from the box. Meanwhile Evershaw was getting the passengers down.

When they had all the people lined up my master stood over them, a pistol in either hand, the reins knotted on my neck, while Evershaw searched hurriedly through the mail bags and swore at Billy Hind to stop blubbering about a ball through the arm.

Finding the bag he wanted, Evershaw swung himself up on Harkaway and placed it across his knees. My master was engaged in collecting a few guineas from the passengers, when the sound of approaching hoofs was heard and three young men came riding through the dusk. The passengers called out for help; the guard broke away and was shot down by Evershaw. The young men drew pistols and charged. The commotion was terrible. Pistols banged, ladies screamed, men shouted. The black smoke from the gunpowder hung in the air. There was no time to reload, so they closed in, using their whip handles and pistol butts as cudgels. Hats were knocked off, men swore and shouted, we horses reared and plunged in fright.

Above the uproar my master called to Evershaw to break away and gallop for it. We were heavily outnumbered and he had seen the coachman pick up the guard's blunderbuss; in a moment it would be reloaded.

'I'm going, Evershaw,' my master called again. 'Break it off, you fool.' Then to my relief he did go. We took to the fields. Never had I galloped so willingly. Shouts and thudding hoofs followed us, too close for peace of mind. I hoped that they had had no time to reload.

The country was strange to us but my master rode as though he had a place or point in mind and we took the obstacles that appeared in our path as best we could. I was

not sure of myself as a jumper, but I managed to scramble
over several ditches and hedges and when we came to a
stretch of grass, I covered it at full speed, confident that
no ordinary horse could keep near me.

But it was darkness coming down that saved us,
though we were soon lost ourselves, in a strange place
with no moon.

My master dismounted and led me, walking boldly
until he came to the darker blackness of a wood or hedge,
then he felt his way as best he could, stumbling over
rough ground, tripping over roots and losing all sense of
direction.

Our progress was very slow and there was no light or
other sign of habitation to make for. At length he gave
up.

'We'll rest and hope for a moon, Shady,' he said, slack-
ening my girth and taking the reins over my head. 'You
must graze as you can for I fear a shelterless and supper-
less night lies ahead; at least the rain is warm.'

I cropped the grass which was short and sweet, he ate
some crumbs of bread and cheese from his pocket and we
waited.

There was no moon that night and though once or twice we moved on a little, it was more to warm ourselves or to find me fresh grazing, than in the hope of making any progress.

Dawn found us cold and wet through, but at first light my master began to lead me forward and, as the sun rose, he mounted and we went on, heading south-west towards a heath. On the heath he stopped to look at his map, while I listened to the birds, all singing noisily at the sight of a new day.

When Jem was certain of his way we set off again, still going south-west, and we kept going steadily for several hours. We halted once or twice to drink at streams, but not for food, and I began to wonder if we would ever be able to enter a comfortable inn again.

We came at length to the Weymouth road and, crossing over, made our way into the hills of North Dorsetshire and, beyond them, we came to a vale. Here we were quite unknown and when we stopped at a small inn I was more hungry and more weary than I had ever been in my life.

We rested there in the vale for several days and then, our money beginning to run short, we began to rob again.

King George was at Weymouth taking the sea air, so many fashionable people belonging to the Court and politics were travelling up and down the road, and my master seemed well satisfied with his takings. Away from Evershaw he had resumed his former polite air and we had no shouting or threats. But I think he was in some anxiety about his friends for he went out of his way to get hold of newspapers and looked through them in a very apprehensive manner.

One day we rode right into the town of Weymouth. It was very early in the morning, but there were people everywhere and all the shops open. When my master enquired the reason they told him that the Queen, who was a strange old body and wore a cloak and bonnet just like any other old woman, rose up at five every morning and went sea-bathing with her daughters. And the whole population feeling that they must rise with her, the shops were all open by half-past six.

I was very much taken with the sea, never having seen it before, but my master seemed more excited by the people parading about in fine clothes and the bands which appeared as the morning progressed, and played for the king. Farmer George, as he was called by the populace, had been very ill and many people were pitying the poor old man and wishing that he might be left in peace. But the music went on all morning; we heard *God Save the King* played six or seven times and the trumpets being sounded as he went down to bathe.

From that day my master had no peace of mind either. For, while still in Weymouth, he got hold of a newspaper that announced the capture of Edmund Evershaw. He had been arrested in the act of changing bill notes taken in the robbery and was in prison awaiting trial. But, worse than this, it was now known that my master had also been involved and a reward of two hundred pounds had been offered for his capture.

He read this several times, turning very pale, and then he began to curse the day that he had met Evershaw. Until, suddenly recollecting where he was, and realising the danger, he mounted hastily and hurried from the town.

'Two hundred pounds, Shady,' he said, slowing me to

a walk as we reached a quiet byroad. 'Two hundred pounds! It is a great deal of money – a fortune to some. Shall I ever be able to trust anyone again?'

The next few weeks were very uncomfortable. We travelled great distances and lived rough, sleeping out at nights and stopping at small inns for but one meal a day. Otherwise I lived on grass and became quite lean.

We robbed solitary travellers on the byroads, choosing those who would not put up a fight. My master swore at the paltryness of the sums he took and was very sad and restless and irritable.

Then came more bad news. Evershaw and Billy Hind had been tried and sentenced to death. It seemed they were in prison near London and my master suddenly resolved that he must go there; he must see Evershaw before his end.

By this time we were both very rough-looking and my master's fine clothes were very much the worse for wear, but staying only at the lowest sort of inn, 'dogholes' Jem called them, this did not attract attention to us. It was only to those who knew a good horse, that I looked too superior for my station, and for them my master had an answer ready: I was a broken-down racer he had bought for a song.

I do not know if Jem managed to see Evershaw in prison. But he was desperately low spirited for days on end and, not knowing what to do with himself, hung about a disreputable tavern gaming and drinking Geneva spirits.

When the day for the execution came we rode to the common near London where the gallows had been set up. There were four of them, for Evershaw, Billy Hind and two other wrongdoers.

I did not see the horrible business myself. Jem left me to be baited at an inn and went on foot, for together we were more likely to be recognised. But I had seen the great crowds of people gathering and, when the wagon carrying the prisoners appeared, I heard the shouts and boos that greeted it. I heard the terrible excitement of the people enjoying the spectacle of men being hanged.

When my master came to fetch me he was pale and much shaken. 'Oh God, Nightshade, this will not do,' he said, as we hurried away from the place. 'I could not bear an end like that. To be hanged like a dog for all the world to see. And now his body is to be gibbeted! Hanged in irons from one of the gibbets on the heath. Horrible!

'To think of his body swinging there until it rots away and bits of him stolen by the old witches for their spells. Oh God, I could not bear such a fate. And Billy's is little better. His body has been given to the surgeons for their dissections.'

My master rode on towards London in this very agitated mood and then gradually he seemed to come to a decision.

'I must leave the country,' he told me. 'I must go to the colonies, the Indies, America, anywhere, and start again under another name. I must sell you, Shady; it grieves me, but it has to be done. You will pay my passage to a new life.'

I was apprehensive at the prospect of a new master, but I did not see how things could go on as they were for, without a settled existence, we would starve or freeze to death when winter came.

I do not know how my sale was managed, I suspect it was through a friendly inn-keeper, but a buyer was found, and as Jem Lovelace gave me a quick pat and hurried away, a brown-liveried groom, who said that he was Mr Samuel Packington's man, came and took me in charge.

CHAPTER SEVEN

A more respectable life

I soon learned that Mr Packington lived in one of the suburbs of London where the newly rich merchants and owners of manufactories were building large modern houses. I also learned that Joseph, his groom, had been sent to London on two errands.

The first errand was to buy a riding horse, my predecessor having died of colic, the second to escort a party of parish children from one of the London workhouses to Mr Packington's manufactory in Kent.

Joseph was a neatly made, small featured man, wearing his own black hair. He was a fair rider and a good judge of horses and, being of superior intelligence, was entrusted with many business matters by his master.

Greatly dissatisfied with my appearance, Joseph soon began to trim me up. He also put an ostler to work grooming me and a stable boy to cleaning my saddlery, with the result, that when we set out next morning, I felt and looked a different horse.

We went straight to the workhouse. A huge grey, gloomy building in a dismal street, it housed the poor, the old and children who had no parents to see to them. Orphans, foundlings, unwanted bastards and children whose parents were too poor to keep them, were all shut away and paid for by the parish.

As Joseph told his business to the man at the door, our two wagons, drawn by six horses apiece, came trundling up the street.

'You've got the leftovers,' said the man on the door. 'All the best ones get taken as servants or apprenticed to trades. Very rough lot you've got, and mind you keep 'em, we don't want to see 'em back in London. The Poor Rate's 'igh enough as it is.'

The children came marching out in a very orderly fashion, boys being directed to one wagon and girls to the other. They quickly piled in, as though glad to get away. They were very young, about eight or nine years of age, with pale faces as though they never saw the sun and, though clean and not ragged, their clothes were of very poor quality and seemed either much too large or too small.

As soon as they were settled we set off, Joseph and I leading the way through the busy streets. Carts and carriages were crowding us all the time and some of them becoming very impatient at the lumbering pace of our wagons.

The children were all in a great state of excitement and fighting for places where they might look out, round and under the wagons' canvas awnings. They seemed as happy as if it were a pleasure trip. They sang songs and hymns and shouted remarks at the passers-by.

Their favourite shout was, 'Guinea pig!' for since powder had been taxed one guinea, to help pay for the war, many men had given up wigs and it was the fashion to wear your own hair and unpowdered. Men of the old school who stuck to their wigs were nicknamed guinea pigs.

The two carters, who wore brownish smocks and carried whips, mostly walked beside their horses and from time to time Joseph dismounted and walked with me, which rested my back and stretched his legs.

Towards dinner-time, we went on to warn a small country inn of our arrival and then while Joseph ate in the inn and I was baited in the stable, the children were given bread and cheese and tea in the barn.

They seemed very disappointed with this fare and it gradually came out that the overseers at the workhouse had given them great expectations of their new life. They'd been promised roast beef and plum pudding every day and told that they would earn enough money to buy gold watches and fine clothes.

Joseph was very much shocked at the wicked lie. He told one of the carters that the unfortunate children were going from the prison of the workhouse to the slavery of a factory, and that Mr Packington would not pay them a penny until they were twenty-one. Until then they must work long hours for their clothes and keep. And poor keep it was.

A coach would have accomplished the journey to Critley in a few hours, for the better roads and the quick and constant changes of horses, enabled them to cover eight or nine miles an hour in flat country. Our wagons' steady plod, with the same horses taking us all the way, could not do better than three miles an hour and so it had been arranged that we should spend a night on the road, Joseph and I putting up at an inn, the children sleeping in the wagons.

Bred in the city, the children did not seem to like the look of the country overmuch, but when at length we reached Critley and drove through gates, with *Packington & Tucker* writ very large on the archway above, and they saw the factory, a great, tall, ugly building, with the noisy thump of machinery never stopping for a moment, they were very cast down indeed. The sight of the two bleak,

grey barracks they were to live in was an even greater disappointment and many of them burst out crying.

Joseph was very unhappy at their distress, but there seemed to be nothing he could do for them, so when he had handed them over to the overseers and seen them counted, he said we must be off at once for we had a long way to go.

Mr Packington's house, number 22 Park Drive, was a good deal closer to London than it was to Critley and I was very tired by the time we turned in at the gate and saw the tall modern house standing in a garden, with a coach house and stable to one side. In front it looked across a common, but there were no cattle or geese grazing there. Instead avenues of trees had been planted and walks laid out, but the air was fresh and not thick with smoke and dirt as the city air is.

I soon found myself in a stall, with companions on either side, and a boy called Rob unsaddling me.

I was quite glad to have a regular stable again and soon settled down in my new home. Mr Packington did not keep a very large establishment, Joseph being coachman as well as head groom and Green helping in the garden as well as the stable. Rob was a dull, sandy-haired boy with light eyelashes, who had to be given every order twice, but even so the place was run in a very orderly manner.

The carriage horses were a well-matched pair of bays, called Madcap and Tomboy, but they did not live up to their names being very staid animals. There was also a small pony, a sturdy, cheerful, dark brown called Jolly Roger, and a larger grey, Snowstorm, who was rather a weary, grumbling sort of pony, much afflicted by worms.

In the general way Mr Packington took the carriage when he went to the city, for there, Joseph said, he had to look the big man, but when he visited the manufactory, which was three or four times a week, he rode me.

Joseph rode me a good deal too, generally on errands for his master, and Mr Sidney, the elder son, was to ride me when he came home from school.

There were four other children: Violet, Rosamund, Myrtle and a little boy of five who was the curled and spoiled darling of his Mamma. According to Jolly Roger, Master Clarence was a good deal too free with his whip and when Rob, who was his riding master, took the whip away he made a great outcry and said he should tell his Mamma that Rob had not treated him with proper respect.

At first I much enjoyed the rides to Critley, but, as I grew used to the road, they became rather monotonous. Mr Packington, who was a well-built man in his forties, with black, bushy eyebrows, a large nose and a severe mouth, never thought of changing his route or giving me a gallop. He was not much of a rider, being unable to get into the rhythm of the thing, and always pulled on the reins as though force was needed. But, worst of all, he never spoke to me and we would go all the way to Critley and back in perfect silence.

When I had lived at 22 Park Drive for some months a great outcry against the conditions of factory children was raised and taken up in Parliament and the newspapers.

It came out that the children at Packington's worked for twelve hours a day, six days a week and the men whom they assisted, being on piece work, would do almost anything to keep them awake and busy. They often beat them and soused them with cold water if they were slow, or dropped off to sleep.

It seemed that such great labours at a very young age (some of the local people sent their children to work in the factory at six or seven years) often caused malformation of the bones and many had crooked knees and grew up quite lame and crippled. The heat and dust also brought on consumptions and many of the children died young.

Mr Packington did not seem much perturbed by this outcry. He pointed to his two grey barracks and said that they were well-conducted by respectable overseers and the boys and girls kept strictly apart. That the children were given a plentiful supply of bread and porridge, with either bacon or cheese every day and meat on Sundays. Every child attended Sunday school or church and the long hours of labour at least kept them from idle habits and mischief. And many people, agreeing with him, and feeling that the parish children should earn their own bread from the age of nine onwards, the protest died away and nothing was done.

I think I had been with Mr Packington about two years, when disaster struck his own family.

As the spoiled Master Clarence grew older he had

become more and more disobedient and one day, when being taken out for a walk by his nurse, he ran off and, in a moment had entirely vanished. The poor woman hunted high and low for him and then, hurrying home in a great state of distress had called on the whole household to assist in the search.

When they failed to find the boy, Joseph mounted Madcap and rode to Critley at breakneck speed to bring Mr Packington the bad news. I was saddled at once and we hurried back to Park Drive to find Mrs Packington in hysterics and the boy still missing.

Mr Packington went off with Snowstorm in the gig to tell the magistrates and have the Bow Street Runners informed, for it was now feared that the boy had been stolen.

It was quite a common thing to steal little children for their fine clothes, which could be sold, and sometimes gipsies took them away to distant parts of the country and they were never seen again, but Mrs Packington feared that Master Clarence had been sold to a chimney sweep. It seemed that the newspapers had reported a shortage of climbing boys, for the tall modern houses had narrow chimneys with small flues (nine by fourteen inches was said to be the usual size, but some had been built only eight or nine inches square), which needed a very small child indeed.

With all the master sweeps wishing to advertise 'Little boys for small flues' on their trade cards, they were paying parents as much as two guineas a child and taking them as young as five or six. But, since the better sort of parent did not want to inflict such hardships on their own children, a trade in stolen children was thought to have grown up.

Green, who was frequently in and out of the house with flowers and vegetables reported all that took place there to Joseph, so we were kept well informed of Mrs Packington's fears and vapours, of Mr Packington's rages and of the dismissal of the poor nurse without references.

When the first shock and upheaval was over a more systematic search was organised and a handsome reward was advertised for the return of the boy safe and sound.

I found myself constantly searching some squalid quarter with either Joseph or Mr Packington, for there were many poor areas between Park Drive and the centre of London and some very desperate districts near the river.

To relieve Mrs Packington's fears we called on every chimney sweep that we could hear of and, though I had stayed at low inns with Jem Lovelace, nothing I had seen hitherto had prepared me for the misery and stench of the dreadful streets I now visited.

The buildings were all crushed together without gardens or fields and every house was crowded with people; incredible numbers packed into every dirty, damp room, and frequently without proper beds or any sort of furniture.

Outside there were middens or dungheaps close to the houses and they were piled high with every sort of refuse; dead cats and dogs, as well as soil from the privies, all decaying together and stinking most horribly, while the open drain that ran down the street smelled far worse than the dirtiest stable.

The sweeps worked very early in the morning. This was so that the fires might be put out at night, and the chimneys have time to cool down, and yet the whole operation be over and the fires lit again in time for break-fast. We began our search in the late morning expecting to find them returned home.

But, though the master sweep was often there, waiting for his dinner, the poor boys had frequently been sent out to walk the streets crying 'sweepo, sweepo,' in an attempt to get work for the future and we did not see them. This made us change our tactics and we began to go out at all hours in order to get a look at the boys themselves.

Black all over, ragged, barefoot and carrying the great, heavy sacks of soot on their backs, they were a sad sight. They were all thin and starved, for a well fed boy would not be able to elbow his way along the smaller flues, and with their red eyes and coughs, bent backs and swelled knees, they looked a good deal worse than the factory children.

One day Mr Packington stopped and talked to three little sweeps walking without their master and he asked them how they came to this work. One had been appren-ticed by the parish when eight years old, another by his father when his mother died and the third said he was the master sweep's stepson. He looked just as ragged and dirty and starved as the other two and he told us that his stepfather ill-used him, his mother did not want him to be a sweep, but was powerless to stop it.

Another time we saw a little curly-headed sweep cry-ing pitifully and I felt Mr Packington's hopes rise that he would find his son under all that dirt and soot. It wasn't Clarence, but when Mr Packington asked him why he cried, he answered that he had only just started as a climbing boy and, being afraid of the dark, could not bear the long climb up, the scraping and brushing away, all the

time in the black stifling chimneys. And yet, if he did not climb, his master threatened him with beatings, pinched his feet or, lighting damp straw in the fireplace below, half choked him with smoke. He showed us the raw wounds on his elbows and knees caused by climbing.

But the bigger boy who was with him said he'd get used to it by and by and after a few months his elbows and knees would heal and the skin harden. Then he showed his own scars. Some were caused by falling down a chimney. The others when he had lost his way in a connecting flue and got by mistake into the chimney of the next door house. There he had knocked down soot into a lighted fire, causing it to flare up and burn him most severely.

Though a hard man, Mr Packington seemed much affected by the misery of the climbing boys' lives, but, beyond handing out pennies, he did nothing for them, though, Joseph said, he was spending larger and larger sums advertising rewards for the safe return of Master Clarence. He also spent many hours out looking for the boy and, when his own presence at business was essential, he sent Joseph out on me to search in his stead.

Joseph would rise early and we would be on the road at dawn. So I became accustomed to seeing the sweeps at their work and hearing the cry of 'All up!' and seeing an arm and scraper waved at the top of a chimney, to show that the boy had done his duty and gone all the way to the top.

One day we had the address of yet another sweep and, going to his dirty, tumbledown house, we found a little boy lying in a cellar on a bed of soot sacks. He said he was ill with sooty wart, a horrible disease confined to climbing boys, but did not want to go to hospital. He said his master had taken on a new little boy in his place, quite lately and told us the street where they were working.

We gave him a penny and left. Joseph said he was certain to die, for without an operation soot wart was fatal, and hurried me through the streets in search of the new little boy.

We found the house easily enough for the back door was open and the place in an uproar, with servants running about not knowing what to do, for the climbing boy was stuck fast in a flue and could not be shifted. The kitchen window was open and we could hear the sweep shouting at the boy. He was threatening to fetch a barrel of gunpowder and blow him out if he did not come down immediately. When this failed the sweep told his other boy to strip off his clothes and fetch the first one down. So, wearing but a hood over his head, he vanished into the chimney too.

Joseph hitched me to the railings and went down the basement steps into the kitchen. The sweep was telling the second boy to tie a rope round the first one's ankles and, when this was done, he began to pull on the rope in an attempt to drag the child free. But the boy could not be moved an inch and his screams were terrible to hear. Joseph was trying to prevent further use of force, the kitchen maid was in hysterics, when the master of the house, awakened at last, came down in his night clothes. He took command and while a servant was sent running for a doctor, Joseph and I were dispatched to fetch a mason, who lived further afield.

We hurried through the early morning streets, fearing all the while that it was our Master Clarence stuck fast in the flue. We knocked up the sleepy mason, throwing stones at his window, and Joseph impressed on him the urgency of the matter, but he was dreadfully slow and we had to wait while he wakened his boy and loaded his handcart with tools.

We found everyone at the house waiting in great anxiety, for not a sound had been heard from the boy for some time, and the mason was hurried to work, knocking a hole in a wall with his pick, somewhere up on the first floor.

At length the poor boy was brought out and the doctor arrived in time to pronounce him dead of suffocation.

He wasn't Master Clarence, but Joseph and I rode home in very low spirits all the same.

Our search went on all summer without success and, as winter followed, the hardships suffered by the climbing boys were much increased.

We found that frequently they had no coats, no shoes or stockings and went to work at two or three in the morning without so much as a slice of bread. It was terrible to see the shivering little boys walking barefoot on frosty ground, or through snow.

One day when we came upon a bigger boy carrying a little one on his back, Joseph stopped to ask the reason. The big boy said that the little'un had been crying so dreadfully about his feet and displayed them to us, all red and raw. Joseph asked if the people at the large houses did not give them the cast off shoes and stockings from their own children? The boys said that this often happened, but, as their master immediately took them away and sold them, they preferred to be given food.

As time went on we all began to give up hope of ever seeing Master Clarence again. In his absence all his faults and spoiled ways were forgotten and even Jolly Roger mourned his loss.

The troubles of the country were also in the forefront of everyone's mind, for the war was sending all prices bounding up and up and now the French were thought to be contemplating an invasion of England. Joseph said that Mr Packington was much taken up with raising money for the defence of the country and had subscribed very handsomely to the Lord Mayor's fund for this purpose.

Mrs Packington had less to distract her and, as her hopes of finding her son faded away, there began to be fears for her health. First they tried ass's milk, then the doctors said that there were symptoms of a consumptive decline and she must be taken on a sea voyage.

After much discussion, Mr Packington decided on taking his whole family to Lisbon and, since the future was uncertain, and his wife could no longer bear the house with its memories of Clarence, he dismissed the servants and put both the house and the horses up for sale.

CHAPTER EIGHT

'The French have landed!'

In a very short time the establishment at 22 Park Drive was split up and we all went our separate ways.

Mr Tucker, who was to run the business in Mr Packington's absence, decided to take on Joseph; Rob was sent home to his parents. Madcap, Tomboy and the carriage were put in a sale, Jolly Roger went to some children living near and Snowstorm found a comfortable situation with two elderly ladies.

I was quite well known locally and several offers were made, but a close friend of Mr Packington's was determined to have me for his brother-in-law and brought him to try me.

I liked Mr Maitland directly. He was a thin, spare man of medium height and a great deal lighter than Mr Packington. He wore his own silver hair quite short and was exceedingly courteous to those around him.

He congratulated Joseph on my general condition, Rob on the cleanliness of my coat and me on my manners and paces, but, to the disgust of his brother-in-law, he seemed very doubtful about making the purchase.

'What should I do with such an elegant animal?' he asked. 'I do not propose to join the fashion parade in Hyde Park, or lead a regiment, or dazzle some beautiful lady. All I need is a steady conveyance and you find me a magnificent thoroughbred. Neither I nor my horsemanship are worthy of such an animal.'

'Nonsense, Maitland,' the brother-in-law was very

firm, 'I know that you are unworldly, but other men judge each other by appearance and you will procure far better attention at an inn, riding a horse of his stamp, than on your usual decrepit nags. In addition you will find a well-bred, well-made horse far less tiring to ride; a man who travels the distances you do, should not condemn himself to the joltings of a common animal.'

In the end, this second argument prevailed, for my new master admitted that, as he grew older, he did have to look more to his comfort. So I was sold and it was settled that Joseph should ride me to my new home, which was some distance to the south of Critley and not far from the sea.

In London, where there was constant talk of invasion, nothing much seemed to be done about it, but as we came closer to the coast there was a great deal more activity. We saw semaphore signalling devices on the hill tops, looking very much like gibbets, but said to take the news of a landing to London in an unbelievably short space of time. On every church lych gate and nailed to a tree on every village green was a poster headed INVASION with instructions on how the people were to burn the crops and drive the cattle with them and many other things.

Here and there we came across materials for building barricades piled at the roadside, ready to be pulled across and obstruct the approaching army. There were also many little fortifications, made where a bridge was to be defended or a crossroad held.

When Joseph stopped for ale the talk was all of armies massed along the French coast, only twenty miles away, and of the thousands of flat bottomed boats that were to bring them across the channel. It was said that there was hardly a tree left in that part of France; they had all been cut down for boats.

Everyone seemed a good deal afraid of the French leader, Napoleon Bonaparte. Boney they called him for short. All day long you could hear mothers using him to threaten their children. In London they were threatened that the sweep would get them, here it was Boney.

When we reached my new home, The Croft, there was quite a party of people to welcome me. Mr Maitland smiling and joking about how much in awe he was of my elegance and how he must mend his ways and buy a new coat. Mrs Maitland saying that she wanted a kind horse that would bring him home safely and she could see from my eye that I was just the thing. Three maidservants all crying out in admiration at my appearance and, to my great surprise, a black man. I had seen quite a few in London, runaway slaves who begged for a living and were known as St Giles blackbirds, after the district where they congregated, but never one who came up and, patting my neck, made jokes about the master riding in the St Leger now he had a racer.

I was led into a stable, where a pony neighed greetings to me, and put into a loose-box which to my great joy had a half door so that I could look over and see the rest of the stable and the row of stalls where the pony was tied.

Joseph handed me over to my new groom, Mr Howard. He was a short man with white hair, a long serious face and even older than Mr Maitland. There was also a boy called Pat with a screwed up, monkey-like face and dark hair. He seemed very pleased at my arrival, but whenever he tried to do anything for me Mr Howard drove him away, saying that he was to see to the pony and that a scamp like him was not fit to look after a thoroughbred.

When I had been watered and fed I was left to rest and Joseph, saying goodbye to me, was taken into the house for a meal.

My fellow horses at The Croft were two stout mares called Jenny and Poppy. Jenny was a very irritable brown, who would bite at the least thing. She said she had suffered very cruel treatment from a farm boy when she was young and could not forget it. She often bit Pat when he was grooming and harnessing her, but he took his bruises in good part.

Poppy was bay and a hand taller, so they did not match very well when they drew the carriage, but for the greater part of the time they were employed on a little farm that was attached to the house. Poppy was sweet-tempered, but when she moved she threw out her forelegs in a very ugly way, called dishing, which would not do for a carriage horse in smart circles.

The pony was a piebald, called Magpie, who did the errands and was driven by Mrs Maitland in a pretty little cart.

I soon learned that Mr Howard was a great singer, but only of hymns and psalms. He thought songs very wicked. He was a chapel-goer and lectured Pat a great deal about the error of his ways and the certainty that he would go to hell and be consigned to the flames. The boy took it all in good humour and did not seem at all in awe of Mr Howard, answering back very pertly at times and making faces behind his back, in a way that Mr Simpson would not have stood for a moment.

After a day's rest, Mr Maitland took me for a ride round the neighbourhood. The whole of our village,

Hurstmore, seemed very excited by the event of a new horse and the people all left what they were doing and came to give an opinion on me. It seemed to be generally agreed that I was a great improvement on any horse Mr Maitland had owned before.

My new master was constantly apologising to me for what he called his 'ambling ways' and hoping that I was not hankering for my life as a racer. He also apologised for his horsemanship and sometimes I wished that I could speak and set his mind at rest on both counts.

To me, absent-mindedness was his only fault. He seemed to ride in a dream, his mind entirely taken up with other things, and would frequently lose himself through lack of attention. I did not like retracing my steps so, when I grew to know his habits I would take charge. But when we went on longer journeys into strange neighbourhoods I had no idea where to take him and I began to shy a little, jumping sideways at the rustle of a bird in the hedge or the bark of a dog on a chain, when I wished to regain his wandering attention.

Jenny, Poppy and Magpie were not much interested in the nature of Mr Maitland's work. Having been born and bred-up close by, they had seen very little of life and all three had a very rustic outlook, but I gradually learned from the conversation of the people around me that my new master was very taken up with reform. It seemed he had modest private means and so was able to give all his time to societies for the improvement of the prisons and the abolition of the slave trade.

He was also a very religious man, but in a different way from Mr Howard; I never heard him threaten anyone with hellfire or eternal damnation.

One week when Mr Howard was called away to Tunbridge Wells in a great hurry because his brother was very ill and like to die, Mathew the black man was constantly in and out of the stable.

He was a very cheerful person full of jokes and stories. When he groomed me he talked all the time, so from this and what I heard him tell Pat, I gradually pieced his history together.

It seemed that he had been born in Africa and, being captured by another tribe when very young, had been made a slave as was the custom there. He had served a black mistress in Africa until he was eleven or twelve years old, but then she had sold him to a white man. In the black family he had been treated more as a servant than a slave, but now he was dragged away to a slave ship and forced into the stifling hold with hundreds of slaves, packed tight and chained, so that they could scarcely move.

Without exercise, or fresh air or proper food many, more than a third, had died on the voyage, but he being young had been allowed on deck a good deal and so, though frightened, sad and sick, had survived.

They arrived in the West Indies, where they were intended for the sugar plantations, but a British naval officer had liked the look of him and bought him for forty guineas.

He had then gone to sea with the navy, serving the officer, learning to set the sails and to fire the guns and even to navigate the ship, of which last he was very proud.

He had grown very fond of his master and served him well. As a slave he received no pay and even his prize money (all the crew had a share when they captured a ship in battle) belonged to his master. But he had not minded about this for he expected that when he was twenty-one he would be set free. There being no slavery allowed in Britain he thought he would be treated as an apprentice and they were always free to work for whom they pleased from that age.

When the time came, they were in an English port, but when the ship's company was paid off he was not allowed ashore. His master, now a Captain, held him prisoner, the law on slavery not applying to ships, and sold him to another Captain who was returning immediately to the Indies. When they reached a West Indian port he was sold again, this time to a merchant.

It had been very terrible to find himself a slave again, with all his expectations dashed, and, as he had looked upon his master as a friend he felt that it was a great betrayal of trust.

However, his new master had given him a responsible position and had not objected to him doing a little trading on his own account, so, after another fifteen years slavery, and saving every penny, he was at last able to buy his freedom.

The white men there, hating and distrusting freed slaves, he had come to England, and Mr Maitland being well-known for his efforts to have slavery abolished, had sought him out.

He was employed in quite a lowly position, but he made himself very useful to Mr Maitland, who was inclined to neglect his own affairs in favour of reform, and they worked for the abolition of slavery together.

Mathew told us many stories of the cruelty with which the slaves were treated on the plantations. How they were flogged for the most minor misdeeds, had all their teeth pulled out as a punishment for eating the sugar cane, and how, if any black man ventured to strike a white man, he was tortured and hanged, even though the white man was in the wrong.

'They treat them far worse than horses, Nightshade,' he told me. 'Though I can see that you have been ill-used by these white hairs on your sides.'

Mr Maitland made good use of me in his own quiet way. We often went miles to see some lady or gentleman of influence who might help his cause, or to discuss his latest pamphlet with a fellow worker.

We also visited many prisons up and down the country and I would be put in the stable while he was shown round. He took many notes and was always full of ideas for improvement of the conditions, which were often very bad as you could tell by the stench, it being worse than any farmyard or pigsty.

Some were damp dungeons with little air and the poor prisoner lying there, fettered, on dirty straw, he would tell me, and at some the jailors were dishonest and did not give the prisoners even their meagre allowance of bread. He was always much affected by seeing bad conditions and would talk about them all the way home, musing as to what could be done.

The worst of it, as he was always saying, was that these prisoners were usually foolish or unfortunate men who got into debt and, instead of being allowed to work and pay what they owed, they were confined in these dismal circumstances until ill health or jail fever carried them off.

It seemed that felons: thieves, murderers, highwaymen and the like, were only kept in prison until their trials, then they were either hanged or transported, while minor offenders and runaway apprentices, were sent to bridewells where they had to work very hard, but only for a short period.

Sometimes we went to London to see members of Parliament about new Bills and Acts, but more often Mr Maitland took the coach, a thing rather frowned upon locally, for men of his standing, carriage folk were expected to travel post and hire expensive chaises. But being unworldly and not caring the least for show, he could not see the need.

Pat was always happy when our master was away for he was the only other person to ride me. Mr Howard, though too old and stiff to take me out himself, could not bear to see Pat on my back. He was certain that the boy would let me break my knees on the road or over-gallop me on the grass and we never went without terrible warnings or returned without an inspection of me from head to tail.

Except for the war and bread going up to seventeen pence a loaf and a mad dog going through the village and biting dogs and pigs, all of which had to be killed, our life went on smoothly.

Then came a great surprise. Peace with France was

declared. At first it was not believed, there having been no suggestion of it until that moment, but when the coaches from London came through our little town bearing banners saying *Peace with France!* and the coachmen and guards wearing sprigs of laurel in their hats, then we began to think it could be true.

There was great excitement everywhere with the Militia firing cannons in the market places and church bells ringing everywhere and those who could afford it putting lighted candles in their windows at night.

In London, it was said, the Post Office had lighted six thousand lamps, but in Hurstmore we contented ourselves with a bonfire and ale. It was very different from the Lovelace celebration, there being only two people too drunk to get home and they being much frowned on by the chapel-goers. Mr Howard threatened poor Pat with hellfire for days, because he had seen him at the bonfire, a pot of ale in his hand, singing *Rule Britannia* at the top of his voice.

Soon after this all the notices about invasion came down and all the part-time soldiers were disbanded and stopped drilling on the village greens.

Mr Maitland, feeling that people would now have more time to consider the horrors of slavery, arranged a great many meetings. Mathew came with us on Poppy, leaving Jenny to do the farm work, and spoke on the misery of being a slave from his own experience.

Mainly the speeches were given in Town Halls, but once or twice they spoke in market places, telling of the dreadful slave ships, of the toil and floggings, of the fetters and chains, of the shocking fact that in America it was a crime to teach a slave to read or write.

Once a man shouted that factory children were slaves

too, and nearer home, but most people agreed that slavery was very wrong and that something ought to be done. The difficulty was to *get* anything done and sometimes Mr Maitland became very despondent, but this would pass quite quickly and soon he would be making new plans and full of hope again.

So life went on very happily until, after a year had passed, England and France fell out again and the war re-started.

Many people felt that the peace had been a trick and that France was now all the more ready to invade us. Rumours came every hour of armies and boats gathering in France for the crossing.

In our part of the world all the arrangements for defence had to begin again. The Militia was recalled, the Fencibles or Home Defence re-enrolled, the invasion notices put up again.

This time Mr Maitland, being one of the chief men locally, was asked to take command and I was kept very busy taking him hither and thither, for he seemed to have to spend every minute of his day at some drill or meeting.

Mathew joined the Home Defence. Pat was very angry that he was too young. They would take no one under fifteen years or over sixty. Mr Howard seemed quite glad to be too old and did not at all object to driving Jenny and Poppy in our largest wagon and going in the parson's party. It had been settled that in every village the women and children should be put in wagons and carts, and, led by the parson or curate, should drive inland to safety, keeping to the lesser roads and lanes, so that they did not slow up our army advancing to battle with the invader.

The skilled men, blacksmiths, wheelwrights, masons and such trades, were put into a pioneer band. They were to knock down bridges and build barricades to slow up the enemy advance, and yet another group were to drive the cattle inland and fire the ricks so that Boney's army found little or nothing to eat.

Then we got down to making our beacon on Hurstmore Hill. There was to be a chain of beacons covering the whole country. When the watchers on the cliffs saw the enemy ships approaching they would light theirs, and, seeing theirs, we would light ours and all the people would know to leave off work or rise from their beds and take up arms.

In the daytime wet hay was to be used to send up a smoke signal, at night it was to be a good blaze.

Jenny and Poppy and some of the neighbouring farmers' horses dragged up the wagon-loads of mouldy hay, faggots, old barrels and pieces of old timber that would make a sudden blaze. The children all thought it rather a holiday and begged rides on the wagons so that they might come up and help build the beacon. But Mr Maitland was very serious about it all and said that he prayed God we might not have cause to light it, for he feared we were very ill-prepared to meet an invader.

Every week we held drills and once there was a parade, which included all the wagons and carts that were to take the women and children. Jenny and Poppy were fetched from their hay-making and Mrs Maitland drove Magpie and they all paraded round the village green before lining up. Mr Howard caused great annoyance by singing *Soldiers of Christ, Arise* very loud, and keeping it up after the military gentlemen who had come to inspect our efforts, had arrived. However the Home Defence men with their six muskets, proudly carried by the best shots, in the lead and followed by those armed with staves, while those with pitchforks brought up the rear, marched very well and behind them came the pioneer band with axes and picks over their shoulders.

On Saturday we had a sham fight with the Home Defence men of several other villages and quite a few old scores were settled when the men began to battle with their staves. Mr Maitland was riding up and down the line calling, 'Steady, there' and, 'Let us not be too realistic, we want no broken heads,' in the hope of calming things.

At night we manned our hill and put a guard on the road by the bridge and I would take Mr Maitland on his inspection of these outposts. When there was a good moon I enjoyed it, but on dark nights scrambling about on the hill was not so pleasant.

The fear of invasion was very real and some of the older folk could scarce sleep at night for anxiety. People feared for their lives and their children and their money which it was said they were drawing out of the banks and burying in their gardens. Every day there were new rumours, a plot to capture the King, landings in Ireland, landings in Wales, to keep the people in a perpetual state of fright. It was a good summer with a fine crop of corn, but it was said that we were only harvesting it for Boney.

Then, one warm October evening, ships were sighted out at sea, and it was the fish ponies, galloping their fresh fish to London in relays, that passed on the news that the French had come.

It was after dark when the news reached Hurstmore and it caused a dreadful panic. People were running from cottage to cottage crying out that the French had come. Men, boots in one hand, weapon in the other hurried into our yard shouting for Mr Maitland.

Mr Howard, already abed, for he thought late hours ungodly, appeared very flustered in his nightshirt and cap and called for Pat to come down at once and saddle the horse.

Pat came, dressed but half asleep, and saddled me with Mr Howard shouting all the while for him to make haste and harness the pony.

I could hear Mr Maitland's voice outside, telling people to calm themselves and asking how the news had come and whether it was from a reliable source.

Pat led me out with my bridle all twisted, the throat-latch round the cheek-piece, and forgot to tighten my girth. So when Mr Maitland tried to mount the saddle slipped round and added to the general confusion.

However, gradually things began to be sorted out and the men were assembling in the churchyard while the wagons gathered on the green.

Then it was found that many of the women were bringing great bundles of household possessions, and in some cases birds in cages, as well as six or seven children and a baby in arms. When they were told the wagons could not take all of it there was a general outcry and complaint. This added to the babies' crying and the mothers calling for the bigger children, who constantly wandered away into the dark and were soon lost, made the most terrible uproar.

Mr Maitland kept calling for order and silence and tried to keep the two parties apart so that the men might concentrate on defence rather than lost children.

At last, having collected most of our force, we marched away to the bridge. It was pitch dark, there being no moon, but a good many of our party carried lanterns. Mr Maitland asked everyone to be quiet and listen for the sound of church bells and to watch the south for the sudden flaring of beacons. Then he reminded everyone that we were to hold our position on the far side of the bridge as long as we could, but when forced to retreat we had to knock the bridge down, in an endeavour to slow up the French advance.

We had not been long at the bridge when it was discovered that Pat, armed with a pitchfork, was with us. He said that Widow Todd from Well Cottage had been forgotten by her wagon and finding her screeching that she'd been left to be murdered by Boney, he'd given her his place in Magpie's cart and come to join us. He made himself useful holding me while Mr Maitland settled which of the great elms was to be felled across the road

when the moment came, posted two men further down the road as look-outs and some more in the fields on either side, and then inspected our first casualty, a ploughboy who'd put his pitchfork through his foot in the general excitement.

By this time we had settled down, all were outwardly calm, and there was great laughter when Thatcher Brown was heard to challenge one of Farmer Chapman's cows.

But then there was a sudden glare in the black sky and everyone called out that the beacons were lit, that Boney really was coming and panic broke out again.

Mr Maitland called for order, very sharply for him, and pointed out that it was *our* beacon on Hurstmore Hill that was lit. 'Can any of you see any other beacon burning?' he called out urgently, as he climbed on me to look from the greater height.

We scanned the hills to the south carefully, but there was no other fire to be seen. Mr Maitland said, in great distress, that our men must have done it without waiting for orders and now the whole country would be thrown into a state of panic through our error. 'Every beacon to the north of us will be lit on our signal,' he said, 'and what Frenchmen have we seen?'

We all began to feel a great sense of shame that our village should have done such a thing and several men offered to run up the hill and put the fire out, while others suggested that a messenger be sent to Bilbury Hill to explain the mistake. But it seemed that both actions must be too late to be of any use, until the blacksmith thought of me.

'Yon Nightshade were a racer,' he said, ''e might do the distance in time. 'E's our best 'ope anyways.'

'Our only hope,' agreed Mr Maitland, 'but who's to ride him? I cannot leave my post. Is there anyone here who can gallop a thoroughbred?'

Lanterns were held up as the men looked at each other's faces, but for most of them a jog trot was the fastest pace they used.

'I'll go, sir,' said Pat's voice.

Mr Maitland did not seem very happy to send such a young boy, but there was no one else and so, as Pat climbed up and shortened my stirrups, he wrote a note and signed it plainly. 'Give that to the men on Bilbury Hill,' he said, 'provided the beacons to the south have not been lit meanwhile. Are you certain of the way?'

Pat said he was and we set off, both very pleased at the importance of our mission. It was dark away from the lanterns, but not as dark as it had been earlier for the moon was rising. We cantered through the deserted village and took the track to our hill. From there we would follow the drovers' track that led over the hills for miles.

We galloped up the track to the hill, for we both knew it well, and came quickly to the blazing beacon.

'Douse that fire,' shouted Pat in a commanding voice. 'Mr Maitland's orders.' He waved the note, 'It never ought to 'ave been lit.'

'But Mr Howard said . . .' figures, black against the orange flames, came forward to argue.

'Who can read?' asked Pat, waving the note again. 'The fire is to be put out immediate.'

As soon as they were convinced of the order we galloped on. The hills looked wonderfully dramatic, very strange and mysterious under the climbing moon. I could see where I was going, but not where I put my feet; I hoped that we would not find ourselves in a rabbit warren and turn head over heels.

Then Pat found a wide track, mercifully it was dry and not too poached by the hoofs of the droves of cattle.

We galloped as I had not galloped for years, pulling up pretty sharply once when the moon vanished behind a cloud, but setting off again the moment it reappeared.

Pat let me choose my own speed. At first I think he was a little frightened by our pace, never having ridden at racing speed, but he grew to enjoy it and only slowed me up once, saying that I must take a breather, I was an old horse now, and the master wouldn't want me galloped to death even for the good name of the village.

All the time we watched the hill ahead, waiting for the flames to burst forth and pass on the false alarm, knowing that when that happened our gallop would have been in vain. We knew it *must* be a false alarm now for, every so often, Pat looked to the south and nowhere could he find the smallest glow in the sky.

Our reckless speed brought us to disaster at last. We had left the main track and were going down into a hollow before beginning to climb Bilbury Hill itself, when I felt a forehoof sink into a rabbit hole and sprawling forward collapsed upon my nose, pitching Pat over my head. He landed heavily, but fortunately the turf was soft and, though both much shaken, we quickly scrambled to our feet.

Pat felt my forelegs and then led me forward, looking with great anxiety to see if I was lame. The leg seemed undamaged and he looked round for a hollow to stand me in so that he might climb back into the saddle.

We went on more slowly, convinced now that we must be too late. As time passed it seemed more and more extraordinary that the Bilbury beacon was still unlit. Had the guard been asleep, or had they had reason to disbelieve our signal?

As rather blown and tired I climbed the last stretch of hillside, we could see torches and hear the angry voices of men cursing each other. A thin spiral of smoke rose from the beacon and the ashes of burnt straw smouldered below a great pile of unburnt wood.

We cantered up and delivered our written order.

'Well that do be a mercy for sure,' said the rustic in charge and burst into a loud cackle of laughter. 'Here lads, the Hurstmore beacon shouldn't 'ave gone up at all. "It were lit in error". There b'aint a Frenchie in the place. Perhaps it were a good job arter all that old skinflint Thomson sent up green wood.'

'Green and wet too,' said an indignant voice.

We learned that they had been struggling to light their beacon for the past twenty minutes, but had burned every bit of their straw without getting the green wood to catch and the poor men had become quite desperate in their efforts, feeling that through them the whole country would go unwarned and hundreds be murdered in their beds by the advancing French army.

We parted in a state of great mutual relief. Pat and I made the homeward journey at a very gentle pace and found Mr Maitland and his troop much pleased with our success, though quite unable to guess how it had been achieved.

Pat and I were sent home with some of the other men, no longer needed, for it seemed certain now that the alarm had been a false one. The Mail coach had brought a report to town that the ships sighted were East Indiamen.

Next day the villagers, the bundles, the children and the birds in cages all came home again and gradually things settled down. With much grumbling Jenny and Poppy hauled another load of wood up the hill and we rebuilt our beacon.

It soon got about that it was Mr Howard who had caused the trouble. It seemed that the old man, feeling certain of invasion, had thought the beacon forgotten in the excitement and taken it upon himself to give the order to light up. It was said that Mr Maitland had taken him to task very severely, speaking uncommon sharp and calling him an interfering old man.

Pat and I were more fortunate. We came in for a good deal of praise for having ridden so fast and saved the good name of the village. Not a great deal was said about the green wood.

About the same time as our false alarm Admiral Nelson had been fighting a great sea battle and a week or so later, news reached us of a glorious victory at Trafalgar, where the French navy were totally beaten. But the rejoicing over this was very much dampened by news, that came at the same time, of the death of Lord Nelson. This was a very heavy loss and was felt by many as though it were the loss of a member of the family.

The war was by no means over, in fact many hard battles remained to be fought, but, from that day there was no longer any dread of England being invaded, for our navy had control of the seas.

All the Home Defence were disbanded again and Mr Maitland went back to his prisoners and slaves and his endeavours to improve the lives of one and abolish the other. I continued to carry him on his journeys until we were both so old and grey that we were forced to retire, he to his armchair and papers, I to my paddock, where I spend the days happily enough, thinking about the past and those far off days when crowds roared my name or I carried a highwayman.

BLACK ROMANY

by Diana Pullein-Thompson

I wish to thank *The Times* and the *Leicestershire Chronicle* for their reports on the visit of Queen Victoria and Prince Albert to Belvoir, and also Miss Barbara Smith of Hodder and Stoughton who kindly transcribed much of them for me.   D. P-T.

CONTENTS

❦Black Beauty's Family❦

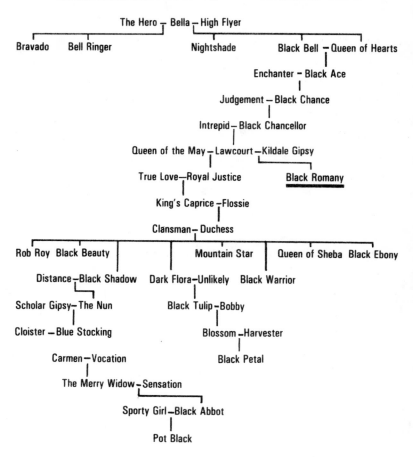

The Hero — Bella — High Flyer

Bravado   Bell Ringer   Nightshade   Black Bell — Queen of Hearts

Enchanter — Black Ace

Judgement — Black Chance

Intrepid — Black Chancellor

Queen of the May — Lawcourt — Kildale Gipsy

True Love — Royal Justice   Black Romany

King's Caprice — Flossie

Clansman — Duchess

Rob Roy   Black Beauty   Mountain Star   Queen of Sheba   Black Ebony

Distance — Black Shadow   Dark Flora — Unlikely   Black Warrior

Scholar Gipsy — The Nun   Black Tulip — Bobby

Cloister — Blue Stocking   Blossom — Harvester

Carmen — Vocation   Black Petal

The Merry Widow — Sensation

Sporty Girl — Black Abbot

Pot Black

CHAPTER ONE

A visit from the Queen

Looking back now I see that my life began to change in December 1843 at the time when Queen Victoria and her German husband, the handsome young Prince Albert, visited my home at Belvoir Castle in the county of Leicestershire.

Up till then the days had run smoothly into one another, and I can truthfully say that the first six and a half years of my life passed with few worries and only small mishaps.

I was born in a large stable kept for foaling mares. My mother, a Cleveland Bay thoroughbred cross, was pitch black apart from a sparkling white diamond on the centre of her forehead. My father was pure thoroughbred, black, too, with a remarkable turn of speed and a proud nature. I inherited strength of physique, depth of girth, wide cannon bones and a placid temperament from my mother and a slender curving neck, long sloping shoulders and swift action from my father. I was black, too, with a white diamond on my forehead exactly like my mother's, but I would rather have been bay or, best of all, grey with dapples and a steel-dark mane and tail. However, the Duke of Rutland particularly liked black horses especially to pull his carriage and to carry outriders on grand occasions.

I grew up in meadows near the park in view of the castle which was partly castellated, but had been largely rebuilt and redesigned after a fire some years earlier. And there was always much to see, people coming and going, horses being schooled and jumped, shooting expeditions, hounds being exercised or the hunt actually crossing our fields with the sound of horn and the cry of hounds echoing across the countryside.

After I had left my mother, my chief friend was my half-brother, Pioneer, a handsome bay with black points. We shared the same father, but his mother was without thoroughbred blood so he was heavier than I was, but fast and nimble for his size and with high spirits that matched my own. We were broken-in at the same time by old Mark Bampton, a gentle teacher who took us slowly, step by step, so that we were never frightened or dismayed. Of course we were accustomed to seeing our friends and relations pulling all kinds of vehicles or being ridden, so none of our training came as a surprise to us.

Paddy, my groom, a cheerful and affectionate Irishman, took me hunting for the first time when I was five and a half and afterwards I was usually ridden by one or other of the Duke's sons, being too strongly built to take his daughter; my favourite being the intelligent Lord John Manners, who stammered. Meanwhile Pioneer was used mainly as a carriage horse, although sometimes he would carry a rider to hounds for half a day. In the summer of 1843 he was sold and disappeared from my life, and in the autumn when I was six and a few months I was allowed to stay out with hounds all day if a second mount was not available.

Then at the very beginning of December there was a tremendous air of excitement at Belvoir among the servants and tenants of the estate. Carriages and chariots were brought out and cleaned, extra stables, some of them recently built, were prepared for visiting horses.

Carts, vans and drays delivered extra provisions to the Castle, the Duke's private band practised at all hours, and the gardeners were busy clipping shrubs into perfect shapes and tending the flowers. Paddy seemed to take longer each day in grooming us and much time was spent cleaning bits, buckles and stirrups with silver sand until they shone like silver.

The grooms talked over the impending royal visit and we learned from them that the Prince was coming to hunt with a fast pack, so that the British people could see that he was a brave and accomplished horseman. Our stud groom said that some of the gentry and also a few noblemen suspected that the Prince was a cowardly and ineffectual horseman partly on account of his nationality, for they believed that the English were the only people who could truly understand horses and hounds, with the Irish coming a poor second. A German might ride beautifully in a ménage, but would show little sense, skill or courage in the field.

On December 3rd six of the Prince's best horses arrived with two grooms and later one or two belonging to the Duke of Wellington – I cannot recall the exact number – and there was much discussion about the decorations which were being put up to celebrate the visit. We heard that the Prince intended to hunt his thoroughbred, Emancipation, but there was some uncertainty about whether the Queen would go to the meet. A triumphal arch was built of evergreens at the entrance to the park, and the tenants made plans to acclaim their Queen.

On December 4th the quietness of the morning was broken by the boom of guns, and an old war horse threw up his head and neighed a warning, but we heard later that the noise was only a royal salute being fired at

Nottingham Castle in honour of the Queen's arrival in the town. She had come by train from Chatsworth to be greeted by hundreds of people and companies of soldiers. Horses were harnessed and away she went with Prince Albert, escorted throughout by relays of troops of the Enniskillen Dragoons. The first carriage horses were exchanged at Bingham for fresh animals and soon after eleven our master, the Duke of Rutland, set out to meet the royal carriage and I learned later from his horse that there was much waving and cheering by Belvoir tenants, two hundred of whom had lined the road near Red Mile, and that a local gentleman, named Norton, of Elton Hall had come too with his own tenants and had also escorted the royal party right to Belvoir, which they reached with a great clatter just before half past one. Afterwards there was a flurry and bustle in our yard as the steaming carriage horses were rubbed down, watered and fed. And later they, too, described to us the triumphal arches, the decorated houses and all the bunting and flags.

'Had we not been blinkered we most certainly would have shied,' one gelding told us, 'for the bunting was very frightening when the wind caught it.'

In the late afternoon the Duke's second son came to the yard accompanied by a young man of fresh complexion, with a friendly smile and gentle manner, whom he introduced to Paddy as Charlie Daintree, saying that the Duke had decided that he should hunt me the following day. The young man stroked my neck and patted me, saying that I was a fine beast, and Paddy asked whether he was staying at the castle and he replied that he was and explained that he was related to the Duke through his mother's side. Then he talked merrily of racing, a subject close to Paddy's heart, and stroked a black cat sitting on a mounting block, and I saw that this man was an animal lover and as a result I felt quite happy about carrying him to hounds the next day.

In the evening the Castle, which stands on a mound, was bright with lamps and candles, the fountains gushed water and carriages and coaches rolled up the private road. Paddy said a grand dinner party was being given attended by many noblemen and their wives, including Sir Robert Peel, the Prime Minister.

The next morning soon after seven o'clock as our grooms were bringing us out to drink at the trough a handsome elderly gentleman walked into the yard, and a whisper went round. 'It's the Duke of Wellington!' The hero of Waterloo was still tall and walked like a soldier; his face was remarkable with fine eyes, and a hooked nose and his charm of manner was evident in the way he spoke to the grooms. I felt him looking me over as I walked across the yard and raised my head higher and lifted my tail, wanting his admiration.

'He bends well to the bridle, your grace,' said Paddy turning to smile politely at the Duke, who nodded solemnly, his hands behind his back.

Presently we heard that the Queen had decided to attend the meet and would drive over in a landau with the Queen Dowager, who had arrived at four the previous day, and the Duke of Rutland. So four of Belvoir's best black carriage horses were prepared and others to carry the outriders who dressed themselves in the Belvoir livery. Soon afterwards Paddy saddled me up, for Charlie Daintree had decided to ride me over himself. He was now splendidly clothed in scarlet coat, white stock, breeches, boots and a top hat and his face and eyes shone with youth and excitement.

'I was presented to her Majesty last night,' he said excitedly. 'I had not realised she was so enchanting and so *kind*. She has the loveliest blue eyes! I actually *liked* her, almost *loved* her!' And Paddy unaccustomed to young men talking so frankly and freely to him, merely smiled and advised Charlie to be gentle with my mouth which, he announced, was as soft as a ripe peach. As my rider sprang into my saddle a chariot set off to the Castle to take Prince Albert, the Duke of Wellington and Lord George Manners to Croxton Park to mount their horses which had gone on ahead.

'I should hurry, sir,' said Paddy.

Soon I was trotting along the private road in the wake of the groom who was hacking Emancipation over for the Prince. Meanwhile the Queen drove to the meet along public roads lined again with her subjects, and everywhere there was much cheering and, as she went, more and more people joined her until the cavalcade was at least three hundred strong. When I arrived at Croxton Park which was only a short distance from the actual meet I saw lots of decorations and mottoes such as 'God Save Queen Victoria and Prince Albert', and bunting running from building to building. Prince Albert and the Duke of Wellington were just mounting their horses surrounded by thousands of people and riders, for now another three hundred horsemen and women from a neighbouring hunt had joined us. However the Prince made his way through the crowd to join his wife and rode beside the landau as it was driven through Croxton Park to Waltham where hounds awaited us. He cut a fine figure on horseback, tall and slim, yet wide-shouldered with large blue eyes in a face hedged by sideboards. A thin brown moustache crowned his red upper lip and his

hair was the same light brown as the Queen's. She looked in contrast very tiny and young, sitting straight and demure in the landau beside her old aunt, Queen Adelaide. Her hair was parted in the middle and her blue eyes seemed to be watching the Duke as he cantered beside the landau dressed like Charlie in a red coat and top hat. At Waltham the cheers that greeted the royal pair were so loud that the Duke of Wellington's mount, which had been lent to him by the Duke of Wilton, became so disturbed that the old soldier had to dismount and ride one of his own instead, which fortunately had been brought over by a groom. Then we saw hounds and my heart began to beat wildly with excitement, and Charlie's time was taken up keeping me still. Someone proposed three cheers for the two Queens and at this my black friends pulling the landau threw up their heads and danced with excitement while the outriders were kept busy keeping the crowd back from the Queen.

Fortunately only a few minutes passed before the huntsman gave a toot on his horn and hounds moved off towards Melton, with almost six hundred riders in their wake.

Hounds found three foxes in Broom Covert and after a time, when one had left the wood, we all started galloping madly across the fields to the sound of their music. Charlie urged me forward until I was almost level with Emancipation, who was going like the wind with a long effortless stride, but, with so many people around, the fox was soon headed and we all turned back towards Melton. Soon we moved on to another wood where we failed to find, and riders drank from flasks and ate their sandwiches. Then hounds drew Waltham Pasture and found again and we had a ten minutes run jumping hedges, ditches and timber. We lost that fox in gorse but found another and then there followed a long run, with Charlie digging me with his spurs so that he could ride beside the Prince, whose horse was one of the fastest in the field. Now we thundered over the turf, five hundred or so behind us, the hounds streaming before us and the notes of the huntsman's horn ringing across the landscape.

We jumped a tall hedge with a ditch below, galloping a few yards behind the Prince, and a horse beside me fell, and then a post and rails. And, afterwards, a long meadow stretched out before us with the hounds moving closely together as though a table cloth could have covered the whole pack. Cries of 'Tally Ho!' came from a distant lane, beyond which we could see ploughed fields climbing to meet the grey sky; for an instant the whole of England seemed to lie before us, dreaming and beautiful with the trees dark, still and leafless and the sky pale as a pigeon's back. Oh, it was so lovely and so exciting that I felt the sweat breaking out on me all over! I strove then to make my legs move faster until I was beside the Prince and Charlie's hand was on my neck patting his thanks.

More hedges rose before me and wide newly dug ditches (for landowners were beginning to drain their fields) and timber fences and even a closed gate which Charlie put me at to get out of the way of other riders who were jumping the nearby hedge. All the time the noise of hounds and horn acted wildly on my brain driving me to greater efforts so that I would gladly have galloped until I dropped. Coming abreast of Emancipation I saw his ears flatten with annoyance, and his nostrils extend as he blew at me fiercely as though trying to say, 'You can't overtake royalty, keep back!' Then I felt Charlie's hand on my rein, 'Steady there!' At the same time a man in a top hat on a beautiful grey frowned and I dropped back a few paces, and catching my breath saw that the Prince was well accompanied by other young men: the Duke of Rutland's two eldest sons and also the Lords Wilton, Forrester and Jersey, all riding superb horses, and behind me there galloped a lone lady side saddle on a blue roan.

We leaped over a wall into a park across which we galloped like race horses our hearts pounding, our necks stretched out, our legs moving like clockwork, and then we came to ploughed fields and saw ahead of us a fine team of shires, their manes plaited with ribbons of red, white and blue and we realised by the way hounds paused and swung back that this team had headed the fox. Now our quarry turned off in another direction but was stopped by a dog, and changing his mind again made his way back towards Waltham, and then the huntsman's long wail on the horn told us that he had reached an earth and gone to ground. I looked around again at that moment and saw that the Prince was still riding determinedly and skilfully, sitting straighter than the English horsemen and interfering less with his mount on take-off. We jumped one last fence and were the first to arrive at the earth after the huntsman, his whipper-in and the Prince. And now I paused at last with my sides heaving and my hot breath rising like steam. I gulped and drew in a long sweet draught of air and, dismounting, Charlie turned my head to the wind.

'You're a great horse, Romany, and I wish you were mine,' he said and then Lord George Manners came across to congratulate him on his horsemanship and he replied that he was all right when his blood was up. 'But I was just a passenger today, this willing beast did it all.'

Men drank from their flasks again and horses stretched their necks and nibbled what grass they could find. The Prince, whose cheeks were red now from his exertions, commended the huntsman on his skill, and everyone talked about the run which had actually lasted forty minutes. Presently the Marquis of Granby suggested that we called it a day and we set off for Belvoir along with the Prince while hounds took a slightly different route. Charlie was most attentive and opened all the gates for the other riders, until two ladies joined our party and then, after being introduced, he chatted and joked with the prettiest all the way home with hardly a pause.

Gradually the intoxication caused by galloping in the wake of hound and horn died in me and by the time I reached Belvoir I was as quiet and calm as an old donkey back from a regular journey, but pleased none the less to see Paddy and plunge my muzzle into the warm gruel which he had prepared for me. The Duke of Wellington's hunter was anxious to know about the day as his master had turned him back after the first covert was drawn and the landau horses were interested because they had seen the start of the first run before returning the Queen to

Belvoir. So there was much blowing and talking between the bars that separated us that night while the band played at the castle; and, when dawn sent her first grey shaft through the window, it seemed only an hour or so since we had thundered so wildly across the Leicestershire fields as though we would die rather than be left behind in the chase which men call hunting.

CHAPTER TWO

I hear news of a journey

The next morning Paddy took me for a short walk in the park to loosen-up after hunting, and we saw the Queen, wearing blue velvet trimmed with white fur, walking arm in arm with the Prince who was in shooting dress. They looked to me like ordinary lovers and, although both were attractive, I could not understand why everyone made so much fuss about their visit.

Back in the yard, the grooms were discussing the Prince's horsemanship all over again, declaring that though he might be a German he did not lack courage. In fact he rode and walked with the stiff bearing of a soldier and, someone said, the proud valour of a Prussian.

There was another meet in the district that day and so the grooms were busy again hacking horses over and making gruels and mashes for their return. The Queen went with the Duke of Rutland to see hounds draw the first covert, while the Prince went shooting with the Duke of Wellington and the Duke of Bedford. I cannot sympathise with man's love of killing and was as usual greatly upset by the sound of guns firing, and the thought of the poor, beautiful birds falling to the ground with bloodstained plumage.

The next day the royal party left in the landau at eight o'clock, the Prince's horses having gone on ahead. They went to Leicester this time and were again cheered by great crowds. One triumphal arch, crowned by two stuffed foxes, bore the inscription 'Albert, Prince of Wales,

England's Hope', referring to the Queen's baby son whom the English expected one day to be king.

By this time I was tired of all the excitement and the endless talk of the royal family, and was looking forward to more hunting, without, if possible, any foxes being killed.

My wish was granted for Charlie Daintree rode me to hounds the next day, but, without the incentive of keeping up with Prince Albert, he proved to be an indecisive rider. He put me, for example, at a black bullfinch and then changed his mind and all but turned me back, and I only saved myself by snatching the reins and bounding forward to take off a stride too late. Then I nearly fell as I hit the top. Afterwards Lord George Manners angrily told Charlie that he should let me go on at the fences or risk an accident. But Charlie only smiled and said he was deuced sorry and would try to do better next time.

'I'm not in the saddle more than two or three times a month, so you must forgive me my occasional mistakes. I will try to mend my ways and would be much distressed if I were to damage Romany in the slightest,' he said in his light charming voice, which was hard to dislike, even when the words were irritating.

By the next day most of the house party had gone and the stables were getting back into their usual routine, with only members of the family driving or riding the horses. I love the place to be run like this, in the same way day after day. It makes me feel safe and secure and when I listen for Paddy's footstep I know he will not fail me. I can look forward to regular meals, and the chimes of the stable clock fill me with happiness for they seem to regulate the day and keep everything in proper order. Before first light each winter morning I hear the pump going up and down, as the sleepy grooms and stable boys wash under its gushing water, and the mewing of the black cat asking for milk. Lanterns swing in the murky darkness and feet crunch on the gravel or clatter on the cobbles, and then I hear Paddy's cheerful whistling and know that another day has begun. I raise my head and neigh for the hay he will put in the rack for me to nibble as he mucks out my stable, and I think of the food that will follow, the broad flakes of bran and the fine full oats, and the dull chaff that stops me gobbling. But this year of 1844 wasn't to be like that right through the winter.

In January I heard news of a change, when Charlie's name cropped up in conversation. There was talk of a bet, a wager to save his honour, and it was said that the Duke had agreed to lend me to him for a long ride down to Cornwall. My master had said such a trek might be the making of the young fool, who meant well but had no spine or perseverance. The Duke was a betting man himself, who often lost money on horses, so could understand Charlie's troubles. 'But he shouldn't play the tables,' he said. 'He hasn't the brains for that.'

Paddy was clearly upset at the thought that I was to be taken out of his care and left in the hands of a young man with 'as much sense as a louse', as he put it. 'Why, that young gentleman couldn't find his way from Red Mile to Nottingham, let alone from Leicester to Tintagel!'

Other grooms said that Cornwall was a wild and dreadful place, where I should doubtless fall into the hands of gipsies. They said the Duke was making a mistake in letting me go, and that he was too kind hearted, and that Charlie Daintree came of an unreliable family and had bad blood in his veins. Paddy said the fool was too fond of the bottle and a stable boy said he reckoned the ladies would be the young gentleman's downfall. Then Charlie came to the yard again and rode me out on the roads and tracks and across the fields for three hours, and spoke in so friendly a way to the grooms that for a time they began to relent and say that he wasn't such a bad young gentleman after all. Paddy told him that I needed feeding every four hours during the day and must always be offered a drink first, never afterwards. He told him I must wear two rugs at night and never be galloped over stones, and he warned Charlie that the Duke would be very angry if I was returned with any blemishes or splints or spavins. 'You've got a valuable 'oss there, a good 'un, who must be cared for like a child.'

Charlie promised that he would do all that Paddy told him, and that he wouldn't make me go too far, or let me sleep in draughty, dirty stalls. He said that he would make the ostlers at the inns clean my saddle and bridle so that they were always supple and comfortable. And, feeling better, Paddy said he would see that I had a fine set of strong shoes that would last me the whole journey, so there would be no problem about finding a farrier; he also said that he would take me for long rides every day at a hound-jog, so that I would be as fit as an athlete in training. He said I was just the horse to make a long journey and that I could beat any horse to be found anywhere in the whole length and breadth of England, and that Charlie's rival, Archie Hickstead, would not be able to find a comparable animal.

I heard that the journey was to start in February and that Charlie hoped to retrieve his lost fortune by winning and that the wager had been made before witnesses when Charlie and Archie were under the influence of drink.

The grooms said that in their grandfather's days the two young fools would have fought a duel instead. They then made several rude remarks about *young bloods* and *tom-foolery* and Paddy wished that the Duke had let Charlie have any other horse but me.

Such changes of attitude were unsettling. And I didn't understand exactly what was wanted from me, only that somehow I had to behave well and work hard for the honour of Belvoir, and that a long and arduous journey was before me; a ride which would be safe and easy enough if I was cared for by Paddy or his like, but would undoubtedly be difficult because of the poor judgement and unreliable nature of Charlie.

It was all very disquieting and yet in a strange way exciting for although the routine was, as I have said, comforting and pleasant, the prospect of change suddenly seemed to stir me. I began to paw the ground in the morning if my hay did not come quickly enough and to nudge Paddy when he was slow tipping my feed into the manger. I suppose I realised that there was a challenge in the air and that quickened my blood and gave me a new impatience and feeling of importance.

January came to an end with rain and high winds, and my mother, who was expecting another foal, was kept in night and day, and there was much talk of a new drainage system for the fields. The Duke came to see me and feeling my muscles, declared me to be fit.

'The sure winner, if young Charlie keeps his head,' he forecast. 'I have a mind to lay a bet myself that he will be first at Tintagel.'

'But what a time of year to choose, your Grace,' the stud groom said.

'Ah, it would be far too easy in summer. These young

men want to test themselves, that's natural at their age. I admire them for it, so let it be.'

And that was the last time I was to see my true owner for many a month.

CHAPTER THREE

Lost in the dark

Three smart young men wearing fancy waistcoats, checked trousers, cut-away coats and top hats, witnessed our departure, their noses reddened by the keen February air. Charlie wore breeches, boots, a stock, plain waist-coat, beaver hat and leather gloves.

'Archie's riding a weed, you'll win easily my dear fellow,' said one of the young men twisting his beautiful fair moustache.

'I *mean* to be there first,' said Charlie. 'I must win or flee the country. My debts, ah how my debts haunt me! You've no idea, the nightmares. Pray for me my friends.'

'That we will do!' exclaimed the owner of the fair moustache. 'My thoughts will go with you.'

'I back my brother as you know,' answered a man of sanguine appearance with dark sideburns, while the third who was neutral patted my neck. 'I wish you a safe journey and God's speed,' he said solemnly. 'It's a bold man or a fool who undertakes so long a journey at this time of year.'

Now Charlie turned and, with a little bow, wished his companions goodbye.

'I'm neither a fool nor a courageous man, just half way in-between.'

'Good luck! Keep away from the tables and the ladies and no tippling!'

His fair friend's warning seemed to follow us down the twisty lane that wound its way between hovels and better cottages as though made by the straying feet of drunken men. Clipped and cold, I was glad to trot briskly with my breath rising like steam in the cold air. Soon dark clouds rolled up across the sky and balls of hail fell, beating a tattoo on the hard surface of the road and the roofs of the cottages. Charlie turned up the collar of his cloak and pulled his hat lower on his head. Then quite suddenly the sky cleared and a sunlit patch of blue lay before us like a grotto in a dark cave.

At midday we stopped at an inn where a young ostler fetched me water and rubbed me down in a stall, hissing and muttering about the long journey that lay before me. I buried my head in a moist feed in which split beans had been added to the oats to give me extra energy. Meanwhile Charlie also ate well and came out about half an hour later with a swagger to his walk.

'To horse!' he cried dramatically. 'No time to waste!' The ostler put on the 'furniture' as he called my saddlery, and in no time we were on our way again, trotting and cantering down lanes and tracks through flat countryside almost empty of leaves and birdsong. I loved my home and did not want to leave Belvoir. The further I went the less eager I was to continue until Charlie used his spurs and I had no alternative but to go on.

We came to another inn at dusk and another ostler led me away to a warm stall where I stood next to a big chestnut who had just been taken out of a stage coach. He had galloped down hard roads and now his legs ached and he hardly seemed to know which to rest first. Later he lay down with his head stretched out breathing heavily, but I remained standing all night. I do not like lying down when I am tied or in a strange place. I dozed and was wakened by rats scuttling in the straw under my feet.

Big brown fellows they were with intelligent beady little eyes, bright as boot buttons. Had rats been found at Belvoir the head groom might have been dismissed, but that inn was a miserable place with holes in the walls and not a cat to be seen. In the morning my feed tasted of mice and the hay was yellow and rank. I had eaten what I could when Charlie appeared smiling with his cheeks still fresh from yesterday's ride.

'How's he doing? He's a nice horse and a great one with hounds,' he told the ostler, who replied that I was 'a fine 'oss, gentle as a baby.'

Presently I was saddled-up and another day of the journey began. A light drizzle of rain fell softly from steel-grey skies and Charlie sang old ballads. And I was happy then, for I love singing.

'On to the sea and I'll wager you've never seen the sea before,' declared my rider.

But he could not know that I had heard horses talk of it, especially a little mare who pulled the Duke's phaeton and had once lived in Brighton, taking a trap up and down the Promenade.

'We are going to win,' Charlie now went on. 'Two

hundred golden sovereigns, my dear Romany, think of that! And then I'm going to change my ways. I'm going to become a respectable country gentleman. I shall no longer be seen at the gaming tables nor the races. I'm going to marry a nice girl with a fine dowry, and settle down and rear a family.'

He patted and stroked my neck as he talked and for a time I almost forgot about Belvoir and Paddy.

That day we took a long time to find an inn for lunch and it was past three o'clock before I was settled in a stable with my muzzle deep in a manger, and, as I ate, it started to sheet with rain.

In no time at all Charlie was with me again.

'Just five more miles, Romany,' he said, as he swung himself into the saddle. 'I've looked at the map.'

He soon turned me into fields where he galloped me before the wind and the wild driving rain, until my heart was pounding with excitement and my sides heaving. At last he brought me back to a trot. 'Had enough?' he asked, his breath heavy with the smell of wine. My hot, wet body steamed, but Charlie complained of the cold.

'You are lucky not to have been born with fingers and toes. Man is most stupidly constructed.' He put a hand inside his cloak and took a few gulps from his brandy flask. 'Ah, that's better.'

We went through a gate and came out on a rough road, and presently we heard the rumbling of wheels and the clattering of many hoofs and a few moments later a coach and four came into view. In a trice Charlie had me standing in the middle of the road. Waving his arms he brought the sweating horses to a halt. They leaned forward trying to stretch out their tired necks, but their bearing reins were too tight to allow it; a little foam lay like cherry blossom around their mouths and flecked their wide chests.

A pretty girl with kiss curls leaned out of the window while Charlie asked the coachman how far it was to the next town.

'Five miles, sir.'

'Five miles?' Poor Charlie was incredulous.

'You must ride like the wind to get there before dark,' said the girl teasingly before drawing back into the coach.

'We will. Never fear!' said Charlie taking off his hat to her as the coach raced away into the gathering dusk.

'He can't be right,' said Charlie, bringing out his map. 'And I can't gallop you along that road or you'll spring a splint and then there will be no two hundred sovereigns to get me out of a hole. In actual fact I shall be ruined.'

He dismounted and, screwing up his eyes, tried to read the map in the fading light.

'We've taken a wrong turn. Ah, here's a short cut, up over a bit of downland, that couldn't be better. Can you gallop on a bit, Romany? You must or we shall be caught in the dark without a light.'

He stuffed the map away under his cloak, took another swig of brandy, sprang into the saddle and dug in his spurs. Away we went then with mud spattering our faces, rain whipping our backs and the sky above turning black as tar. And I longed for Paddy, who would never have allowed himself to be caught in such a situation.

After a mile or so we turned down a track into a wood, a deep wood with dark firs and the scent of wet pine needles. It was very quiet and the track seemed to go on and on, while the darkness came down through the trees and blackened everything. The night grew very still, as the rain stopped. And the boughs dripped, pitter patter on the sodden earth. Then the track petered out and we were simply moving through trees, hundreds of trees, all slender and dark and not yet large enough for the forester's axe. Charlie shivered and I knew from his smell that he was frightened and that made me nervous. He stopped me and drank again from his flask and cursed, and his voice seemed very faint and young in the darkness of the wood. There was no moon nor stars only the rolling clouds, and the horrible quietness which seemed to suggest that we were miles from open fields or roads and tracks. Not a chink of light proclaimed a thinning in the trees which were now hard for me to see so that I was constantly brushing Charlie's legs against their trunks. Then, all at once, I felt a path under my feet and those regiments of trunks parted a little to allow a passageway. The air freshened, a tiny night breeze wafted the scent of lavender through the darkness, and I saw before me the solid form of a building. I stopped. It was very strange and I cannot now explain the sensation which came over me because there are no words to match my feelings. The trees seemed to move slowly away to reveal to my startled eyes a little dingle in which a tiny deserted cottage stood. And then I sensed that a strange being was with us. My heart thumped and my eyes seemed to strain in their sockets. A snort, my snort, rent the silence with the savageness of a pistol shot; the splintering of twigs told me that some wild animal was fleeing before us. I stood with legs straddled then, my skin flapping with fear. I saw a luminous figure dressed in ragged clothes rise from the walls of the cottage, and as she levitated her sad grey eyes seemed to look straight at me. Her lovely red hair lay about her narrow shoulders, and over her arm she held a basket full of lavender tied up in bunches ready

for the market. But she wasn't alive; she was transparent
and through her ragged skirts and shawl I could see the
darkness beyond. And I knew that her lily-white face was
bloodless. The poor girl was neither dead nor alive. She
was for ever between the two states.

'Romany, my dear fellow, have you seen a ghost?'
Charlie's voice came to me like the voice of sanity and
commonsense. More calmly I watched the tragic figure
float away among the still trees, while my eyes began to
feel more normal and my flesh settled. He had seen
nothing but the solid form of the cottage, the dripping

trees and the blackness of the night, to which his eyes had become accustomed. I straightened my legs. I tossed my head as though to cast out the memory of that ghost.

'There now,' said Charlie, dismounting. 'Dear me, you are in a sorry state. Fear not. Let me lead you on.'

He pulled my ears affectionately, stroked my neck and rubbed his bristly cheek against mine. 'Be a brave fellow. See, there's a hut where we can take shelter.'

He coaxed me forward, kindled a light with his tinder and found the door. The scent of lavender had faded to be replaced by the more natural smells of wet fir wood and damp earth. It started to rain again.

'Come on, inside.'

The cottage had just one room with a broken window and a pile of sacks or rags in one corner.

'A miserable place,' said Charlie, 'but at least it will afford us some shelter.'

He took off my saddle and bridle, rubbed me down with a handful of rags and patted my neck.

'Sorry my old friend but I am afraid you must go hungry tonight. Thank God for my brandy or I might have expired with the cold.'

He latched the door, drained his flask, wrapped himself up in his cloak, lay down on the earth floor and was soon fast asleep. But I could not forget the ghost and that night was full of fears for me. I could hear noises that no human ear could detect, and I stood close to Charlie until the dawn, wanting the comfort of a breathing, living thing.

I nuzzled him, as the light came through the little window, glad to break the loneliness of my vigil, and he awoke smiling.

'Oh heavens, where am I?' his voice was heavy with sleep. 'Oh Romany, what a night! I was dreaming. I was

in London with the most wonderful girl with dark flashing eyes and such hair! But you're only a horse, you
wouldn't understand, and I'm an idiot to speak to you in
this way. Heavens, I'm cold!' He stretched. 'And stiff too!
What a miserable place this is. I bet Archie managed
things better, a hotel bed for Archie I'll be bound. And
you're cold too,' he added, looking at me. 'Oh dear me,
what a pickle, and all my own fault for drinking too
much wine at that inn and not reading the map accu-
rately. Have you seen any more ghosts, my dear fellow?
You were rigid as a plank.'

As he spoke he picked up my bridle and looked at it
with a perplexed frown on his face. 'Which way up? Well,
the bit must be at the bottom. Open up, Romany, now
you must be patient and good.' He spent a long time
saddling and bridling me and when we left the cottage
my bit was too low in my mouth and my girth back to
front.

CHAPTER FOUR

I swim for my life

Now in daylight the wood seemed a friendly place, full of singing birds and flashes of green where clearings allowed the grass to grow. The path from the wood-man's cottage led us towards a break in the trees through which the early sun shone.

'That means we are heading south-east,' said Charlie. 'We should keep a little more to our right but I'm hanged if I'll leave this blessed path.'

I was hungry. My tummy rumbled and I longed for a bite of spring grass to freshen my dry throat. All the same I cantered willingly, being careful not to trip on roots and each moment the wood seemed to lighten so that we knew we were moving towards open country. Then at last we were out of the trees and galloping down a track towards a farmhouse which nestled against a brown hill, like a wild animal sunning itself on a ledge.

Soon Charlie was knocking on the old front door. 'Anyone at home?'

A woman came with a grey shawl over her shoulders. 'Yes?'

In a few moments Charlie had explained how we had spent the night and the woman had promised him a fine breakfast of bacon and eggs. A man was summoned and soon I had drunk deep at a trough before being settled in a stable with a good feed and a rack of hay. An hour later we were on the road again.

'It *was* a ghost you saw, Romany,' said Charlie. 'Poor

Mary, the lavender girl, who was betrayed by her lover, Joe the forester. No one will live in the hut now on account of her presence. It's very singular that you should have seen her and I should not.'

Feeling better for my feed, I trotted willingly enough and we soon reached the town where Charlie had intended spending the night. Here he left me tied by a public drinking trough while he went to buy a compass. When he returned a small crowd had collected around me.

'Is this the 'oss what's a travelling all the way down to Cornwall?' one swarthy man asked.

'Indeed, indeed,' replied Charlie with his good natured smile. 'But I was not aware that we were famous. News travels fast in these parts and no mistake. Have you heard of my rival, a dark haired fellow riding a mare with two white socks?' But no one had news of Archie, not here nor in any of the hamlets through which we passed during the afternoon. We kept to one road and the day passed uneventfully, and before nightfall we came to a manor house owned by Charlie's cousins.

'I promise you safe lodging this night. No ghosts, no haunted houses to set your flesh flapping, and I believe there's a horse from Belvoir to keep you company,' said Charlie as he turned me up a well raked gravel drive flanked by yew hedges.

The front door of the house opened and a stout barrel-chested man in breeches and gaiters looked out.

'So you are here on your mad escapade, Charlie Daintree,' he said gruffly. 'Our other guest overtook you on the road and brought news of you. Your horse will be in need of fodder and a good rub-down. Stanley! You must be patient. Our servants are getting old like us and don't move as fast as they did.' At that moment an old bow-legged groom came shuffling round the corner of the house. He took my rein, grunting disapprovingly at the mud and earth on my coat, and led me away.

He put me in a loose-box with a floor of blue Stafford-shire brick from which, looking through bars, I soon addressed my neighbour, a fine bay shining like mahogany. My whinny of welcome was returned, the long elegant head turned; fine nostrils were pushed between the bars.

'Romany!'

'Pioneer!'

How pleased we were to see one another. And how we longed to be closer so that we could feel each other all over with our muzzles. It started to rain as we began to talk.

'What's brought you here?' asked my friend.

And I told him my story and all the news from Belvoir, and then he explained to me that the Duke had sold him to Charlie's cousin at the Manor House.

'I am a horse of all work now. I carry him to hounds and pull the trap, and I have even pulled the mower that cuts the grass on the lawn, with rubber boots on my feet so that I should not spoil the turf. Oh, it's a quiet peaceful life, with just Joey, who taught my master's children to ride, to keep me company now and then. Yet I'm bored, Romany, really I am.'

'But you were bored at Belvoir,' I reminded him.

'Yes, but this is worse. But I hear that Master is short of money and I may be sold. They say I'll fetch a lot, because I'm reliable and lively and up to weight. I'm heavy without being clumsy.'

'I know, I know. That is what Paddy always said,' I cut

in. 'He talks of you even now. He says you are a great beast, a grand hunter.'

'And now I want to be in a larger place again, an estate, with carriage horses as well as hunters and all the bustle of a busy yard. How I hate these bars! Will men never learn that horses like to have windows, too? I want to push my head out into the fresh air and smell the spring! Oh, how well I remember the oaks at Belvoir, and all the excitement before a great house party. Standing here all day looking on that passage I hear so many noises, yet I cannot tell what they mean. I cannot see what's going on. Everyone is kind. No one ill-treats me. But Romany you are the first visitor for ever such a long time! And although Stanley is a good man he doesn't talk to me as Paddy did.'

'Charlie is kind, too,' I said. 'He talks and sings to me and I am growing to love him, but he's foolish, Pioneer. I can't trust him and I'm not sure where he will take me next. And he drinks too much liquor and yet and yet, there's something about him which makes me very glad of his company.'

We talked through much of that wet and stormy night, sniffing each other's nostrils and when I was saddled at nine o'clock next morning we looked longingly at one another and were sad to part.

The day was damp and grey. Standing outside the Manor House waiting for Charlie I felt the keenness of the February wind biting at my clipped flanks.

Stanley soon started to grumble. He threw a rug over my quarters and led me up and down, and every now and then he stopped to beat his arms across his breast against his sides to warm his hands. Ten minutes must have passed in this way, then fifteen, then twenty. A maid came out of the house with a tankard of frothy beer for Stanley. 'Don't let the master see it, drink up quick,' she said.

'I'll be in need of brandy soon!' he said.

Then we heard a familiar tinkling laugh in the garden and seeing the girl who had looked out of the carriage so prettily I knew the cause of our delay. Walking across the lawn with Charlie, she wore a long brown coat and a fur trimmed bonnet, and her eyes sparkled as she laughed up into his face. Presently they both went into the house through a side door and the church clock struck the half hour, and Stanley muttered something rude about 'young bounders'. I thought of Archie and the bay mare that I had never seen. And I remembered that the people and horses at Belvoir expected me to win. I wondered whether my rivals were already on their way and I recalled the warning given by Charlie's young friend about keeping away from the ladies.

''E'll be driving you that 'ard to make up for lost time, that 'e will,' said Stanley. 'Master should give 'im the boot.' Then it began to drizzle with rain, and the old man found another rug to put over my saddle to keep it dry. Pioneer neighed and I neighed back to let him know I was still around. And then the little old grey pony in the field neighed too, and a Newfoundland dog started to bark.

At last, as the church clock struck ten, Charlie came out full of apologies.

'I was delayed,' he said, pressing a silver coin into Stanley's hand.

'And we all know what by, that we do,' snarled the groom, keeping the money. 'I'm an old man to be 'anging about while a young bounder plays with the ladies.'

The girl stood on the steps smiling.

433

'Bon voyage,' she said, tossing her head and making a rude face at the groom's back.

'Au revoir! On to Tintagel and the ghosts of King Arthur and all his knights,' cried Charlie dramatically, swinging into the saddle and pushing me straight into a trot. At the bottom of the drive he turned and waved to the girl who stood on the doorstep looking like a brown china ornament.

'And now for the road!' he cried to me as though he were an actor playing a part rather than a real man on a long and arduous journey.

We had thirty miles to cover after a late start, but my rider remained cheerful. Indeed he soon started to sing and invent crazy poems about beautiful girls. Every now and then he stopped to consult his compass of which he seemed very proud.

'We won't get lost with this bit of magic on board! Oh, Romany, have you ever seen such a girl!'

Soon we took a gated road which led us through pleasant hilly countryside. We came to a farm where Charlie paused to buy me a feed, and soon afterwards we stopped to eat, Charlie having brought sandwiches and a bottle of ale from his cousin's house. Scenting food a little

dog came begging scraps of bread from my master. A terrier, mostly white, he had a brown patch over one ear, bandy legs and a short stumpy tail. He stood only about twelve inches high, but his eyes were spirited and he looked as though he could walk for ever, for his little limbs seemed to move automatically. Charlie made a great fuss of the dog, talking to him as though he were another human being, and patting and stroking him.

When the last morsel of sandwich had disappeared down the terrier's throat, Charlie mounted me.

'Now, home, dog!' he said. 'Go on, home!'

But the little dog only gazed up at us with astonishment, as though amazed that we could be so cruel and unfeeling as to send him away after he had offered us his adoration for life.

'Oh don't be silly, you must have an owner somewhere,' said Charlie.

But the little dog came with us, his bandy legs working like clockwork and his eyes full of admiration for Charlie and happiness that he had found himself a master.

After a time my rider dismounted and lifted up the dog so that he could ride on the pommel of the saddle.

'We'll call you Skip until we find who you belong to,' he said, and the little dog licked his nose, as if to say thank you.

Presently we came in pouring rain to a village perched on a hill above a rushing river. Charlie hitched me to a post and went to a shop with Skip in his arms. I turned around until I had my back to the wind. A carrier's cart passed by and a timber wagon pulled by three enormous shire horses, with brasses shining on their harness, and a couple of dogs yapped at me through a fence. Then Charlie returned still carrying Skip.

435

'It seems you will be staying with us for a while,' he said, patting the terrier. 'Can't *you* tell us where your owner is?' He fetched his map out from under his cloak and consulted his compass.

'We're behind-hand. Can you manage a ford, Romany? It will be quite deep.'

Feeling cold and impatient to be off, I pawed the ground.

'I suppose that means yes,' said Charlie, tucking away map and compass and turning up the collar of his cloak. 'And there's no time to waste. I've news of Archie; he's five or six miles ahead of us on the upper road.'

He mounted quickly putting the dog in front of him perched on the saddle with his paws on my withers.

'You're a fine brave horse and ten miles further on there's a capital lodging house with good fare for man and beast. But we can cut that distance by a third if the ford is passable,' he said, urging me into a trot.

Soon we took a lane which wound between bare thorn hedges, where the puddles lay like little lakes overflowing here and there to rush ahead of us down towards the valley. The sky rumbled with thunder while the clouds rolled above the hills and valley, and the trees shuddered under the fury of the wind.

We came to a fork with a choice of two lanes running almost parallel, before curving away from one another towards the river we hoped to cross.

'Right or left?' asked Charlie. 'I can't dig out the map in this rain.'

He threw down my reins and drove me forward, and I took the left for it seemed to lead towards woods and I wanted shelter from the storm. Now thunder growled like the guns of war, and lightning cracked the sky and lit the waving treetops. Our lane ran beside the woods not through them and Charlie was loath to lose time taking shelter. We had been climbing upwards for a while, but now we started to descend and the lower we went the wetter was the ground underfoot until the water came above my fetlocks. Little Skip, who had jumped down from the saddle earlier on, was all but swimming so Master pulled him up on to my back again, from which he saw the swollen river foaming and rushing before us and the trees tossing either side.

'The deuced thing is flooded – this, my dear Romany, is the ford!' cried Charlie. 'Just my luck!' He pulled me to a halt, fetched out his flask and drank deeply from it, then he poured a little liquor into each of his boots to warm his wet feet.

'Dammit! We should have delayed until April, waited for fairer weather. What fools we were, what hot-headed idiots to choose February fill-dyke, the wettest month of the year. Dear Romany, I am sorry but you may have to swim.'

He leaned down and patted me on the neck. 'They said in the shop that the river was passable. Ah well, nothing venture nothing win!'

I had crossed rivers before but never one so deep and fierce, and now I was frightened of those dreadful rushing waters which bore sticks and branches along as though they were bits of straw. I blew through my nostrils and danced from side to side and Charlie said, 'Only cowards turn back.' Then he spurred me forward.

'God spare us,' he cried. 'Spare us, and I'll never gamble or drink heavily again. I'll mend my ways, dear Lord. But please first take us safely across this river!'

Behind us streams of water raced down the hill to join

the flood like children running to catch up with the crowd at a fair. The wind drove us from behind, sending my tail between my legs. Skip barked as lightning zig-zagged in the crazy sky. I hesitated, blew again through my nostrils and then plunged into the swirling waters. Charlie, knowing that a swimming horse must use his neck, threw down the reins. Skip barked more wildly standing up on my back to admonish the river for its fury. On the other side the trees swayed away from us, creaking and groaning like old men. The water pressed

hard against me as it rushed downstream. It rose up to the stirrups. It climbed Charlie's legs. It reached my mouth as the floor of the river seemed to give way under my feet. A moment later there was nothing but the water and myself battling against one another. The force of the river toppled me over on to my side. My mouth and throat filled with water and I thought that I should drown. I heard a stifled cry from Charlie and, with a choking snort, righted myself, then found that I was swimming for the first time in my life. My tail fanned out in the water to act as a rudder, my legs moved in the right motions without directions from myself. I forgot Charlie, Skip and the ride to Cornwall and thought only of reaching the other side where the lane led upwards between trees to meet the wild tempestuous sky.

A moment later my feet felt firm ground. I scrambled and plunged forward and came into shallower water covering the bank which had once marked the edge of the river, and then I was out and standing on the lane. I shook myself like a dog, I snorted to clear my nostrils and throat while my wet sides heaved up and down. My saddle was empty. Where was Charlie? And what should I do? My first impulse was to gallop until my legs were so tired that I could go no further. But where to? I stared at the raging river. I looked downstream where young trees were being dragged up from their roots by the current, where weeds and undergrowth were flattened and fencing posts split. I looked up the lane along which we had come, in case Charlie had somehow turned back, and into the darkness of the trembling wood. There was not a cottage or building in sight, not a human voice to guide me. I neighed and my neigh rose above the storm and hung for a moment in the air. I neighed again. And then I saw the little dog lying panting on a brown patch of sodden earth a few yards downstream, and Charlie still in the water hanging on to a tree, his black cloak swirling madly round his body.

I turned as another flash of lightning lit the sky and trotted up the hill, and at the top was a tiny thatched cottage. I neighed again and a little door opened and a wrinkled old man came out. He looked at me, at my soaking body and shaking sides, and then turned to find a sack to put over his head and shoulders. Then he took my reins and led me back down the hill with all the vigour of the storm beating in his face.

'Someone drowned,' he muttered. 'Some poor soul.' He turned his head, looked up and down the swollen river and spotted Charlie white and hatless with his wet hair plastered to his head. He left me then and climbed a fence and went to pull him out. But he wasn't strong enough.

'I'll die of cold, if I don't drown first. Make haste, get a rope. Help me, man, help me!' gasped Charlie between chattering teeth.

The old man leapt the fence with the agility of a mountain goat, jumped on my back and galloped me back to the cottage. He found a rope, broke down a bit of fence and led me to Charlie. He tied the rope round Charlie's chest, hitched the ends around the flaps of my saddle and urged me forward. The saddle moved. I pulled again. The old man pulled. The saddle slipped back but my well sprung ribs held it from passing over my flanks. I pulled again and with a cry of gratitude Charlie came to rest on a lump of undergrowth.

'Brandy in my cloak,' he whispered hoarsely.

And the old man found the flask and held it to my master's lips, and watched the colour come back into his face. Then the old man went to Skip and opening the little dog's jaws, persuaded him to drink also. And after a few moments the terrier got to his feet and shook himself as though he had just been for a pleasant dip on a summer's day.

Charlie sat up. 'I think I owe you my life,' he said simply.

'This 'oss fetched me,' the old man said. 'He neighed outside the cottage.'

'God be praised,' exclaimed Charlie with a fervour which was not natural to him. And then he laughed. 'I wager I look like a drowned rat!'

The old man said we had taken the wrong lane. The other ford was usually passable whereas this one was only useful in midsummer or at times when there was little rain. It was particularly treacherous because of a shelf which made the floor of the river fall suddenly away. He helped Charlie to climb on my back and we returned to the cottage with Skip trotting cheerfully and a little drunkenly at my side. Then the old man explained that he had a rabbit stew with dumplings hanging in a pot over the fire, but nothing that would adequately feed a horse. He could only give me chicken feed and a bit of straw. He took me to a hovel leaning against the cottage and, after removing various garden tools, he led me inside and fetched me a little water, maize and straw. He rubbed me down and made a rough rug for me out of sacks, using a jack-knife to slice them open and sewing them where necessary with a large needle and string. As he worked a plump black cat sat on his knees purring softly and looking with adoring emerald green eyes at his master's wrinkled face. And the old man talked to the cat and to me as though we were people.

Meanwhile Skip and my master were inside the cottage drying themselves before the wood fire, waiting to be joined by their host when he was sure I was comfortable.

'I'll have another think and if I can conjure up any more food for you, I'll be back,' said the old man before leaving.

The roof of that little hovel rocked terribly in the wildness of the storm, but it was well-made and nothing split or came apart, and I remained dry and snug all night. At dawn the old man came back, moving as softly as his cat and carrying a bucket which steamed and smelt delicious.

'I remembered that I had a little linseed put aside in case I needed a poultice, so I've made you a mash which will set you up for the day and make your coat shine like a jewel,' he said, speaking in the way of an educated man and moving like an animal of the woods accustomed to stalking its prey or escaping silently from enemies.

I whinnied politely for I loved that man, and he stroked me kindly as though he liked the feel of my coat.

We bade him goodbye as the sun streaked the eastern sky with ribbons of gold and red, and the country lay quiet at last after the tumult of the storm.

'I owe you my life,' Charlie said again, squeezing his hand.

'Don't say such things, that's blasphemy,' the old man said. 'We do not decide these things.'

'Please let me give you a sovereign. It would afford me such pleasure. You have looked after us capitally,' begged Charlie.

But the old man refused to accept anything, saying that he hoped to reap his reward in heaven and that money was of no importance to him. He lived all alone, Charlie said later, snaring rabbits and growing his own vegetables and earning a big hedging and ditching when that work was available. Perhaps in his heart he knew that Charlie was actually in debt with no money of his own to spare. Perhaps he knew many things without being told. There was something unforgettably wise about that brown wrinkled face which haunts me to this day.

CHAPTER FIVE

Trouble at an inn

After that frightening episode Charlie vowed that he would take no more risks and the next two days passed uneventfully. We stayed at inns with Skip sleeping in my manger as soon as I had finished my evening feed. Then every morning at daybreak the little dog would lick my muzzle and dance round me barking as though he was celebrating the dawn.

On the third afternoon we caught up with Archie on his weedy bay mare with two white socks.

'I thought you were lost. I heard bad news of you,' he told us. 'What a life!' he grinned, showing long white teeth. 'Is the dog your mascot, Charlie?' His voice mocked; his hazel eyes were heavily lidded and his nose curved like an eagle's beak.

'Just a little friend who has chosen to adopt us.'

'Oh, now you are being sentimental. I should part company with that cur, otherwise you are only adding to your weight and responsibility.'

'Romany is a substantial fellow. I only weigh eleven stone,' retorted Charlie. 'He's a nice little dog with engaging ways, and the word cur is objectionable to my ears.'

'Running out of money?' asked Archie with an impudent grin.

'Not at all, not at all, Archibald,' replied Charlie with his disarming laugh. 'You must not worry so much about me. We have been living very carefully.'

'No liquor?'

'Just enough to keep the wicked cold at bay.'

As the two men continued to exchange remarks of this kind half in mirth and half in earnest, I looked at my rival. She possessed, I noted, a finely cut head, rather nervous protruding eyes and a long slender neck. Her skin was so thin that here and there you could see the veins standing out like string, and her cannon bones were too narrow to suggest stamina. She walked nervously, looking more like a three year racehorse than a seven year-old hunter, her small hoofs picking their way daintily over stony ground. In contrast my own feet looked large as sunflowers and my cannon bones like fencing posts.

'I'm going to gallop to freshen up my mare. Coming?' asked Archie.

But Charlie declined saying we were taking the journey steadily. And we called goodbye to our rival, as Archie spurred the mare into a gallop, and presently we heard her hoofs on the stones growing fainter as she disappeared into the distance.

That night we took lodgings at an inn noisy with merrymaking. Someone played an accordion and there was much fine singing and many ribald jokes. Then around ten o'clock there was an uproar outside and I heard voices raised in anger, threats and curses and the sound of clashing sticks and thrown stones. Our ostler came running down from his loft and joined in the fray and occasional cheers contrasted with the groans and angry shouts of injured men. Little Skip barked wildly in the stable, jumping at the door as though he hoped to break it open and get out to join in the fray. Tied as I was with a rope and ball, I could see nothing although the noises seemed to tell their own story and I guessed that a fight between two different factions was going on.

Presently the latch of our door was lifted and Charlie came in, saying, 'Down, Skip, down, sir,' as the little dog tried to welcome his new master. 'There's been an affray,' he went on, as though we were humans who would understand. 'A lad is badly hurt. For heaven's sake, Romany, where is your bridle?'

A rough-looking man with blood on his arm, who had followed Charlie, said, ''Ere it is. Stand still, my beauty,' and as he spoke he gently took off my headstall and slipped the bit between my teeth. 'Now, sir, go right up this 'ere road till you get to the turnpike, then turn left and it's a white 'ouse 'alf a mile down close to an old oak tree. There's a brass plate on the door. If Jack kicks the bucket 'is Missus will be in sorry straits with a new baby and all.'

He led me out into the murky night, where bricks and stones and wooden sticks, upturned benches and a couple of knives glinting on the ground showed evidence of the fight.

'Say no more, I'll gallop as though my own life depends on it,' said Charlie dramatically, as the man gave him a leg-up on to my back.

He slapped me on the flank and aware of the urgency I sprang into a gallop, and people cheered or mocked as I raced up the road along which men were limping home-wards, some supporting one another, others singing wild songs. Little Skip ran in our wake causing some amuse-ment among some of those we overtook.

Charlie made a fine noise banging the doctor's knocker on his fine oak door and presently a white haired woman with a candle drew back bolts, unhitched a chain and lifted a bar to open up.

445

'Gone to bed,' she said, peering at us. 'Had an early morning delivering Rosie Greg's baby, he's that tired.'

'There's been a fight,' Charlie said. 'A lad's dying by all accounts. Two different factions trying to settle an old score . . . down at The Three Bells.'

'And who might you be?'

'A wayfarer, belonging to neither side. I'm only interested in saving life. The lad needs a surgeon, he's little more than twenty years old.'

'I'll go and see. Wait a moment,' the old lady said.

She came back some moments later with a stout bleary-eyed doctor, who held a black case in his hand.

'No peace for the wicked, they say,' he remarked. 'The Three Bells, did you say? Well if it's that urgent I had best have your horse. Martha, look after the gentleman until I get back. I daresay he would not say no to a dram of whisky. A leg-up, sir, if you please. It's not the first time I've ridden bareback.'

The doctor's hand was light on the rein and he spoke to me softly as we jogged the mile or so back to the inn, where he sewed up the boy and dosed him with medicine. 'He'll live,' he said, simply. 'He won't lose the scar but a few cold compresses on the head would assist his recovery. Tell him to keep out of fights in the future, for he might not be so fortunate next time.'

The ostler had saddled me for the return journey, so the doctor trotted me briskly back and in no time his place was taken by Charlie, who was in high spirits after the glass of whisky. I was back in the stable just before the church clock struck twelve with faithful little Skip panting beside me, and was glad to find that the ostler had left a little feed for me in the manger and had filled my rack with fresh hay.

446

But I missed a proper night's rest and the next morning when we started I was tired. Indeed I yawned right in front of Charlie's face. And where was Archie and his bay mare? My master asked everyone he met. Eventually a farmer driving his cob to market told us that he was five miles ahead on the higher road. 'Saw 'im myself on a thoroughbred mare riding like the very devil.'

'He'll wear his horse out,' said Charlie. 'It's the story of the tortoise and the hare all over again. We'll win in the end.'

''E's no horseman or he wouldn't be galloping over them stones, enough to bruise the mare's soles,' the farmer said.

The sun came out and put my rider in good humour and he started to sing again with his arm round the little dog who was sitting on the pommel of the saddle.

'You animals are both such good friends to me,' he said, between one song and another. 'You are better than people, you don't scrap and fight.'

We stopped at an inn at midday where the stables were full and, tied outside, I watched Charlie eating at a table by the bar. Three ragged orphan girls came to the door with outstretched hands begging for bread. The inn-keeper's wife turned them away, but Charlie came out and gave them a few pence and they curtsied to him. 'Thank you, sir, thank you.' Then they ran off on their bare brown feet to buy bread at the baker's shop.

'Who looks after them?' asked Charlie.

'They look after themselves and sometimes the Rector spares them a bite of this or that and they begs the rest,' the woman said. 'But if I was to give them bread I should have every penniless man, woman and child at my door.'

All afternoon riding through Somerset Charlie was

trying to write a poem in his head about those orphans. He said he could not forget their little white pinched faces and dark troubled eyes. 'We look after our horses better than our children,' he told Skip.

So the day passed and another and we heard no more of Archie while we came through Devon and on to Cornwall, a wild place, where the men spoke with a dialect we could not understand. There was no railway here and much of the land was bare and uncultivated, and there were tin mines, in which children and adults worked from first light until dark.

Riding across a moor we came upon a man walking unsteadily, tripping over clumps of heather and boulders. He was wearing tweeds, a deerstalker hat and laced brown boots, and there was a drip at the end of his purple-veined nose.

'He must be drunk,' Charlie said, while Skip barked and leapt in the air with excitement. 'The poor old gentleman has lost his bearings altogether.'

As we drew nearer Charlie called out: 'Permit me to help you, sir. Can I be of any use?'

'That you can, for I canna see a thing,' answered the man in a loud clear voice.

'Scottish,' muttered Charlie. 'Come on.'

I cantered up to the lurching figure, who turned and showed us his scarred and rugged face, dominated by a large bushy moustache.

'I'm blind, ye perceive,' he said. 'I lost my sight at Waterloo.'

'But a moor is no place for a sightless man!' cried Charlie in great consternation. 'Can you ride?'

'Aye, I can ride, but let me have hold of your stirrup, that will serve me well enough.'

'No, I'm the younger man,' said Charlie, dismounting.
'I'll do the running if you please, sir.'

'I canna see you, but I ken you're a fine lad right
enough,' replied the blind man, putting out his hand for
guidance. 'Could you be the young lad I've heard tell of,
the man who's riding from Leicestershire to Tintagel for
the sake of a bet to, to, well, I'll not be going into
that.'

'That's me,' replied Charlie eagerly, taking the man's
hand. 'Have you heard news of my rival, Archibald
Hickstead?'

'I've heard say that his horse is lame, lad, and he's
raving like a frustrated bull.'

As we continued across the moor with the blind man on my back and Charlie at my head, we heard of our new friend's plight. A few miles back three men had ambushed his coach, knocked out his driver, and driven the horses to the moor where they had stripped the blind man of all his valuables and his bag of gold before dumping him in a clump of heather.

'It's a terrible place Cornwall to be sure and I wouldna have ventured so far had I not had a sister who's been waiting these ten years to see me, poor soul; she wed a sailor from Penzance and has been repenting of it ever since. But ye have a great journey in front of ye and will not be interested in the chatter of an old blind man. If ye could take me to the nearest inn I shall thank ye from the bottom of my heart. I have guid letters of credit with me right enough so will not be wanting my gold. I would not want to be slowing ye down.'

'With Archie's horse lame we can relax a little,' Charlie answered. 'And we're not the kind to leave a blind man on a moor, whatever the odds.'

'No, I ken that, I ken that, you're a great lad,' the blind man said.

So we walked on across the bleak sweep of moor that men call Bodmin and came at last to an inn where we left the Scotsman with a kindly innkeeper in a small town before continuing our journey at greater speed through unsheltered countryside, which lacked the pretty cottages, the little dells and dingles which had made much of Devon so pleasant for us. It grew very cold as the dusk fell on the rough fields and meadows and snow came with an easterly wind, so that we were glad to find lodgings in a posting house for the night. A kind groom rubbed me down and rugged me up and finding myself loose in a stable, I lay down and Skip cuddled up against me for warmth.

It was a rowdy place with much drinking and coming and going far into the night. Sometimes I could hear Charlie's voice as he joked or laughed with a crowd of other young men, and there were many toasts drunk.

CHAPTER SIX

I become a wild horse

In the morning several of Charlie's new friends came with much merriment to see him off and promised to meet him for a midday meal fifteen miles further on. They were going to catch a regular coach within the next hour.

I was glad to be on the road again and, trotting briskly, soon warmed up. My clipped coat had started to sprout little wiry hairs in an effort to protect me against the cold. The air was keen and invigorating, the landscape stark and bleak with the winding gear of the tin mines etched against a pale steely sky. Brave little Skip ran at my side, his bandy legs serving him well. Every now and then he looked up at Charlie and wagged his tail. He seemed so pleased to have found himself an owner.

By and by we overtook a little girl riding to school on a donkey. She was sitting sideways on his back and every now and then she shook a bunch of keys in his ears to urge him on.

'What a capital idea!' cried Charlie. 'My dear Romany, shall I try keys with you?'

We came to a grey slate-roofed inn just after midday and here I was tied in a shed next to a large white sow who lay wallowing in filth. The smell of her sty and the drains from the cow byre were very strong. There was no ostler but the innkeeper gave me a bit of chaff to eat and an armful of hay, while little Skip found chicken bones in the back yard and made a great show of eating them, growling most ferociously as though crowds of dogs were waiting to snatch them from him. The place was alive with rats and later he caught and killed three large males, leaving them in a heap by the back door as though wishing to draw attention to his skill. Meanwhile Charlie was drinking heavily and presently we heard him singing:

> Archie's horse is lame,
> Isn't that a shame?
> And who must we blame?
> Hickstead is the name.
> He galloped over stones,
> Ignored his horse's groans,
> And now he's full of moans,
> For he will need some loans
> Unless his granny dies.

Several other young men took up the refrain. The inn-keeper's girl was busy refilling glasses, and every now and then a cheer went up.

It was three o'clock before we took to the pitted road again; the sun had drifted downwards in the west, and a few dark clouds were gathering behind us. We trotted between rows of hovels where whole families of ragged children and parents seemed to live, and we met a team of red oxen with a man sitting sideways on the leader. Then we came into a wood where Charlie started to sing his ridiculous song again. It was a strange rough place full of stunted trees, boulders, and, here and there, a collapsing wall or remains of a cottage. I hesitated, wanting to turn back, then suddenly Skip started to bark and at the same moment two men emerged from behind bushes. They had dark hair and small rat-like faces and looked as stunted as the trees. They spoke to Charlie in a dialect he could not understand.

'What's that? I'm sorry I can't catch what you are saying?' He leaned forward good naturedly the better to hear and in that instant, quick as a monkey, one of the pair leapt on my back behind the saddle and held a long bladed knife at Charlie's throat.

'Hand over the money. Come on before I slice you open and leave you to die like a suckling pig.'

'Money?' replied Charlie keeping his nerve. 'My dear fellow, I am a gentleman with many debts.'

I wanted to gallop off, to throw the evil smelling man from my back but his accomplice held me firmly by the bridle. And the next moment my poor silly master was on the ground, too drunk to fight. They dug in his cloak and found his little bag of coins, his brandy flask and his compass. Then they hit him in the jaw and, after seizing his cloak for themselves, they jumped on my back one behind the other and galloped me back the way I had come. Making a detour round the inn they came to the moor on which we had found the blind man, where eventually they reached their hideout, an old pit which they had covered over with branches and slates and stones, so that it merged with the landscape. Here they dismounted and, giving me a resounding wallop on the haunches with a stick, told me to be on my way.

I should have returned to Charlie, of course, but instead I galloped wildly and senselessly with the cold wind lifting my mane and stinging my eyes, across those wide acres. The moon rose. Winding tracks led in all directions, myrtle and broom bent under my frantic feet, stones jarred my pasterns and tendons. My heart pounded and my breath came at last in gasps. And then I could go no further. My sides were heaving as my throat tightened. My legs slowed down, grew weak as cotton-wool. And yet nobody was following me. My panic was unnecessary and ill-founded. I stopped and from my body there came a loud and desperate neigh which seemed to belong to that desolate moor rather than to myself; and caught by some outcrop of rock it came back as an echo, mocking me. I hung my head, ashamed that I had panicked and left my master and little Skip. Then, miraculously, I was answered by a little whinny of friendship. Excitedly, I strained my eyes but at first could see nothing except emptiness meeting the troubled grey sky. Yet I felt a presence and could smell ponies. I knew that I wasn't alone. Calming down, I now perceived that I had been looking too far ahead, scanning the horizon while in front of me there was a dell lower and cosier than the plateau on which I stood. A curly path led down into this haven, a small sheltered place with boulders and leafless trees bent and twisted by storms and tempests; and, picking my way down, I saw a group of ponies nibbling at a few jaded blades of grass that grew sparsely between rocks and boulders. They were thin little animals with hips jutting out like cliffs and sweet dish faces from which shone large eyes soft as velvet; and they reminded me of a Dartmoor pony I had met in my youth. As I drew nearer, a dark bay mare with a little white star whinnied gently and a young colt approached me mouthing in play as youngsters often do. He sniffed me from head to foot, paying special attention to my tack.

'You are tamed,' he said. 'You carry man. I shall never let them catch *me*!'

'Hush, he is a horse not a little wild pony. He was bred by man, his father and mother chosen for mating no doubt,' said the mare.

Now the leader of the herd, a dark brown stallion with neat hoofs, high crest and wide-cheeked head stepped forward.

'Where are you from and why have you no hair?' he asked. And then I told them my story while night lay over the land and the moon turned the moor silver. And, as I talked, they all looked at me with wonderment through their long forelocks and pricked their delicate ears which were full of fluffy hair.

At last a yearling stamped a foot. 'What a terrible life, no freedom, no chance to be leader of a herd!'

'But plenty of food,' the dark bay mare commented, swishing her tail which swept the ground. 'He never goes hungry; see how fat he is compared with us. He is beautiful.' She came across to sniff muzzles with me and to run her whiskered face across my shoulder and down my sides.

'You smell of man, not of the moor,' she said, 'and this saddle? How can you bear it? It is strapped on so tight! I think I should burst under such constriction.'

'Roll on it,' advised the youngster. 'Break it into pieces. And bite through that iron in your mouth. Kill it!'

'I love my home,' I said simply, 'and I am thin-skinned. I could not survive a winter on this windswept moor. I need a warm stable and Paddy's kindness. How I would love at this moment to plunge my muzzle into one of his warm bran mashes, and to be covered in rugs, to have him fussing round me to make sure I was comfortable. We horses at Belvoir live better than many a human child, and I work willingly in exchange for such care and cherishment.'

'Your mane is stupidly short and as for your tail – what help is that pathetic thing against the storms of winter and the flies of summer?' asked the youngster.

'That is enough,' said the little mare, 'Romany is tired. Let him be.'

'You can stay with us, but I warn you to leave the mares alone. This is *my* herd,' said the stallion, 'every female and every foal is *mine*, and I give the orders.' He tossed his lovely dark mane which fell inches below his proud neck and wheeled around in a pirouette as if he wanted to demonstrate his beauty and strength.

I told him he should have no fear. I would not wish to stay long, for I couldn't live on lichen and old grass nor stand the bleakness of the moor. My master needed me and I was bred for work not breeding, so I would not touch his wives.

We remained in the dell all night, talking and dozing and at dawn the stallion led us up on to the moor where grass could be found among the stones.

Here, exposed to all the vigour of a biting wind, my poor clipped hair stood on end in an effort to protect me from the cold, and I must have looked a sad sight with broken reins, coat covered in dirt where I had rolled, and saddle askew. Several of the herd came to sniff at me as the dark bay mare had done, feeling my body and sampling my smell, as though I was something new in their experience. They asked me where my fetlocks had gone and how I came to have no whiskers and beard and, when I explained about clipping, they snorted and declared that *they* would not allow themselves to be treated in such a way. They needed their beards they said to protect their faces from the snow when they searched in winter for grass, and their whiskers helped them in the dark. I loved them, in spite of their derision and criticism, admiring their looks and the way they climbed over rocks and boulders with the agility of goats while I followed slowly, my big hoofs slipping on hard surfaces, my fetlocks twisting as I stumbled over crooks and crannies.

Towards evening I followed the herd to a farm where, the youngster said, a man put out food for them each day during winter.

'He thinks he owns us, but we belong to the moor and each other, and when I'm older I shall go off with some of the fillies and make a herd of my own,' the youngster told me. Not far from the farm gate we found a long curving line of hay, poor stuff compared with the fine mixture grown at Belvoir, but palatable enough to a horse as hungry as myself.

'Sometimes he only gives us straw, which is bitter and hard but better than nothing,' the dark bay mare said. 'Young Mountaineer sees himself as king of the ponies, but if he's chosen for breaking-in instead of breeding, he will be as much a slave as you are whether he likes it or not. It is the farmer who decides now whether or not we shall be free. He comes with other men on tall, fast horses like you and rounds us up and takes away most of our foals leaving just a few for breeding. We can't gallop fast enough to escape, however hard we try.'

I spent a second night with the herd in the same dell which had protected us from the wind and rain the first time, and tried to satisfy my empty stomach with twigs and lichen and what old grass I could find. It wasn't enough and I was glad when the next afternoon came and we started to make our way down to the farm again. This time the farmer saw me and came out of his yard calling softly.

'Whoa there, my beauty, whoa. Come along sweetheart.' He rattled a sieve of oats and walked lightly over the sodden earth while the herd of ponies began to move off.

'Don't go to him,' a dark bay two-year-old advised. 'If he catches you, he'll put ropes on you and throw you down and burn you with a red hot iron. See how I am branded with this terrible letter on my flank! I shall carry his mark for life and that means that he thinks I belong to him. And I don't want to belong to anyone. I want to be free.'

But I was tired of the moor. I was cold and hungry and the sound of the shaken oats made me long for a decent meal, and I knew that animals like me were never branded; we were too valuable to be mutilated.

The farmer was tall and well built. He walked with the step of a man accustomed to striding across rough ground and surmounting every kind of difficulty, and he spoke with an accent which belonged to the Shires of England rather than Cornwall. I was tempted to approach him, but the little mare who had been kind to me from the first neighed enticingly.

'Don't go, stay with us, be wild!' she called. I turned and saw the herd watching me, so many pairs of dark eyes peering out from under bushy forelocks, their nostrils wide, their little furry ears pricked and sharp.

'Come on, my beauty,' called the man. 'Come up. Let's take that saddle off.'

'We're going,' neighed the little mare. 'Follow us. Soon it will be spring with bright tender grass everywhere and sunshine to warm your back.'

A vision of Skip with his endearing brown patch over one ear and another on his flank, flashed before my eyes, and of Charlie with his fresh complexion and pleasant amused expression, and his foolishness.

'We're going,' called the mare. 'That man is dangerous.'

And then I pushed back the vision and turned to follow the herd, even though my stomach felt empty as a used bran sack.

Yesterday had been fine, but now it started to rain again, and the cruel wind howled relentlessly. The stallion took us to another dingle where we nibbled at dry stalks trying to keep our backs to the wind and rain. I started to shiver and then I started to cough, and the stallion said I was too delicate for their way of life. This moor was worse he said than Exmoor or Dartmoor. You had to be exceptionally strong to live on it.

'Look at our coats,' he said. 'It takes hours of rain to reach our skins, but you have nothing. And your legs are too long and slender and you still have that dreadful saddle, and those slippy shoes.' And now, standing there with the rain beating my quarters and the wind whistling round my short pulled tail, I was very homesick. I wanted Belvoir and Paddy and all my friends, my warm rugs and deep bed of straw.

'You are going,' the little mare said. 'You can't stand this. You're too large.' She looked at me sadly, her head on one side.

I stared at my little friends as they stood so stoically in the storm, their thick coats flattened by the rain, the water trickling from their manes and their untrimmed fetlocks, and I knew that they were right, so I went to the mare and sniffed her neck, which was my way of saying goodbye, and the youngster came again with his baby-mouthing and said, 'You were not born to be free,' and the little mare ran her muzzle over my flank and her breath was warm. And then I turned and trotted from the dingle up on to the main part of the moor. And here I galloped until I found the farm house. I came to the open gate and went into the yard and my shod hoofs made a clatter on a brick path that led to the house. The farmer saw me through a window and hurried to shut the gate so that I was trapped.

'You changed your mind, then,' he said. 'Whoa there!' I stood while he took my broken reins and stroked my wet neck. 'You're a fine horse,' he said. 'And your young master is fair demented with the worry of having lost you.'

He took me to a stall, removed my saddle and bridle, rubbed me down, rugged me up and then went to make me a bran mash. And I was very happy to be free of a saddle and to have a fine surcingle holding a jute rug instead of a tight girth and lopsided tack.

Much later in darkness Charlie arrived, driven by a man in a dog cart.

'He gave himself up, walked into the yard of his own

461

accord,' the farmer said. 'You're fortune he's not caught the pneumonia.'

Meanwhile Skip looked up at me with shining eyes and barked his greetings.

CHAPTER SEVEN

Charlie says farewell

Charlie and Skip spent the night at the farm. My master was still feeling confident of winning the two hundred sovereigns because he had further confirmation that Archie's mare was lame, and one of the conditions of the race was that the winning horse must be sound in wind and limb.

The farmer made a sweet-tasting paste for my cough and showed Charlie how to put it on my tongue with a wooden spoon. He also oiled my tack so that it would be supple and comfortable for me to wear, and gave Charlie a pair of reins to replace the broken ones. He told us that he had been born in Northamptonshire and knew Belvoir, but had moved to Cornwall when he inherited the farm through his mother's side of the family.

'The Cornish are a peculiar people,' he told us, 'very deep and devious. I find it hard to get along with them, for they are like foreigners to me. Some are hardly better than outlaws. When I heard of your race to Tintagel I was naturally interested. Quite a number of people have been laying bets on who will win.'

'I do believe it will be me,' replied Charlie most earnestly. 'If it isn't I shall be ruined, I tell you truthfully, for I'm up to my ears in debt and had to go to the considerable expense of buying a new cloak and hat after I was robbed.'

'Well by all accounts the mare is lame and you are only a day's ride or less to Tintagel, and by God's grace your horse has not suffered from being out on the moor two nights. Did you see the herd as you came across? Lovely little fellows they are, the colts as courageous as bantam cocks and the fillies when broken gentle as kittens. They make capital ponies for children and are grand in a governess cart. Why, one I bred pulls the invalid carriage for Lord Carter's daughter and looks after her crippled mistress with the care of a nursery maid for a child.'

We had just over twenty miles to go and started before dawn, the farmer walking with us carrying a hurricane lantern to set us on the right road. Like the little old man by the river he would accept no payment for his hospitality.

'It's been a pleasure,' he said. 'And it was grand to converse again with a man who knows the Shires.'

The smell of the sea was in my nostrils and I could see the coastline meeting the pale sky as dawn broke over flat countryside. The roofs of the houses were blue in this early light and the grass and first flowers sparkled as the night frost melted and the sun rose flooding the eastern sky with pink and gold. Charlie started to sing again, and people came to garden gates and doorways to see us go by. We saw a group of children going to work in the fields and a man sitting sideways on a donkey who was laden with straw, and oxen ploughing. I trotted and cantered for the sea air made me lively and the farmer had fed me well with plenty of oats. When the Cornish sun comes out it is very warm and where we were sheltered from the wind it was hot on our backs and for the first time on the whole journey I was glad that I was clipped.

Charlie wanted to find out more about Archie, but the people we met were all taciturn and reserved. Their eyes and their straight faces did not seem to invite questions as

464

they watched us in silence, deep, it seemed, in their own thoughts. This was the last day, these the final miles of the journey, yet my master did not hurry me. He seemed wrapped in optimism and hope. He had convinced himself that Archie was out of the race on the strength of information gathered from people he did not really know. And nothing would change his mind. He was already deciding how he would use the two hundred sovereigns, or rather the few which would be left after he had paid his debts. It must have been the same insane optimism which had made him lose so much at the gaming tables, a sort of fatal flaw in his character. But, of course, I did not understand all this at the time, only later after I had heard many people discuss the race and its outcome.

He stopped briefly for a glass of ale and a pie at midday, watering me at a common village trough which would have annoyed Paddy, who always claimed that horses caught dangerous diseases from drinking from such places. And then we continued on the road to Tintagel striped now with sunlight, and deep in woodland and forest. I could not resist contrasting this untended landscape with the green beauty of Belvoir with its great trees and its gardens so bright with flowers and shrubs of all kinds. I longed to see a copse again lying warm and brown on some winter hillside or a spinney winding its way like a dark muffler across the landscape. Now as we drew nearer to the sea the wind seemed to rise and rush towards us, but the low stone houses stood steady as rocks and the women we met on the road looked solid too with shawls over their heads and their faces rugged and brown with no spare flesh to soften the lines of age.

'We shall spend the night at the inn, a capital place by

465

all accounts,' said Charlie, 'if my information is correct. And I'll buy you a steak, little Skip, for you have been a faithful friend and companion and I confess I've grown to love you.'

Now we could see the castle standing out to sea on cliffs, grey and mighty, and a nearby ruined church and other buildings. We could hear the roar of the waves and the thunderous crash as they broke on rocks, and the cry of the seabirds. And, although the sun still shone, the strength of the wind defeated its warmth and whipped our faces and whistled over the fields and the blue roofs of the cottages. We overtook a farmer in a gig with a fine high-stepping horse and three donkeys pulling carts which seemed too big for their thin little bodies, and a waggon loaded with dung.

Now and then Skip went into backyards to bark at chained dogs and taunt them with his own freedom, until Charlie took him up in front of the saddle again.

'To keep you from making mischief, you little tyke,' he said. 'Anyway, should you not arrive riding like a knight? Romany, my dear fellow, do you not see the ghosts of King Arthur?'

As we came nearer to the village we noticed a group of people standing outside the inn including the three young men who had witnessed our departure from Leicestershire. I could not see Charlie's face as he waved, but I suspect it wore a smile of happiness and triumph. But there was no cheer in response, only a mocking cry from all but the young man with the fair moustache, who looked disconsolate. And then my master swore.

'Surely,' he cried, 'I have not been pipped at the post?'

'Archie arrived yesterday, he's drinking now in celebration,' the fair young man said. 'What kept you?'

'Robbers, and a lost horse, but Archie's mare is lame. I had reliable information,' said my poor master in a voice heavy with despair. 'I'm lost, Cedric.'

'I know, and I can't lend you even a sovereign for I betted on your winning and now have lost it all. You had the best horse Charlie but the least sense.'

'I lost him on a moor, but twenty-two miles from here.'

Archie came out of the inn then, his saturnine face split in a smile.

'Sorry, my dear Daintree, but I am the winner. But I do congratulate you on the condition of your horse. He looks remarkably fit.'

My master dismounted, lifting down Skip.

'I've hardly a sovereign left,' he said weakly.

'You can give me a letter of credit,' replied Archie Hickstead.

'I've no credit.'

'What a miserable fool you are, Charlie Daintree. Your

debts are renowned, your stupidity notorious. Perhaps it's time you saw inside a debtor's prison, for I'll not leave till I have the money or see you in jail. It's a matter of honour between gentlemen, my dear fellow. Have you no sense of decency, sir?'

'Let me see your horse, bring her out,' cried Charlie in desperation.

'Ostler!' yelled Archie.

Presently a mare with two white socks came blinking into the sunlight. She stepped daintily, her eyes bulging a little with apprehension, her nostrils distended. Her tail was high, and the veins stood out on her forearms like string.

'Her sole mended then?' said Charlie.

'It was nothing, just a prick, a farrier soon dealt with that,' answered Archie. 'It was no more than a trifling annoyance.'

'She looks full of life,' added Charlie miserably.

'A good night's rest does wonders with a tired horse,' replied Archie. 'Now I've waited sixteen or more hours for you, and I want satisfaction on one way or another.'

By this time a little crowd had gathered, farmers and local people who had heard of the race, and a short swarthy faced man shouted: 'Come on sir, pay up!'

I looked at the mare and she looked at me and I knew she wasn't the same horse as the one I had seen earlier in the race. The shape of her head was different and the way she carried her tail and, most plainly of all, her smell. But everyone else except Archie seemed to be deceived.

My master's friend went inside the inn and came out with a tankard of frothy ale. 'Drink that while you decide what to do,' he advised. 'A man with an empty stomach is likely to make unwise decisions.'

'I wish I was dead,' said Charlie. 'Truly I do. Has anyone a pistol? – for I would happily blow out my own brains.'

At this moment a small dark eyed farmer approached him.

'It may be that I 'ave the answer, sir,' he said. 'I'd gladly 'elp you out of this little difficulty by giving you two hundred sovereigns for your horse.'

'But, but. Oh heavens, pray sir let me think a little,' poor Charlie said. 'I am somewhat confused, for I am not at all anxious to part with such a loyal friend as this horse has been to me.' He took another gulp from his tankard. 'Ostler, take this horse and look after him while I talk more seriously inside. This wind is no pleasure to man nor beast.'

I knew then that he was going to lie and allow the farmer to think that I belonged to himself rather than to the Duke of Rutland; and as they walked towards the inn, I heard my master say, 'I could not part with such a fine beast for less than three hundred and you would have to take the dog as well, for the little fellow is devoted to that horse.'

Tied up in a stall, I was able to look at the mare properly although I could not speak with her, and knew for certain then that Archie had swopped mounts. Indeed I could see that her white socks had been made by man not nature and I could only suppose that he had bribed a number of people to remain silent. And now I despaired at the thought that I might never again see my beloved Belvoir. Miserably I played with a feed of oats, bran and chaff and nibbled at the musty hay in a rack. The stables here were dirty with the urine running straight out into an open drain where it remained until rain washed it away, or it overflowed into the yard.

Presently a chastened Charlie darkened the doorway carrying Skip in his arms.

'It's farewell,' he said simply and sadly. Then he patted me on the neck, fed me two lumps of sugar and chained the dog at the end of my stall. 'I wish you both good fortune,' he said, 'and I'll never forget you nor fail to rue this day.'

Standing there he looked very small and suddenly rather weak, as though a gust of wind would topple him over like a tree without proper roots.

Skip whined and barked as Charlie left us, furious to find himself chained like the dogs he had mocked as we had walked so merrily down that last stretch of road to the sound of the breaking waves.

CHAPTER EIGHT

Life on a Cornish farm

My new owner, William Pardoe, was small, dark and as silent as Paddy and Charlie had been talkative. He fetched me out of the stall in late afternoon, hitched me to the back of his gig, invited Skip to share his seat and set off for home the way we had come, for he lived not far from the moor where he had a flock of sheep and a score of bullocks which he was fattening. He also grew potatoes and daffodils and kept a hundred or more hens. His grey house was long, low and shabby, and, looking at the place, you would not expect the owner to have been able to hand over a credit note for two hundred or more gold sovereigns without so much as blinking an eyelid.

As I arrived, after a brisk trot for the best part of twenty-one miles, I heard several cocks crow and out of the house came three rather dirty, dark haired children, and a mongrel collie dog who growled ominously at Skip who was standing up in the gig with his ears raised.

Seagulls swooped and called above the house and not far away in the twilight we could see a river hurrying on its way to the sea. A westerly wind blew across the moor and the pale impatient clouds were high in the sky sailing across the wide grey expanse like ships on calm water.

The three little girls stroked my legs and rubbed their faces against my chest. They had peat-brown eyes, bright cheeks, short noses and pointed chins and in their ears they wore gold rings like gipsies. They were called

471

Winifred, Rosalie and Mirabelle and seemed almost as wild and carefree as the young ponies I had met on the moor, for their dark hair fell over their eyes in almost exactly the same way and they were generally unkempt in appearance.

They greeted Skip with cries of delight, but he was overwhelmed by their welcome and hid under the gig, causing our new master to give a sardonic smile.

Soon I was installed in part of a cow byre standing in a pen fenced by hurdles with a sweet smelling brown cow as my neighbour, while the dun mare who had pulled the gig so briskly was put in a stall in a building that adjoined the house, which she shared with five brilliantly coloured bantam cocks who crowed almost incessantly and threatened each other through the bars of their cages.

Later in the evening Will (as he was known) came with his wife to see me, carrying a fisherman's lantern in his hand.

'And why would you be wanting a great horse like that and you such a mite of a man?' she asked him.

'I've always longed to own such a beast,' the Cornishman said. 'It's just because I'm small that I admire the big strong animals. Look at those legs, Rosabel!'

He stared at me, his little dark eyes bright with pride of ownership. Then he told his wife that he had promised not to sell me for a month while Charlie looked around to see whether he could raise the money to buy me back. 'And the little dog will keep down the rats,' he added, 'for old Floss has grown lazy of late.'

Spring comes early in Cornwall and next day I saw that there were already primroses and violets out in sheltered spots and Will's daffodils were nodding bud-laden stems in the warm breeze blowing across the moor. In just twenty-four hours the weather had changed dramatically.

After a few days I saw that my new master was nearly always busy. When I arrived his sheep were lambing and he was up at all hours of the night looking after his ewes, and in the daytime he mended fencing, dug his garden and trained his fighting cocks. His wife, a sluttish looking woman with dark hair hanging half way down her back, cared for the hens, and the three girls were sent into the fields most days to hoe around the potatoes. Each morning if it was fine I was turned out in a long meadow to rough-off, as Will put it, sometimes accompanied by the dun mare, Daisybell, and the cow, Buttercup.

Occasionally Daisybell would go out at night pulling a wagonette, and come back in the early hours her hoofs muffled with felt and rubber boots, and then kegs, barrels and boxes would be carried from the cart down into a small cellar at the back of the house. When I asked Daisybell about these journeys she said, 'I go to the sea and a rowing boat comes in, down in a little cove between rocks, and they unload the liquor and the tobacco and I bring them here for Will. And there are ponies taking loads away on their backs. That is all there is to it.'

But a man came one evening enquiring about the kegs and barrels, only it so happened that Daisybell had taken them all away to another farm the previous day, and when he searched the cellar he found it empty. Nevertheless, Will was obviously much distressed by the man's visit and an hour later he saddled me up and galloped me across the moor, down by the River Fowey and on towards the sea. In darkness I picked my way nervously along the edge of a cliff with the great ocean lashing the rocks below. Presently we saw lanterns down on a beach and we heard the splash of oars, muffled rowlocks and men's voices raised above the sound of the water. Will jumped from my back, tied me to a bush and made his way down to the shore along a dangerous twisting path. Staring down I could make out a boat and several figures in dark clothes and tall boots, and then I heard Will cry out like a sea bird and the men stopped and looked up towards the cliffs, and waved their arms and then signalled with a light. So steep was the path that I feared Will would fall, but he reached the bottom, and, immediately he arrived, the men started to carry kegs, boxes and barrels back to the rowing boat. They moved silently as though their lives depended on the job being done as quickly and quietly as possible. And the moon came out from behind a blanket of cloud and gave us a silver sea.

Presently Will started back up the path and, as he neared the top, the boat pushed off and disappeared round the corner of a great rock that jutted out to sea, and

then by the light of the moon I could see a small masted sailing ship anchored a mile or so from the shore.

Will lay down in the sparse cliff grass beside me, watching the cove. I could feel the tenseness in his body and knew that he was afraid. I nuzzled him gently but he bade me be quiet. After about half an hour he got up and led me down into a dell from which we could watch the path, and presently we heard men's voices and feet. And then Will held my nostrils so that I could not neigh. Four soldiers went by with guns slung over their shoulders, and two darkly clad men whom I was told later were customs officers. They took the path that Will had taken and when they were half way down and could not see us, Will jumped on my back and trotted me back the way I had come. I reached home in the early hours of the morning and great was Skip's welcome, for it was the first time we had been parted since my time with the herd of wild ponies, and he was afraid that I had gone for ever.

In the morning out in the meadow with the sun dappling the young spring grass, Daisybell said, 'So you went out smuggling last night. I heard you come in.'

'I don't know what a smuggler is, but you make it sound special,' I replied. 'I do know that Master was very frightened!'

'It's to save the tax. There's something called a duty on drink and other things that come over the sea. If you smuggle, you fetch it in secret and don't pay the tax. That's all I know. Don't ask me what tax is for; I can't answer. But I think you saved him from getting caught. That man who came was looking for trouble. He was a customs officer.'

We were half way into March now and there was no

news of Charlie and Will talked of selling me to a Sir George Wrightson-Smith who lived in Devon. Apparently Will knew the man's stud groom who was from Cornwall. The gentleman was rich he said and well accustomed to paying from three to four hundred guineas for a good horse and the stud groom would take Skip as his own and so Will would not break his promise to Charlie.

A strange contentment had crept over me down at this Cornish farm between the moor and the sea, where the days seemed to fold into one another and all around me was the fragrance of spring. Apart from the bantam cocks all Will's animals seemed calm and comfortable. There were few excitements and as a result few worries. There was no bustle, no aim at perfection as there had been at Belvoir, and Will himself was always the same: quiet, expert and kind. He never spoke to us except to give orders, but his hands were gentle and he never made mistakes. After the strain of living with Charlie and his foolishness, the Cornishman gave me peace of mind. And, although I longed to see Belvoir again, I grew fond of Daisybell, with whom I could have easily and happily spent the rest of my life. She wasn't beautiful, being plain in colour with a long face and rather ugly black stripe down her back, but she possessed such an air of calm friendliness that she was pleasant company, and I loved to stand with her under the trees.

However, it was not to be, for although Will admired me for my looks he had no real use for me and was never adverse to making a bit of money if the opportunity arose. He had bought me on the spur of the moment and was willing to sell me on a similar impulse.

In March the stud groom came in a coach to see

me, along with his master, the plump Sir George Wrightson-Smith.

The stud groom, a man of middle height with a lean boney face and hazel eyes, ran his hands down my legs, opened my mouth to check my age and inspected the lower lids of my eyes to see that my blood was red and strong.

'A beautiful hoss, sir,' he announced. 'Shall we see him out?'

Will had put up my mane and groomed me until I shone like a polished walking stick. My hoofs had been tarred and my mouth washed. I felt worth hundreds of guineas, yet I didn't want to leave my new home, and I didn't like the red faced Sir George, with his bristling grey moustache, his bloodshot rheumy eyes and his fat soft body. I left my pen reluctantly.

'Not nappy, is he?' asked the groom.

'No, willing as a sheep dog,' said my owner, giving his friend a meaningful glance.

The stud groom mounted me, swung me round as though I was a cow pony and sent me straight into a trot, so that I knew he wasn't a horseman, for a truly knowledgeable rider always lets a horse that has been standing in a stable warm up slowly. I swished my tail with annoyance and offered to canter. Presently the groom sent me into a gallop to test my wind and then he brought me back to his employer, pulling me up sharply to halt beside Will who looked none too happy about the way I had been handled.

'Rides all right, sir, and he's well up to your weight. See what bone he has! Going to have a try, sir?' The man dismounted. 'Got a mounting block?'

'No, never had need of one,' Will said.

So the stud groom legged the fat Sir George into the saddle and adjusted the stirrups for him and checked the girth. And after Charlie and Will he felt like a sack of turf. He dug me with his spurs and I moved off, shying a little at a twig that was blown in my direction by a little gust of wind from the moor. Sir George stuck his legs forward and his hands moved up and down as I trotted, jerking my mouth. He made himself seem even heavier than he was by sitting too far back in the saddle, but he was firm and I didn't misbehave, because I had been well broken and trained to obey instructions automatically. He cantered me in circles, first one way and then the other, neck-reining me as though I was a polo pony. Then he asked for a jump and Will and the stud groom fetched three hurdles and drove them into the ground with a wooden mallet.

'You've taught him to go leap then?' he asked Will.

'He's been a hunter down in Leicestershire, jumping bullfinches and the like,' Will said.

Sir George galloped me at the hurdles and at the very moment when I wanted to stretch out my neck he raised his hands as though to lift me up, but hurdles are nothing to me, so I sailed over just the same and he seemed well pleased.

'A great leaper, no doubt about that,' he said, very proud of himself. 'Well, Ted, I leave you to check him over again. Look inside his hoofs, and take him out once more after he has stood in the stable for a while. Now Mr Pardoe let us talk business. I want to know more about his home in Leicestershire. I always like to know about a horse's background and pedigree. Indeed I never buy an animal without checking his credentials and antecedents.'

Will said he had a little bilberry wine inside and a

noggin was a good pick-up on a blustery day like this one. And then the two men went into the house, and Winifred, Rosalie and Mirabelle came out and put their arms round my neck.

'You are never going to buy him, and what about the little dog, Skip?'

The groom said that curiosity killed the cat and that it would be best if they held their tongues, but they continued to pet me, and to gaze up at the man with their appealing dark eyes. Unmoved, he looked inside my hoofs and pushed me with a stick to see whether I would grunt and peeped under my tail, and then he left me in the byre and went outside to smoke a cigarette.

The door of the house opened and Sir George came out followed by Will, who looked very grave.

'I shall write to the Duke,' Sir George said. 'I've met him on more than one occasion and an enquiry from me will be in good order. I recollect a piece about the race that appeared in *The Times* and, if my memory is not at fault, it was stated that this horse ridden by young Daintree was the Duke's property. If there's been any funny stuff it's best sorted out. But don't worry, my man, it goes without saying that you bought in good faith and shall be repaid, whatever the facts of the matter are.'

'The young man was a fool,' Will said. 'Why, a horse like this could cover fifty miles a day without coming to harm and he just played around doing twenty or thirty. And it's said the other fellow changed horses and the white socks on the mare he rode at the end were bleached, but I don't know the truth of it.'

'Trust me to get to the bottom of the business,' said Sir George puffing through his moustache like an overweight walrus. 'I'm not a man who stands any nonsense.'

Meanwhile the driver who had brought Sir George reappeared as if by magic with the coach and horses, and a moment later with a clatter of hoofs and the rattle of iron wheels on the stony lane, they were off with Skip barking in their wake. And somehow I knew then that their visit was going to mark the beginning of the end, and another change in my life would soon take place.

CHAPTER NINE

A happy ending

Of course it was all very disturbing. It is horrible for a horse to feel that his future is uncertain and frequent changes of home often make us nervous and unreliable. Charlie or Paddy would have chatted to me so that I should have known how things stood, but Will was as usual as silent as a bat in the rafters.

Two weeks passed like months and, with Daisybell busy taking eggs and flowers to market, Skip either ratting or trying to make friends with the unresponsive Floss and the three little girls busy in fields or garden, I was much alone.

By April my summer coat had grown, sleek and glossy as a raven's wing, and Will rode me over to the smithy to have a new set of shoes put on my feet. I thought I might learn something of the future from his talk with the farrier, but he only spoke in a general way about the potato crop, the price of daffodils and so on.

Then, two days later, everything changed again. I was in the long meadow with Daisybell talking sleepily about the plight of animals at the hands of men.

'Think of Master's sheep,' she said. 'Man takes everything from them. First their coats for wool, then their dear lambs for meat, and, last of all, their very skins for coats or rugs.'

'Yet all but the last comes again,' I objected. 'The ram gives them more lambs and nature provides them with new fleece. My mother for example loses her foals, one by one, but each time she is expecting another to arrive, so that although she may neigh and gallop up and down the fence she is soon happy again.'

'I don't agree,' began Daisybell. 'But what is that? Listen – a man is coming.'

Raising my head and pricking my ears I heard a merry whistling and footsteps brushing through wet grass, and the tune was wonderfully familiar. Indeed at the sound of it my heart seemed to jump and miss a beat. It was the *Londonderry Air*.

'Paddy! It's Paddy!' I said. 'I would know that whistle anywhere.' I galloped to the gate of the long meadow and almost hurt my eyes gazing through the mist in search of my friend.

'He's come for me,' I said to Daisybell, who was soon at my side. 'Isn't it a fine whistle?'

'It sounds to me very like any other whistle,' the dun mare replied. 'I can't see or hear anything special about it as a matter of fact, although I confess it's not a tune I've heard in these parts.'

'It's Paddy,' I said again. 'I know it's Paddy.'

Then I saw him walking with a light step, a knapsack on his back, and strong boots and gaiters on his feet and legs. I whinnied, pressing my chest against the gate, and the soft Irish voice said, 'It's me, Romany, for sure. Top of the morning to you!' And there he was standing before me like a person out of a dream, with his shock of red hair, freckled face, blue eyes and snub nose.

'Hello stranger,' he said with a merry laugh. 'It's been a long time, and the Duke has been making enquiries, and you're the winner, Romany, as I knew you must be.'

He patted my neck, as he spoke, and gently pulled my ears, and I nuzzled his pockets for tit-bits.

482

Then Will came across to us, a cap on his head and a rabbit snare in his hand.

'So you've arrived and came to the horse before the house,' he said with his sardonic smile, looking small, dark and wiry beside my Irish friend. 'He's been well cared for. You can see that with your own eyes.'

'He's grown a fine coat for sure,' said Paddy, looking me over with a critical eye. 'It's a fine thing that he's been in such good hands. Is this your mare, too? She's a handy sort.'

'Yes, that's old Daisybell, fifteen years old this May and always as good as gold.'

Paddy told the Cornishman then that three hundred guineas was waiting for him in a bank some twenty miles distant.

'I'll give you the note; just take it. They know what you look like, so don't send anyone in your place or he might be clapped in jail.'

'And Mr Charles Daintree?' asked Will.

'He fled to France, with the change without paying his debts, a wastrel for sure, good-natured enough, but weak as water. He's cleared, of course, and the other young rascal has paid up, but it's a bad man who sells another man's horse right enough.'

As he talked Paddy ran his hands down my legs.

'He's in fine fettle and he'll take me to the railhead all right. It'll be a welcome change from walking, for my feet are awful sore.'

'And the dog?' asked the Cornishman, looking up at Paddy from under the peak of his cap.

'What dog? Dammit man, no one spoke of a dog to me.'

'Didn't Sir Arthur tell the Duke that it was part of the

bargain? This horse can't go without that little terrier – I gave my word.'

'To a scoundrel.'

'It was my word, never mind to whom I gave it. My word is my word,' said the Cornishman, looking at Paddy with the full force of those dark slanting eyes. 'He's a grand terrier, and will not hold you back.'

'I'd be a grateful man for sure if you would have the charity to explain,' said Paddy.

So Will told him more about Skip and described the bay mare who had replaced Charlie's lame mount and the cruel way in which her fetlocks had been bleached.

'There's a lot round these parts who now know the truth about that, but we are not a people to talk unless we are asked. It was for the young man who rode this horse to spot the difference, but a drunk man is a poor judge and a poor master to a horse, too, and there it is. I expect you would like a nosebag, and a meal just now for yourself, so come along and we'll see what the wife will find you. I can give you the name of a farmer who'll put you up thirty miles from here, and when you've eaten I'll saddle old Daisybell and put you on your way.'

The two men went off to the house then, both talking in their own dialects, which I have not tried to reproduce here, for they are hard to understand until you have lived with them for a while.

An hour later we set out with our heads turned towards the moor, with the mist lifting as the midday sun broke through and lit the way with hazy gold. We came to parts which I had not crossed before, strong with the acrid scent of gorse, the distance dominated by tors which stood like mountains, their peaks shrouded in the last remnants of mist.

484

Later we reached a deep valley where we drank in a stream that fell from rocks in a cascade of white, pretty as blossom, but foaming like the froth on the crest of a glass of beer. We saw great crags standing like guardians either side of a ravine and in the distance a forest where men were cutting down trees to use as pit props in the tin mines.

We must have covered almost ten miles when we came upon a herd of wild ponies, their manes ruffled by the wind which never seemed to leave the moor, their winter fur falling to reveal the splendour of smooth summer coats, their bodies plumper now as they flourished on the spring grass. Startled, they looked at us with raised heads and pricked ears. And I realised that this was *my* herd and over to the west was the farm where I had spent a night. I stopped then, and the little mare recognised me and whinnied gazing at me again with those wonderful soft velvety eyes under a wild and tangled forelock. But the stallion wheeled around and started to urge the herd away and, after I had whinnied my greeting in return, the little mare turned too and followed the rest as they galloped across the moor, their tails streaming out behind them.

Soon afterwards we came to a turnpike where Will and Daisybell left us to make our own way, and then a long lane stretched before us leading through deep woods with not another soul in sight. I thought of the robbers and shied at shadows and jumped every time a twig cracked or a leaf rustled. But grooms are not robbed like gentlemen and we came to our first night's lodging without mishap.

Each day then passed more or less the same, without incident, for although Paddy could barely read he had an uncanny gift of knowing which way to go. Like a collie dog he knew his way home, and once he was given directions he never forgot them. Three days later fresh and relaxed we reached the railhead and I was persuaded to step inside a van, where I was tied. The movement of the train and the hiss of steam frightened me, but Paddy, close by in the groom's compartment, calmed me down and fed me oats, and by the time we reached Leicester many hours later, I was quite accustomed to bracing my legs to take the sway of the van on the lines.

The great moment came when I stepped out into the light of day and smelt again the air I knew so well, and then it was only a few hours' ride to Belvoir down the roads where a few months earlier the carriage horses had taken the Queen so quickly from Brooksby Gate to her train for London. The day was now overcast, with a thin, kind drizzle blowing in our faces, and the wild flowers smelling sweet on the banks. We stopped at a farm, where Paddy was known, for food and drink and then at last we saw the castellated walls of Belvoir Castle. And, as though to welcome me home, the sun came out, and the clouds cleared to show a sea-blue sky. Just before we reached the stable yard we rode under an arch made of laurel, like those constructed for the Queen and the Prince Consort, and on this arch a board cried out in white paint: 'Welcome Home Romany – The Winner.'

Paddy must have been told of it beforehand because he read it to me, although, as I have said, he was no reader. And in the yard lots of grooms and servants came out to see me as though I was a hero. Then Paddy said, 'And now, my friend, I have a happy surprise for you.' And he led me to a field and there, standing under a tree, was Pioneer. 'The Duke bought him back to replace you,' said Paddy with a laugh. 'And we have the pair of you again.'

I neighed and Paddy said I could go out there presently when I had been fed and given a drink and rubbed down, and so on. And he fussed around me as though I was worth a million pounds, while the stud groom's wife took Skip off for a meal of rabbit.

Much later when I was grazing with Pioneer the old Duke came across and looked me over, and said that I had come to no harm, and that I'd be all right for a full season's hunting next winter. And then he ordered beer to be brought out to the yard so that all the stable staff could drink my health, and there was a sing-song.

Skip soon attached himself to the stud groom's wife and lived in her cottage instead of my manger, which was just as well because I slept out for the rest of the summer. But in the winter when I was stabled he spent a good deal of each day with me and always danced around me first thing in the morning when work started.

One day about two years later I heard a familiar voice in the yard, and there was Charlie with the girl whom he had met at his cousin's house.

'May I introduce my wife,' he said.

Paddy was cold and unfriendly at first, but once again the young man's humour was infectious, and soon the grooms had more or less forgiven him his dishonesty. He had, it turned out, made himself useful to a rich nobleman whom he had met in France and somehow come into some money, so that he was talking of buying a place and settling down to farm. He made a great fuss of me and asked whether I would overlook his careless behaviour. Soon he told everyone of our adventures on the journey and with so many jokes against himself that presently Paddy was laughing against his will, and other grooms were asking, 'What next, sir?'

Now as I write I am near retirement. Times have changed and steam engines thresh the corn and roll the roads and more crops are being grown in the fields, but Paddy, who has married, is still my groom and, though old and lame, Skip still visits me most mornings, licking my legs as though to express his undying friendship. The old Duke has died, and his eldest son has taken his place and chosen me to be his special hunter. And now and then in the evenings, after a glass of beer, the servants still talk of the Queen's visit and the way Prince Albert rode to hounds and proved to them his worth as a horseman and Queen's Consort.

BLOSSOM

❀

by Christine Pullein-Thompson

CONTENTS

𝕏Black Beauty's Family𝕏

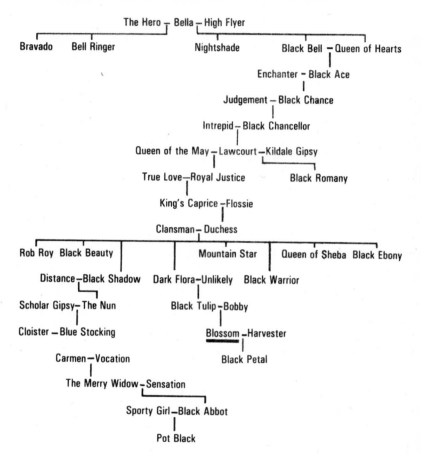

The Hero — Bella — High Flyer

Bravado   Bell Ringer   Nightshade   Black Bell — Queen of Hearts

Enchanter — Black Ace

Judgement — Black Chance

Intrepid — Black Chancellor

Queen of the May — Lawcourt — Kildale Gipsy

True Love — Royal Justice   Black Romany

King's Caprice — Flossie

Clansman — Duchess

Rob Roy   Black Beauty   Mountain Star   Queen of Sheba   Black Ebony

Distance — Black Shadow   Dark Flora — Unlikely   Black Warrior

Scholar Gipsy — The Nun   Black Tulip — Bobby

Cloister — Blue Stocking   Blossom — Harvester

Carmen — Vocation   Black Petal

The Merry Widow — Sensation

Sporty Girl — Black Abbot

Pot Black

I am born

My first memories are of my mother, tender, warm, black as night, with a star which gleamed white as snow on her dark face. Her name was Black Tulip and she had been well-known in the hunting field before becoming a brood mare. I was her sixth foal and her first filly. I came into the world on an April day, but it was not until June that I learned of something which was to affect my whole life. My mother and my master knew straight away, and my master never forgave me for being what I was. I remember him looking at me in disgust, his waxed moustache twitching. Once he said, 'She's fit for nothing but the tinkers and I thought we were going to have a good 'un this time.'

I was born on a small stud farm where there were twenty mares all with foals. They stood together under the trees when the weather was hot, talking about their offspring. On these occasions my mother always remained silent, though she would turn and nuzzle me from time to time trying to tell me how much she loved me. It was an old mare with grey hairs on her shoulders and a small, mean eye who finally revealed why I was so disliked by my master.

'Love matches are all right,' she said, looking at my mother, 'until your foal arrives. Now look at yours, Black Tulip. She will never be a beauty. You may be related to the great Black Beauty, but because you fell for a common young colt, she's piebald, and her fetlocks are growing already. She'll never be fit for gentlefolk. She'll be a common work horse all her life, and worn out by the time she's ten years old, and all because you wanted a change; because you were tired of Firecrest, one of the best stallions there's ever been; you had to run away with a useless young colt.'

My mother looked at me with sad eyes, but I was too young to care or understand. I butted her ribs with my black and white muzzle and stamped my tiny hoofs, two of which were pale coloured instead of the usual black.

'It is true of course,' said my mother at last. 'And my poor filly will grow to hate me. But it was love at first sight and there's no controlling that!'

My master refused to give me a name, so Luke, the old man who looked after us, called me Blossom. 'You and I are alike,' he said, stroking my forehead. 'I was an ugly little boy by all accounts, and my father used to beat me something terrible. But you do your best, Blossom, and you'll be all right.'

The other youngsters were always teasing me about my long fetlocks and soon my neck grew thicker than theirs, and my muzzle broader. I could see despair in my mother's eyes when she looked at me, but, though I could not gallop as fast as the other youngsters, I was stronger than them if it came to a fight, and in a kicking match I was always the winner. None of this pleased my master. 'She's going to injure the others,' he said one day, leaning against the field gate in frock coat and gaiters. 'She won't be hurt herself, that sort never is. I want her put on her own, Luke. And I want her tail off, and no fuss. Just fetch the chopper and take it off.'

'I'll put her in the paddock then,' said Luke uncertainly, 'I will have to get someone to hold her while I take her tail off.'

'Yes, of course,' snapped my master. 'Get young Tom. He's as strong as an ox and he's no good in the garden.'

'Yes, sir.'

So that afternoon I was separated from my mother and put in a small paddock beyond the walled garden which was by the house. I was quite alone now and I called to my mother for hours. I missed the other young horses too, and every sound frightened me. Luke came to see me often. One day he said, 'My family never cared for me neither. I was the odd one out.'

It was August and the little paddock was full of flies. 'We can't take your tail off now,' he said, 'not when it's so 'ot. It might get infected.' So for a time my tail was spared and I lived a lonely life, not knowing of the ordeal to come.

There was plenty of grass in the paddock and a pond from which to drink, but the only shade was that given by the wall, and I missed my friends more every day.

Sometimes I could see them playing in the distance, and I would trot up and down the fence neighing until I was exhausted.

Then, early in September, my master came to the paddock and stood staring at me, his face growing red with anger. After a minute, he started to shout, 'Luke. Come here will you. Come here at once.' And after a time the old man came stumbling and wheezing, crying, 'Yes, sir.'

'I thought I told you to take her tail off,' yelled my master. 'And it's still there. I've a good mind to sack you, Luke. Turn you out, and then where would you go?'

'I was waiting until the weather changed, master,' replied Luke. 'The flies won't do the stump any good.'

'Use something to seal the ends then – put some tar on, but take it off,' shouted my master, hitting nettles with the cane he always carried. 'If it isn't off by tomorrow, you'll have the sack, Luke. You're getting old for the job. I could do with a younger man.'

So, later that day, Luke came to the paddock with Tom, a rough lad of about sixteen. I trusted Luke and I let him slip on a halter and lead me to a gate. 'What you want to do, Tom? The chopping or the 'olding?' asked Luke.

'I might not chop it straight,' replied Tom. I don't want trouble with the master.'

'It seems a shame, doesn't it?' asked Luke.

'Let's get it over with,' replied Tom.

Luke stroked my head. Then he moved to my quarters while Tom twisted a cord round my lip and held my head steady. I was not ready for the pain which followed, but Luke's arm was strong and the hatchet was sharp, and in a moment it was over. He put something on the stump,

talking to me all the time, and I could see a tear running down his wrinkled, weather-beaten cheek. 'It's over now,' he said. 'It's done, Blossom. You won't feel no more pain,' and he threw my tail into the nettles.

But the pain was still there and I had nothing but a stump left now, nothing to swish against the flies, nor to protect my quarters from the wind, nor to hold high above my back when I played with other horses. It was gone for ever, and with it I lost my trust in human beings. In the distance I could see my former playmates chasing each other, their fluffy tails held high, and life seemed very hard indeed.

Luke visited me every day with oats in a sieve, but I was wary of him now. If he approached my quarters I kicked; if he tried to put the halter on I reared up. My master came once more to see that the job was done. He looked at me and gave a sigh of satisfaction. 'You will make a cart mare now,' he said. 'And your dam is in foal again, and this time she'll have a beauty, I can see it in her eye.' He turned away leaving me alone again with no tail to defend myself against the flies, and with all my trust in human beings gone.

CHAPTER TWO

Nutmeg

In the autumn Luke found a donkey to keep me company. He was a rough, tired animal, who had spent his life pulling a cart. Now he wanted nothing but rest. He taught me to eat the nettles when they were dry and the sting had gone from them. When he was not eating, he dozed, with his back to the wall. He was no company for a young filly, but at least I was no longer alone.

In December we were moved to another field, where there was an old thatched building where we could shelter in rough weather. I was much larger now and my mane had grown long and tangled. I had three white legs and one black, and my head was black except for a white streak down it. My mane was both black and white, as were my sides and quarters. I could still see my old friends in the distance, bigger than I was, but with slender legs and fine necks. They lived in a yard at night, and there were other horses near the house which were used to pull my master's carriage. Often I heard them stamping and neighing to each other, and sometimes I saw the carriage pass along the road below the fields, but we never spoke to one another. So, a whole year passed and now my mother had another foal, a colt as black as herself, but not the filly my master had desired. Luke had grown older during the winter, and now he coughed incessantly. Like me he was lonely, his wife having died, and he would stand in the paddock talking to me as though I was human.

'Your master's selling you,' he told me one day. 'You're going on Tuesday. He can't bear the sight of you. If your mother had had another filly it would have been different, but he's a hard man and he wanted a filly to carry on the line. Colts are no good he says, he can't be bothered with them, it's a filly he's wanting.'

Two days later he caught me and, putting the halter on with difficulty, led me away from the only home I had ever known. I saw my mother in the distance and neighed. The fields were dappled in sunlight, the trees were breaking into leaf. The brick buildings looked mellow. I was losing my coat which was blown hither and thither by the wind. Luke wore his trousers tied below the knees and a tattered shirt. An old cap covered what was left of his hair. 'It's a long way. The Master is a hard man,' he grumbled. 'I'm turned fifty and it's twelve miles to walk.'

At first we travelled along a road past cottages bursting with small children, past commons where geese plucked at the grass and goats were tethered. I stopped to look at everything. Luke was very patient. I was nervous and unsure of myself; the slightest rustle and I jumped. Carts passed us and once a carriage with the horses' heads strapped high and froth rising from their lips. I stood and stared, quivering in every limb.

Then we turned off the road and walked down a long straight track where nothing seemed to move but the wind. It was here we stopped while Luke ate his lunch – a piece of bread and half an onion. It was a strange silent world now. In the distance a pair of oxen were ploughing. The fields were flat, separated only by dykes. Far away something turned in the wind. I stopped and stared again. 'It be nothing but a windmill,' said Luke. 'Come on, my old darling. The Master's sending the gig for me at three and I can't keep it waiting.'

Women were hoeing in the fields, their long skirts billowing in the wind. The sky was full of dancing clouds. 'That be your new home, Blossom,' said Luke, pointing at a range of low buildings in the distance. 'You won't be lonely there; they keep a fair number of horses, I'm told. Not the fine sort we've been used to, but work horses.'

The ground was wet underfoot. I felt very nervous for it seemed to be drawing me down, but at last we reached a hard driveway. 'Not much further now,' said Luke, stopping to cough and then to spit. 'This be your new home, whether you like it or not.'

A carter met us, dressed in a smock. 'She's a bit small, ain't she?' he said.

'She's only a young 'un, and she's got good blood in her veins,' replied Luke.

'It's not blood we want, but strength,' answered the carter.

'She's got that too,' replied Luke. 'Give her time.'

A wagon filled with sacks was leaving the yard, drawn by four enormous bay horses with white fetlocks. Brasses hung on their chests. A carter led them, with a boy walking behind.

'That be wheat going to the mill. We've been waiting for a wind,' said the carter who had met us, whom I later learned was called Giles. 'We used to mill it here in the old mill house yonder, but it's easier to send it to the mill, and the master says it does a better job.' And he pointed to the windmill in the distance. 'It be the last of the wheat,' he said.

The farmer appeared now, a large man with a red face.

'This be the filly then,' he said. 'I don't like the colour, but since she only cost me ten pounds, I can't complain. Put her in the bottom meadow with old Nutmeg, Giles. What's her name? Or hasn't she got one yet?'

'We call her Blossom,' said Luke, handing the halter rope to Giles. 'I had best be getting along then. The Master's sending the gig for me and they don't like to be kept waiting.' He patted my neck and then was gone, walking along the drive into the distance. I never saw him again.

Nutmeg was a strange dark colour. 'So you've come to take my place,' she said, looking me up and down. 'I should be in foal, and I'm not, so it will be the knackers for me. I'm twelve, that's a good age, isn't it, for a work horse?'

'I wouldn't know,' I answered, walking round the field.

'That's the river down there,' she said. 'Lots of things happen on the river, you'd be surprised. Yesterday two boys drowned a dog down there. They tied a stone round its neck. How it struggled and how they laughed! It whined and pleaded for its life, but they had no mercy. When it was drowning, they threw stones at it. I see your tail is docked too. Do you suffer much with the flies?'

'Yes. Why do men do it?' I asked.

'It keeps our tails out of the way of the harness, and they don't have to be brushed any more. I wish we could cut their hands off,' said Nutmeg.

I felt very depressed by Nutmeg's talk. She had been alone for a long time with a swollen fetlock and was glad of company.

'You should be with gipsies,' she said. 'They like a piebald.'

'My mother came from a great family,' I answered, 'but my father was a common cart horse, so I am nothing, neither strong nor fine.'

'I am the same,' replied Nutmeg. 'And like me you will be a jack-of-all-trades. You will pull the muck cart and the hay rake and the pigs to market. You'll wear the worst set of harness which is stuffed with straw, with blinkers so big they hide everything, and breeching so low that you can't hold a load on a hill without almost breaking your legs in two. It will be the worst brush for you, without any bristles, and the youngest carter will learn his trade on you. Your manger will be dirty, and you will have the worst of the straw, and the oats which the rats have chewed. There are prize horses here, great Shires, and they have stables finer than the carters' cottages; but we are the misfits, born to slave day in, day out, to breed foals while we work to pay for our keep.'

'Foals?' I asked. 'Have you had many children?'

'Nine,' she replied. 'One a year and no rest in between.'

'Where are they now?'

'All gone – sold for meat or work. Oh, the master has made good money out of me, but I'll never be in foal again, the work has seen to that, and you are here to take my place.'

I refused to be further depressed by Nutmeg's talk. I was young and everything was new to me. I rolled over and over on the wet ground. I smelt the air and, cantering to the river, I drank and drank.

Nutmeg stood under a tree resting a leg. 'Rest when you can,' she said. 'Don't wear yourself out. You'll work soon enough.'

'I'm too young for work,' I answered. 'I'm not yet two.'

'They work children here,' she replied. 'Last year they were picking up potatoes all day in the pouring rain. How they cried. Then a policeman came and asked their ages. Their mothers told them to say ten, though you could see they were younger. It was a terrible day. I was glad of my stable in the evening, but they left in the dark to walk five miles home. Oh, it's a cruel world,' finished Nutmeg. 'The masters may be comfortable but their servants aren't.'

'Where do we live in the winter?' I asked.

'In stalls, tied day and night, except when you're working. You're let loose when it's time to foal, but after that it's work again. Often I've wanted to die. Working all day long when your foal is waiting for you, not knowing when he may be taken away for ever, that is the cruellest thing of all. Then one day he's gone and you know you'll never see him again. Oh, it's hard.'

'But soon you have another one,' I answered.

'But the worrying's always there until the next time comes and then it starts all over again. Why can't our masters leave us in peace? Why can't we keep our foals for a little time? Why must we always be separated?'

I trotted down to the river again, wearied by her talk. There were horses on the other side. I galloped up and down calling to them, but they soon grew bored with me, and dropped their heads to graze again. I looked back at the farm house, red–bricked, with a slate roof, newly built. I galloped round the field twice more bucking to try and impress the horses on the other side, my poor stump of a tail standing straight up.

I jumped a branch and kicked at a butterfly.

The next day was the same, only a boat passed along the river drawn by a horse and I saw the Shire horses working in the fields. And my master brought the mistress to look at me, and later his children, who were well dressed and clean. They laughed when they saw me.

'What a funny colour she is,' they cried. 'Like a patchwork. And her tail is so short. They cut it too short, didn't they, papa?'

'They never work in the fields,' sniffed Nutmeg, after they had gone.

So the days passed. Small incidents remain in my mind. I was very young and still full of youthful joys; even so some things affected me strongly. There was the day I saw the beautiful stallion who served all the mares on the farm, and the day a young woman threw her baby into the river and ran back across the meadow weeping, 'Better dead. Much better dead.'

There was the day when boys threw stones at us, and the day Nutmeg started work again and I waited for her all day by the fence. They were all days I would never forget. So, slowly, the days turned into weeks and the weeks into months. Another summer came and I suffered horribly without a tail. Nothing would rid me of the flies on my flanks and I spent much time galloping up and down the field to shake them off; only to be tormented by them again the minute I stopped. Nutmeg, who had more tail than I, suffered them in silence when she was not working in the fields from dawn to dusk. When winter came we were taken in each night to stand tied up in stalls in the large airy stable where the Shire horses lived. They were tall and proud and I think they looked down on us, though one of them, a tall horse called Admiral, would sometimes tell of the days when he worked in the woods clearing whole forests with his strength. He would describe the people who lived there. Kind, decent people, he said, who made their living by making barrels, chair legs, even clothes pegs. 'It is a different world,' he said, staring at the flat fields outside.

I found being tied up all night caused my legs to swell and I grew bad tempered as the weeks went by, but at last spring came again and Giles, the head carter, announced that it was time for my education to begin.

CHAPTER THREE

I start work

Giles was a patient man. He started my training by making me wear a bridle. It was a stiff dirty thing with a thin bit and blinkers across my eyes which stopped me seeing anything but that which lay straight ahead. It was very unpleasant. Next he put on my harness, talking to me all the time, for I was very nervous. One of the younger carters held my head while another held up a front hoof while he slipped the crupper under my tail. The collar was very heavy, even though the hames and traces had been taken off, and the pad across my back was broad and smelt of sweat. It was not the fine harness carriage horses wear, but a work harness, heavy for the most part with broad straps and dull unpolished buckles. When it was on, I felt frightened and uncomfortable, but Giles talked to me all the time, calling me all sorts of pretty names, like 'his little cherry', and after a time I felt less nervous and followed him round the yard only trembling occasionally. The next day I wore the hames on my collar – heavy metal bars which were attached to the traces – and Giles made me walk while one of the young carters, who was called Ted, hung on to the traces, making me pull him along. I had seen Nutmeg in harness and I did my best, but I was still very nervous and disliked the blinkers intensely, for they made me feel half blind and shut out the sunlight. The crupper was not much better, and the breeching felt uncomfortable against my haunches.

Giles was very patient, but Ted, who was to be my carter, was always in a hurry. It was his job to brush me now, and instead of being gentle he would scratch me all over with a metal tool called a curry comb. I look coarsely bred but I have my mother's fine skin and I found the curry comb difficult to bear.

After three days I was harnessed to a plough alongside Admiral. I was nervous of him and nervous of the plough and the work was very heavy. Giles drove us himself, walking behind the plough and Admiral snapped at me when I went too fast and kicked at me when I went too slow. He liked to plough with his partner, Consort, who matched him perfectly in size and strength.

'You'll never make a plough horse,' he said. 'You haven't the stamina. I am pulling you as well as the plough. Throw your weight into your collar.'

Giles shouted at me from time to time and used a whip on my quarters. I found the work unbearably hard, and soon my shoulders and quarters were aching. Then I started to stumble. By midday I could hardly walk and I was soaked in sweat. I was taken out of harness then and allowed to rest; but three hours later Ted put me in the tip cart and I spent two hours trotting round a field with Ted and his friends jumping up and down inside. I had no spirit left by this time and was now considered broken to harness. The next day Giles took me to the farrier himself to see that I was treated kindly but I was too tired to resist and in an hour I was shod.

Days began early at the farm. The carters arrived first at five a.m. and by six we were on our way to the fields. Ted usually overslept, so my breakfast of oats and chaff, tipped into the manger, had to be eaten in a hurry. Often he forgot to water me and I would go all day without a

drink. This was almost worse than the work, which was hard enough. We would all break off at midday and either we were allowed to graze or were given nosebags. If there was a pond nearby we would be watered, if not we had to wait until dusk when our work ended, and how we drank then! Sunday was our day of rest when we were turned out to pasture. Many the talks we had then, standing under the trees resting. Nutmeg was a great one for stories. She had a way of tossing her head and saying, 'Men! If there were no men in the world what a happy place it would be!'

But my most interesting friend was Dewdrop, a grey mare, whom the Master rode. Sometimes she was turned out in a field next to ours and we would talk over the fence. She was grey with small ears and a sweet face. One day she told me not to grumble too much about our home. 'There are worse places,' she said. 'Here we have enough to eat and, though you may work all day from dawn to dusk, it is slow work. I have seen horses galloped to death in the hunting field. I have seen them whipped and spurred to death over fences they knew they could never jump. I have met ponies which have worked under the ground, never seeing grass or light of day for years on end, some only coming up to die. Nutmeg grumbles, but their lives are worse than hers.'

'But carrying the Master cannot be as hard as pulling a plough all day. Why, sometimes you leave at midday and are back before dark,' I answered.

'But I go much faster. Often we gallop and I am expected to show my paces, to hold my head high and step out. You can go as you like,' replied Dewdrop. 'I wear an uncomfortable bridle, because that is the fashion. I have two bits in my mouth and a chain round my chin. And I used to carry a side-saddle when all the weight was on one side, or so it seemed at times.'

'So I shouldn't be sorry to be a work horse?' I asked.

'No, it is a more peaceful life. You will never wear a bearing rein; and on farms there is always plenty of everything. You need never go short of food or bedding.'

I felt better after this conversation. I started to look at life in a different way. I was determined to do my best and, as winter came and the work grew less, I remembered what Dewdrop had said and knew it was true, for we were never short of food nor bedding, and when Giles caught Ted feeding me before I had had water, there was a great to-do and it never happened again.

CHAPTER FOUR

A foal

Several months passed in this way. Hard weather came and the roads were made impassable by snow. We stayed in our stables for several weeks, while the carters polished the harness and cleaned the windows and painted the walls. Giles kept an eye on us seeing that our hoofs were picked out regularly and that we were given bran mashes to compensate for lack of exercise. It was warm and friendly in the stable, and the yard was cleared of snow so that we could be led up and down it twice a day to stretch our legs. Of course it was irksome to be tied up for hours on end, especially for us younger horses. But when the snow was gone, spring came and Giles insisted that we started work gently as our muscles had grown slack with lack of work.

I shall never forget spring coming. The grass was suddenly miraculously green, birds sang from dawn to dusk, hens cackled, calves frolicked. Even the Master seemed more cheerful than usual. Then one day the stallion walker came with his stallion. He was a little man with bandy legs who came every year and slept in the loft above our stable. The stallion was called Harvester and was well known. He was a chestnut colour with three white socks. And I think I fell in love with him at sight, which was just as well, for he had been chosen to be the father of my first foal.

With spring and summer came more work. Once again, we were in the fields from dawn to dusk, pulling the hay rake and the plough. It was about this time that a sad thing happened. Nutmeg was taken away. She had been expecting this to happen ever since I had been announced in foal. 'I won't be wanted any more now,' she had said, shaking her worn dun head. 'You can do my work and produce the foal a year our master wants. I shall go to the horse slaughterer. I have known it ever since you came.'

Giles was fond of all of us and sad to see her go. 'It's a pity she couldn't have a last summer here in peace,' he said. 'She's worked well all these years; but there it is, that's money for you. The more men have the more they want and the beasts and the poor must suffer for it.'

And young Ted, who was growing into a fine young man, said, 'One day things will change. It won't go on, because many of the poor won't stand for it any more.'

I missed Nutmeg. The Shire horses were kind enough. There were eight of them. They had been together for several years and were related to one another, so were very close, most of them having been born and bred on the farm. They found me young and ignorant. With Nutmeg gone, I had all the casual work to do. I took animals to market, and carted muck to the fields. There was hardly a day when I was not busy from dawn to dusk, and by the winter I was heavy in foal and the work seemed harder. I would lie down in my stall now whenever the opportunity arose. We were carting potatoes at this time and the fields were full of small children who earned sixpence a day for their labour. They picked up the potatoes and put them in sacks, which I carted to the barn. Often they were crying with cold, for a cold wind blew all the time bringing with it sleet and hail. They wore no gloves and their boots let in the rain. I felt very sorry for them. The Master would come to see how the work was going and sometimes he would cuff one over the ear if he wasn't working hard enough, and their mothers were always shouting at them to work harder or there would be no supper. The girls suffered more than the boys, being even smaller. There was ale for the mothers when we broke off at midday, but nothing for the children, although many of them managed to get at the ale.

Nobody needed to lead me now. I would walk on and halt to order while Ted walked behind picking up the sacks. After the potatoes were lifted, there were cabbages to be cut and carried; and threshing to be done in the big barn. One of the carters left to better himself and Ted left me to work with the Shire horses and a new boy came called Jack. He was a silly young man and given to teasing, which made me very bad tempered. He would hold out a bucket of feed and when I put out my nose for it, he would snatch it away. Or he would tickle my nose with a piece of straw when I was tied up and unable to move away. Ted caught him at it one day and boxed his ears. After that he only teased me when no-one was about.

Jack was a very rough driver. When he wanted me to move off, he would jerk the reins and shout at me, which hurt my mouth. When he wanted to stop he would lean back and haul on the reins nearly pulling my lips in two. When we went to market, he would forget to put the drag on when we came to the hill above the town, which meant I had to hold all the weight on my haunches, which was very tiring. He would forget to water me and hang about the town instead of returning immediately, and then he would drive very fast home to make up for the lost time. My harness was very heavy and the cart had iron wheels and was not made for fast travelling and, being in foal, I grew very tired. I would arrive back sweating and exhausted. After a time there wasn't much spirit left in me.

My foal arrived in April, after a long and painful labour. Giles sat up with me all night sponging me with cold water where I sweated, feeding me a bran mash with his own hand, talking kindly to me. He helped my foal to suckle and for several days we lived in peace in a shed where I was free to turn round and get up and lie down as I pleased, and how pleasant that was! My foal was black like my mother with all her slender grace. 'A real throw-back,' said the master happily. 'We can sell him for a hunter.' And he gave me something sweet to eat, which he called sugar.

They called my foal Black Petal and our master came often to look at him. He had grown much stouter and his side-whiskers had turned grey and his face was very red. I think he drank too much, for often his speech was slurred and he smelt very strongly of drink. After a week, I started work again. At first only for a few hours, but how long they seemed, for all the time I was yearning for my foal. Sometimes I could hear his little voice calling to me. Then, when work was finished, how I rushed back to him, hardly stopping to drink though I was very thirsty. I would rush into the shed with my harness still on, whinnying to him, fearing he might be gone. Gradually, as I worked longer hours, my fears grew worse. I could hardly concentrate on my work and whenever I could, I would call to him across the fields hoping he would hear me. So what Nutmeg had foretold came true. I think Giles knew how I felt, but he had no choice in the matter. The Master set the rules and he needed money to keep up his fine house and servants and drink.

So weeks passed and one day in the evening my foal had gone. How I neighed then! If only men could know how sad it is to lose a foal. When they are older we can bear it, but to be separated from your own child when he is still small and needs you, is unbearable.

I couldn't eat. Next day I went to work again, but all the time I was calling for my foal. My eyes searched for him, my heart ached for him. I remembered what Nutmeg had said to me. I knew it could go on year after year, and I wished myself dead.

CHAPTER FIVE

Jimmy Reed

Shortly after my foal was taken away from me, the Master died. People said it was drink that killed him. At any rate, the farm was put up for sale, and we were all to be sold too. I wasn't sorry, because I was still pining for my foal. But the carters were very upset.

'We'll all be looking for jobs then,' said Giles, 'and with these new steam engines coming in, there will be less jobs about.'

He had lived on the farm for a long time in a small cottage by the gate. Now he was to lose his home and his job. It was very hard. The Shire horses were to be bought by a neighbouring farmer, but I, like the carters, was to go to the next fair in search of a home.

I shall never forget the fair. The pleasant town was completely transformed. The market place was full of tents; gipsies were everywhere; the inns were bursting with people. Men stood in lines looking for work, the carters and the thatchers with twisted cord and straw round their hats, the shepherds with crooks in their hands. It was a sad day for Giles after fifteen years as a head carter. There were cows mooing, and small ponies straight from the moors, wild-eyed and untamed. There were mares searching for their foals, and foals searching for their mothers. There were proud thoroughbreds who had come down in the world through no fault of their own, and odd coloured gipsy horses, and old cart horses, their lower lips hanging, their fetlocks swollen by years of work. There were gipsies telling fortunes in booths, and performing fleas, and the fattest woman in the world on show. There was cock fighting out of sight in the courtyard of an inn. Nearly everyone seemed to have a beer tankard in their hand. I was tied up and left. I was very nervous. I neighed for friends. I searched with my eyes for my foal.

Horses were run up and down. Men cracked whips to drive them faster. There were horses with swollen withers and horses which coughed. There was a horse which lay down and would never get up again. Dogs ran between our legs. A lady in a fine dress walked up and down among us begging everyone to be kind to dumb animals. 'Think of the Lord,' she said. 'Do as you would be judged. Be kind to these poor animals. They are God's animals.' She stopped to stroke my nose. Her hand was very soft and white. Her eyes were full of tears.

Men came and pulled open our mouths. We were trotted up and down. Our legs were picked up and put down again.

Soon the air smelt of sweat and drink. Men's faces grew redder. There was one man who liked me particularly. He kept returning to feel my legs and pick up my hoofs. Finally he said, 'I'll give you eighteen guineas for her,' and after some haggling I was sold.

'Blossom; it's a pretty name,' said my new master. 'I hope you and I get on well together. You're a little on the small side, but you look strong enough.'

My new master was a carrier by the name of Jimmy Reed. He lived in a cottage with an orchard and the neatest stable you've ever seen, with a level floor and a door I could look over. He had a dimple-faced wife and five children. His horse had just died and he had bought me to replace him.

When we arrived after walking six miles through the dusk, his wife and children came running out to meet us, crying, 'What have you bought? Have you bought a good one?'

They fetched a piece of bread for me to eat, which was something I had never tasted before, and the two little girls were put on my back.

'Now, keep quiet,' said Jimmy. 'Remember horses have feelings too. She'll need a bit of time to settle down. Don't rush her.'

'Can I feed her?' asked one little boy.

'Can I brush her?' asked another, while their mother stood smiling, saying, 'I think you've made a good choice Jimmy, for she has a sweet, kind eye.'

I looked at the orchard. The boughs on the trees were heavy with apples. There were bee hives under the trees, and a cat sitting on a window ledge. The children were bedding down the stable now and filling the rack with hay. There was a carrier's cart in the shed next to the stable. Jimmy took me to a pond to drink before turning me loose in the stable. Everything smelt fresh and clean. The hay was sweet and when I had eaten my fill I lay down, thinking that I would be very happy.

CHAPTER SIX

A carrier's horse

My new master was a kind man. 'Treat others as you would be treated yourself,' was a favourite saying of his and he would add, 'Man or beast'. My stable was always clean, the hay sweet and the oats in my nose bag were never musty. His cottage was small but always neat and tidy.

The day after my arrival was Sunday and I was turned out in the orchard to rest. The elder children sang in the church choir and I could hear the church bells ringing on and off all day.

The next day I was fed and groomed early and soon after that the children came to bid me and my master goodbye. The little girls were called Meg and Rosie and they kissed my nose while the boys, trying to appear more manly, patted my neck. Henry was the eldest, closely followed by Mark and John.

The covered carrier's cart was heavy, but my master always walked when we came to a hill, and never forgot to put the drag on when needed. He was very well known in the district and on this first morning, all his regular customers came out to look at his new horse. They were a merry crowd; there were plump women with baskets who wished to be transported to town, and others who wanted us to call and take parcels to the station. After three miles we were nearly full, with four women in the back, a baby, two young geese and half a dozen parcels. Whenever we saw a sign put out on a gate, we stopped to pick up something. At eleven we reached the town, a distance of some nine miles, and I was taken to a small inn, unharnessed and tied in a clean stall and given food and water. 'This is where you stay, Blossom,' said Jimmy, 'until we start for home again.'

I wondered what he did all day in the town. There was one other horse in the stable, a tired bay, who had once been an army horse, but was now used for delivering and fetching drink.

'So you are the new carrier's horse,' he said. 'The last one never had anything to say, but you look a bit more sprightly.'

'Except for losing my foal, I am a very happy mare,' I answered. 'I could have borne it if he had been a little older, but he had only just begun to nibble grass when they took him away for good, and I cannot forget him.' And I fell to wondering where he was now and whether I would ever see him again.

'They took off a lot of your tail,' said the old horse, next. 'I was a gunner's horse before I came here, but I never saw battle, which is just as well for it's terrible I am told.'

At three o'clock my master harnessed me again and drove me to the newly built station. I was very frightened of the great steam engines, for I had never seen one before, but he talked quietly to me, and after a time I grew calm. Once again, we were soon loaded with parcels and people, and two tiny kittens in a basket, and now we completed the journey the other way round, stopping to leave parcels at homes and for people to get out. Several of our passengers remarked on my good looks and I think Jimmy was pleased. 'At least we can see this one coming,' cried one little old lady. 'And she has such a kind face.'

'Yes, the other was a sour old horse,' said a child.

'He had a hard life,' replied Jimmy, 'with never a kind word till he came to me. He wore a muzzle I know, but he never bit me, because he trusted me.'

Jimmy stopped to light the lamps on my van and when we reached home the children were waiting for us. Jimmy took me to the window of the cottage and they fed me titbits from inside, and what a pretty sight it was, with a clean cloth on the table and lots to eat and everyone merry and smiling and full of fun. My spirits rose immediately, for we horses don't mind work if we are well treated; it's doing our best and being punished just the same that breaks our spirits.

Soon I was well known in the area. People would look for 'the black and white horse'. Some ignorant people even thought I brought them luck. At first I was lonely, but after a time I grew used to being alone. I became part of the family. The work was hard but Jimmy was a kind, patient man. If the passengers were in a hurry, he would say, 'This is only a one horse van, if you're in a hurry catch the stage coach, or one of those new fangled steam engines in the station. Only it will cost you more than sixpence.' The town was always full of horses, gentlemen's horses which pranced, high stepping butchers' ponies, sad cab horses, greengrocers' ponies. I never had time to talk to them. I still looked for my foal, but I never saw him.

As I've said before, I never knew what my master did when I stood comfortably fed and rested at the inn. But I am certain he did not rest, for sometimes he came back quite morose, while other times he was laughing and joking with the passengers all the way home. On these occasions he usually had presents for all the family and extra oats for me. He did not smell of smoke or tobacco, but when he was merry, his pockets were full of money.

The village where we lived was quite small with a thatched church, a row of cottages, a baker and some outlying farms, all of which belonged to The Hall, the property of a Lord Chadwick. Sometimes we called at The Hall. We went round the back and my master would be given a cup of tea before collecting whatever we were required to take to town. The stables were very grand and there was always a great bustle going on with stable boys running here and there and fine horses being led backwards and forwards, and everything clean and tidy. There was a great array of harness in the harness room, polished to perfection, and many magnificent carts and carriages. The coachmen wore liveries and there were footmen in the house and butlers, housemaids, laundry maids, parlour maids, cooks, kitchen maids, pantry maids, scullery maids. Everyone seemed to know their place, but it must have been a happy place because they were always laughing. Once I saw Lord Chadwick himself. He asked Jimmy Reed how my mistress was and was very friendly and quite ordinary to look at. Of course the horses there didn't talk to me, considering themselves very superior and not stooping to talk to a mere carrier's horse. I didn't mind this, for I was perfectly happy to look at them from a distance, and, since I was content with my humble stable and pretty orchard, I did not envy them their fine stalls.

Gradually I learned where to stop for parcels and my way round the town, so my master hardly needed to guide me. I knew my stall at the inn and the way to the water trough. So two years passed; happy years. I was accustomed to my way of life now and wanted nothing better. As Christmas drew near I was very busy. Everyone wanted to shop and often my van was so full, that passengers had to dismount and walk up the hills. It was my second Christmas as a carrier's horse and it was about this time that my master started taking me out at night and disaster befell us.

CHAPTER SEVEN

Disaster!

It happened like this: I had finished my day's work and was resting in my stable, when my master came in with a lantern and saying, 'Come on, Blossom, we've still got work to do.' I raised my head and saw that there was a moon shining down on us, and everything had turned white with frost. It was not the first time my master had taken me out like this at night and I knew what to expect. Before we left, my mistress came out and pleaded with Jimmy not to go. 'Blossom has done enough,' she said, 'and you know what you are doing is wrong. None of us mind about a Christmas dinner, so please stay with us and forget the job you are doing tonight.'

'I've given my word, and I won't break it,' my master said, pushing her away so roughly that tears started to well up in her eyes.

'If you didn't gamble, it wouldn't be necessary,' she said in a voice so low it was hardly audible. 'You are trading with the devil, Jimmy.' And with that, she went inside and shut the door.

I was much perturbed by this conversation. But my master went about his work briskly, and I was soon harnessed and trotting along the road without time for thought. He was always in a hurry when we went out like this at night. It was as though he couldn't wait for the job to be finished.

Soon we turned down a rough lane full of stones and there was no sound now but the creaking of the wheels on the van. The lane turned into a track, which led through a wood and then to a cottage which stood quite alone at the edge of a field. Here we stopped and Jimmy gave a long low whistle. A man came out carrying a tea chest. 'Dead on time,' he said. 'Now, don't let anyone see them. And you know where to go tomorrow. Don't waste time. If anyone asks what's inside, say you don't know. I've sealed it up, and here's a brace for you,' he said, handing my master a pair of plump pheasants. 'The money will be waiting for you at The Four Bells tomorrow night,' he added. 'And then we'll lie low until after Christmas, for I think his lordship is growing suspicious.'

'Aye, he'll want a good shoot for Boxing Day,' agreed Jimmy.

The man was a rough, unshaven fellow who smelt strongly of drink and tobacco. The tea chest was hastily loaded into my van and Jimmy jumped up in front. 'The Four Bells tomorrow, then,' he cried, using the whip across my quarters. 'I won't be late, you can be sure of that. And thanks for the Christmas dinner.'

There were stones on the track and the moon had moved behind a cloud and everything was dark. We had gone barely a hundred yards, before we heard the barking of dogs and loud voices. 'We're done for, Blossom. Gallop, for God's sake,' shouted my master.

I threw my weight into my collar, but we had no chance, for in a moment the lane was full of men, some with lanterns, some without, but all of them bearing sticks or guns.

One grabbed my bridle. Another seized my master, crying, 'So, we've caught you, Jimmy Reed. You'll be in trouble for this. You'll get six months for certain.'

Two men climbed into my van and levered the tea chest open. 'I didn't know what was inside, I swear I didn't,' pleaded Jimmy.

'What? With a brace beside you on the seat? Come off it, Jimmy,' cried the man at my head.

'Think of my missus and children. I'll never do it again. I swear I won't. It was only because of Christmas,' pleaded Jimmy.

But no one listened. Two men came along the lane now, dragging my master's accomplice. 'That's it,' they said. 'We'll take them to the station.'

A man drove me home. He was quiet and gentle with me and obviously used to horses. We soon reached the cottage, and he called, 'Missus, are you there? I've brought your mare back.' And my poor mistress came to the window, her hair in plaits, a candle in her hand.

'Has there been an accident?' she called, though I think she knew the truth already.

'If you want to know about your husband, you had best go to the police station. I'll put the mare away for you,' said the man.

'I'll do that then,' she called back in a faint voice, trying to pretend that she knew nothing.

Next day the children came to the stable early and wept into my mane. The van stayed in its shed and there was no one to take passengers and parcels to the town.

Later, Henry, the eldest boy, turned me out into the orchard for exercise and cleaned my stable. My mistress was beside herself with grief. After a time she put on her best bonnet and went to see his lordship, but it can't have done much good, for she came back crying, 'We're all disgraced. There's nothing but the workhouse for us now.'

Later some men came with a fine looking horse in a dog cart and took away the tea chest. 'His lordship wants his property back,' they said.

'What will become of us?' wept my mistress.

'They say he'll get three years,' said one of the men. 'But it will soon pass, missus. He's lucky not to be transported.'

'It was the gambling which did it,' she said. 'Why must men gamble? We were quite comfortable. We wanted for nothing. Why did he do it?'

CHAPTER EIGHT

A bad time

After a few days, bailiffs appeared at the cottage and took away the furniture. Apparently my master owed many people money, which he had lost gambling. My mistress was often in tears, and when a dark haired gipsy-like man took away my oats, I had little to eat.

One day my mistress put my halter on and led me to the river. At first I thought she intended throwing herself in, for she stood looking at it and muttering, 'It would be the best way out.' I remembered the girl who had thrown her baby in the river, and was very nervous. But presently my mistress led me on along the towpath and soon

we came to a row of barges moored by a little inn called The Sparrow's Nest. Horses were tethered near the barges and they raised their heads and whinnied to me. A man climbed out of a barge and looked at us; brown-eyed, brown-skinned children followed him.

'What is it, missus? What be you wanting?' asked the man.

'A home for my mare,' replied my mistress. 'She's

good and kind and I don't want a lot for her. We've fallen on hard times, otherwise she would not be for sale. I think she would be happy with you.'

The man started to laugh. 'Buy your mare?' he cried. 'Just take a look at our barges, missus. They are half empty. There's not enough work for our own horses, missus. Our children are nearly starving. The railways have taken the work away from us; they've killed our trade. I'm sorry, missus, for she looks a good mare.'

'So am I,' replied my mistress, turning away, 'for there's no home for her now, but the coal merchant, and he's a hard man if ever there was one. And she will have to work in the town, and the streets are cruel to a horse's legs I'm told, and she's been a good mare.' She was sobbing now. She put an arm over my neck. 'It's the end of us all, Blossom. Just a little dishonesty and we're all finished,' she said.

The children were crying outside the cottage when we returned. 'Our beds have gone. They even locked the door,' cried Mark.

'I tried to stop them,' said Henry. 'But they were too big and strong.' He had a black eye and he looked crest-fallen. 'If I had been a man, they might have listened,' he added.

My mistress started to weep and wail, then crying, 'What will become of us? Blessed Lord, how did it happen? Is there no kindness in this world?' while Henry put me in my stable.

The next day the coal merchant came to look me over. He pulled my mouth open and knocked my knees with a hammer. Henry trotted me up and down the road.

'She's too small,' the man said. 'And I don't like a

piebald, you can't keep them clean. Her neck looks weak too. And isn't this a spavin on her hindleg?'

My legs were as clean as a whistle, but my poor mistress knew nothing about horses and became very downcast. 'I can't give you much for her because I don't think she'll last more than a year on the coal carts. Her hocks look narrow and you need good hocks for the hills,' he said.

'She's never been sick or sorry with us,' said Henry stoutly. 'She's a good mare and willing. Ask anyone around here.'

'Why don't they buy her then?' asked the coal merchant, turning away.

'Because they're too poor,' replied Henry.

'I thought you wanted to sell her, but I see you don't,' said the coal merchant, looking angry.

'But we must,' cried my mistress. 'We are in terrible straits. Have pity on us.'

'That sounds a bit better,' said the coal merchant, 'and a lot more like the truth. Now, you said you wanted twenty pounds, but I haven't that sort of money for a mare like her, for she's small for our carts and will have to be given the easy runs, unless there's a cock horse available on the hills. So I can't give you much. She needs shoeing too. One way and another, it's ten pounds or nothing,' he finished, stroking his chin as though giving the matter great thought.

My mistress turned a little pale. 'It's very little for a mare just turned six,' she replied. 'Couldn't you make it twelve, for you can see we're in a bad way.'

'No,' replied the coal merchant, starting to walk away, 'for I'm not keen on the mare at all. I was looking for a different animal altogether. I like a bay myself, and failing that a chestnut. You know the saying about white legs? "One buy him, two try him, three suspect him, four reject him".'

'What does that mean?' asked Henry.

'That three white legs mean trouble,' cried the coal merchant. 'On second thoughts, I don't want the mare at all. I see nothing but trouble with her. My men won't like her white legs – too much work keeping them clean.'

'Oh, please buy her,' cried my mistress. 'Please. We have to leave here tonight. I will accept anything, only be kind to her.'

'Ten pounds then,' said the coal merchant. 'Here's the money, my dear and I will send a man for her in the morning.' And he pinched my mistress's cheek. All the children were weeping now. They clung to my neck and cried, 'Don't go, Blossom, please don't go. Run away. Hide. You will hate pulling a coal cart.' Then the girls clung to their poor mother's skirts, saying, 'Must she pull a coal cart? Isn't there anyone else who wants her? Can't we try at the big house?'

'After your father stole his lordship's pheasants?' asked my mistress. 'Come, help me. We have to be gone tonight.'

'What about Blossom?' asked Henry.

'She must stay in the stable until the morning. And then take her chance. Hurry now. We must get our things together and leave.'

Henry gave me the last of the hay. His whole bearing had changed. He slapped my neck and said, 'Goodbye Blossom,' and turned away with tears running down his face. There was much crying coming from the cottage, but at last they all came out of it with small bundles over their shoulders. They turned once to look at the cottage, and then they were gone, walking away in the dark, and I was alone with nothing left to eat, waiting for the morning.

CHAPTER NINE

A rough journey

Morning came, wet and dismal. There was no one to feed me and no merry voices coming from the cottage. Horses have small stomachs. We need to be fed often. I neighed for help but no help came. Soon I was both hungry and thirsty. I walked round and round my stable and banged the door with my knees. Henry had shut the door completely, top and bottom, and I could hear nothing but the falling rain. I had grown used to a regular routine and we horses like a routine; it suits our stomachs and gives us confidence. After a few hours I feared I would be forgotten for ever. Then at last, towards evening, I heard hoof-beats coming up the road, and presently a small man wearing breeches and gaiters and a tweed coat looked inside my stable. I was mad to get out now, but I had to wait while he forced my head into a bridle with blinkers and a Liverpool bit and led me out. A horse and cart were waiting by the cottage. He tied my reins to the cart and, with a click of the tongue to the horse, we set off. I felt very nervous for he had not spoken one word to me. I had no choice but to follow the cart, which was pulled by a black horse with a fast trot. Soon I was cantering to keep up and, because I was accustomed to nothing more than a steady trot, I was soon drenched in sweat. After a time we stopped outside an inn and the man went inside. I was very tired by this time what with no food inside me, no water and a lot of worry. To make things worse, it started to rain again and the sky grew dark.

'He's Jacob,' said the horse pulling the cart. 'I am called Nobby. What is your name?'

'Blossom.' Nobby was a black horse of barely 14.2 hands, not highly bred but well put together, with a long mane and tail.

'I am a Dale pony,' he said. 'For a long time I was a pack pony bringing slates down from the hills. There were twenty of us working together and it was pleasant, peaceful work; but there are trains now, so we are not wanted; and I was sent to a fair, and here I am driven to death by Jacob or the Master, badly fed, badly shod and always dirty.'

'You don't pull the coal carts then?' I asked.

'No. I am not big enough, though sometimes if there's a rush on I deliver small loads. Mostly the Master drives me. I miss the hills. Sometimes I think that I shall never see them again.'

Jacob came out then and we set off again, hammer, hammer on the hard road for three more miles, until we reached another public house and stopped again. It was dark now and Jacob smelt of drink. I felt very miserable, hot one minute, cold the next.

'Are our stables comfortable?' I asked Nobby.

'If you don't mind being tied up all the time, staring at nothing but a blank wall,' he answered, shaking his mane. 'If we could go out to pasture sometimes, I could bear it . . .'

I felt very disheartened by this time. Jacob returned again and drove us very fast and so, at last, we came to the town which was lit by lamps. It was a very big town and a great pall of smoke hung over it. In spite of the hour the centre was full of horses and carriages. Cab horses waited in a long line by the station for the last train to come in. I was too tired to be nervous and soon we left the centre and trotted over cobbles, down mean streets with houses so close that there was barely room for a horse and cart to pass between. The windows had no curtains and everything looked dejected and poor. The air was very unpleasant after the country air I was accustomed to. My shoes were nearly worn out and I found it difficult to stand up on the cobbles. We passed a public house where children sat on the pavement waiting for their parents to come out. Finally we turned into a yard and stopped. My new master, who was called Hudson, came out with a light.

'You're late, Jacob,' he said. 'Have you been drinking again?'

'No, sir, it was the mare; she wouldn't come along. She kept jibbing, sir. She needs a lot of whip. I was afraid she might break the reins, the way she hung back.'

'Well, dry them off properly, Jacob,' said my new master. 'And see they are given grub and water, and here's two shillings for your trouble.'

I felt very disheartened by what Jacob had said for I have always done my best, and he had given me a bad name to cover up that he had stopped to drink. He led us into a long stable which consisted of nothing but stalls. Everything smelt of coal, the horses, the bedding, the very wood on the partitions which separated us. Nineteen tired heads turned to look at me. Most of them had no forelocks or manes, having had them cut off to save trouble. Some were resting forelegs, others hind legs. They were all tied short and the stalls sloped down to a centre drain. Jacob tied me up and fetched me water and hay. I was wet and cold but he made no attempt to dry me. A chestnut horse spoke to me over the partition

which separated us. 'You smell nice,' he said. 'You smell of the country. Are the trees in blossom there? Is there much grass? I have almost forgotten what it is like to graze, or roll, or simply stand under a tree. We only leave here for the knacker's. Have you ever pulled a coal cart?'

'No,' I answered, much perturbed. 'I am a carrier's horse.'

Jacob shut the double stable doors and went away. I could hear the rumbling of a train. Most of the horses were asleep now standing up. But even in their sleep, they moved from one hoof to another trying to relieve the strain on their tired legs. I ate for a long time. The hay rack was built for a tall horse and as I ate the hay seeds fell into my eyes. I found the slope of my stall very trying. I wanted to lie down, but I was tied too short. A little thought and we could have been saved much misery and discomfort at no cost at all. But Mr Hudson was not a clever man and it never crossed his mind that horses come in different shapes and sizes, so hay racks should be hung lower for ponies and small horses. He never looked to see how tightly we were tied and the drivers tied us tight so that, in the morning, we were clean, not having lain down all night. We would have lasted much longer, with a little thought, but though Hudson was careful to sell underweight sacks of coal, it never occurred to him that there were also honest ways of saving money. We were shod with calkins on our shoes to help us pull our laden carts over the cobbles, but these caused terrible strain to our legs. And because of the coal dust, most of us soon developed a cough which, in time, would break our wind.

The morning after my arrival I was given to a man named Ralph to drive; a thin, haggard man, with a perpetual stoop from carrying coal. 'She's called Blossom, and she's got a lot of wear in her yet. Her legs are clean all the way down, not a splint or a spavin anywhere. She needs shoeing and the farrier will be here this evening. I want calkins behind. I'm told by Jacob she's stubborn, so remember to take a whip. I think that's all,' said Hudson.

'Yes, sir,' said Ralph.

And so my life as a coal cart-horse began.

CHAPTER TEN

I become a coal horse

I won't dwell too long on the hardships of my life as a coal cart-horse. Some horses have good, considerate drivers who make work possible to endure; others have cruel, thoughtless drivers who make work a torment and a misery. Ralph fell somewhere in between. He was an underfed exhausted man with nine children to feed. He worked seven days a week, doing the other men's work on Sundays when they wanted the day off. He suffered from rheumatism, and was worried about his wife, Bessie, who was always ailing. Often he would drive to his house when we should have been having a rest and something to eat. She would come to the door, still in her night clothes, clutching a baby, with three or more children behind her, barefoot and badly clothed. Washing hung across the street. It was a completely different life to that which I had known in the country; there, the children had had rosy cheeks, here they were mostly thin and pale and undersize.

Most of our time was spent carting coal from the station to the great steel works on the outside of the town. At first, I was terrified of the steam engines and even more of the great steel furnaces, where men worked naked to the waist, sweat glistening like drops of rain on their bodies. We would stand by the trains while the coal was loaded and then we would trot through the cobbled streets to the steel works, where it was unloaded again. Sometimes we would do as many as ten trips a day and, as the distance was some three miles, we would be quite exhausted by the end. Hudson also supplied coal to private houses and this was usually delivered on Saturdays. Sundays we stayed in our stalls resting our exhausted bodies.

Soon I was as dirty as the other horses. I smelt all over of coal. I longed to roll. Rolling is as good as a bath to a horse and if I could have rolled in a green field, or in wet earth and then shaken myself, I would have been much happier, but this was impossible being kept as we were. We all suffered a good deal from never having enough to drink. Often we were watered when we came in from work and had nothing to drink again until next morning.

On Sundays, when the stables had been cleaned and we were fed and watered and shut up until the afternoon, we would talk. None of us had been in the stables for more than a few years. Dauntless, a sixteen-hand dark brown horse was the exception. He had worked at some brick works before in a village called Nettlebed. 'There were twenty of us,' he said. 'And the work was hard, but we didn't mind because we were well treated. There were fields all around, and whenever possible we were turned out to rest. The Master was fair to the men who worked for him, so they were fair to us, and we were well fed and well shod. Once a year the brick works shut down completely and we had a holiday, and how well that suited us!'

'I worked as a brewery horse,' chipped in a big bay with three white socks. 'We had a holiday every year. We were walked six miles to a farm and turned out for a month; our master said it was worth it, for it added ten years on to our lives.'

'I worked on the buses,' said a bay mare, with a small

neat star on her forehead. 'But I was too highly strung. I could not bear the stopping and the starting and I always wanted to go before all the passengers were on board. It was terrible work. No horse lasts longer than three years on the buses. But I never learned to endure it, so I am here.'

'The trams are little better,' spoke up a mealy coloured horse, 'though I've never worked on them, for I worked for a baker before I came here. It wasn't a bad life, except my master drank and when he had had too much he became a different man.'

'We've all gone down in the world then,' said Dauntless. 'I've been here seven years and I think I have navicular; my off pastern aches very much at times. If we had level floors and more bedding, and were turned out sometimes to rest, it might be less painful, but there is little hope of that. Last week a lady spoke to my driver about it, for I was resting my hoof. She said that I should be turned out for a rest and that in three months I would be a changed horse. But my driver just said, "Yes, m'lady, and no m'lady" and that is as far as it's likely to go. He doesn't care; and the Master doesn't care, because he knows he can buy another horse for twenty pounds when I'm no use any more.'

'There was an accident yesterday in the centre of the town,' said the mealy coloured horse. 'My driver had taken me there because he wanted to meet a friend, when I should have been resting with a nose bag. A fine young horse came galloping down the High Street driven very fast by a young man, just as a carriage and pair came out of New Street, and a shaft went right through the young horse's shoulder. They were all down in the road with gentlemen crying, "Sit on their heads", and "cut the

traces", and women screaming. It was a terrible sight.
They shot the fine young horse. The carriage horses had
their heads strapped high with bearing reins, and hadn't a
chance of getting up. Both their knees were broken, so
they'll never work for gentry again. And all because of a
young man showing off!'

'What about the passengers?' I asked.

'Oh, they were all right of course, though the ladies
were escorted to a posting inn so that they would not see
the horse shot. Very grand they were, clutching smelling
salts and the like. I wish they would try pulling a cart for a
day or two, it might teach them a lesson. My driver was
helping everyone, and was given a handsome tip, but I
had no nosebag and no drink all day. And he lost a lot

more time looking for his friend, a kitchen maid in one of the big houses, so I had to go at full speed for the rest of the day to get back here on time for him to meet the young woman somewhere else.'

'If money was shared out a bit fairer we would all be better off,' said Dauntless. 'If our drivers were worked less hard they might look after us a bit better, and if they had a holiday, we would have one too.'

Three days later Dauntless was led away. We all missed him for he always seemed to lead us into conversation. There was no time for saying goodbye. He came in from work tired and dusty, his head low, limping badly, and presently Hudson came in and said, 'Take him away, Jacob. He's no more use to me.' And we never saw him again.

In his place came a spirited black mare called Midnight. She was known for her flighty manners and for her bad temper and Hudson had bought her cheap because of this. 'We will soon break her spirit, Jacob,' he said. 'You take her out tomorrow with an extra full load. Don't spare the whip, and she'll be a different horse by the evening.'

And so she was, a poor exhausted animal, soaked in sweat, with heaving flanks and weals from a whip across her quarters. She came staggering home in the dusk with Jacob shouting at her, though he must have known she had no strength left.

CHAPTER ELEVEN

Midnight

One Sunday Midnight told us about her life. 'I was born across the sea in a place called Ireland,' she said. 'It is very wild there and I grew up roaming the moors with my dear mother. In the winter we went to the farmstead for food and shelter, the rest of the time we went where we pleased. It was a rough, carefree life and I was happy. At two years old I was broken in and drew the plough and my master's cart. It was hard, for I was not fully grown, but I did my best. The harness was old and tied together in places with string, the stables were tumbledown and we shared them with pigs and hens, but I never saw any cruelty there and the grass was always green and the hay sweet. So I grew up believing that men were my friends. Then one spring day, I was led to some crossroads by my master. Other farmers had gathered there and each of them had hold of a black horse. I discovered why, when a man appeared and started to look us over. "She's got to match his lordship's mare, and nothing but a mare will do; a mare with a blaze right down her face and with a snip between her nostrils. This one should do," he said, slapping my neck, "she's the right size and the right age. Now what about the price?" My master and this man, who had come from England, haggled for a long time, but I think my master got a good price for me for he sang all the way home.

'It is terrible to leave the place where you were born and it was a long tiring journey to the coast. The last part I

545

travelled on a train, which was terrifying, but mostly I
was ridden, which was tiring enough for I was barely
four and had never carried a saddle before. When at last
we reached the sea, I was put in slings and raised high in
the air and then dropped into the hold of a ship where I
was tied so tight I could hardly move. It was very dark
and the ship seemed to be shaking all the time, and you
know how we like firm ground under our feet. There
were several other horses and we were all sweating and
trembling. I was the youngest there, most of the others
being hunters.

'After a time the ship started to move and then we
could hardly stand on our legs at all. I won't dwell too
long on that journey. I felt very ill and I couldn't eat or
drink. Several times I neighed for my dear mother, but I
knew now that I should never see Ireland again. Then at
last we were lifted out of the hold on to firm ground
again, shaking and trembling, our heads sore and aching
from swaying against the ropes that held us in the hold. I
was led away and left at an inn for the night. I was too ill
to eat much but the ostler there persuaded me to drink
some gruel. He was a very kind man; if all men were like
him, I think we would all be happy. I couldn't bear him to
touch my head, but he sat talking to me, rubbing my
aching muscles, calling me "a poor wee mare".

'The next day his lordship arrived by carriage to look
at his new horse. I was still very tired and frightened.
"She's had a bad journey," the ostler said. "They're all
like that when they come off the ships; it takes weeks for
them to settle down."

'My new master was middle-aged, with narrow lips, a
strong chin, and side-whiskers. He looked at me with
dislike. "She's too heavy, and I never said anything about

white socks; she's got two behind and that won't match my mare. Jeffreys, where are you? Come here at once."

'The man who had chosen me in Ireland appeared, suddenly humble. He had been a sprightly man in Ireland, but now he seemed much cast down.

'"You won't get anything a better match," he said. "She'll slim down with work, and we can black out her socks, your lordship. But you never said anything about legs, sir. I swear to God you didn't. She's the right size, your lordship, and the right age, and her blaze is right too, right down to the snip here, sir. You won't do better, sir. I swear to God, sir, I searched all Ireland for her, your lordship."

'"I won't pay three hundred guineas for that mare and that's my last word," shouted his lordship. "She's more suited to a hearse than my carriage. I want quality. I repeat it, Jeffreys – quality."

'And with that he climbed into his fine carriage and was driven away.'

'What happened to you then?' I asked.

'The ostler said he knew of a home and two days later I was led to a fine house set in a park, and then to stables which were like a palace after my home in Ireland. But I was still very nervous. I was frightened to step off one piece of ground on to another for fear it might move like the hold of a ship. I wouldn't let the grooms touch my ears, so they put a twitch on my lip which was very painful and made me more nervous. I hadn't worn blinkers in Ireland and they frightened me, for I couldn't see what was happening on each side of me, and I was afraid to go under a railway bridge. The stud groom was called Johnson. He was a very handsome man more interested in impressing the ladies than in how we horses were cared for, and he had little patience. He would whip me without mercy when I was afraid, when a kind word was all that was needed, and the more he whipped me the more nervous I became. Finally, one day when I was in the dog cart, I bolted. Johnson was driving me with a message for the vicar, because he wanted a word with the parlour-maid there and was happy to make this his excuse. I galloped for two miles and, when I stopped at last, there was only one wheel on the dogcart, and no one holding the reins. I think Johnson was badly hurt for I never saw him again. Three days later I was sent to a sale with no reputation and our present master bought me for twenty pounds. So here I am for the rest of my life, through no fault of my own, for I always wanted to do my best. A little kindness and I would have been all right, but ever since I left my old home it has been nothing but whip, whip all the time. And how ever hard I try, I can't cure my fear; Jacob may whip me all he likes, but I can't change myself. I was very young when I went on the ship, straight off the farm with no experience of life. I can't forget that journey and no amount of whipping will erase it from my mind.

'In Ireland my master was my friend and the hard work didn't worry me, and if our stable was like a pig sty, that didn't worry me either. It was a lot better than a fine stable loaded with cruelty.'

Three days after this conversation, Midnight bolted again. We were waiting by the station with nosebags for a train to come in, when a factory hooter went off, and she must have thought it was a ship's hooter. She hadn't been eating her oats and chaff, but standing fretfully as she always did throwing her head up and down. She broke her reins and, although the drag was on the cart, it was empty and she still managed a gallop. We neighed to her to stop but, scared as she was, she didn't hear. Her cart turned over some crates and knocked over a child, and the child's screams frightened her even more. Her driver caught up with her and started to whip her and she seemed to fall to the ground with fear, and never got up again.

Her driver said she had broken her neck in the fall, but I think she died of fear. We all felt very sad for some time afterwards, for she was only five and, handled properly, she could have lasted a long time and been happy, but being tied up at night and worked all day was no life for her. If there was nothing else in store for her, she was better dead.

CHAPTER TWELVE

At the forge

Hudson was angry at losing Midnight and we were now one horse short, which meant more work for all of us. My fetlocks were swollen with wind-galls, which were very painful at times. Summer had come and the town was always hot and stuffy and full of flies. I was finding the loads very heavy, being not as large as the other horses and part thoroughbred. Struggling up cobbled streets with a heavy load behind you is hard at the best of times, but after a night standing up on a sloping floor it becomes even harder. Ralph did his best to make my life easier. He always walked when I had a full load, and he put tassels on my bridle to try and protect my eyes from the flies. In his own way he was quite fond of me, but his wife was often ill, and sometimes he would be in such a hurry to get back to her he would neglect to pick out my hoofs or check my shoes. So, one day I found myself without a shoe and Ralph was forced to take me to the nearest farrier. We had to wait some time. Three farriers were working and I was tied to a ring while Ralph sat telling everyone of his troubles.

'There's rats in the house,' he said. 'And I can't get rid of them. And my wife's ill with a cough and I can't afford the medicine. What sort of life is that, I ask you? Times have got to change; there's no other way. I've got nine children to feed on twenty shillings a week, and three of that goes on the rent. If I had a bit of ground I could grow something.'

Nobody paid much attention to poor Ralph and presently a fine black horse came in and was tied next to me. He wore a rug with initials on it and was led by a young groom.

'The Master said he was to be done at once,' said the young groom. 'For the Mistress is to ride him in the park in half an hour. If you shoe him straight away there's a shilling extra for you,' he added. There was something familiar about the horse. He reminded me of my mother.

'And where do you come from then?' I asked.

'I have two homes,' he answered. 'One is in the country and one is in town. I like the country one best, but I am kindly treated in both. I am my mistress's favourite horse. I have come up in the world for my mother was a simple cart mare, piebald like you, though my father was finely bred, and my grandmother was related to the sire of Black Beauty, I believe. I am in fact half good and half bad, but my mistress sees nothing but the good in me and I am very happy.'

'And where is your mother now?' I asked, my lip trembling a little.

'I don't know. I was taken away from her when I was very young and put with finely bred colts. I have no idea what has become of her. She was only a simple farm horse but kind and good I believe.'

My shoe was now replaced. Ralph untied me. I turned to look at the young black horse. He looked very fine and I was proud to think that he was my son and glad that he was happy. I wanted to say one last word to him, but we had been in the forge a long time already and Ralph was in a hurry. 'Get up,' he shouted. 'What's the matter with you, Blossom?' At the word Blossom, the young horse turned and looked at me, his eyes growing wide with recognition. But there was no more time for words. I was pushed between the shafts, the traces were attached, the breeching straps and the belly band fastened, and then it was back to the railway station full speed, hammer, hammer, on the road and that is how it went all day; Ralph trying to make up for the time he lost at the forge, driving me fast with a full load. As the days went by I could feel my strength failing. Ralph's wife's health was growing worse and he would rush through the day's work in his haste to get back to her. He grew absent-minded with worry; he would forget my nosebag, to put the drag on the cart until I was half way down a hill, and the time he spent grooming me grew less and less. All this helped to undermine my strength still further.

My hindquarters grew thin and I found the cobbled streets increasingly hard on my legs. I had a perpetual cough now, due to the coal dust, and was given cough powders by Jacob. Ralph was ordered to damp all my food and to make sure that my oats were free from dust. My legs were bandaged at night to try to reduce the swelling and Hudson, who was afraid of losing another horse, inspected me daily. But it wasn't just the work that was undermining my health; it was the lack of green grass and sunshine and the unhealthy state of my skin and coat. If I could have been turned out for a few weeks in lush pastures I would have come back a different horse, but the air we breathed was either thick with coal dust or with smoke, and it got into our coats and into our lungs. This affected our drivers too and their health was little better than ours. Sometimes they even fared worse; most of them were bent by middle age, with lined faces and shabby clothes. They shambled rather than walked and nearly all had money troubles of one kind or another.

I don't know how much longer I would have lasted as a coal horse. I was only seven but I looked and felt much older. I had not been bred for such heavy work and I had not the strength of the other horses. And in a way this saved me, for Hudson ordered that I was to be put to the easier work of carting coal to private houses. 'She'll have a cock horse to help her up the hill,' he said. 'And the air will be better for her a little way out of town.'

CHAPTER THIRTEEN

I break my knees

The next day Ralph loaded my cart from the stack near our stable and we set off for the pleasanter part of the town. Soon we had left the drab streets behind and crossed the railway by the fine new bridge. Next we crossed the river. Then we came to a steep hill. Here Ralph stopped and gave a long whistle and almost immediately a man came from under some trees leading a fine chestnut horse. This was the cock horse, a horse used to help pull a load up a hill. This one was called Jack, and his driver was known as Walter. You could see they were fond of one another and, though Jack was hitched in front of me in seconds, no cross word was spoken. And what a difference Jack made! He was seventeen hands high and I think he could have pulled two coal carts up the hill. When we reached the top he was unhitched and Ralph said, 'I wouldn't have made it without you.'

'Yes, many a horse has died trying to get to the top of this hill. But the ladies, God bless them, decided it had to stop and I'm here as a result and paid by charity – Jack too. It just shows what a little good will and charity can do. Now if you'll excuse me, I'll go back to our little house under the trees,' replied Walter with a smile.

After a few days I knew Jack well and the pleasant air above the town did much to raise my spirits, though I did not lose my cough. Pulling the cart up the hill was no effort with Jack in front, and returning, it was always empty. The outskirts of the town were full of pretty

houses and there was a common with a windmill. I think
the air did Ralph good too. But some weeks later he came
to the stable very sad and disturbed, with a black band on
his arm, saying that his missus had died, and one of the
children was sickly too, and there wasn't a lot of hope for
her. He wanted to stay away but Hudson insisted that he
had to take a load of coal to the Manor on the common.
'Mr Heyworth is a good customer of ours and he asked
particularly that the coal should be delivered today, for
they have barely enough to cook on. If you had come
early we could have made other arrangements, but seeing
you are late and all the other carts are out already, there's
no two ways about it. Old Mrs Wison at Sunny Side
wants two bags too, so you can put them on the back and
kill two birds with one stone,' he said. 'And make haste,
my man, the sooner you are gone, the sooner you will be
back.'

Ralph was in a dreadful state. His hands were trembling so much he could hardly buckle my harness. But
eventually we were ready and he jerked my mouth and
shouted at me to get going. And how we raced through
the traffic, narrowly missing other carts! There was such
a jam of vehicles on the railway bridge, we were forced to
stop. I was dripping with sweat by this time, the load
being unusually heavy owing to the extra two hundred-
weight on the back.

'Steady on,' called a driver. 'What's the hurry, mate?
You'll kill your horse driving like that. Have a little
sense.'

But Ralph was in no mood to wait and as soon as there
was a space in the traffic, he laid into me with the whip
again. By the time we reached the hill, I was sweating all
over with my breath coming in sobs. Ralph gave the

usual whistle and then started to shout, 'Cock horse' in a loud, demanding voice, which I had never heard before. But no cock horse came. 'Drat them,' he shouted, after barely a minute. 'We can't hang about.' And he whistled again, louder this time.

'Well, we can't go back,' he said after a moment. 'Where is he, the fool?' And then, when no one came, he said, 'Well, the Manor must have its coal or there will be the devil to pay; so we will have to get to the top of this hill, Blossom, cock horse or no cock horse.' And with that he seized my bridle and shouted at me to get moving. The first part of the hill was quite a gentle slope, but it grew steeper. I did my best, but now I was moving more and more slowly. Ralph was frantic by this time, pulling at one shaft and shouting, lashing me with the whip, even kicking my stomach with his feet. Half way up, the surface became very slippery; it was easy enough with Jack in front, but without his extra power the iron on my wheels wouldn't grip. I threw my weight into my collar.

I strained every sinew of my being. My heart pounded inside me like a hammer, but I could not move the cart another inch.

Ralph put the drag on and waited for me to get my breath. Sweat dripped off me like rain. I hung my head. My legs trembled. My sides moved in and out like bellows. 'Now then,' cried Ralph, after a moment, 'get up, Blossom,' and he leapt into the cart and laid into me with the whip like a madman. I strained and struggled, too distressed to feel the whip cutting weals across my quarters. There was a humming in my head, and then I felt my hoofs slipping from under me and I knew I was going down.

I heard Ralph shouting at me as though through a mist, his voice growing more desperate each passing second. I heard hoofs going along the footpath by the road and Walter calling that he was coming. Then I was down on the road with blood spurting from both my knees, my collar choking me, the traces broken.

I don't know how long I lay there. It felt like a minute but it could have been much longer. I think all the breath was knocked out of me. Then I heard Walter's voice. 'Steady there, steady. Not to worry. Steady.'

I heard a horse neighing and it sounded like my own son. I thought I was dreaming or dying as I lay there, the road wet with my blood. Then there was a crowd around me, all talking at once and above it all, a lady's voice crying, 'I'll have you summoned for this. If it hadn't been for my horse, I would never have stopped, for I couldn't see you through the trees. But Black Petal would not go on. He knew what had happened, and people call beasts stupid! He knew there was a horse down and in trouble and he was trying to tell me.'

Walter was sponging my head now with cold water. 'Couldn't you wait? I would have been there in five minutes. I had only gone for some water,' he said.

'Don't summons me, please, Madam,' said Ralph. 'My wife has just died and I hardly know what I am doing. I've got to make the funeral arrangements, and one of my little girls is desperately ill too. I should have the day off. I'm sick with grief, but the Master said I had to work. It's a cruel world, Madam.'

I was on my feet now. I felt very weak. 'I'll take her to Jack's stable and bathe her knees; she's losing joint oil and will be scarred for life,' Walter said, stroking me.

'The Manor wants the coal,' said Ralph, wiping sweat from his face. 'I don't know what to do.'

'They will have to want the coal. Now, where do you come from? I am going to see your master. This mare isn't big enough to pull a coal cart, and hers was overloaded, as you know yourself. Now, you go straight home, my man, and I will speak to your master and see that you are not out of pocket. It's a terrible thing when a man can't have a day off to arrange his wife's funeral,' said the lady.

Walter led me down the hill to Jack's stable under the trees. It was made of wood with a tarpaulin for the roof. He only used it in the day time, but it was cosy enough inside. He took off my harness and sponged my knees, talking to me all the time in a quiet, soothing voice, which made me feel better straight away. If men only knew what a difference a kind, friendly voice makes to a horse, they might not shout at us so much. While this was going on, Jack stood outside as good and patient as a horse can be. Then Walter made me a warm mash and bandaged my legs with wet bandages to stop the bleeding. After that he made himself a cup of tea and sang a song called 'Dolly Gray', before a whistle summoned him and Jack back to work.

He stopped to pat my neck before he went and, when he was gone, I lay down in the straw to rest my legs. It was very peaceful under the trees and I think I slept.

Later, Jacob came for me. I was very stiff by this time.

'I should turn her out as soon as the wounds have healed,' said Walter. 'Otherwise she'll never be the same again.'

'That's for the Governor to say,' replied Jacob. 'He might rather send her to the knackers than have the bother of getting her right. I always said she was too small for our job.'

'She's not an old mare either,' said Walter. 'She might breed a nice foal. She's a good natured sort, too, by the look of her. It would be a pity to have her destroyed.'

It was a long painful walk to Hudson's yard. Jacob let me go at my own pace. It was tea time and the streets were quiet.

Hudson was waiting for us in the yard. He was in a bad humour.

'She's caused us plenty of trouble,' he fumed, looking at me. 'The young lady who called is threatening to summons me for cruelty. Was it my fault the cock horse wasn't on the hill? And now there's another horse ruined. If Ralph had had a bit of patience it would never have happened.'

'If you had given Ralph the day off, Blossom would still be sound,' muttered Jacob, leading me to my stall.

CHAPTER FOURTEEN

Back to the country

The young lady called the next day and the day after. She brought a groom with her, who held Black Petal and his own horse, while she looked at my knees. Her hands were very gentle and she talked to me as though I was a child.

'I know who you are,' she said. 'You are Black Petal's mother. You've fallen on hard times, but I am going to have you taken from here quite soon.'

She looked strange in the yard in her riding habit and veil, and Black Petal would grow impatient to be gone after a few minutes. My knees were painful; if it hadn't been for the young lady, who was called Florence, I believe I would have been shot. While Florence was visiting the stable all our conditions improved. We were watered more often; our hoofs were picked out without fail and we were groomed more thoroughly. The men touched their caps to her and Hudson would inspect the stables before each visit, putting everything in order. She had a sharp eye. She complained about the sloping floors and had my hay rack lowered. The groom, who was tall and good looking, always stayed outside in the yard, a look of disapproval on his face.

After her third visit, she had a long talk with Hudson. 'If you turned your horses out for a holiday each year, they would work much better,' she said. 'They would return full of strength and vigour. As it is, they are all coughing and all poor. Now I am going to give you fifteen pounds for Blossom, for I've found her a home. I want her taken to the station tomorrow and put on a train. It is quite a long journey, but she will have a happy home when she gets there and a long rest. Will you bring her out into the daylight so that I can look at her. She needs to move about. She will never get well confined in a stall.'

Slowly and painfully I hobbled out into the sunlight, which hurt my eyes. Black Petal whinnied to me and pricked his ears. 'Try to walk, try,' he said.

I was very stiff. 'Walk her up and down or she'll never make the station tomorrow,' cried Florence in great distress.

'You can't replace joint oil,' said Jacob. 'She will never be the same again.'

'She'll be as right as rain in a week or two,' replied Hudson, afraid of losing fifteen pounds.

'Oh, I do hope so,' cried Florence. 'And I'm sure Black Petal does too.'

Next day Ralph came back. 'Just to say goodbye,' he said. 'Who said piebald horses weren't lucky? My little girl is better and the young lady has found me a gardening job in the country, so I shall be all right. I'll be making a new start.'

He led me to the station himself. My friends were waiting there in their coal carts, hanging tired heads. Nobby looked rough and tired. He tossed his head and called, 'Goodbye.'

Ralph talked to me kindly and the stall in the carriage was comfortable and bedded thickly with straw. He fetched me water and tied me up. 'Goodbye. Do your best,' he said.

It was not a very long journey, but my knees were

painful and I found the shaking difficult to bear. When I came to the end of it, a groom was waiting for me. He looked at my knees and said, 'Well, you are in bad shape. And piebald as well; that won't please the Master. Come along now, gently does it.' The air felt fresh and clean. Birds were singing. Trees hung pink and white with blossom. I felt better already.

It wasn't a long walk to my new home. On my arrival, the head groom rubbed ointment into my knees and I was then turned out into a shady paddock with a mare in foal. I smelt the ground and rolled over and over trying to rid myself of the coal dust which had been in my coat for so many months. The head groom watched me over the gate. 'The master won't like her colour and he won't like her scarred knees, but he'll do anything to please that particular young lady, so she'll stay,' he said.

'Fair enough,' replied the young groom who had fetched me from the station and was called Percy. 'She deserves a rest. She looks as though she's had a rough time, and when all is said and done, she's God's beast, just the same as the thoroughbreds.'

My new home was a stud farm for thoroughbreds. It had bred several winners. My master lived in a pleasant house with fine pillars and a beautiful garden. He was bearded and usually wore a top hat and carried a cane. When he saw me he said, 'Is this Miss Florence's good deed? Hide her away, will you George. I don't want her out with the brood mares. I shall be the laughing stock of the neighbourhood.'

'She's only resting, sir. Later on she can cart the hay and straw. I want her close by so that I can keep an eye on her knees,' replied George, the head groom.

'She's a disaster. There's nothing fine about her. Even her tail has been docked too short,' said my new master. 'As soon as her knees are better, see if Farmer Collings will have her with his cart colts.'

'They'll chase her, sir,' said George.

'The Mistress mustn't see her from the windows of the house. She'll think she's a gipsy horse. Move her as soon as possible. And if you must use her for carting later on, hide her round the back somewhere. I don't want her in the front. Whatever will my customers say if they see her in a fine loose-box? It's unthinkable,' said my master. 'Is that understood?'

George touched his cap. 'It doesn't seem fair,' he said later to Percy. 'She's just the same as the other horses, only a little less fine.'

Three days later I was turned out on Farmer Collings's farm. He was a large, bluff man with broad shoulders and side whiskers, but kind enough. My field had a pond in it and a little coppice where we could shelter. The cart colts were rough and given to biting and kicking and I kept away from them as much as possible. My knees were completely healed by now and my stiffness was going. Farmer Collings would visit us every day and I grew quite fond of him. There was plenty of grass in the field and my jaded spirits soon rose and my coat grew sleek and glossy again. I was hardly the same horse by the autumn. When George saw me he exclaimed, 'What a few months at grass do for a horse! You look a different mare altogether, Blossom, my dear. Surely, even the Master will not mind so much about your colour now.' He slipped a halter over my ears, talking to me kindly, and led me across the fields to the stud farm. The stables were very grand. The horses were all in loose-boxes and there was not a piece of straw to be seen anywhere in the yard. I lifted my head and whinnied.

'Not there,' said George. 'You are to live round the back,' and he gave my halter rope to Percy. 'Put her in the shed, and don't tie her too tight,' he said.

There were chickens in the shed scratching in my manger. 'This is your home now,' said Percy. 'It's not any great shakes, I know, but a lot better than a coal merchants no doubt.' And with that he tied me up and went away.

The roof was so low that if I raised my head I banged it on the ceiling. My manger smelt sour and of chickens, and a hen had nested in my hay rack. I missed the cart colts, for we horses hate being alone and any company, however rough, is better than none. The window was shrouded with cobwebs, but I could just make out horses in the distance roaming free. After being free myself, it was very irksome to be tied up hour after hour with little to see and only chickens for company. I pawed the ground and whinnied. I stamped my hoofs on the floor. I pulled with all my might on the halter rope. But nothing gave.

In the evening Percy came to feed me. He was tired and in a hurry. He gave me hay and a bucket of water and shut the door after him. The chickens started to perch on my hay rack. In the distance I could hear the clatter of buckets and men's voices. I neighed again and again, but only the hens cackled. If only men knew how we suffer, tied up hour after hour. How lonely it is! I was still quite young and no longer exhausted by work. I neighed and stamped all that night, but by dawn I had become resigned and, in spite of the work and the coal dust, I almost wished myself back in Hudson's yard. Later that day I was put to work. My driver was the odd job man, Albert. He wore a broad brimmed hat and was old, with bandy legs and a weather-beaten face. His job was to repair the fences, to cut the hedges and to cart the hay and straw to the yard when needed. He had made a great bonfire in one of the meadows and I carted the hedge trimmings to it. I did my best and I didn't mind the fire, which greatly impressed Albert. Later I heard him telling Percy that I must have worked for the fire brigade. ''Cos she don't mind fire at all,' he said. 'She'll come right up to a fire, so close it almost singes her coat. She's a funny one.'

'More like a gipsy horse; they have fires, don't they?' asked Percy.

'Either way, she don't mind, that's the wonder of it,' said Albert.

My harness did not fit well, but no one troubled. It was not that they did not know how to fit a set, it was simply that they were busy with more important things and could not be bothered. The breeching was too low and the crupper too tight, causing it to chafe what was left of my tail. The tugs were set wrong, so that too much of the weight fell on the shafts putting strain on my back. But otherwise the work was easy, and often I would stand a whole day in my shed with no work at all, which I found most irksome. When I had been a carrier's horse I had been alone, but I could turn round in my stable and was put out to grass on Sundays and on fine evenings, so I could endure the loneliness. Now it was almost unbearable. I became very headstrong. Once untied I could not wait to get out into the daylight. I grew snappish and would refuse to pick up my hoofs when required, because I wanted to delay Percy, to make him stay longer. My head grew tender straining against the halter and I became difficult to bridle. I wanted to do my best but I could no longer control my temper. There was plenty of good food, and water was always available. It was not that I was badly looked after; it was boredom which was ruining my temper. I knew I was becoming peevish and ill tempered, but I could do nothing about it. I don't know how vicious I would have become with time, had something not occurred which was to alter my life. I had a very bad name by this time and Percy and Albert disliked me for it. Albert would shout at me and twice Percy hit me with a whip to try and curb my temper. I knew I was going down hill fast. I think if Florence and Black Petal had seen me at this time they would scarcely have recognised me.

CHAPTER FIFTEEN

Frances and May

One afternoon when I had no work to do and was standing tied in my stable, I heard children's voices in the distance. I had heard them before but this time they seemed to be coming nearer. Presently I heard a little girl calling, 'Nana, what lives in that little shed over there?'

'Nothing, May,' answered the nurse. 'It's a hen house.'

'Yesterday I heard a horse's whinny. Do let's look,' cried another voice.

'Frances, May, come back. That is no place for girls in pretty frocks. Come back at once. I will tell your Papa,' called the nurse.

'It moves. It's a rocking horse,' cried May.

'It's real, it moves. Oh, Nana, it's a lovely black and white horse – all alone, poor thing.'

In a moment the two little girls were in my stable fondling my nose with soft hands, running out to pick me grass. 'Why is it here all alone?' cried May, who was the smallest with ringlets and a pretty pink frock.

I remembered Jimmy Reed's children; all my bad temper faded away. I nuzzled their hair while they cried with delight. 'It must be a girl. She's so soft and sweet,' cried Frances. 'She's not like the other horses.'

'She's cuddly like a teddy bear,' said May. 'I shall ask Papa why she's here all alone. I shall ask him tonight. Why should she be here – it's a hen house.'

'She is only a common cart horse May,' said Nana.

567

'She isn't fit to stand in a fine stable, any more than a common man is fit to live in a palace.'

'It is not the same, and she should not be tied up,' said May. 'Not one of the other horses is, not even the carriage horses. Papa always gives orders for them to be loose at night and when they are not working. He says it is better for them. So why is she tied up? It is not fair. I shall speak to Papa tonight.'

'So shall I,' said Frances.

'Your hands and dresses are all dirty now,' said Nana. 'You look a proper sight. Come indoors at once.'

'I don't care. We love this horse. Don't we?' asked May.

Nana took their hands and pulled them away from me. She wore a starched apron and her hair was piled on her head in a neat bun. 'Your Papa is a busy man. He won't wish to be bothered over a cart horse,' she said.

The next day Albert fixed a bar across the doorway of my stable and let me loose. I stretched my neck and all my legs in turn. Now I could see the house in the distance, and the sky, and the trees, and everything which was happening around me. I shook myself and felt easier all over. Later that day the children came again with carrots and lumps of sugar for me. They put their arms round my neck. 'Blossom, lovely Blossom,' murmured May.

'You are our horse now,' said Frances.

After that they came every evening with titbits for me, usually with Nana in hot pursuit. Once they fetched a bucket and climbed on to my back and sat untangling my mane with their fingers. I started to look out for them, to whinny when they came.

Albert told them that I was not safe. 'She'll bite you,' he

said. 'She'll bite your fingers right off and then what will your Papa say?'

'She won't. She's not like that,' said May.

'You make her like that. You are a horrible, cruel man,' retorted Frances.

'She should be with the other horses. She is lonely here,' said May.

The children changed my life. They complained that I had a sore under my chin from straining against the halter, and it was treated. They complained when I was dirty. They tried to teach me tricks and were always in trouble for the state of their frocks.

One day I heard their mother calling, 'Children, where are you? Come away from that dirty old horse at once. She is nothing but a gipsy horse. Next year Papa will buy you a pony – your very own pony.'

It was Nana's day off and in a minute she stood looking at me, her eyes filled with disgust. 'She's just a common cart mare,' she said. 'Come indoors at once.'

'She is a circus horse. She is not afraid of anything. Look, I can even light a match in front of her nose and she does not mind,' retorted Frances.

'How dare you have matches? You will set the yard on fire,' said their mother, who was a very fine lady dressed in silk and wearing fine gloves. 'Give me those matches at once. I shall tell your Papa to forbid you to come here.'

Slowly, a whole winter passed. I carted hay and straw and sacks of oats. I fetched bran from the mill. Albert was a slow patient man. He never hurried me, for he liked a job to last as long as possible, because that way he had less to do. I was much more comfortable now, but I saw the little girls less in the winter, and I grew lonely again. When spring came my head was filled with daydreams. I neighed to imaginary horses in the distance, and imagined that every hedge held a strange animal inside it. I took to chewing my stable door to relieve my boredom. Often there was no work for me for days at a time, which would make me very restless. I was stabled behind all the other buildings and there was little to see, and now everyone was busy with mares foaling. I was often neglected and left unfed until dark.

May became ill and when she recovered both the little girls were taken to the seaside for a holiday. Percy suggested that I should be turned out, but the master said that I was not to be with the brood mares and that every paddock was taken. 'I am sorry. She is too ugly for one thing,' he finished. 'Everything is wrong with her; look at her tail. Whatever made anyone dock it so short? And her fetlocks need trimming. I know she comes from a good line, but it doesn't show, does it?'

I felt very miserable after this, for the fields were full of buttercups and I was bursting with health, but there was nothing to be done. I was not well bred enough to be seen among the thoroughbreds.

Then the little girls came back and their visits began all over again. I felt much better then. They had something new for me most days – sometimes a bit of cake smuggled from the tea table, or some morsel from the kitchen when cook's back was turned. They would throw their arms round my neck crying, 'We don't want a pony. We only want Blossom.' One day they dressed me up in a bonnet. They put ribbons in my mane and draped my quarters with a table cloth. Nana was very angry when

she found them. But in the end she could not help laughing for I looked so comic.

I did my best to be patient, but sometimes I felt sorely
tried by the strange games they played. One day I was a
highwayman's horse, the next a fine lady on her way to
the races, another day they dressed me in their father's
top hat. They tied my legs together with rope and I
became a robber. I liked it best when they sang hymns to
me and lullabies. I dreaded the thought of winter coming
again, for then their visits would grow less frequent and I
would watch for them in vain. But something happened
before then which was to change my whole life.

CHAPTER SIXTEEN

Grandma!

I shall never forget that day. I had been carting wood in the afternoon from the spinney to the house ready for the winter. Albert had been even slower than usual, grunting and grumbling over each log of wood which had to be lifted into my cart. There was a keen wind blowing and the trees were turning yellow and brown. I was feeling frisky and I found Albert's slowness very trying. When we had finished, I was put away as usual, but the children didn't come that evening so I was quite alone. The night came early without a moon. Percy was going to a dance at the village hall. I think it was to do with the harvest festival. He had little time for the horses, and neither did George. They kept discussing the girls who would be there. Later, I could hear music coming from the village and laughter and a great clapping of hands. I stood by my door dozing, while the night grew blacker. Sometime later I heard a crackling noise and smelt smoke. It seemed to be coming through the cracks in my stable and the hens started to flap their wings and cackle. I was very nervous now. Next, I heard a great shouting coming from the yard, my master's voice the loudest of them all. 'Where are the men?' he shouted. 'Get the horses out. Don't worry about anything else, just get them out.'

I heard later that he had gone into the stables himself, but none of the horses would move for him. The grooms were still at the dance and not to be seen. And Albert had no understanding of horses and none of them trusted him. Soon the smoke was seeping into my stable, filling the air. Then I was coughing and distressed. I threw myself against the door and neighed. I could hear a great clatter coming from the yard and more shouting. I knew I would be forgotten and I became frantic. I charged my door again and again and suddenly it gave.

The next minute I was in the main yard, and what a sight it was there! Flames were leaping out of the lofts and the horses below were whinnying with terror, but they were too frightened to move in any direction. The Master was frantic and the Mistress was sobbing as if her heart would break and crying, 'We're ruined. There's no hope.'

Frances and May were standing with Nana and when they saw me, they let out a great cry. 'Blossom will save them. She is all right in fire. Look she's come to help. They will follow Blossom. Try, do try.'

The grooms were coming from the dance now having seen the smoke and the flames bright in the night sky. Someone put a halter over my ears and led me into the stables. The doors were all open, but the horses wouldn't move. Some had been blindfolded but it made no difference. I was not afraid because I had seen so much smoke and fire in my life and it was no worse than that of the steel furnaces; so I neighed to them, 'Come out. Follow me. Come out before you are burnt to death.' And one by one they followed me. I think I went back three times and by then the timbers were cracking. Another minute and the whole stable collapsed, but the horses were safe. I stood in the yard and coughed. My throat and my eyes were sore with smoke. The grooms' faces were black. The Master came across to me. 'You have done a good night's work, Blossom,' he said. 'And it won't be forgotten.' He patted my neck and pulled my ears. As he had never touched me before, I was very surprised.

The horses had to be taken to fresh stables on Mr Collings' farm. They were not nearly as grand, but somehow they were all found somewhere to sleep. Everyone wanted to know how the fire had started. Several of the grooms smoked when the master was not around, but none of them confessed to it. Albert said there had been a tramp about and George said that it had been done on purpose by someone who was jealous of so fine a stud.

In the middle of it all the fire engine arrived pulled by two fine black horses who pulled the hearse at other times. The firemen put out the last of the fire while I was taken back to my stable and given a feed of oats. Everyone kept patting me. I had never been patted so much before. Frances and May were beside themselves with delight. 'She is a heroine now,' May cried. 'You must love her now, Mamma and Papa. You must love her for ever and ever.'

After the fire my whole life changed. The stables were rebuilt and in the middle a special stall was built for me with a door I can look over and a hay rack which is neither too high nor too low, and a level floor, and a manger which is always clean. On the door there is a plaque which reads BLOSSOM. THE BRAVEST OF THEM ALL. The smart visitors who call to see the thoroughbreds, stop at my stable and read it and then the master explains, 'She saved them all. There wouldn't be a horse left if she hadn't gone in among the flames to bring them out.'

The hard work when I was in foal has made it impossible for me to be in foal again, but I spend my time in the summer with the brood mares. I am a great favourite with their children who call me Grandma, for though I am only ten, I feel old having seen so much. They love to listen to my stories about the great city where I worked.

So I hope to end my life, not as a piebald misfit, but as a horse much loved. I don't pull a cart any more, and Frances and May still visit me daily. One day last summer we had special visitors – Florence and Black Petal. He was looking very well and before he left he told me, 'I am proud to call you "mother". For handsome is as handsome does and you have done so much.'

So all my troubles are over and I have nothing to look forward to but peace and happiness. I only wish that all the horses in this hard world could say the same.